PRELUDE

Book 1 - Prophecy's Daughter

Susan L. Alandar

Apropos Press

Published by Apropos Press

Print ISBN: 979-8-9900576-0-9

"The optimist proclaims that we live
in the best of all possible worlds.
The pessimist fears this is true."
—*James Branch Cabell*

CONTENTS

PART 1: DESCENT FROM EDEN

"There's a story in the Bible about a place called Eden,
and how we fell from grace and were cast out.
I wonder now if it is meant as a history or a warning.
If in fact Earth is our Eden and we are cast out,
where will our descent take us?"
—*Father Verity Rowan*

CHAPTER 1

S handiin had met him once, on a long-ago day before the world died.

Standing on a busy street corner waiting for the light to change, she'd felt a presence and turned around to find him there. Shandiin was six feet tall, but his greater height barely registered while gazing into his inhumanly brilliant emerald eyes. The strange, jeweled eyes were framed by black velvet brows and lashes. His thick black hair brushed the shoulders of his leather jacket.

He was stunning. The most beautiful man she had ever seen. She told herself later that was why she remembered him, but the expression in those strange eyes was what held her. They held a commanding presence, and a warmth that could only be...unaccountably...love.

She'd jolted when he spoke her name.

"Hello, Shandiin." He'd spoken softly, and she had thought that low voice also held power, but didn't understand why.

"How do you know my name?" she had demanded.

"I have known you all of my life." He had hesitated a moment, as though to say more. But he'd shaken his head, seemingly at himself, and turned away from her to disappear into the crowd.

The crowds were gone now, as time had depopulated cities no longer supported by supplies from a dying world.

She dreamed of him occasionally. Sometimes she wanted to remember the dreams even as they faded. Years later, when she thought she saw him again, that meeting on a street corner came back to her.

His hair was different, now traditionally short. And he seemed to have lost that strangely commanding presence.

Which wasn't surprising, because he was being arrested.

She was a cop, for now. What was left of law enforcement was less than rudimentary, and the police were scarcely able to protect themselves, much less the citizens. In addition, the laws were changing, and she knew she would not enforce the new ones.

So when she saw him cuffed, face down over an aged black-and-white's hood, she walked up and frowned at the arresting officer. "What is this man charged with?" she demanded.

"He's one of them," the cop sneered. "Did you see those eyes? He is one of *them*."

She knew what he meant, ignored that while her body tensed. "What is he charged with?" she repeated.

"Being an abomination!"

"That isn't a law. Not yet. You can't arrest him for something that isn't a crime. Let him go."

"It's been passed! It just isn't in effect yet for some technicality. I'll have you know I have applied for membership in the Right Church!"

"Why the hell are you here, then? Why aren't you behind the Wall with the rest of the assholes? I don't give a shit what circus you belong to, Officer. There is no law in effect allowing you to arrest someone for being genetically enhanced. I am telling you to *let him go*."

She faced the man down while he glared. Middle-aged WASP, broad of face, broad of body, arrogant in his righteousness. She bared her teeth, almost hoping he would dare to assault her and give her a reason to take him down.

She was bigger—and she had a vicious rep. He grimaced finally, unkeyed the cuffs and yanked them off his prisoner before walking away.

Her handsome stranger stood up, rubbing his wrists. "Thank you," he said.

"I strongly suggest that you get some contacts to make your eyes less noticeable."

He smiled wryly. "I know. I forgot to put them in this morning. And they don't always help."

She regarded him thoughtfully. The strange eyes were a giveaway, but he was handsome to the point of beauty, certainly genetically enhanced.

"It isn't wise of you to be walking around here, Mr. ..."

He smiled. "It's Doctor. Zion Alexander."

She recognized the name. "You're the scientist. The one they said is smarter than Einstein. But they have never shown your picture. I see why, now. Beauty makes people more accepting, and they want to demonize you. You should get away from this city, probably out of the country, Dr. Alexander. It's not safe for people like you."

He seemed to study her face. "May I ask your name, Officer?"

"I thought you knew it." She scowled at his puzzled expression. "I have a good memory for faces, and yours is frankly unforgettable. We met on a street corner, and you called me by name."

He studied her for a long moment. "Would you join me for dinner?" he asked.

"Awkward timing for a pickup line, doc."

"Wow." He looked embarrassed, and she found that somehow charming. "I apologize. I guess it did sound that way. Officer, I believe you think we've met before, and I would like to talk about it somewhere off the street to get more information. Did this person have long hair?"

"Yes. So you do remember."

He shook his head. "No. It wasn't me. Apparently I have a double, because someone else met him too. Can we talk, over coffee, perhaps, if dinner is too much? I was on my way to a place where I am...more welcome than others."

She considered. Wherever it was couldn't be far, as there wasn't much livable city left. "You can buy me dinner. I'll be off duty in an hour, and can meet you where you are welcome."

He gave her the address, and she watched him walk away, her curiosity piqued. Same face, same weirdly beautiful eyes, same powerful build and height. Perhaps genetic enhancement had created two of a kind...a very tasty kind.

She finished her shift, changed from uniform and helmet to her usual jeans and tall boots, pulling on a navy turtleneck, then a Kevlar vest and a grey blazer over her shoulder holster. She always wore body armor, always kept her service weapon with her. The streets were seeded with the homeless, too hungry and desperate not to be dangerous. The reigning government kept its churched constituency behind a wall with its own well-equipped army to protect them; everyone else had to fend for themselves, as local police were few and barely funded. Helicopters made daily supply deliveries, but not outside the Wall.

She would never go unarmed in this hell that had forgotten civilization.

Most of the city outside the Wall had been abandoned, the rest haunted by the last dregs of humanity. The living core had receded to a few square miles, where attempts at normalcy failed daily along with any connection to the rest of the world.

But there were attempts. She walked into the small hole-in-the-wall restaurant, dimly lit and fragrant with the scents of good Italian food, and saw Dr. Alexander stand up to beckon her to a table in the corner.

Heads turned as she walked through, but she was used to being stared at. Shandiin had never been fashionably thin, but was built in statuesque harmony with her unusual height, full curves and trained muscle. Her unruly red hair, freed from her uniform's helmet, bloomed like a fiery chrysanthemum around her face and shoulders.

He smiled as she approached, and she lifted an eyebrow at his open regard. She knew what he saw. Her face was planed by mixed heritage to an exotic near-beauty. The faint lines at the corners of her piercing silver-grey eyes proved she was no youngster; the strong chin showed she was tough enough not to care.

"Thank you for coming." He pulled out a chair for her. As they settled in, his eyes never left her face. "I never did get your name."

"Shandiin Haskie."

"Shandiin is Navajo for sunshine, isn't it? Are you part Navajo?"

"My grandmother was a Navajo medicine woman. I am surprised you know the meaning. And you are part...do you have any idea?"

He laughed. "I am a little of everything. I have ordered a simple Chianti, Officer, but of course you may have coffee or anything else you wish. I hope you like Italian food? It's the specialty here."

She nodded, lifting her gaze to the chalked menu on a blackboard behind him. "I will have the rigatoni, and that Chianti, and please call me Shandiin. I will not be a cop much longer anyway."

He blinked at that, but looked up at the waiter who brought the wine. "Thanks, Roland. We'll both have the special."

Shandiin looked up at a striking black man with a sparkling smile and locs.

"Certainly, Zion. Glad to see you finally got a date. Welcome, ma'am, and thank you for your charity to the lonely homely." He poured the wine as he spoke, and winked at her before he walked off.

Shandiin grinned appreciatively after the waiter. Zion ignored him to ask, "Why will you no longer be a police officer, Shandiin?"

"Because I will not enforce the new laws that include the attack on your kind. I don't plan on staying near a Church stronghold. Which is the plan I already suggested to you."

"So you have no problem with genetic enhancement."

"It has done away with many of the diseases humanity has suffered."

"That's genetic modification. Enhancement is defined differently under the new law. The Right Church doesn't think we are human, because we have been changed to be—forgive the bluntness—in some ways superior to those resulting from untampered natural conception."

"God forbid," she said sourly, "that anyone should be superior to a low IQ middle-aged white man like the one who just tried to arrest you. I understand you are fighting the movement against the enhanced, Dr. Alexander, but you must realize it's a losing battle now, since the Right Church has taken over the government."

"You aren't religious?"

"No. I always respected those of true faith who practiced the golden rule, but those that are left are hiding from the fucking righteous."

He lifted his eyebrows. "You seem particularly angry about it."

"Zion..." she hesitated, then continued. "I am a lot older than I look. I watched this country change from the land of the free to the divided travesty it is now. It started with little things, like politicians saying we needed to bring God 'back' to government...where religion never was intended to be to begin with, and what they called God meant their religion only, not to be sullied with anyone else's. It has escalated over the years to what we have now, and the result isn't only the harm to people like you, and the loss of individual freedom, but the loss of everything. As if they expect God to magically reverse the damage we have done to our planet, and to save us from the bombs everyone keeps building. We live with the sword of annihilation hanging over our heads, but no one will look at it."

She scowled, lifted her wine, sighed. "Sorry for the soapbox rant. I guess I *am* angry about it. I'm an army vet. I fought in a war with the belief I was helping to keep us free. I watched friends die for that noble cause, which has been undermined until there is nothing left of it. Yes, I am angry, and obviously bitter." She sipped her wine, set it down, shook back her fiery mane. "I thought you wanted to talk about your double."

He looked at her thoughtfully, topped off her wine glass. "How old are you?" he asked.

She snorted laughter. "How dare you ask a woman that question?"

"They say I'm not human, so I figure I can have different rules. And you brought it up. But, of course, you don't have to answer." He looked up as their waiter brought their dinner. "Thanks, Roland."

"You're welcome. Just don't try to skip out on the bill again."

Shandiin watched the waiter walk away. "He must be a friend."

"Whatever makes you think that?" Zion smiled, picking up his fork, and she laughed, following suit, realizing she rather liked this genetically engineered man.

"So who else met your double?" she asked.

"Roland. He said the man looked like me, but he knew it wasn't me."

"How? Because of the long hair?"

Zion frowned. "No. He said the man almost scared him, but he couldn't explain it. An aura, he called it, of overwhelming authority."

She considered. "A commanding presence," she agreed.

Zion sat back. "So you saw that too."

She nodded, frowning. "But he wasn't scary. He was actually...very friendly to me."

"Maybe he just doesn't like black men?"

"No. Something more personal...toward me." She shook her head. "I probably imagined that."

Zion was quiet for a moment, studying her face. "Perhaps he was reacting to the fact that you are a very beautiful woman."

She let the compliment pass. She could tell it hadn't been easy for the unusually genteel man who gave it. "No. It was not a flirtatious or admiring look. Women know the difference. It was more...familiar, like he knew me, like he...cared about me."

Zion raised his eyebrows. "You saw that? But you think you imagined it?"

She said nothing in response, concentrating on her food.

"What was he wearing?" Zion asked.

"A black leather jacket open over a plain white tee, dark jeans, scuffed black work boots. He wore leather gloves. He smelled faintly of soap...and horses."

"Horses?"

She nodded.

"That's odd...and you are obviously a trained observer. Was there anything else?"

She looked up, into the weirdly beautiful emerald eyes that were watching her very closely. She picked up her wineglass, held it motionless while she met that gaze.

"It was only a few seconds, on a busy street corner. He said 'Hello, Shandiin,' and when I asked how he knew my name, he said he had always known me. It makes no sense." She frowned. "His voice was as strange as the eyes. He spoke softly, but it...it was like...like it could carry without a microphone." She shrugged. "Again, probably my imagination."

"Did you see where he went?"

"He walked into the crowd, and I lost sight of him quickly. Is Roland the only other person who has seen him?"

"As far as I know." Zion looked up as the restaurant door opened and three men walked through.

Roland stopped them within steps of the door. "Hey there," he said cheerfully. "I have a table over here for you!" he gestured widely, and walked to the corner opposite from Zion and Shandiin.

Shandiin watched this with peripheral vision. "He's heading them off. Protecting you, Zion?"

"Not just me. One of them spotted you the minute they walked in. He's looking back at you now."

She turned around at that, looked. "Well, shit."

"You know him?"

"Yeah." She started to get up.

"Shandiin, where are you going?"

"To help Roland head him off. Your eyes are too noticeable, Zion, and he's a minor church leader; I've been dodging him for days. He has his bodyguards with him, and would do whatever he damn well pleases to you—with no accountability."

Zion moved as though to stop her, but she was already on her feet, walking toward the heavy man in the white suit of a Church Elder. He had shoved Roland aside and started toward her, watching her approach with a broad and lustful grin.

"Elder Benson," she said. "Good to see you again."

"You never answered my calls, honeybuns."

"You called? Are you sure you got the right number?" She reached into her pocket, pulled out a small notebook, jotted something down. "Here. This is my personal cell phone, and it's still working. Call me tomorrow for sure, okay?"

He took the paper she offered, but was looking over her shoulder at Zion. "Who's that?" he asked.

She walked closer to the man, took his arm, turned him away. "Confidential informant. Don't spook him, okay? It's a big case. I'm excited to hear from you, sir. I'll talk to you tomorrow." She gave him her best smile, turned and started back to the table.

He snagged her arm. "You'll come have a drink with me."

"I'm on duty." She smiled now through her teeth. "You understand."

"Nope. I'm tired of being put off. Come on, sweetheart." He tried to pull her toward him, looking surprised when he couldn't move her.

"Tomorrow," she said.

"Now," he demanded.

The two bodyguards were watching with barely concealed amusement.

She sighed. "Well, shit. Are you really going to insist?"

"Yes, I am," he grinned, tightening his hold on her arm.

"That's too bad."

Her free fist went straight to his throat. He dropped like a stone, and his surprised bodyguards began moving in. She rammed her elbows into the first man's collarbone, clasping the back of his head in her hands as he staggered, unbalanced, which allowed her to swing him to block his partner. She followed a knee to his gut with a bootheel to the kneecap; he went down screaming and she faced the other, who made the mistake of coming at her directly without putting his guard up. Her right cross broke his jaw; his eyes rolled up and he dropped next to the screamer.

The restaurant's few patrons were screaming as well, but she ignored them and turned to see Roland holding open a door; he bowed as though presenting it to her, grinning. She followed Zion and Roland through the kitchen, snatching a basket of breadsticks with a smile for the startled cook, and into the alley where they were already getting into an ancient car. She slid into the back seat and the car accelerated as she treated herself to warm bread.

Zion turned to peer back at her with a bemused expression. "Krav Maga?" he asked.

"Breadstick?" she offered him the basket, and he took one. "Sorry we didn't get to finish that excellent dinner, Zion. Roland, thanks for the getaway."

"I hope you killed that bastard." Roland glanced at her in the rearview mirror as he drove.

"I tried. I intended to crush his larynx. He slums with his bodyguards in tow, prowling for young girls. As a Church Elder, he's immune from arrest."

"This was better than arresting him." Roland's voice was cold. "I know him too. And I knew a fourteen-year-old girl who disappeared for good the last time he was in my restaurant."

"Your restaurant? I am sorry for the damage, Roland."

"It was worth it. We were ready to close it anyway, with the new laws. Just moved up our timeline, that's all."

"You have a timeline? And who else is on your timeline?"

The two men looked at each other. "You could say we are partners," Zion told her. "Were you really planning to leave the police force, Shandiin?"

"Yep. It appears my timeline has been moved up, too. You can drop me anywhere, guys. It's me they will be after, not you. Zion has already had one close call tonight; he should go to ground."

Zion shook his head. "I count two close calls. And you made the save both times. I would prefer that you come with us, Shandiin."

She saw Roland give him a sharp look. "I was headed to the bus terminal," he said. "There's still one bus running, so she could blow town. You want her to come *with* us?"

"She saved me twice, Roland."

The men locked gazes. "We don't know her." Roland was grim. "And she's a cop."

"She's not one of them," Zion said stubbornly.

"Hey," she put in. "Just drop me off."

They both ignored her.

"You can run a check," Zion suggested. "And if that's clean she still has to get past Sarnath. Quit being so paranoid."

"It would be better if you were a little more paranoid," Roland snapped.

Shandiin rolled her eyes. "Roland's right on all counts. I'm really an alien with an anal probe. Just drop me off, guys."

Zion turned to look back at her again, his strange eyes reflecting neon green from the headlights of a car behind them. "You just took down a Church Elder. They will be waiting at your residence, Shandiin. You will be safer with us."

"Well, crap." Roland sighed. "What's your full name and date of birth, Shandiin?"

"You might find me under several names, starting with Sunny Begay and Lily Haskie. My age is also subject to change. Drop me off." She saw that Roland was typing into a computer console while he drove, and swore. "Don't you get it? A security check won't do you any good. I work around the net...or what's left of it."

"That's not the kind of check we do," Zion said. She was relieved when Roland slowed to pull over, angry when she realized the car door wouldn't unlock. "Hey!" she exclaimed. "I have a gun, remember? Let me out!"

"I got a flag." Roland sounded surprised. "Egypt's been looking for her."

"That settles it." Zion looked back again. "Do you know Egypt Jones? Sometimes alias Khadijah Jones?"

Shandiin's hand was already on her weapon, but she dropped it. "Egypt? Big beautiful black woman, about six foot three, mean as hell?"

"That's her."

Shandiin grinned. "I'll be damned. Okay, I'll go with you." She sat back to finish her breadsticks.

CHAPTER 2

T he two men fell quiet as Roland maneuvered expertly over streets that had been disintegrating for years. The few cars they passed were as old as the vehicle they were in.

Shandiin was surprised to see the wall that divided the city rise ahead of them. It was called the White Curtain, usually with an unflattering epithet thrown in, for behind it lived the most privileged members of the Right Church. She was sure the roads on the other side of that wall were maintained, and that its restaurants were numbered with stars, having none of the simple charm of Roland's lost eatery.

Those inside the White Curtain only came out to prey on the less fortunate. Those on the outside of it lived on the edge of losing everything, often including their lives. Shandiin had stayed on the failing police force in an exhausted attempt to protect what she could...and for one personal reason she knew she had to face before she could leave.

She stared up at that graffitied, many-storied wall as they drove next to it, knowing her attempts to protect had been futile in the long term. Looking at the wall made her tired. She'd lately felt a dimming of her spirit that she wasn't quite able to fight.

They had turned off the main thoroughfare that gave entrance from the center of her lost city through the White Curtain, and were running alongside it to the abandoned outskirts of that city. What had once been a thriving place was in these latter days a carcass where slunk the scavengers. There were no angry young men here, as there had been throughout history when the human spirit still burned high. There was no one fighting for a home for themselves or those they loved. The criminals here were unopposed killers. The rest were the destitute, the diseased, the dregs.

The police never came here. Even Shandiin kept clear of this place.

She sat back and waited curiously for what came next, but was surprised when their car turned, nosing down into a tunnel that appeared to go under the White Curtain.

Zion looked back at her. "Out of breadsticks?" he asked, and she laughed.

"Yep. Are we nearly there?"

"*Yep*, as you say. You are very stoic about all this."

"That's actually a philosophy, you know."

"Yes. Stoicism is the essence of wisdom, courage, justice, and temperance. There is more to you than being a cop and once a soldier, Shandiin."

She just smiled, looking away at the lights strobing by in the tunnel.

"Is philosophy a hobby, or did you study it?" Zion asked.

She sighed. "I have a master's degree," she admitted, "in Philosophy. Almost another in history, specializing in the Medieval period."

His eyebrows went up. "The first is an unusual choice of study for a warrior. The second...I am not sure how that fits in."

She shrugged. "Medieval history has always fascinated me."

Roland asked, "Is that the time of the Spanish Inquisition?"

"That was later. The Medieval Inquisition was in the 12th century, targeting mostly Jews and Muslims."

"Someone wrote that religion has caused more misery throughout human history than any other single idea."

"And here we are," she agreed, "in misery once again."

Roland slowed the car. "Here we are in more ways than one. This is our first stop."

The tunnel was blocked by a concrete wall, apparently added to close it to unidentified traffic. There was a gate just wide enough for a car, guarded by a soldier in full white battle gear with an ankh insignia on the armor's chest. The helmet's black glass faceplate obscured his face.

"Wow." Shandiin sat forward. "That looks like a Warrior of God."

"Looks like." Roland rolled down his window.

The soldier approached, scanned the car's interior, nodded, pressed a button over the helmet's earpiece. The gate slid open.

They drove through and a second gate opened at their approach. "Interlock," Zion explained briefly. "If unauthorized, a car gets held here."

"Yeah, I guessed that wasn't a real Warrior of God. I'm also guessing you guys have an underground bunker of some kind, and Roland is right to be cautious about who you let in. What happens to unauthorized cars?"

"The passengers don't get past the second gate," Zion said quietly. Roland just kept driving and Shandiin crossed her arms, thoughtful. These men weren't playing games.

Shandiin leaned forward as the tunnel's lights and their headlights revealed her old friend walking down the tunnel toward them.

"Stop and let me out," she demanded. Roland obeyed and she got out.

Egypt Jones was the only woman who had ever made Shandiin feel small, and now the short hair Egypt had worn years ago had bloomed into a full aura of black curls adding another three inches to her height. The afro stood almost as wide as her shoulders.

And as she neared, Shandiin stared in shock at the jeweled emerald eyes that seemed almost brighter in that beautiful dark face than they did on Zion. "What the hell, Egypt? Are you for real? Were the brown eyes contacts?"

Egypt laughed, held out her arms for a hug. "I am so glad to see you, girl! You vanished into thin air."

"It was either that or face a court martial. Sorry I didn't keep in touch, Egypt. I figured it was safer for you if I didn't. Shit, you haven't aged a bit in what...fifteen years? Twenty?"

"I can say the same for you, girlfriend. I think you might be related to me, which is even weirder than being a redheaded Indian."

"That's Native American to you, bitch. By related you mean genetically enhanced, right? The eyes tell me you are...but I don't think I am."

Egypt just grinned. "C'mon, in the car."

They slid into the back seat, and Shandiin looked from Egypt's emerald eyes to Zion's, as he had twisted around to see both of them. "Army buddies?" he asked.

"Served together," Egypt grinned. "Shandiin saved my sorry ass once, before she refused to kill innocent civilians and went AWOL. You joining up with us, Shandiin? Please say yes."

Shandiin shrugged. "I had plans and I have no idea what I would be joining. Do you all have those weird green eyes?"

"I don't," Roland put in with a laugh. "I'm the infiltrator, the spy, the James Bond in this adventure!"

"Right," Egypt said dryly. "You tell all the women that as often as you want, Roland. You still won't get laid. And as for you, Zion, I am pissed at you. You shouldn't have been out there. How did you find Shandiin?"

"Shandiin found me," Zion replied. "Saved me, too...twice. Shandiin, we will explain about 'joining up' in a while. And I was out there because I wanted a last look at the city, and had, as an excuse, a tip that someone had seen Lilith."

"Who is Lilith?" Shandiin asked.

"She's a sister abomination," Egypt answered.

"I'd rather go with the witch label," Roland put in.

"Some of us," Zion said, "are both abominations and witches, because we do witchy stuff like medicine, physics, astronomy, engineering, and other heretic practices outside the authority of the Right Church."

Shandiin circled her hand to indicate the tunnel. "So you have an underground network."

Egypt laughed. "We surely do. And welcome, Shandiin. I'm glad you didn't go over to the dark side."

"You mean the Right side," Shandiin punned on the Church's name, ducking her head to see bright lights ahead. "Are we there yet?"

"Just about." Roland was slowing the car. "Do the honors, Egypt."

Egypt slid out of the car as it stopped in front of brightly lit hydraulic doors. She looked into a retinal scanner. The massive doors were sliding open as she returned to the car, and Roland drove through. Shandiin felt the sudden drop that told her they were in an elevator. When it stopped Roland pushed a button on his steering wheel. The second elevator door opened.

"Wow," Shandiin breathed. "Can anyone other than you weird witches open these doors?"

Zion turned back to look at her. "Yes. All of our key people. All but one are already here though, so this entrance will be shut down soon. It will all be explained, Shandiin."

Roland continued to what appeared to be an assigned space in an underground parking garage. Shandiin got out, gazing around curiously at the well-lit structure, and fell into step with Egypt behind the men as they headed toward another elevator.

She looked over at Egypt, thinking she was as beautiful as Zion was handsome, but Shandiin had never wondered about her being genetically engineered. Egypt had mentioned a poor family life when they had served together...and back then she had worn brown contacts.

"Was it all a lie?" she asked Egypt. "The family, growing up in the slums, instead of being a custom-made rich kid?"

Egypt didn't meet her eyes. "Most of us...of our family, you could say...come up with stories that makes us seem like naturals. Even before D.C. burned, before the Church took over, we knew there was danger. Zion saw the future best, though. He has been our leader and has accomplished some amazing...well, you will see." She looked over, studied Shandiin for a long moment. "I often wondered if you were like us."

"Engineered? Not that I know of. I told you the truth about being adopted on the reservation, so I'm very likely not one of the custom-built variety."

"Adopted by the Navajo?" Zion asked.

"Long story. I am more interested in yours, at the moment."

Zion peered into another scanner, opening elevator doors. Inside, Shandiin noted it was equipped with cameras, like the parking garage. "Lots of security," she observed. "More than any government operation I ever saw."

"The government isn't as efficient as we are."

"I believe that, having been a government employee. They mistake bureaucracy for competence. I'm surprised you only have the one fake Warrior standing guard in the tunnel."

"We have cameras on him," Egypt explained. "And very lethal gas to protect him as needed; his equipment would save him, but no one else. We don't mess around, Shandiin. There is too much at stake, and not just for us. For the world."

Zion threw her a warning look, and Egypt fell silent.

Shandiin frowned. "I thought you trusted me."

Zion shook his head. "It's not about trust, Shandiin. I'm more concerned about scaring you off with too much information too soon. There's a lot to know, and not many people have guessed that the new laws are just another symptom of a fatal disease." His emerald eyes met her grey gaze. "You called it something else. You said most people don't look at it, though it's hanging over our head."

She remembered her words on the sword of annihilation, and felt a chill. "You think war is coming?"

"Half the world is already at war," Roland pointed out. "They just haven't gone nuclear yet. If they do...shit, considering the world leaders in charge these days, *when* they do...nuclear firestorms will release soot and smoke into the upper atmosphere.

When that blocks sunlight, there's crop failure around the world. People who managed to survive the war will starve. The world's average temperatures will drop like the last Ice Age. And it doesn't matter who is bombing whom. With the world in paranoia, one bomb will trigger everyone, and there will be a firestorm."

He looked meaningfully at Shandiin. "You don't want to be here when it happens."

The elevator stopped, but Zion put his hand over the panel, and the door did not open.

He turned to Shandiin, his expression grave. "What you are about to see is the biggest secret of this world, which connects directly to the world's other biggest secret. Any of us would die to protect this, Shandiin. I will expect the same from you."

She stared. "I think you should take me back. I can't give a promise about something I know nothing about."

He smiled. "I know. But you will, when you see it."

"How can you know such a thing?"

"Because you have already shown me who you are."

"And if I turn out not to be who you think I am?"

Egypt dropped a hand to her shoulder. "I know you are. But we have someone who can verify it, and if you aren't what we think, we will take the necessary steps to correct our error."

Shandiin glared in suspicion. "What the fuck does that mean?"

Egypt was laughing as the elevator doors opened, but Shandiin wasn't fooled. Here was danger. She wondered if they would wipe out her memory...or herself.

Then she blinked in shock. The elevator opened on what appeared to be a grassy field circled by connecting buildings, with sunset gilding clouds in a dusky sky. It took her a moment to understand the sky was an amazing hologram.

Children were playing a game of softball under that sky while stadium lights came on around the field. As she stepped out, she saw that the elevator was next to an ordinary set of open bleachers where adults sat cheering a kid who had just hit a homer and was rounding to third base.

A man even taller than Egypt stood in front of the elevator with his back to them, hands clasped behind him as he watched the young boy slide home to shouts and applause. The man had hair of pure white that fell in a long braid down his broad back. As he turned around to look at them, she saw he was powerfully built, and while not young, he was not old enough for that white hair to be the result of age. He was dressed in loose white clothing.

This man didn't have emerald eyes, but eyes so dark the irises appeared as black as his pupils. They were unreadable, and there was something ancient hidden behind them, something that made Shandiin both wary and fascinated. Though his hair was white, his upswept eyebrows were black. His golden skin, much like her own, told her he too was of mixed blood.

"Welcome," he nodded to them, those black eyes settling on Shandiin in alert interest. She found that focus unnerving, and in fact had to stop herself from stepping back.

"Shandiin, this is Sarnath," Zion introduced. "He's kind of our local sage. Sarnath, this is Shandiin, who is joining us, but who has no idea what she is joining yet."

"I see." The huge man offered a hand so big Shandiin found her own almost lost within it... and his touch brought a strange jolt that made her try to pull away. Before she could, he quickly trapped her hand between his two. His dark eyes widened, and for a puzzling instant she read joy. "You have seen him!"

"I have?" She freed her hand and looked from the man called Sarnath to Zion, who looked as puzzled as she felt. "Who do you think I saw, Sarnath?"

Sarnath hesitated, seeming to collect himself. "He was gone as quickly as he came. Just for an instant I knew more. All I know now is you have a connection to destiny."

Shandiin scowled. Her cop instinct told her he was holding something back, but she couldn't imagine what it could be.

He looked at Zion. "He resembled Zion, but he was not him."

"Longer hair?" Zion asked.

Sarnath's eyes moved back to Shandiin. "The difference is far greater than that," he said profoundly, but did not explain. "Welcome, Shandiin. You have traveled long and far in your life, and your spirit is in chaos. I am glad you have found us at last."

He made her edgy. He reminded her of the medicine woman who had been her own adopted grandmother, and beliefs she had painfully discarded when she'd been taken from her and thrust into a world she could not trust. "Okay. Did you just read a fortune cookie?"

He smiled warmly, and she realized for the first time that he was attractive in his own way, rugged and strange though he seemed.

Shandiin was surprised at his warmth. She knew she'd been rudely flippant. She also knew Sarnath had recognized that her rudeness arose from nervousness.

She turned away from him to Egypt. "I know we must be underground, but there's the perfect illusion of sunlight and sky. Is this place built to escape the war you think is coming? Is this your secret?"

Egypt looked to Zion, who explained, "This facility is part of our secret. The bigger secret is out there playing a game of baseball." He indicated the children.

Shandiin looked at the kids, frowned. "Kids are a bigger secret than your survivalist site?"

Egypt smiled, put her hands by her mouth and yelled "Hey, Khandor! Come here!"

The home-run kid of about twelve years looked up at her call, grinned at his buddies, and trotted toward them. He took off his baseball cap as he neared, and shook back shoulder-length black hair. When he stopped in front of them, smiling, Shandiin saw he had emerald eyes like Zion and Egypt. Maturity, she thought, would make him heartbreakingly handsome as well.

But he was still just a child. "Did you see my homer?" he asked Egypt.

"I did. Great job as always. Khandor, I would like you to meet Shandiin, and tell her what you have planned for your life."

He looked a little surprised, but nodded respectfully to the tall redhead who studied him so carefully. "Hello, Ms. Shandiin. I am going to be a leader for the colony."

"What colony?" Shandiin asked.

"The colony on another world. Sorry, ma'am...Egypt; I gotta go. The inning's over, and I'm pitcher."

"And I see you have changed teams again. Go on, then." Egypt flipped a hand at him.

The boy grinned broadly and ran off to join his friends.

Shandiin stood watching them, saw that Khandor was the tallest of the children, though he didn't appear to be the oldest. She was still trying to digest what he had told her, so she put it aside for the moment in favor of the simple and mundane. "Why did he change teams?" she wondered aloud.

Zion replied. "Khandor is athletically far superior to the other children. Switching teams evens out the chances for each team to have a win. He won't play otherwise...and he only plays team sports. No one would have a chance against him in track, for instance, so he just doesn't compete."

"He does that willingly?" Shandiin asked in surprise.

"He's the one who thought of it."

"Wow. That doesn't seem...normal."

"Khandor is special," Egypt volunteered. Shandiin heard a mixture of pride and concern in her voice. "A specially engineered bloodline. And just special in general. Many of the others are genetically enhanced...but he and one other are the only ones of this specific bloodline." She paused, watching a tall man approach. "And here comes the other. Khalen, this is Shandiin. She is an old friend of mine, and she just rescued Zion from a Church cop."

Once again Shandiin looked up into inhuman emerald eyes, and for an instant thought she saw her street-corner stranger again. But when she blinked, she saw that he looked less like him than Zion did.

He was nevertheless stunning. Full black hair fell to his jawline, a few stray locks loose around his face. His jeweled eyes held hers for a long moment before he offered his hand. She took it a little nervously, and found it warmer than his expression. Those strange eyes considered her with chilling intelligence.

He didn't release her hand. "Welcome, Shandiin. And thank you for saving Zion, who shouldn't have been out there in the first place."

Zion straightened, obviously offended. "That's not for you to say."

Khalen's smile took him from handsome to beautiful. His eyes continued to hold Shandiin's as he lifted her hand and touched his lips to her knuckles, causing a disconcerting shiver. "Thank you," he repeated. "Zion doesn't like being called out, but sometimes he needs it. I'm just glad you were able to get him home in one piece."

He released her hand and turned to Zion. "Perhaps it's not my place to say it, but that doesn't change the truth. The chances of finding Lilith in that wilderness outside are nil. She is either dead or captive, and you need to accept that, sad as it is. You need to be more careful, Zion. You are too necessary to everything we are trying to do."

"You have no right to lecture me." Zion's voice was edged with anger.

"Especially in front of a new recruit you are hoping to keep," Khalen responded with an arched eyebrow, "if I don't miss my guess. But I sense that she has a mind of her own. You might be careful of that." Khalen nodded politely to a speculative Shandiin, turned and walked away.

"He's such an arrogant boy," Zion said irritably.

Shandiin was surprised. "He doesn't look like a boy. He has to be at least mid-twenties."

"Zion doesn't like the fact that Khalen grew up," Egypt laughed. "Or that he's probably as smart as himself. Cool it, Zion. He likes to get your goat and you know it."

"Yes. And he does it very well."

"Is he Khandor's father?" Shandiin asked curiously. "Khandor looks like him."

"No," Egypt said. "Khandor's the second of the bloodline, but more like a little brother to Khalen."

"And a lot less irritating," Zion noted. "Khalen's always been arrogant and critical. I'm just glad Khandor doesn't show the same traits."

Shandiin glanced at Egypt, who rolled her eyes, and guessed that this was an ongoing feud. So she changed the subject.

"Were all these children born here?"

"Most of them," Zion nodded.

Shandiin looked up at the bleachers. "Are those their parents?"

"Some of them are parents. Some, like us, are just workers."

"Just workers." She narrowed her eyes at the handsome man who smiled at her, waiting. "Zion, I am quite certain you are downplaying your role in this. Since when is an Einstein-level scientist just a worker?"

He shrugged. "When his work is done in support of the children. They are our hope for the future, Shandiin. There are more children than you see here, many at other places around the world that are similar to this one. About half of the children—and workers—have no genetic tampering. But all of us work together on a project to colonize another world and save whatever is left of humanity. This world is coming to an end, Shandiin. The end comes faster and closer every day."

Shandiin was silent. The idea of colonizing another planet was still too big a bite, so she thought she would chew on it after she had addressed what was already in front of her. She watched young Khandor wind up for a pitch. "So," she pronounced finally, "you have created a group of genetically engineered kids to replace humanity?"

"Ouch. Is that what you think?"

"It's what the Church will think. It's the kind of thinking that pushed people over the final edge that destroyed Washington

D.C. and put the Church into power. I admit even I was shocked to learn about a secret project that was creating people like you."

She turned to Zion, met his unnatural eyes. "You aren't some designer kid that had a few improvements bought by rich parents, are you? You're from that secret project, a completely engineered human. I thought you were all destroyed in the final riots. But here you are, creating more people like yourselves."

Zion met her challenging gaze solemnly, showing none of the anger he had given to Khalen. "The public's reaction to the project was fear based on the history of eugenics...such as flashbacks to the Nazi's experiments on people. The Church warned against changing what God had created, illogically ignoring the fact that modern medicine has already done that to increase health and lifespans. There's a belief that people will always use science for evil purposes. It reflects the teaching that all people are sinners and only God can redeem them."

He turned to watch Khandor pitching a no-hitter. "That secret project was called Aztlan by its creator. He believed the opposite. He believed science is essential to humanity's continued existence. With the help of other good people, he worked to engineer us, with the hope that our intelligence could save humanity from the misery it produces for itself. His name was Damon Alexander. I took his surname as my own."

He turned back to her. "Most of the engineered were killed in the riots. There are five of us left to continue Dr. Alexander's work. We are not trying to replace humans, Shandiin. We are trying to save them. Some of those children have been enhanced with our own DNA...meaning the five we call family; that includes me, Egypt, Roland, Lilith, and Sarnath. We believe those children have certain traits that will increase the colony's likelihood to survive, and even flourish. The other persons will come along as well, and most of them do not have the advantage of enhancement, but if necessary they will be protected by those of us who do."

"I'm surprised about the others."

His eyebrows went up. "Why?"

"Because I wouldn't think you would want those others involved in your plans or your colony. People without genetic enhancement are often your greatest enemies. Even without religion, humans are suspicious of anyone different. Why would you help those who might prefer to see you dead?"

"Those who work alongside me are not enemies. Like you, they are the better part of humanity, and genetic enhancement has nothing to do with that."

"It is a matter of the spirit," Sarnath agreed. "We believe that humanity has the potential to become what is good and right. That is spirit, not genetics."

Shandiin shook her head. "You work with scientists. I doubt they will agree with you."

Zion frowned. "Most of us agree with Sarnath, at least in theory. It's why we are doing this. We believe in the potential of the human spirit, given the right opportunity."

"Most of you agree? Not all of you? Aren't you the one who engineered these kids, Zion?"

"Partly. I built on the work of Dr. Alexander. But after Khalen, much of the work has been carried on by a brilliant scientist who has a different belief. She thinks that the needed traits can be created through restructuring DNA, that anything called 'spirit' is mysticism. Some of her work has actually proven her DNA theories correct, but I disagree that she is creating those traits; I think she is bringing forward what has always been existent but recessive."

Egypt snorted disdainfully. "She thinks she can create a messiah with her science."

Zion sighed. "Egypt, I know you don't like her, but we do want a leader who cannot be corrupted, and who cares for the people. I think she's succeeding."

Shandiin chuckled. "What, an incorruptible politician? That seems as far-fetched as your new planet."

"Leadership is critical," Zion said. "If you look at history you find all governments failing eventually, because of the constant war of politics. Democracy, republic...it doesn't matter; it crumbles in the face of corruption. The only efficient form of government is a dictatorship, but a corrupt dictator is even worse. So we hope for an incorruptible leader, a dictator if you will, who puts the needs of his people ahead of all else. Putting all that aside for the moment...what do you think, Shandiin? Will you join us, or do you prefer to leave us abominations behind?"

Shandiin crossed her arms, returning her gaze thoughtfully to the boy pitching a no-hitter. "I had plans of my own out there, which I can't just set aside. I have an awful lot of questions, and don't see how I could fit in here. I am not a scientist. I don't think I am one of your enhanced people. What good would I be to you?"

It was Sarnath who spoke. "What good is any person to any other? You are one of us, Shandiin, and everything you will give is yet to come...but I see your great potential. Your spirit is a beacon."

She blinked. "I bet you say that to all the girls."

She turned away as he chuckled, watching the young boy walking from the mound after pitching a perfect game. Wondered what potential was hidden there.

She realized she would like to belong here. Her own spirit shone brighter here, with these people. Watching that beautiful boy, she thought he could be a step toward an ideal she also wished she could believe in.

But she knew she couldn't. She feared their plan used the same kind of wishful thinking that had created the hopeless world she lived in. "I have to think about it. I would ask you to take me to your leader..." She looked at Zion, who was smiling at her warmly. "But I am guessing I have already met him."

"I don't lead alone," he told her. "We are a family. I imagine you are tired, Shandiin. It's much later than our sky indicates, and I know you have worked a full shift. Would you like me to show you to your new home?"

"I will take her," Egypt said, and Zion threw her a look that made the woman raise her eyebrows. After a moment he nodded, looking a little chagrined. "Of course." He looked back at Shandiin. "I will see you in the morning," he told her. "Egypt will bring you to breakfast. Have a good night."

"Thank you." Shandiin turned to fall into step with Egypt as they walked toward the closest building. "Buildings inside a...what would you call this place? An overgrown bomb shelter?" she shook her head. "Wonders never cease with you people, huh?"

"I think I just saw the biggest wonder of all," Egypt smirked. "And Khalen picked up on it too, which is one reason Zion was so annoyed with him for speaking out in front of you. We both saw the way Zion looks at you. I do believe he is smitten. He doesn't do that."

"You've got to be kidding. But—what do you mean he doesn't do that?"

"He doesn't do that kind of emotion," Egypt shrugged.

"What about the brilliant geneticist he was talking about, that you obviously don't like?"

Egypt scowled. "That one would give her left tit to get a chance at Zion, but she will never get it. He is not drawn to her; if he were, I would probably have to do something unthinkable to stop it. She is brilliant—but she is not one of the good people, and never will be." She lifted an eyebrow. "Unlike you."

Egypt opened the door into a hotel hallway, and Shandiin was startled to hear a male voice say "Welcome, Shandiin. You are in Room 1010. Just let me know if there is anything you need to make your stay more comfortable."

"Who the hell is that?" she demanded.

Egypt laughed. "That's Phil. It's an A.I. You know, an artificial intelligence, a computer. We call him Phil, which annoys Zion, as he thinks we are trying to humanize it when it is not a sentient being. He says it is no more than layers of electronic files. Files...thus Phil, get it? It runs all of our systems on this level, and some outside of it that you will learn about later." They walked down the long hallway as she spoke, stopping in front of the door numbered 1010.

Shandiin opened the door and walked into a beautifully furnished studio apartment. She stopped and stared around. "Wow. This is better than what I left behind, for sure. There's even a kitchen."

"And a stocked bar," Egypt said.

"Well, that sounds like a hint. Would you like a beer, assuming there are any in that refrigerator?"

"There had better be, or Phil will be fired." Egypt found the beers, popped one open for Shandiin, and the two women dropped into easy chairs.

Shandiin shook her head at the television they confronted. "This place has all the comforts of the people behind the White Curtain, I am guessing."

Egypt popped her beer open. "You would guess right. And they are living a few hundred feet above our heads, with no idea this is here. Everyone thought the only Aztlan project was located somewhere in Washington, which is gone."

"Zion is pretty prominent in scientific circles. Has no one figured out his origin?"

"He has been the Church's pet abomination, giving them plans and inventions that keep them safe and comfortable while he slaves away secretly doing the same for the rest of us."

"They use him," Shandiin frowned. "Is that what you are telling me?"

"Oh, yes. That mind of his..." Egypt shook her head. "He is a polymath. A genius in medicine, in many of the sciences, not just physics, and he has an eidetic memory. They call him a nonperson right to his face, but they are willing to take everything he gives them. They treat him like a beast of burden."

"That means he must go behind the wall, meet with its leaders. My God, Egypt...aren't you afraid of what they might do to him?"

Egypt nodded. "Yes. And he is aware of the risks he takes, but says he doesn't think they will do away with the goose that lays the golden eggs. Khalen is right about him...he takes too many chances."

"But what if they just cage him, make him do what they want?"

"That's always been my fear. He wouldn't tell our secrets, of course; he would die first, and like all of us, carries the means to do so. No, he is betting on a rumor flying around among the Church leaders, the people who are not religious but use the faith of others to keep power and wealth while the rest of the world dies. If there is any truth to that rumor, they will not harm a hair on his pretty head, or take a chance that he would harm himself."

"And what rumor is that?"

Egypt grinned. "That he has the secret of immortality. They know he is far older than he looks, and he has never changed in the fifty years they have known about him." She sipped her beer, tilted her head to study Shandiin. "I am the same age as Zion. You haven't grown older in our years apart. Either you are one of us, or you have really good genes from nature."

"From what Zion said, it's all nature, and science isn't creating anything from nothing."

"Aren't you interested in him as a man, Shandiin?"

Shandiin settled deeper into her chair. "Any woman with sense would be interested. But I don't do smitten, as you said about Zion. And I definitely don't fall in love, Egypt. I wouldn't be good for him."

"Wow. I am mystified. Why not?"

"Let's just say I have a lot of baggage."

Egypt studied her, finished her beer, got up to throw the can in the recycler. "You are tired, and you don't want to talk. That's fine. Get a good night's rest; Phil will get you up in time for breakfast."

"I have no clothes or anything..."

"Sure you do. You'll find a closet provided with what Phil believes you will like, based on what you are wearing. There are toiletries in the bathroom. If you can't find what you need, just say 'hey Phil,' and tell him what you need. He'll send someone to get whatever it is and deliver it to you. See you in the morning, Shandiin...and I am so glad you are here."

Shandiin didn't even get up, just watched the door close quietly behind Egypt. She sat there for a long time. She was exhausted, but knew her mind would keep her awake. She had a lot to think about.

Zion being part of it. She had guessed his interest, seen the warmth in his eyes.

She wondered, even as she pushed the thought away, why it seemed less important than the warmth in the eyes of an identical stranger she had only met for seconds.

CHAPTER 3

The next morning she found everything she needed, as promised, including blazers and jeans like her own. She dressed in black, including her shoulder holster and service weapon under the suede blazer.

Egypt met her at the door. Shandiin realized she was glad to be reunited with a friend. She had known very few in her life, for she was not a trusting person.

They walked across the now-empty field under a sky gone blue with simulated morning; light even sifted through scattered clouds. She was surprised when they entered a busy cafeteria. "Wow," she said, looking around. "I feel like I'm back in high school. Do we get to sit with the popular kids?"

"The food is better." Egypt's eyes scanned the room. "And we are the popular kids. C'mon. They will cook your eggs to order."

"Real eggs? Do you insurgents have chickens down here?"

"We also have access to cows and other livestock. How can you settle a new world without them?"

"My God. You are really serious about that colony thing."

Egypt just smiled. They went through the line together, and Shandiin noted that Egypt was shown deference, though she was friendly to everyone. The servers greeted her and knew her preferences. Shandiin looked back at them as they walked away with full trays. "Are they also to be part of your colony?"

"Yep. Everyone volunteers somewhere. We are taking in as many people as we can because we figure Earth won't be habitable for much longer. But no one gets a free ride; there is always work to be done." Egypt chose an empty table and Shandiin sat down with her. She saw Egypt look toward the door, then frown as several people came through.

"What's wrong?" Shandiin asked.

"Probably nothing. I expected Zion to be here, is all. He's always an early riser." She looked toward the door again, frowned again as Roland came in.

Roland joined them, not bothering with the food line. "Zion's on the phone with the Church," he said. "Some glitch about the ship."

Shandiin set down her fork, picked up her coffee. "What ship?"

"They're building an ark," Egypt said. "A spaceship. They plan to save their flock before things...end."

Shandiin sipped, considered. "So they believe the world is ending, like you do. And they are taking their own, leaving everyone else to end with it."

"Does that surprise you?"

"That they only care about themselves? Not in the least. But the ship is a surprise to me. They have certainly kept that quiet from the world outside their White Curtain. Where are they building it?"

"In space. It's too big to be built on-planet. Parts are built here and sent up by rocket to be assembled there. It kind of looks like the 'Death Star' in that old space-opera movie."

Shandiin laughed. "Wow. And you guys are also building a ship to go to another planet? How do you keep that secret from them?"

Roland shrugged. "The same way we do this complex. It's right under their noses."

Egypt nodded agreement. "This facility is our headquarters, but it is only one of several. Zion's a global science guru, and we have branches, so to speak, all over the world. Scientists have always been more in tune than governments. Our family has been all over, and only reunited recently." She frowned. "Most of us, anyway.

You got here just in time, Shandiin. The last of our people are being called in, and this facility will be sealed."

"Then how will you get off-planet?"

"It's...kind of complicated."

"I bet it is, and I don't expect you to tell me. Egypt...I can't stay here. I have to get out before this place is sealed up. I can't live underground."

"We won't be here forever," Egypt assured her. "I know you are skeptical, but we are serious about relocating to a new world. Zion has been working on this for years, along with some of the greatest scientists on earth."

Shandiin shook her head. "I'm no scientist, but I've read enough popular stuff to know the nearest star with planets is so far away it would take more than a lifetime to get there. I can't live like that, Egypt. Not underground, and not in a ship in space."

Egypt and Roland looked at each other. Roland leaned forward, met Shandiin's eyes as he placed a hand over hers. "Please talk to Zion before you make any decisions. His plan for a colony does not include the kind of time you are talking about. It sounds impossible, but we know him. We know just how amazing he is. He'll do what he says."

Shandiin sighed. "You have faith in him." She looked around. "He...and your family, as he says...have accomplished the nearly impossible already, it seems to me. I will certainly wait to talk to Zion, but I really don't think I can stay." She smiled a little. "But I'll be happier, knowing that you guys are out there somewhere. How long before you seal up?"

She watched them both frown. Egypt answered. "He's waiting for Lilith. She was supposed to be back weeks ago. She left her facility the same time we left ours, but hasn't arrived."

"If she's been missing that long," Shandiin said, "I think Khalen is right. She likely is dead."

Roland's smile was gone. "We know that. So does Zion. But he won't give up on her. He's like that."

"Sarnath says she is still alive," Egypt put in. "I want to believe him."

Shandiin considered. "You used Sarnath to determine if I was good enough to join your club." She caught Egypt's quick grin, ignored it. "He apparently saw a vision when he took my hand. Is he some kind of psychic?"

Egypt nodded. "Yes. Even Zion recognizes he has unusual abilities, though he will not admit they are paranormal. Zion would like to find a DNA marker for his talent, but Sarnath says it's a spiritual rather than a physical attribute."

They all looked up as the cafeteria doors opened and children came through, noisy as any happy children heading for food. Sarnath followed them like a shepherd, with the boy Khandor walking more sedately by his side; the two were in deep conversation until Sarnath gave him a push to join the others.

Egypt followed Shandiin's gaze. "Khandor is special to all of us. He carries all of our genes."

"Did you guys teach him to be altruistic?"

"No. I think it was born in him," Egypt said.

"Part of the breeding?" Shandiin grimaced. "Sounds like we're talking about racehorses or something."

Roland laughed. "I guess it seems that way. People have bred animals for specific purposes for centuries, but let human genetics go as nature willed."

"Nature meaning lust," Shandiin said dryly. "But I guess none of us asked to be born, modified or otherwise."

Roland raised his eyebrows. "According to Sarnath even that is open to debate. Some believe we choose our path before we are born."

"Then I know a lot of people who made some bad choices." Shandiin looked up, seeing Zion walk in. He came to them and pulled out a chair to sit next to her. Everyone went quiet, as he appeared very serious.

He looked at Egypt. "Did you chip her?" he asked.

Egypt nodded, then turned to Shandiin. "I'm sorry, Shandiin. It's protocol."

Shandiin sat back in alarm. "Chip? Did you put a tracer on me? What the hell, Egypt?"

Zion caught her hand, quickly releasing it when he saw the anger in her eyes. "It's my fault, not Egypt's. I designed the biochip and the parameters for use. The computer analysis showed it could be useless for security if a person were aware it existed. But you...I wanted you to be aware, so you could make a choice to stay knowing all the facts."

"What the hell? Some kind of microchip? Was it in my beer?"

"Yes," Egypt said. "It was in your beer, and is live now in your body. But it's more than a tracker. It connects you to Phil. The artificial intelligence. So it monitors everything you do or say."

Shandiin was stiff with anger. "I trusted you!"

Egypt nodded sadly. "I know. But I have one myself. We all do. It's necessary, Shandiin, to protect what we are doing."

"What...your wild-eyed fantasy about going to another planet? No one would believe me anyway. I want it out of me, and I want out of here!"

"That can be done," Egypt said. "But then we would require you to have your memory wiped."

Shandiin shoved to her feet, knocking back her chair. When Egypt looked up at her, waiting, she punched her in the mouth.

Egypt merely wiped blood from her lip, still looking up at her furious friend. "I'm not going to fight you. You can punch away, but I will not fight you. I love you like a sister, Shandiin. You should know that."

Shandiin's anger drained as she read the misery in Egypt's eyes. "You're all weird as a soup sandwich," she complained finally, picked up her chair, and sat down. "What does this fucking chip do if I act against your plans?"

"The computer triggers the chip to stop the heart," Zion said very quietly. "It kills you. We aren't playing a game, Shandiin. The survival of a lot of people depends on us."

Shandiin was silent, plowing her fingers through her heavy mass of red hair. The others were also quiet, apparently allowing her to think it through.

"I'm starting to get this," she sighed finally. "Zion's the science, Roland's a mole and practical advisor. Sarnath is the psychic reader. Egypt is security. Do you really think I would spill your secret to the Church, Egypt?"

"There are ways they can get information out of you. Even you, Shandiin."

Shandiin shook her head. "And that's why you walked me home last night instead of Zion. You didn't trust him to chip me. I get it. I'm frankly not sure why you would trust me without a chip, even inside the compound. The chip is logical, much as I hate it—but you should have given me the option *first*, dammit. It's a matter of ethics. I don't believe the end justifies the means."

Zion leaned forward. "Shandiin...does this mean you will stay, even with the chip?"

"I doubt it. I didn't want to stay even before I knew about the chip. But I'll listen and learn before I decide."

He smiled. "I'm headed to the labs. Please join me? You need to meet some other key people."

"Why?" she demanded. "Why do any of you think you can trust me, Zion, with or without a...biochip? And why am I important enough to meet your key people?"

"Because of Sarnath," Roland put in. Shandiin turned to him in question, and he added, "After you left with Egypt last night, he told us you are key to the future of this project. His premonitions are never wrong, Shandiin. We...all of us who came from the same background...call him 'The Prophet' for a reason. He is certain we need you."

She shook her head. "That makes no sense to me. None of it. But I'll play along—with the understanding I keep the option to leave."

Zion started to say something, stopped himself. Looked at the others. "May I have a minute?" he asked them.

Egypt and Roland got up to leave. When they were alone, Zion turned back to Shandiin. "I want you to know that I want you to stay for more reasons than Sarnath's prophecies. I want time to convince you to stay. With us." He shook his head, inhaled. "With me."

She looked into those strange emerald eyes and saw what Egypt had recognized. "Zion...you don't even know me."

"I feel like I do. I want the chance to know you better. Please, Shandiin. Tell me you will consider it." He put a hand over hers. "Please."

"I've already said I will think about it," she said after a moment. "So I will."

He smiled, and it made him even more beautiful. "Thank you."

They walked out, and Roland turned to him. "We need to talk to Manuel first," he said.

Zion frowned. "Do you mind waiting, Shandiin?"

"You can meet us at the lab when you're ready," Egypt cut in. "I'll walk her over, Zion."

Zion agreed, and the women walked away together.

Egypt shoved her hands in her jean pockets as she walked. "Shandiin, I know you are questioning all of this. And I know your opinion of things supernatural. But I can tell you Sarnath is the real deal. He can read a person...particularly when he can physically touch them, as he did with you yesterday." She looked at Shandiin curiously. "Who was it he saw, when he touched you? Do you know?"

"Half a dream, I think. It hardly seems real, now, briefly meeting a man who looked like Zion...but was inexplicably different. Tell, me, Egypt, did your Lilith not have a biochip?"

"Phil lost connection soon after she disappeared. It's not working."

"They may have found her, and without the chip..."

"I know," Egypt sighed. "Zion knows too. He just doesn't want to believe it. Lilith means a lot to us. She's our sister." She managed a half-hearted smile. "She's a redhead, like you, and almost as stubborn. She hates Phil, hates the chip." She sighed. "But we have already started the protocol to seal the tunnels, so the Church can't get to us even if she talks."

As they neared another building's entrance Egypt stopped, turning to Shandiin. "I'm actually glad Zion's not with us to introduce you to the geneticist. I wanted to warn you not to trust her."

"Why would you keep someone around you don't trust?" Shandiin asked in surprise.

Egypt shook her head. "It's not about the project. It's personal. She's the biggest bitch I've ever met. Nasty bitch, not the good kind like you and me. I prefer you meet her without Zion because when he's around she changes personalities like a whore changes johns."

Shandiin laughed as they walked into an empty lobby. Egypt led her to a large room that looked like what Shandiin thought a laboratory should look like. A woman in a white lab coat sat with her back to them, in front of a bank of computer monitors; she turned when Egypt announced their presence by saying, "Dr. Fairchild, you have company."

Shandiin froze under the woman's gaze. Dr. Fairchild was undoubtedly beautiful, with high cheekbones and long black hair in a thick braid, and a full figure under the white lab coat. Her eyes were dark brown, almost as black as Sarnath's, but they were as cold and hard as chrome.

Those eyes narrowed on Shandiin, and she said, "What the hell are you doing here, Mother?"

CHAPTER 4

After a moment's surprise Shandiin was able to respond. "Hel-lo, Diane. So you are the brilliant geneticist Dr. Alexander told me about. I didn't even know you had gone into that field."

"Of course you didn't know. You didn't bother with either of us, did you?"

"This is hardly the time to discuss our personal history," Shandiin sighed.

"Wait a minute," Egypt put in. " Diane Fairchild is your *daughter*?"

"I gave birth to her." Shandiin acknowledged, crossing her arms.

"And that's all you did," Diane snapped. "I repeat: What are you doing here?"

Egypt put a hand on Shandiin's shoulder. "She is here by Zion's invitation." Her voice was as cold as Diane's.

Diane gave an unladylike snort. "She's worthless. She was a philosophy major, last I heard. We need scientists, not academic fluff."

Shandiin felt Egypt's ire, put a calming hand over her friend's hand on her shoulder. "Apparently Zion thinks differently, Diane. There's a small chance we may be working together. Perhaps you could let go of some of that righteous anger for the cause of this project."

"She is right, Diane." Zion spoke from the open doorway.

Shandiin saw Diane look up in surprise, watched her daughter's beautiful face transform from cold hate to cool concern. Her smile for Zion revealed none of the rancor she had spewed moments before. "Hello, Zion. Did you know who this woman is?"

"I didn't know the relationship to you until this moment," he responded. "It makes no difference, Diane. Shandiin is one of us. The past can't matter. Our future is what's important."

Diane blinked, displaying long eyelashes and a demure expression Shandiin didn't trust. "I see."

He accepted that as agreement. "Shandiin, Egypt...will you come with me, please?"

But Diane stood as they turned to go. "Please, Zion. May I speak to you privately for a moment?"

He nodded for them to go ahead, mouthed "Wait there," to Egypt, closed the door behind them.

"I hope she doesn't jump his bones," Egypt said dryly.

"You're joking."

"Only a little. You saw the change in her. She is obsessed with him."

"Almost understandable," Shandiin sighed.

"Uh-oh." Egypt grinned at her. "You like him."

Shandiin shook her head. "Of course I like him. He's smart, and the nicest man I have ever met, and gorgeous as sin. But I am not going to fall for him, Egypt."

"Whatever you say." Egypt smiled, then sobered. "He's going to want to know about the daughter thing. It didn't turn up in our records. Or hers."

Shandiin pushed her wildfire hair back, crossed her arms. "You shouldn't have been so trusting after all, huh?"

"Bullshit. This has nothing to do with trust. You didn't know the truth about me when we first met, either, but learning about it didn't change your trust in me."

Shandiin had to smile. "You mean I didn't know you were an abomination."

"Are you?" Egypt didn't look around as Zion came out, closing the lab door behind him. She kept her eyes on Shandiin's. "Are you genetically enhanced? Because Diane is almost 50 years old, though she'd hate that I know it. That would put you at around seventy, even if you were just a teenager when you had her. You look like you're in your thirties, just as you did when I first met you."

Shandiin shook her head. "I don't know about my genes. I truly don't, because I was taken in by a Navajo family as a baby, and they didn't know my parents. But I've lied to cover my age more than once, because people get weird when you don't look like they think you should."

"It still should have shown up in our records," Zion said.

He was studying her without his former warmth, and Shandiin realized she was sorry for that. She glanced away.

Egypt scowled. "It's a private thing, really, Zion, and none of our business."

"I realize it seems that way, but Diane indicated her mother is not trustworthy, having abandoned her and her twin as babies. I would appreciate knowing the other side of the story."

Egypt turned on him angrily. "Diane's a fucking manipulator. Take anything she says with a pound of salt. Shandiin is *not* untrustworthy."

"Diane has a right to think so." Shandiin's voice was quiet. "That's really all I can tell you. If you insist on knowing more, I will need to leave."

Zion held up a hand. "Wait. This doesn't have to mean..."

This time Shandiin turned on him, her voice cold. "You obviously have respect for Diane. She must have worked hard to gain that respect, and to come so far in her career that she is working with *you*, Dr. Alexander. I will not do anything to undermine that. Either you accept that as my only answer to you, or I leave now."

He blinked, his emerald eyes sad. "I see."

Egypt shook her head. "There has to be another way...wait. Zion, do you trust me?"

He frowned. "Of course, Egypt. And I know you trust Shandiin. But..."

"But you think we need to know more. I get it." She turned back to Shandiin. "Shandiin, would you be willing to tell *me* the story? And I will decide its merit, and let Zion know…not the details…but whether or not he should accept you, trust you, based on my decision about it?"

Shandiin considered. "Yes. I would tell you, Egypt. With your promise that the story will remain between us."

Zion rubbed his chin. "It has to include the facts about her twin. Diane said Shandiin abandoned them because her sister is deformed and handicapped."

Shandiin's eyes narrowed angrily. "Leah is neither of those things. She is an albino, and she is blind, but her disability does not mean she is 'handicapped.' She has a good mind and a good heart and she does very well in her chosen field."

"Where is she?" he asked.

"She lives near where I met you, with her father."

"Tell me where. We need to get her in here."

Shandiin stared.

"Shandiin," he explained, "we have to get her where it's safe. She is your daughter, but in the eyes of the Church she will be seen as a nonperson because she is different. We can't leave her out there with what is coming. As soon as the laws are effective, I am sure the Right Church will start rounding up anyone they perceive as different. I've already instructed any of our people outside the facility to come back. Hell, you would be one of those they suspect, walking around like some pagan goddess. Do you want her father brought to us as well?"

She shook her head, inwardly a little astonished—*pagan goddess*? "I am grateful you would do that for me, Zion. But it wouldn't work. They live in a church. He is a priest. They wouldn't fit in with your…science."

"Sarnath could better explain what I think of that opinion. Your daughter is your family. She belongs with you. Don't you want them here?"

"I had planned to get them away from this city if I could. They are the only reason I have stayed. I would bring them here if that is what it takes to save them. But neither of them would leave with a stranger, Zion. I would have to go get them, and they may refuse even me."

He frowned. "You must know how dangerous that would be for you. It's for their own good. I can send armed personnel to make them come in, and we can explain to them when they get here..."

"No. I absolutely will not agree to that. This is something I would have to do...if it is to be done at all, since I will be leaving."

"You do not need to leave, and I don't want you to. Your defense of Leah shows that what Diane told me is not true, whatever her reasons for believing it. Tell Egypt your story, if you want; I won't ask again. But please reconsider going out there yourself, Shandiin. We have people..." he sighed and gave up, seeing her shake her head.

Egypt looked from one to the other. "I will go with her."

"Not necessary," Shandiin scowled.

"I'm going if you are, bitchlady. And you just hush, Zion. Between the two of us we have more combat experience than any of our armed personnel. You know I trained them."

The vehicle they used was a counterfeit of the Church's armored transports, and they both wore the uniforms of the Warriors of God. Shandiin was impressed by the arsenal they chose their weapons from. Strapping on an extra sidearm, she said, "Somehow I had the impression this was a less violent organization."

Egypt snorted. "How practical would that be, in the world we live in? We revere human life...but that doesn't mean laying down to die when our reverence is not returned. Even Sarnath, who is the least violent of us, is a trained fighter."

"I wouldn't want to fight him, then. He's huge."

"He's also an empath." Egypt spoke as they got into the transport, made sure automatic rifles were close at hand, buckled in. At Shandiin's look, Egypt added, "Not to the extent Lilith is, but empaths are very real. All of us have empathy, but they feel all the anxiety, fear, and sometimes overwhelming pain of others. He and Lilith use a mental wall for protection. He's training Khandor to use one as well."

Shandiin thought about that as she watched Egypt start the vehicle, test the shields, and drive into an elevator obviously meant for the big transport.

As the huge elevator doors closed and they began to ascend, she said "I tried to call Verity to tell him we were coming. That's his name, Father Verity Rowan. All I get is a recording and no way to leave a message. He has a landline but since most phone service is dead, I guess no one calls it, so he doesn't bother answering." She shook her head. "Egypt, I don't understand why Zion would bring two unknown religious people into the fold. I have no idea how they feel about your breed."

"Zion's done that before. He hates turning anyone away, and he feels deeply about family, since we never had one."

"What do you mean?"

"You'll learn our story, just as I'll learn yours. We'll have time to talk while we wait..." the elevator stopped, and a red light gleamed at them from the exit doors. Egypt sighed, continued. "While we wait for traffic to clear so we can go out unobserved. It could be awhile, then we'll move out quickly. As soon as that light turns green pull down your faceplate."

"Okay. But I am curious. Is empathy truly a DNA thing?"

"We didn't think so until Diane found the marker. And it's use is controversial among us. It seems to me a bigger handicap than a help."

"How many of the children are engineered?"

"There is only one bloodline, as Diane calls it, that is completely engineered...using mostly our DNA."

"So that's why Khalen and that beautiful boy Khandor have the emerald eyes."

Egypt nodded. "They are the only ones other than me and Zion with that mutation. But Khalen and Khandor are like sons to our whole family."

"Are you related—the family? Parents in common, father or mother?"

"We technically have neither."

Shandiin looked at her friend, who was keeping her eyes pinned to the red light. "Is that possible?" she asked. "Was your mother a gestational surrogate?"

"Not even that."

"So that's why Zion reacted so strongly to Diane's story. You were abandoned as babies."

Egypt finally looked at her. "Shandiin, I know you didn't abandon anyone. I know because you just wouldn't. It's not you. So our story is nothing like your daughter's, no matter what you tell me. We were not born. We were gestated in an artificial womb. The doctor...Damon Alexander believed that would ensure that nothing in the environment could interfere with our potential. Then we were raised by a group of scientists. We were raised and educated to be as knowledgeable as our handmade heritage allowed. We were cautioned to be quiet about our origin when we graduated from this facility. That was necessary, we were told, because we had to know what the world outside was like, and that it would be a dangerous place because people would be suspicious or worse if they knew the truth about us. We all had to come up with a surname, and we've changed those as necessary—and like you, we've done a lot of lying about our age."

"That is more than amazing. This is all five of you?"

"Yes. Me, Zion, Roland, Sarnath, and Lilith. There were others, but they are almost certainly dead." She frowned. "Though I think Sarnath knows more than he says."

"I first thought he was from a different country, the way he talked."

The red light flashed green, but immediately back to red.

"Sarnath has strange memories...but his memories sound like some foggy reincarnation. He says he can't explain them." Egypt shook her head. "I know that sounds weird. It's even weird to me."

The light went green and stayed. Both women pulled down their faceplates and the transport launched out of the elevator onto an empty street. Shandiin looked back to see the doors slide closed in the white wall behind them, seams invisible or hidden in the graffiti that covered it. "Cool," she said. "And I see where we are. Keep going; I'll tell you when to turn."

"Yep. Now tell me...why the hell did you make babies with a *priest*?"

"Father Verity Rowan wasn't a priest then, Egypt, he was just a horny sixteen-year-old boy, and at fifteen I was...as stated by the church leader that ran the shelter we lived in...a little tramp. They took my babies as soon as they were born, never even let me see them. Right after that the church shut down the shelter and the rest of us were dumped into the state system. I tried to track the babies down when I finally got out, but the records were sealed. Verity managed to find them through his own church. Diane got lucky; she was adopted by an affluent family, uninterested in the seedy heritage of their little princess. I know because my outreach was shut down by them, then later by her. Verity rescued Leah from one of those awful places that warehouses disabled kids. It's amazing that she wasn't mentally scarred by any of it, but she isn't." Shandiin sighed. "Leah is a truly good person. Twins couldn't be more different than she and Diane. They are my personal proof that the human spirit is not determined by DNA."

Egypt slowed, pointed at transports like their own crossing ahead of them. "The Warriors of God are already out. No warning, just picking up the abominations."

"Damn. Turn here, Egypt. Verity's church is halfway down on the left, but it won't look like a church. It looks like everyone has gone into fortress mode, with the Warriors out."

"You aren't kidding...this whole street is iron bars and sheet metal. What will you do, just walk in and ask them to come with us?"

"Not without getting shot. And it will not be easy even if they recognize me in this disguise. Verity isn't sure he can trust me because of Diane's lies."

"A priest who shoots at people?"

"I'm not sure if it's just a threat or if he'd actually kill, but at least they're still alive," Shandiin said. "Okay, this is it. He has the riot bars up, so he knows the Warriors of God are on the move. Can this thing get through?"

Without answering, Egypt used the transport's controls to lower tank treads while its wheels lifted clear. She rammed their armored vehicle against the iron bars guarding the church's entrance. When the bars yielded they lurched through and crashed the church's big double doors, which were far easier to breach; crunched through the vestibule, finally jerking to a halt in the narthex.

Gunfire met them. Bullets glanced off the windshield; swearing, Egypt engaged the shield before the bulletproof glass lost integrity to the barrage. Shandiin hit the speakers.

Her voice roared through the church. "Leah! Verity! It's Shandiin. We are not the Right Church! I've come to help you!"

Gunfire continued. "Shit," she said.

"Double shit!" Egypt exclaimed. "There's a real Warrior pulling in right behind us! Shandiin—*fire in the hole*!"

She deployed the rear turret, launching an explosive point blank through the enemy's windshield. Both women covered their eyes from the fire-burst, too brilliant even through their black faceplates.

Ears still ringing, Shandiin hit the speakers again. "Believe me now, Verity?"

When there was no answering gunfire, Egypt raised the shields. They emerged from each side of the transport, standing behind the open doors for safety while Shandiin lifted her faceplate. She drew in a breath, stepped from behind it, hands up and empty. "It's me! Listen—there will be more of these damned Warriors coming. We're here to help you. You need to come with us!"

A figure rose from behind the armored pulpit, stepped out. He pulled off his plain helmet as he strode toward them, rifle cradled over one arm of his Kevlar bodysuit. His hair was pure white, falling almost to his broad shoulders. As he neared, his age became apparent in the granite structure of his face, but the golden-whiskey eyes were clear and sharp. He was still a handsome man, even in his seventies.

Egypt whistled. "That doesn't look like any priest I ever saw," she remarked.

Shandiin saw the wariness in his eyes as they took in her uniform, Egypt's, the armored transport.

"Explain," he said.

"There's no time, Verity. Please get Leah. We've come to get you both out."

"Out to where? Those soldiers are all over the place. It's like war has been declared."

"It just about has," Shandiin said. "The Right Church is picking up anyone it deems a potential enemy. Look—you have got to trust me. I wouldn't be here if it weren't to protect you. Please get Leah and let's go."

"I don't know—" he began, but then a softer feminine voice called "Mother?" and he spun around. "I told you to wait!" he exclaimed.

Shandiin ignored him and turned to her daughter. "Yes, Leah. It's me." She watched the slight, fragile, almost beautiful figure who walked toward them, wearing a nun's plain habit. Her white hair fell free over her shoulders. Her skin was almost white. Her nearly colorless blue eyes were blind, but she walked like one sighted, because she knew her way in this familiar place, and because she knew her father's voice.

And, somehow, her mother's. Leah smiled on hearing Shandiin speak, and came directly to her with her arms open. Shandiin fought tears as she embraced the daughter she had only known from a distance. She looked up to see the priest still frowning.

"Please," Shandiin begged him. "Come with us."

"Will you take her somewhere safe?" he asked.

"Yes. You too, Verity."

"No. I can't. I have a basement full of kids relying on me. Their parents sent them here because they want them hidden from the Warriors. Now you've knocked down the bars...."

"Don't you think the Warriors would have done that?" Shandiin hissed. "It's better if you're open. You can tell a sad story about looters."

"How are you going to get that other transport out of here?" he demanded. "They won't believe looters destroyed it."

"We'll manage." Egypt walked over, pushing up her faceplate. "And they know there are armed citizens who will fight back. Your church will be an obvious target for those who hate any religion because of the Right Church."

The priest turned to her angrily. "The Right Church isn't re-ligion, it's terrorism given authority." Then he stepped back in surprise, staring into her face. "Are you wearing contacts?"

"No." Egypt's voice was cold. "Shandiin, we have to go before another transport shows up."

The priest turned to Leah. "Go with them," he urged her.

"I don't want to leave you!"

"It's better if you do. You know they will target you. The new law labels anyone with a birth defect as a misfit. It might even be safer for the children if you aren't here to give them ideas." He put a gentle hand on her shoulder. "Please go with them. I'll feel better knowing you're safe...and seeing these two, I figure you have a better chance with them than with me."

Leah threw herself into his arms, pressed her face into his chest.

The priest put his arms around her, and looked over her head into Shandiin's eyes. "Keep her safe, please." His voice was thick with emotion.

Shandiin swallowed, nodded. "C'mon, Leah."

But it was Egypt who helped Leah into the transport while Shandiin and the priest regarded each other. "I wish you would come with us," Shandiin told him. "We could take some of the children."

He shook his head. "They have parents who hope to be reunited when the Warriors are gone. They figure there will be no interest in the children, so they will be safe even if they are found here. Tell me...have you learned anything about Diane?"

"I can tell you she's safe. She is where Leah's going."

"That's good to know. She wouldn't respond to my attempts to reach her, and then I lost track of her completely." He hesitated. "Take care of yourself too, Shandiin. I have missed you." To her surprise, he leaned in and kissed her lips very gently before turning to walk away.

"Verity..." she called after him. "At least take the landline off of the automatic message. I want to be able to call you. Answer it if it rings."

He only lifted a hand in acknowledgement, kept walking away. Her vision was a little blurry as she turned back to the vehicle.

"Hope the hell we can shove that transport out of the way," Egypt muttered as Shandiin slid into the front seat.

She shifted into reverse, and the engine rumbled, then roared. It seemed hopeless at first, but their treads finally bit through the floor and gave the needed traction to shove the dead transport back through the doors, the ruined bars, and onto the street.

"Lucked out." Egypt switched treads to wheels and turned to retrace their path. "That was the only one on this street. Hopefully this won't be like the movies, and we can get back home without fighting off an army."

"Thank you for coming." Leah spoke softly from the back seat. "Are you the one driving us, Mother?"

"No, Leah. This is my friend, Egypt. She's part of a special family that is working very hard to save people."

"Hello, Egypt," Leah said. "You and your family must be guardian angels!"

"I know Egypt too well to call her an angel," Shandiin laughed. "But she and her people are doing their work."

They all fell silent as Egypt pulled to the side of the street in front of the great white wall, allowing other Warrior vehicles to trundle past while they waited nervously. Egypt used her radio to let her people know they were coming back and bringing Leah, Shandiin's daughter.

When it was clear, the wall opened and they were through.

Leah was quiet as the elevator dropped, seeming relieved when Shandiin opened her door to help her out.

Sarnath waited for them. "So glad you're back," he greeted them. "And welcome to you, Leah. I am Sarnath."

Leah stepped forward and he took her hands. She asked, "Are you part of Egypt's family?"

Sarnath tilted his head, studying her. "We call ourselves family, Leah, but we are not really related in the usual fashion. There are five of us who have been genetically enhanced...abominations, in the words of the Right Church. We are different."

Leah smiled. "I understand very well about being different. I am glad you are doing this work, helping everyone you can, even though some people are so hateful toward you. How many are in your family?"

Sarnath seemed entranced. "At present we are seven, counting our two sons. Two of us are not here right now. Please come with me to meet those of us who are waiting to know you."

He kept her small hand in his as they walked out through the field with the holographic sky. Shandiin watched Leah turn her face upwards and frown in puzzlement. "It seems I can feel the sun on my face," she said, "but I had believed we are somewhere underground."

Even Sarnath looked surprised. "You are right on both counts. Few people notice the rays from our artificial sun that strongly. Of course, your senses are better attuned than most, I think."

"That's what Father says." She turned toward Shandiin. "I wish he could have come with us."

Shandiin took her other hand. "Perhaps we can get him to come in after the children are safe."

They continued walking, and Sarnath led them into the hotel building and an open meeting room Shandiin hadn't noticed before. It was set up with a conference table and a large television monitor.

Shandiin frowned when they walked in. It seemed like a meeting was in progress. She looked around at the table where waited Zion, Diane, Khalen and Khandor. She glanced at Egypt, who took off her Warrior helmet and shook out her magnificent afro as she asked, "What's up? And where's Roland?"

"He's undercover in his role as Elder at the Right Church," Zion explained. "Sarnath sent him, claiming something is coming, and as you know his premonitions are generally valid. We're waiting for him to call."

Shandiin also removed her heavy helmet, noting Khandor and Khalen sat together, the boy placid, Khalen coolly observant. On Khalen's other side sat Diane, who was staring at her angrily.

Sarnath began introducing everyone to Leah as he seated her at the table. Shandiin noted Leah showed no reaction to Diane's name.

The boy Khandor was looking curiously at Leah. "Can't you see?" he asked her.

"No," she smiled, "I cannot. But I can tell you are a boy of eleven or twelve, and there is a man next to you who is very protective. Is he your father?"

Khalen looked up in surprise. "No. I am not his father. But we are sort of related. Khandor, you should not ask such personal questions when meeting someone. It is disrespectful."

"I apologize," Khandor said promptly. "I meant no disrespect, ma'am."

Leah laughed softly. "You are a delightful young man. Just call me Leah, please. And I do not mind answering questions; I have a lot of those myself."

"May I ask how you knew Khalen is protective of me? I mean, I know he is. He's worse than a mother hen. But how could you tell?"

"Mother hen, am I?" Khalen gave Khandor a brotherly slap on the head, causing the boy to grin.

Leah looked thoughtful. "You know, I'm not sure. I just seem to know things, sometimes."

"Are you an empath?"

"Khandor," Khalen warned.

"It's all right," Leah smiled again. "I don't consider that a personal question, as I have often wondered about that term. I have empathy, but I think being an empath is something more."

"It is." Khandor nodded. "And it's a fucking pain in the ass."

"Khandor!" Sarnath exclaimed sternly.

But Egypt was laughing. "Admit it, Sarnath, you have felt the same way. Sorry he picked up my bad language though. That wasn't nice, Khandor."

"Darned pain in the neck, then?" the boy grinned.

"That will do," Sarnath sighed.

Shandiin finally sat down at the table across from Diane and Khalen. She frowned at the menace in her daughter's eyes, decided to throw something into the proverbial fan. "Diane, why did you put that empath thing into the DNA mix?" she asked her. "It seems kind of useless, unless it includes the ability to read minds."

Diane shrugged. "It wasn't my idea, but Zion wanted it."

"Zion ordered it at my urging." Sarnath's eyes were hard on Diane. "It is necessary for a leader to be able to read not the mind, but the spirit of a person...and, when necessary, recognize evil even before it is aware."

Diane rolled her eyes dismissively. "I think evil is another invention of religion."

Egypt scowled at her as she sat down next to Shandiin. When she spoke her voice was like steel. "Our differences in philosophy have no purpose here. The mission for this bloodline is to create a leader for the colony. Zion's work resulted in Khalen. You believe you also included complete incorruptibility and driving purpose in your DNA recipe. I personally don't see how that is even possible."

"It is more than possible!" Diane snapped. "My work will ensure that we will not have a repeat of Earth's history. The colony's leader is key to that. He will be true and honest, strong and incorruptible, with his people as his sole purpose."

Leah exclaimed, "That is so *wrong!*"

"Why?" Egypt asked in surprise. "You mean it's wrong that we have created a bloodline?"

Leah shook her head. She sat back in her chair, looking distraught. "No. But...all of that should not be decided for him! And—it is wrong to make any human have only a single purpose, no matter how ideal! He would have no free will! That...*all* of that is tampering with his *spirit!*"

Shandiin put a calming hand on Leah's shoulder, but she was also frowning. "I have to agree with Leah that this seems to be going too far. However...I also have to say I am very skeptical that any amount of genetic tampering could create a person like you have just described. He sounds like some kind of...of..."

"Like a messiah? A god?" Egypt finished for her. "I have to agree with you. I have mistrusted this plan from the start. Fortunately I also believe it's impossible. Genius and empathetic? Yes. We have that in our Zion, though he is not an empath. But you expect Khandor and his progeny to be purely honest and incorruptible, with no purpose in life but to shepherd the people? No. It's crazy."

Zion sighed. "I have to admit I have my doubts as well. And Khandor's childish honesty is not necessarily the best trait for a leader dealing with a lot of personalities...such as we have here, apparently."

"It's *wrong,*" Leah repeated. "I hope it is not possible, because it is *wrong!* How would such a person feel? No human should be one of a kind. No person should be created to exist so different...so *alone,* no matter how noble their purpose. No one."

She drew in a breath, turned toward Zion. "But...please, sir, what did you mean by the term 'childish honesty?' Isn't that just a way to belittle what is good and right, instead of honoring it?"

Zion looked shocked. Sarnath, nodding, crossed his arms. "Now you see why I wanted this meeting to include Shandiin. I included Leah as soon as I met her, for she has her own special wisdom. Zion, we are leaders with great responsibility for a lot of people who would die without our help. Part of our responsibility is ensuring we look at every side of any issue related to them."

Khalen's hand on the table had clenched into a fist. "You're all talking about Khandor and me like we aren't sitting right here. We aren't just an issue to be resolved. We aren't lab rats. I for one am sick of being treated like one. Obviously a failed lab rat, or Khandor wouldn't be here at all, would he?"

Zion scowled. "Quit being so dramatic, Khalen. None of that is why Sarnath called this meeting. Sarnath, is it your intent that Shandiin and Leah become part of the Aztlan project's leadership?"

Shandiin leaned forward angrily. "Whoa! Just a minute here! I am just one of the people you have taken in, and a last-minute arrival at that; I know nothing about your history or your mission that treats humans as lab rats...and Khalen, I wouldn't blame you for being angry about that, if it's true. But neither Leah nor I have agreed to act in any capacity for your project, much less as part of your leadership!"

"I see your point, but would like the opportunity to make mine. Would you be willing to answer some questions?" Sarnath asked her.

"Only if you are willing to consider my opinion about how you operate," she snapped back. "It seems to me you are pretty high-handed about making decisions that affect someone else." Her glare included Egypt. "Like lab rats, biochips and memberships."

Sarnath nodded thoughtfully. "And that's reason number one why we need you. We are the leaders of what's left of project

Aztlan. No matter how right we think we are, we must guard against becoming a government of tyranny. That could happen without our intent. We need a system of checks and balances requiring us to look at our own actions objectively."

"So I'm your gadfly? Is that it?"

"You can name it as you will," Sarnath replied. "But that would be an important part of your role. Tell me...were you aware of our existence before you found Dr. Alexander outside of this facility and saved him from arrest?"

"You know I wasn't. This whole thing has been news to me."

"Yes. The project that created our family was named Aztlan. Can you tell me what Aztlan means?"

She frowned. "I know the word. It is part of a myth. Aztlan was supposedly the paradise from which the Aztecs came, a land in the southwestern deserts that became part of Mexico and Arizona."

Sarnath nodded placidly. "Where are you from, Shandiin?"

Shandiin narrowed her eyes. "Are you trying to tie me to a myth? I was born in the southwest, on a reservation created to warehouse the native Americans vanquished by the people who invaded their homeland."

"You say you were born there. How do you know that?"

She frowned. "I guess I don't. It's an assumption, because as an infant I was found by a Navajo woman who took me in and made me part of her family."

"Where and how did she find you?" Sarnath continued to press.

Shandiin sat back, uncomfortable with questions hinting at knowledge of her origins...knowledge Sarnath shouldn't have. But she felt she owed answers to the people who had offered safety to her and her daughter. "The Navajo people use dogs to protect the sheep they raise. My Shimá Sáni ...that is, the woman I called grandmother...found me in the desert at sunrise, her dog curled around me, apparently to keep me warm."

Sarnath nodded. "And so, Shandiin, you were named for the sun. Is there anything you would like to share about why sunrise has meaning to your adopted people?"

Shandiin crossed her arms over her chest. "They believe that sunrise is when spirits walk the earth. My grandmother believed they had brought me there. It's a religion, Sarnath. Just another religion. I don't believe in any religion."

Sarnath remained placid. "I see. Do you think religion is based on magical thinking? And if so, do you believe magic exists at all?"

"I do and I don't. What has this to do with making me part of your project?"

"Shandiin, I apologize for invading your thoughts, your history, but my...premonition about you, as Zion would call it...has brought me to believe you are critical to this project in ways yet to be discovered. It's not just as a gadfly. Your story sounds like a tale of magic. Yet you reject the possibility that magic could be involved."

Shandiin looked around the room. Zion and Diane looked vaguely annoyed with the topic. The rest appeared intrigued.

Frowning, she decided she would go along with Sarnath's line of reasoning to find out what he was getting at.

"It's semantics." She sat back thoughtfully. "I don't know why it should matter what I think, when most of you have more education than I do. But you asked. I am skeptical of looking for magic answers to very real problems...like the changes that are destroying our planet. You scientists probably feel the same. But is science the *only* answer to resolving our problems? Science searches for the hidden blueprint of the universe, what it's made of, how it works. But how do you find the 'why' of it all? Hell, the very 'thing' that makes us ask is a mystery to us. Is consciousness a 'thing'...or is it magic?"

She turned back to the others. "Carl Sagan said, and I agree, that the absence of evidence is not evidence of absence. So how can anyone *know* there is no magic? So...no, Sarnath, I can't unequivocally reject the concept of magic, no matter how wary I am."

Before anyone could respond, the computer called Phil interrupted. "I am turning on the monitor. The Right Church is making a televised announcement. I am also putting through a call from Roland."

The monitor turned on to show a room full of people facing an empty stage with a podium.

The room's speakers filled with heavy breathing before a panicked voice came on the line. "Zion," Roland said. "They have Lilith. They've been questioning her. They know about us."

CHAPTER 5

Roland's voice was low, almost a frantic hiss. "They are making an announcement and have Lilith with them. I was only able to speak to her briefly without them hearing. I can't believe her courage. They have had her all this time, and only got pieces of information from her. They know the children exist, but not where they are. They do not know of your location, despite everything they did to her. She has suffered, Zion. I can't let her suffer any more."

Roland ended the call before anyone could respond. Visibly shaken, Zion was on his feet, staring at the television.

Shandiin recognized the church leader immediately. His Eminence Marshall Canard, duly elected President of what was left of the United States of America, took his place at the podium while streaming text announced "the capture of an abomination."

"Dr. Zion Alexander is a nonperson under the laws of God's Right Church," His Eminence was saying. "We have been investigating him for some time on suspicion of sedition. Our suspicions are now confirmed by the word of his collaborator, who is in our custody. Dr. Alexander has been involved in the unholy breeding of abominations with the intent of ruling humanity. This will not be allowed to continue."

The news conference was being held at the Temple that had replaced the destroyed White House. The congregation there rumbled and howled at this pronouncement. The camera panned away from His Eminence to show the audience, then came back to him, but the new angle was far enough away they could now see the people moving to stand at the back of the stage.

"Dammit!" Egypt exclaimed.

"Is that Lilith?" Shandiin asked as she stared at the monitor, but she hardly needed an answer. The woman standing behind His Eminence was obviously a prisoner between two Warriors of God. Her hair was a tangle of brilliant copper falling over the shoulders of a cloaking gray gown. She was beautiful beyond measure, even though her face was a battered mask of grief and fear. She started to sink down as though her legs were too weak to stand; one of the Warriors jerked her upright.

Roland, wearing the white suit of a Church Elder, went to her in apparent sympathy to offer water. Lilith looked at him, and Shandiin saw open gratitude. Lilith drank while he held the bottle for her.

His Eminence indicated the captive behind him. "This witch has given us information…"

Lilith collapsed. The church leader turned back to look as the Warriors again tried to pull her upright, but it was like holding a rag doll. They gave up and dropped her to the floor; another man went to her, checked her vitals. He finally looked up and shook his head.

Zion's cry of grief tore at Shandiin's heart. She thought of his benevolence, his compassion, and felt he should never have to know such pain.

His Eminence stood for a moment before turning back, his face carefully composed. "God be praised," he intoned. "He has allowed us to witness the smiting of evil, striking this witch down to show His strength and glory. Let this be a warning to all who would follow evil…"

Egypt spun away from the television, fighting tears. "Smiting of evil?" She almost choked on the words. "Lilith was the most honest person you could know. And it wasn't God who took her, but Roland. He gave her the water, and it was poisoned and she knew it—I saw it on her face—the relief, the gratitude."

"I am so sorry," was all Shandiin could say, but Egypt just shook her head.

His Eminence rapped the podium. "This is a sign that we can wait no longer for the last sheep to find their way home. Membership of the Right Church is hereby closed. The new laws are now in effect. The Warriors of God will arrest all abominations, including these misborn children, to ensure they cannot do harm to humanity. Have no fear, you of the faithful. All will be well."

"The children!" Leah cried, snatching at Shandiin's hand. "Mother, they will find the children in the church! They will say they are abominations!"

"She's right," Egypt agreed. "Shandiin, we have to go back."

But Shandiin was already standing to address Phil, giving the computer the phone number of Father Rowan's church, hoping Verity had listened to her, that he would answer the call.

She exhaled in relief when she heard his voice say hello.

"How many kids do you still have there?" she demanded.

"The parents already picked up most of them. There are only seven still here; I think their parents have been taken."

"The Church just declared war on the children, Verity. They will take them all, *any* of them, in the off chance they are enhanced. Hold them there. We're coming for them, and for you."

There was only a brief pause before he gave in with a quiet, "We'll be here, Shandiin."

Egypt was already up and heading for the door, Zion and Sarnath on her heels. Sarnath had both Leah and Khandor in tow. Shandiin followed them out but remembered the helmet she had left on the table, and turned back.

She stopped short in the doorway, seeing Khalen and Diane confronting each other. They stood intimately close.

"You can't go with them," Diane was saying. "Zion won't let you, Khalen."

"He doesn't own me. I'm not taking his orders anymore. Or yours, Diane." He turned away from her angrily, headed toward the door.

But he hesitated and spun back to her, taking her shoulders to kiss her so ardently Shandiin blinked. Then he shook her, whispered something, kissed her again but briefly, and came toward Shandiin.

"I'm going with you," he declared to Shandiin as he walked past.

Shandiin stared at Diane, who just smirked at her. Eyebrows lifted, Shandiin grabbed her helmet and turned to follow Khalen out.

They walked briskly toward the elevators. "You're coming along is fine by me," Shandiin said to Khalen, "but have you ever been outside this facility?"

"Not yet," he shot back.

Zion stepped in front of them. "You can't—"

"Out of the way," Khalen snarled.

Shandiin moved between them. "Zion, I am sorry about your loss, but you need to stand down. Egypt and I are going to get those kids out of that church, and Khalen is going with us."

She stood with her eyes on his while Khalen walked past to join Egypt.

"Why are you taking him?" Zion asked her.

"Why shouldn't I? Doesn't he know how to fight?"

"Of course he's been trained, but—"

"Then I see no reason to keep your lab rat in its cage."

"Shandiin, that isn't fair. You don't know the whole story."

"And I don't have time for stories right now. You have a noble mission, Zion, but Sarnath is right about needing to look at more than one point of view."

He caught her arm as she started past, immediately let go, seeing the warning in her eyes. "Be careful," he said inanely to her, and then turned to Khalen. "I understand more than you think," he told him. "I love you. We all do, Khalen."

Shandiin went to Leah, gave her a hug. "I'll bring your father." She looked up at Sarnath. "Please take care of Leah."

Khandor took Leah's hand. "I'll care for Leah, too. And you can trust Khalen. He always does what's right."

They all stood watching as the elevator doors closed on the three rescuers.

Egypt tossed Warrior body armor to Khalen while she and Shandiin loaded the transport with more firearms. He pulled the armor over his clothes and climbed in behind the women, where he strapped on weapons as the transport elevator went up again.

They waited for the light to go green. "Shandiin, Egypt...I want to say thank you," Khalen said quietly.

"For what?" Egypt snapped. "Letting you have an adventure?"

"I'm not just having an adventure."

Egypt snorted. "So, why did you come? Are you running away from home? You haven't any idea what you're going to find out there, Khalen, and you don't have a plan."

"He needs to see the outside before he can plan for it," Shandiin put in. "And he has a perfect right to leave if he wants. Egypt, you must realize that."

Egypt huffed. The light turned green; they closed faceplates as the transport lurched out.

After a few moments Egypt shifted her gaze to the rear view mirror, to the young man she considered her son. "Khalen, of course you have a right to leave. You are not a lab rat. I know Zion is hard on you, but he cares about you. We all do. I guess we've been as overprotective of you as you are of Khandor. I'm sorry for that. I'm doubly sorry if we have treated you unfairly."

"It's not about anyone being unfair." Khalen was studying the street. "It's about feeling like I can be of some use...which I can't, to the project. Khandor is what Zion and Diane wanted. He'll be a great leader."

Egypt grimaced. "He's *twelve*! Are you abandoning him, Khalen?"

Shandiin looked back in time to see the shock on Khalen's face, nodded when his expression went thoughtful.

"You are all Khandor has, aren't you?" Shandiin asked him. "The closest thing to true family he has. The other engineered are one entity. You and Khandor are another. Right or wrong, you belong to each other, or I miss my guess."

"Heads up," Egypt warned as she turned down the street toward the church. "There are lots more Warriors out here, and some are swarming the transport we killed."

They pulled up behind another transport; four Warriors were indeed climbing over the one Egypt had taken out earlier. When Egypt opened her door they could hear the pops of nearby gunfire, people shouting.

"Have your weapons ready," Egypt warned. She got out, leaving the driver's door open, and strode toward the enemy. For the first time Shandiin noticed she wore Lieutenant bars on her counterfeit uniform. She was surprised to hear a male voice issue from Egypt's helmet. "I have word this was done by rebel troops," the gruff voice said. "You follow." She pointed down the street. "Go about six blocks, then turn north; it's suspected their headquarters are in that area. We will search this heretic church and join you shortly."

Used to following orders, the Warriors climbed into their transport. Egypt slapped their rear fender as they drove off, turned back.

"I put a jammer on their fender so they can't transmit or receive," she said, scanning the street. The noises of warfare continued, too close for comfort. "That should buy us time. I'll stand guard. You two go in and get the kids." She pointed at Khalen. "Stay behind Shandiin. She knows this priest, you don't."

He said nothing, but followed Shandiin through the ruined church entrance. She shouted for Verity.

He came through a rear doorway, followed by children.

Too many children.

The priest came to her, obviously distressed. "More were brought to me, and open fighting started right after the President's pronouncement. Please...you have to take them all."

"That's more than the transport can hold," Shandiin said.

"They can sit on each other's laps or cram onto the floorboards." Khalen spoke as he shoved up his faceplate, kneeling to a small boy who was crying. When the child looked into his emerald eyes he stopped crying...and to Shandiin's surprise, he returned Khalen's smile. Khalen picked him up, crooked a finger at the rest, and they followed him out obediently.

He was helping them onto the transport while Egypt goggled.

"Can Khalen drive this thing?" Shandiin asked her.

"No. Not part of his training."

They both stared as Khalen turned back to them. The kids were all in, but there was barely room for the driver. Khalen told Egypt, "You have to take them. Just go."

"Dammit, Khalen..." but she stopped herself. She pulled an ankh on a pendant from under her shirt and shoved it into his pocket. Then she put her arms around him, hugged him for a moment, and leaned back with her hands gripping his arms. "I'll come back for you."

Khalen shook his head in denial. "Zion has to seal up. Don't let him try to wait for us. The Warriors are on the hunt and they'll find at least one of the entrances. Seal up and don't come back for us."

Shandiin stepped in. "It's not safe here, Egypt. The fighting's getting closer, and that other transport will be back. You have to go, get the kids clear."

Egypt took a deep breath. "I'll go. But that biochip you hate can track you, so I will find you wherever you end up. When Zion has the ships..." she broke mid-sentence, shook her head. "Shit, that's too much to explain right now, but know that I'll come for you. It may be awhile, but I will come for you. Take care of yourself." She nodded toward Khalen. "Take care of him. He's the son of my heart, Shandiin. Take care of him."

Shandiin thought she saw the gleam of tears before Egypt turned away and climbed into the transport.

They couldn't watch it drive away; the fighting was getting closer. "Come with me," the priest ordered, starting back to the church. "I have a place we can hide, and I have some things set aside for emergencies." Shandiin and Khalen followed on his heels.

"Your church has a priest hole," Shandiin remarked as she watched Verity open a trap door in what had appeared to be a solid stone basement floor. "I should have known."

"Yes. Just like in the old days in England, and just as necessary. It seems someone is always being persecuted. There were too many very young children to get them out this way, but I was going to try if you hadn't come."

They climbed down a ladder and Verity closed the door above them, flicking on a light to reveal a small cave-like room, it's walls shelved with supplies.

He looked at them both. "I suggest you take off the Warrior uniforms. They would make the Warriors hesitate before they shoot, but the rebels would take you down in a minute."

"No chance the rebels would be on our side?" Shandiin asked, stripping down to jeans and a tank top.

The priest regarded her as she shook back her wild red hair. His narrowed eyes scanned her body, studying her toned shoulders, the muscles smoothly sculpting her arms. His gaze lifted abruptly to her face, which showed not her seventy years, but mid-thirties. Then he turned to look at Khalen, who had muscles more obvious than hers under his faded jeans and blue tee shirt.

As well as those inhuman emerald eyes in a face even more beautiful than the woman's.

"You are both enhanced," he declared.

"Is that a problem, Verity?" Shandiin asked.

He shook his head. "Not for me. But it won't help us with the rebels. The people out there right now hate everyone they don't already know. And they are suspicious of the enhanced." His eyes went back to Khalen's. "I pray they didn't mix animal genes with yours, young man."

Khalen shoved his hands into his jean pockets, coolly meeting Verity's gaze. "You are thinking of animals whose eyes shine green in the dark. It's from a structure behind the retina that registers light, giving the animal night vision. My genes include a mutation that also combines improved night vision. There are four of us with the same mutation." He lifted his chin. "Just for your information, blue eyes are also a mutation that came down from a single common ancestor. I don't believe I am any more inhuman than a blue-eyed person."

Verity blinked. "My apologies. I didn't mean to be offensive. It's just...a disturbing idea."

Khalen smiled coolly. "I find many ideas disturbing, including those that involve judging other people because they are different."

"*Touché*," Shandiin murmured.

The priest exhaled. "Yes. I forgot my own teachings, didn't I? So I guess I should be praying forgiveness for myself, not on your behalf, Mr. —"

"Khalen. Just Khalen. How should I call you, sir?"

"He's Father Rowan," Shandiin put in. "I call him by his given name Verity because I knew him before he entered the priesthood."

They all looked up at noises coming from the church above them, hands going to their weapons.

There were muffled curses, thuds as large objects were knocked over.

"They will burn it," Verity murmured. "They've learned to hate anything of a religious nature, so they will burn the church. It's best to start moving. Both of you...there is soft body armor on that shelf, along with backpacks that already have supplies."

They donned Kevlar while the priest jostled aside shelving to reveal a narrow passageway. He motioned Khalen to move the shelving back into place after they filed through to the passageway, lit only by the priest's flashlight.

"Where does this come out?" Shandiin asked him.

"It connects to the sewer system, but we can't go past the abandoned gas station on Winslow Street. I don't know if there's anywhere safe to go from there. The city is at war. It's like the end of days."

"'Woe to the earth and the sea'," Shandiin quoted.

"Revelations 12:12. You surprise me, Shandiin."

"I may be a pagan, Verity, but I can read."

The passageway opened to the underground sewage system, which was fortunately not flooded. They all stepped down into a scrim of stinking sludge. "Enjoying your adventure?" Shandiin asked over her shoulder.

"This isn't exactly what I had in mind," Khalen replied mildly.

It was a long and miserable walk. The priest turned off the flashlight when they could finally see light ahead, and Shandiin tapped him on the shoulder. "I go first."

When he opened his mouth to argue, she put her hand over it. "I'm a cop," she hissed. "You're a priest." He looked into her eyes and even in dim light saw her clear warning. He scowled, but he stepped aside.

The light came from an overhead storm drain. The tunnel dropped past it, and they could hear the sound of liquid sloshing beyond, so this was their exit.

She eased up to the grate, pushed it up enough to peer around at ground level. Quickly closed it.

"Shit," she whispered. "Five men in a circle, shoving a woman back and forth. Watch my back."

She pushed up the grate, climbed out, and stalked with gun at the ready toward the laughing men surrounding the sobbing woman. They were so involved in their fun no one even noticed her.

One of the men pushed her to the ground and another held her there. Their intent was obvious. The others watched avidly.

Shandiin shot the first two in the head.

As the other three tried to scatter, she fired three more times.

Then she walked to the woman, who was now sobbing with her hands over her face. Shandiin saw evidence of the struggle, but no blood on her. She turned back to see both Verity and Khalen standing over the dead men, apparently frozen in place.

"Khalen," she snapped. When he didn't respond, she raised her voice. "Khalen! Start scanning the street! This is a war zone!"

He jolted, stumbled back a step, turned away with his rifle ready.

"Verity," she told the priest, "get a shirt off one of those corpses. This woman's has been torn off of her."

He followed her direction, dropping to his knees beside the woman who was taking harsh, gasping breaths while her eyes stared at a horror they couldn't see. She wailed, "They killed him. They killed my husband, my Roy."

"Help her," Shandiin said. "Please, Verity. You're the best at that."

She stood, scanned the street, saw Khalen doing the same. She was certain he'd never seen violent death before, but he seemed to have recovered from the initial shock.

When she turned back the woman was standing, buttoning the shirt while Verity had his arm around her hunched shoulders. When the priest met Shandiin's eyes, his held both shock and anger.

"Is that judgement I see, Verity?" she asked him.

"I can't believe I just watched you kill five people," he said.

"What would you have me do instead? Say naughty, naughty boys, now go and sin no more? Do you think they wouldn't have followed us, tried to kill us in our sleep? The world is different now, Verity. Violent people know there is nothing to stop them. This woman was no more than a toy, and probably then a slave. Civilization is gone. Men like these would kill you for your shoes."

She turned her attention to the woman she had saved, who was peering up at her fearfully. "What's your name?" she asked her.

"Helen. My name is Helen."

"Okay, Helen. Where are you going from here?"

Helen looked around in confusion. "I don't know. I don't know. They...they forced us to stop our car, killed my husband, dragged me over here." She began to sob again. "They killed Roy."

Shandiin looked at the car parked half off the street, doors hanging open. "It looks like we have transportation."

Verity looked shocked. "You would just take her car?"

Shandiin glared at him, turned back to Helen. "You need to come with us. You'll be a lot safer with us."

Helen looked around at the dead, back at Shandiin and the gun she still held, and shook her head. "No. I don't want to go with you." Her voice shook, but it held certainty.

"Then where will you go?" Verity asked her.

"Home. I want to go home."

"Helen...it's not safe. You need to get out of the city."

"I don't care. I want to go home. I'm going home." She pulled away from the priest, her eyes still on Shandiin until she pivoted and started walking away, head down.

"She's terrified of you," Verity said. "I'll stop her."

"We can't force her to come with us, Verity."

Khalen walked past them both, caught up with the woman, who whirled in terror at his touch on her shoulder.

He just waited, speaking soft words they couldn't hear, not touching her again. She slowly lifted her eyes to his.

Shandiin had expected shock. Instead the woman straightened, lifting a hand to place it carefully on Khalen's chest, as though to reassure herself he was real.

Thinking of a handsome stranger on a street corner long ago, Shandiin almost understood.

A moment later Khalen and Helen were walking toward the car.

Verity was looking away, toward his church in the distance. Flames licked the sky above a cloud of oily black smoke. The city's center was burning, including his church.

"I'm sorry for your loss," Shandiin told him.

The priest turned back to her. "People are losing far more than I have. I think you've lost more. You've lost your humanity, like...like an animal who can kill so coldly."

She looked away from him then, and spoke to empty air. "Animals don't kill coldly, Verity. They are innocent creatures who kill as nature dictates. Only humans kill coldly, with full understanding of what they take." Her voice held both pain and anger.

She walked away from him. After a moment he followed.

Even Khalen couldn't talk Helen into going with them. They gave her a short ride to her nearby home, a house gone ramshackle in an abandoned neighborhood that had once been a community's pride.

"You are welcome to the car," Helen said as she got out. "I'm not going anywhere."

"It isn't safe," Khalen repeated to her. "Can't you hear the gunfire, see the flames? The city is at war. Come with us, Helen."

She smiled up at him where he stood with his hand on the car's open door. "You are so pretty. My Roy was pretty too, just not so pretty as you are. He loved me." Her gaze moved from Khalen to her house. "He loved me. I am going home. I'm going to take some pills to sleep, and wait for Roy."

They watched her walk away.

"She's going home to die," Khalen said in disbelief.

"It's her choice." Shandiin sighed. "She won't be the only one. We can't save everyone, Khalen, especially if they don't want us to."

He hesitated. When he finally got back in the car, he seemed lost.

No one spoke as she drove away, through streets empty of everything but the occasional abandoned car. Shandiin looked at the gas gauge, and hoped there were some full cans in the trunk, because gas stations had been closed for a long time.

She doubted there were any cities better off. This was the stronghold of the Right Church, what was left of a government taken down by its own people.

She saw occasional movements in the shadows, but they managed many miles without challenge, and were away from the fighting and at the outskirts of the city as dusk began to fall. Spotting a house with a garage, she turned down the driveway, stopped, pulled out her gun while she studied broken windows and a sagging front door. "One of you open the garage door. I'll cover you."

"Why are we stopping?" Verity asked while Khalen got out. "There's still daylight."

"Not for much longer." She watched Khalen push up the garage door. There was only a golf cart inside, its tires flat. She backed in next to it, then turned back to Verity. "We don't want to travel at night with headlights on," she explained. "It would alert anyone from a distance, and set us up for an ambush."

She got out. Khalen pulled the garage door back down, and she went to the door that connected to the house. Khalen came to her, signaled he would go high while she went low. She nodded, glad of his training. Gun in hand, she stepped through.

The smell hit her immediately. She heard Khalen gag and waved him back.

So it was Verity who followed her into the house, past open doorways to a back bedroom where the smell was strongest, where lay a couple entwined in death. She turned to look back at Verity, and saw pity. "Do you want to give them last rites?" she asked.

"They are already gone. Close the door, Shandiin."

They walked back to the garage. When she didn't see Khalen, Shandiin felt a second of panic.

"Over here," his voice came from a corner where he crouched. He stood as they neared, a tiny ball of white fluff in his hands. It had a heart-shaped black spot on its miniscule forehead.

"You found a kitten," Shandiin said in surprise.

"It's very weak. I can see they left out food and water, but it's all gone." He looked up, his eyes firing citron in the light from the single window. "That smell—are there dead people in there?"

"Yes. Looks like suicide. There's probably a lot of that going around."

"I guess they are choosing that over violence or starvation. I'm sorry I was no help. I won't let it happen again." He looked at the priest. "I understand suicide is a sin in your church."

Verity didn't respond, his eyes on the kitten. "It probably needs water. Hopefully there's some in the kitchen."

They went back into the house, Khalen grimacing at the smell even as he turned on the faucet over the sink. He found a small bowl, filled it, set the kitten on the counter. It lapped furiously.

Shandiin was going through cabinets. She found them empty of food, but there were other supplies she set aside. A pair of mirrored sunglasses went into her pocket. She went to the refrigerator, pulled open the freezer, shut it quickly on the smell of spoiled meat.

"There's dried food in the backpacks," Verity said. He looked toward a bin marked "recycle" which held several empty bottles. "I think we should fill those with water, take them with us. And if you don't mind, I would prefer to stay in the garage, away from the smell."

"I agree," Shandiin said, watching Khalen tuck the kitten down the front of his armored vest, the empty bowl into his pocket. "It looks like looters have pretty well cleaned the place out already, but the garage is also safer if we need a fast getaway."

While the men filled bottles Shandiin found the golf cart still had gas in it, and siphoned it into their car. They ate a small meal from Verity's supplies, Khalen feeding some to the kitten. Without electricity—Shandiin figured that had gone the way of gas stations—dark came fully, but they didn't use flashlights as night fell, deciding to sleep in the car, taking turns at watch.

Shandiin took first watch, sitting on the floor with her back against the wall. There was light from the full moon rising in the narrow window across from her. She wasn't surprised when Verity got out of the car a short time later and came to sit beside her.

"Still pissed at me?" she asked.

"No. You are right, and I need to face the reality of it, which you must understand is a big shift for me. Like Khalen, I will try to do better." He sighed. "I am guessing that you have a destination in mind. You were always a thinker, a planner, even when we were kids."

"Yeah, I do. I figured this war was going to happen eventually. I stuck around the city because of you and Leah. I just couldn't figure out how to talk you into leaving with me. I didn't figure you would even consider it."

"I wouldn't have, at one time. Then Leah found out you've been watching over us. You have police friends in our church membership, Shandiin, but you apparently didn't know it. Leah talked to them."

"Not surprised I didn't know. Everyone keeps quiet about going to church nowadays."

"So where are we headed?"

"North. There's a place overlooking this city, this valley. The car won't take us the whole way, though, even if we had enough gas. We'll be doing some climbing. Is Khalen asleep?" she added.

"I think so. Who is he, Shandiin? Who are these people you are working with?"

"You could say he's the son of a friend of mine," she said. "I can't tell you the rest. I made a promise." *And I couldn't break it if I wanted to,* she thought, *with this thing they put in me.*

"I see. I am guessing he belongs to the woman who drove the transport. She also has the strange eyes. But she didn't seem as innocent as this young man."

"She and I have seen battle together. Khalen has seen none of that. I hate that he's seeing it now. He's young and kind of arrogant, but he's got a good heart."

"Because of the kitten?"

She thought of Khandor's grin when he had looked up at his big brother, and the warmth she had seen in Khalen's eyes when he looked back. "I think there's a lot more to him that that."

"I'm sorry I didn't reach out to you when I found Leah."

"You had your reasons. What matters came a long time before. You were kind to me when all I had known was cruelty, after they took me away from my Navajo family. The do-gooders thought I was 'white' and didn't belong with the people who had found me, taken care of me, loved me for the first twelve years of my life. I hated everyone after that, until you."

"So you no longer hate everyone. What about love, Shandiin?"

She sighed. "I learned that hate only hurts me, and most people don't deserve it. As for love? Verity, there are people I have cared for, still care for. But I'm always an inch away from the kind of love that makes people belong to each other. That inch may as well be a mile. I can't give myself to that."

"Can't, or won't?"

She shrugged. "The results are the same. You should get some rest, Verity."

"Why didn't you ever tell me you are enhanced?"

"I truly don't know if I am. And I don't know why it should matter to you."

He was quiet for a moment, then he sighed. "I guess it doesn't. I love you either way."

"Knock it off."

He chuckled. "You don't think I can love you? I never stopped, Shandiin."

"For crying out loud, quit it. You're a damned priest."

"Yes, I am. But that doesn't mean I can't love you. I thought I would die when they split us up, all those years ago. But I found God, and learned that love is a miracle, and like all miracles it can't be explained. It just is."

"So you loved someone, lost them, and signed up for a life of celibacy. It doesn't compute, Verity. Or are you punishing yourself because of the twins? We were irresponsible idiots, so you gave up sex?"

"Voluntary celibacy isn't a punishment, Shandiin. I chose my life out of love for God, not guilt for my sins. What doesn't compute is society's attitudes, when celibacy is expected of unmarried women, but not men." He patted her hand, the one holding the gun in her lap. "I'll go now, try to sleep."

"You do that. Don't expect me to feel all guilty about the love business."

"I don't. I know your history, so I understand. But I hope for your sake that you find love anyway. The kind that will make up for everything wrong in your life."

She just shook her head. "I don't believe in fairy tales, Verity. Good night."

They left at dawn, and Shandiin turned off the main road onto a tributary that soon became a dirt road alongside a high chain-link fence with concertina wire and warning signs posted regularly. She slowed, seeing low-slung buildings in the distance, and stopped when those were replaced by rows of tall, pointed objects standing against the blue sky.

"Are those *rockets*?" Verity asked in amazement.

"I believe so," Shandiin replied. "And since I've last been this way, I can tell you this complex has all been built in the last year."

Khalen leaned forward in the back seat. "Those rockets belong to the Right Church. The Church is going to use them to save their people, leaving everyone else to die when the planet does. They have a giant ship in orbit just waiting for them."

"How do you know about the rockets, the ship in space?" Verity asked him, amazed.

Khalen didn't answer.

Shandiin twisted to look back at him. "Is this how your people will go? By rocket?" she asked.

Khalen looked from her to Verity, shook his head and sat back.

"Apparently that's a secret," Verity observed.

"Yes, it is. I knew parts of it. You can believe Khalen." Shandiin turned back to drive. The tires slipped a little in the dirt as she pulled out, and she frowned into the rearview mirror, seeing the dust they raised. That wasn't good...and they were very low on gas.

"Uh-oh." Verity sat forward a few minutes later. "That's a Warrior transport up ahead. And Warriors. Can you stop and reverse?"

"They'll have already seen our dust." She took sunglasses from her pocket, handed them back to Khalen. "Put these on in case I have to stop. I can try to drive around them, but..."

Khalen put on the mirrored sunglasses. "Keep going until I say stop. Then just stay in the car unless I need backup." He gave the kitten to Verity, adding grimly "But give me a chance before you start shooting. Trust me."

When she slowed to a stop he stepped out, wearing the sunglasses and the Church's ankh pendant that Egypt had put in his pocket. He strode briskly to the waiting Warriors, snapped a salute and turned to look toward the rockets while he spoke to them.

"Is he undercover with the Church or something?" Verity asked.

"I don't think so. I think he is adlibbing." Her gun was in her lap; she looked to make sure Verity's was also below eye level. Khalen had a Glock strapped to each thigh, but he stood feet apart and arms crossed as though unconcerned about danger.

It was quickly apparent he owned the scene. She watched him in fascination, remembering how quickly he had adapted to a strange new world of violence. He stood now among his enemies with confidence. He had an awareness about him that was missing in Zion, and she thought he was more physically talented as well. Perhaps not a scientist, but certainly a soldier.

More. A leader.

His salute was casual as he turned away; the Warriors were far more formal.

He got in the car. "Just drive. Don't look at them as we pass. Just drive."

She obeyed, tense until they were past and the Warriors showed no sign of moving on them.

Khalen retrieved the kitten. "They are just patrol. Routine for them. They said they haven't had any refugees come this way though there is still fighting in the city. I didn't explain anything about myself, so they figured I was out here checking up on them. This pendant Egypt gave me is a pretty potent symbol of rank."

Shandiin checked the rear view mirror. "I am guessing if there were any refugees, they just didn't see them."

"I agree."

Verity turned back to Khalen. "You looked in command out there. I'm not even sure you needed that pendant."

"Command is what I was bred for."

The priest froze, eyes wide. "*Bred* for? You mean like they breed animals?"

Khalen's eyebrows lifted. "Not precisely, no. But I guess there may be some correlation. Animals are bred for specific purposes, are they not?"

"That's entirely different!" Verity exclaimed. "You can't just breed people! For any reason!"

"They aren't breeding them," Shandiin put in calmly. "Khalen is engineered, not bred."

"I hardly see the difference," Verity scowled.

"Big difference. Precision work in a laboratory. No one is forced to do the dirty."

"But the child...the child has no choice in his purpose!"

Shandiin gave him a sidelong glance. "Do any of us have a choice in our purpose? At least Khalen knows what his is. The rest of us just muddle along trying to figure it out, and most of us never do. I'm one of them." She frowned. "And more importantly, we're running out of gas."

The car stalled, lurched, stalled again and died.

They got out and looked around at scrub brush, dirt, rocks, and a nearby line of mountains, which Shandiin said was their destination. "We'd better load up, and take as much water as we can. There used to be a spring near here, but I'm betting it's as dried up as everything else. It's quite a distance to the river at the foot of those hills."

She took off her soft body armor as she spoke, as it was hot in the sun. Verity pulled out hats and they added water bottles to their backpacks. Khalen tucked the kitten into the pocket of his shirt. It peeked out for a minute, then curled in and went to sleep.

Khalen was smiling when he looked up and saw Verity frowning at him.

"I'm sorry if I offend your sensibilities," he told the priest.

"It's not that, Khalen. I am just wondering how you feel about your situation."

"My situation?" Khalen smiled wryly. "You mean as a lab rat?"

"Khalen," Shandiin put in sharply, "you called yourself that to a family that was created the same way you were. A family that then brought you into the world, and from what I can tell, has cared for you and educated you your entire life. Kids born outside of a lab don't have the good fortune you have had, much less the advantages in good looks, intelligence, and unusual talent. I think your 'lab rat' label is insulting and unfairly critical. Now can we continue this life-or-death journey without any further drama from either of you?" She hitched on her backpack and set off in long ground-eating strides.

It took the men a few minutes to catch up with her, and she set a pace too quick for conversation, which was her intent. She was tired of the tension between them.

The sun was soon high over a desert created by climate change. When she noticed Verity was flagging, she found a pocket of shade and called a break. She watched him lay down and fall asleep immediately.

"Will he be all right?" Khalen asked.

"I think so. He's old, but he's healthy. We'll watch out for him."

"I see you watching out for both of us. I think you have the same purpose I do."

She looked up in surprise. He took out the little bowl and tipped water into it, offered it to the kitten.

"I don't think I was created the way you were," she said finally. "I don't think I have a particular purpose. Are you still angry with the others, Khalen?"

He smiled wanly. "No, I am not angry with them. And I should have considered the impact on Khandor before leaving so impulsively."

"So it was impulse. Egypt said you didn't have a plan."

"She was right. She usually is. She and Lilith..." he looked away. "Between the two of them, I had the best mothers anyone could ask for. You were right, Shandiin, about me being fortunate. The lab rat thing was wrong of me. I was being snide."

"I'm sorry about Lilith." And she could tell he wasn't ready to talk about her, not yet. "I was surprised they had Khandor in the meeting back there while discussing plans and objectives for you both. They plainly made you angry, and he's just a child."

"He's not, really. He's already smarter than I am."

"It's not the intelligence, Khalen. It's the fact he is not mature. A child."

"They have never treated either of us like children."

"But he is a child, nevertheless. Despite the good things about the project, I can't help but feel both of you were cheated out of any normalcy. You've never had a childhood, not a real one."

He lifted his head to look at her, his handsome face gone grim. "Don't you dare pity us. Neither of us are like other children. Being treated like a kid would have just pissed us off. We know our purpose. We have a built-in sense of right and wrong that they tested us for, taught us about. I knew I should never have let Diane..."

She knew there was more when he shut up and looked away again, avoiding her eyes. She straightened, remembering what she had seen when she turned back to that meeting room. Asked softly, "Do you love her?"

He was sitting cross-legged in the dirt, almost knee-to-knee with her. At her question he lowered his head, unpinned the kitten that was climbing up his jeans, ran a hand through his thick black hair. "It isn't me she wants. She wants Zion. I'm just a stand-in." He finally met her gaze, and his emerald eyes held pain. "You should be glad you can't love so deeply, that something keeps you an inch away. I wish every day that I didn't care for her the way I do. I thought if I left...maybe I'd stop."

So he'd been eavesdropping when she talked to Verity. *Probably has augmented hearing too*, she thought with a sigh.

"So she's the real reason you wanted to leave. When did you fall for my daughter, Khalen?"

"I was sixteen." His voice was bitter. "She just walked up to me one day. Didn't say a word. Just put her hands on my face, and kissed me. She took me to her bed. She claimed me, Shandiin, and I've never been able to change that. I can't stop how she makes me feel."

Shandiin was horrified. "Sixteen? Khalen, that's abuse!"

"I know. I've always known. I warned her, before I left that meeting room. I warned her to keep her hands off of Khandor, and I shook her. I'm terrified that he's next. Shit, I never should have left him there. I'm not thinking straight, that's obvious."

"You never told anyone?"

He looked up. "I told Khandor. Not all of it, of course. But I told him to watch out for her, not to trust her, not to be alone with her. I think he figured it out. I hope like hell he did."

Shandiin saw Verity stirring. "So do I, Khalen. But I think if we do reconnect with your people that you should tell them all the truth." After a moment she added, "If you don't, I will. Then I'll knock her damned teeth out."

She got up, stretched, and seeing Verity awake she offered the priest a hand to get to his feet. "We have a lot of ground to cover. Let's move."

They heard gunfire as they traveled, but it was distant and behind them. The spring Shandiin had hoped to find was dried up, so their water would have to be rationed until they got to the river.

Which they did, two days later, but others had reached it ahead of them.

They laid atop a ridge, looking down on the verdant gorge where wound a gleaming river. An encampment was set up on the bank. Sleeping bags, tents, and other equipment surrounded a big campfire. Men worked on a couple of heavy-duty pickup trucks parked with a couple of ratty sedans. Other men were wading in the river, fishing.

"They look peaceful enough," Verity noted. "Is this your destination? Shouldn't we join them?"

Shandiin had pulled binoculars from her pack and studied the scene below. Grimly, she handed them to Verity, pointed at the trees nearest the river. He frowned and followed her gaze, then almost dropped the binoculars.

"Captives." Khalen apparently didn't need magnification to see. "They appear to be tied to the trees."

"Women, tied up." Verity's face was pale, but his golden eyes blazed. "Slaves, like you said would be done to the woman you rescued."

Shandiin sounded unsurprised. "It appears the end of civilization also ended women's rights. A female only has one use now to some men."

She backed down the ridge, stood up to brush off her clothes while the men followed. She waited then, knowing they wouldn't just pass by.

"What can we do?" Verity asked.

Shandiin just looked from him to Khalen. "I suppose you want to do something too. Guys, there's at least ten men down there. I don't want to end up tied to a tree."

"There are eleven," Khalen said thoughtfully. "And you wouldn't, Shandiin. I don't think you would let that happen."

"I'm not a superhero," she snorted.

"Really? How disappointing. We should wait until tonight, when they're asleep. Catch them by surprise."

"And what? Shoot them in their sleep? You'll give Verity a heart attack."

Khalen shook his head. "I wouldn't like that any better than the priest would. I think we just need to release the women. Make sure they are loose and armed. They can take the vehicles to get away. There are five women and three of us against eleven men. The odds are more than even, with you and me in the mix."

"Hmph. How much battle training have you had, Khalen?"

"Believe it or not, a lot. Egypt trained me using holograms. I know the real thing is different, but it's only because of my reaction to it. My stupefied reaction to the reality is being quickly nullified."

"Fine. We'll be heroes and rescue the women. Like you said, they can take the cars wherever they want. But we can't drag them with us, guys. If you want to stay with me...we move out upstream. I have a destination, and it's the other side of that river."

They settled in to wait until nightfall, trading off naps and food and filling water bottles while they waited. Then they put on their soft body armor, and slipped like black shadows through the trees to the camp.

Shandiin and Khalen took the night guard, who was unwisely more asleep than guarding, and who didn't argue with a gun held to his forehead while he was bound and gagged. At the same time Verity was untying the women, whispering reassurances and handing them each a weapon from the arsenal they'd brought with them.

One woman didn't immediately take the weapon he offered, but ran to a young girl tied nearby. She whispered to her while she untied her, then turned back and held out her hand for the rifle he held. There were tears on her face and rage in her eyes. Horrified, he began in a whisper, "Is she yours? Did they..."

She only snarled, and snatched the weapon.

He had thought the women would hesitate, but they each took the weapons they were handed and moved with purpose toward their captors. He grimaced when the child's mother aimed her rifle at a sleeping man and pulled the trigger, but it was the ground that exploded instead of his head.

"Up, you bastard! Up! I want you to see what's coming!" she screamed.

The man sat up, flailing for a weapon that Shandiin kicked out of his reach. Guns were trained on every man who floundered awake. The men watched in horror as their former captives neared, clutching weapons and the ropes that had bound them.

But one man wasn't worried about the ropes. He was looking into the eyes of the mother crazed by the rape of her child, and into the muzzle of her rifle. "Now you die," she snarled, and when she fired into his face the shot echoed down the gorge, repeating over and over until it faded into silence.

Male cries for mercy went unheeded as the women moved in, watched over by the three rescuers who had appeared out of the night.

Binding one man with ankles and wrists behind his back, a woman sneered. "Shit your britches, did you? You'll live in that, for what time's left to you!"

Shandiin went to Verity, tugged at him, but he seemed rooted to the ground. Khalen joined her to take his other arm, and together they walked him away from the camp, away from the sounds that would haunt him forever, including more gunshots that silenced more screams.

They picked up their gear from where they had left it, heading upstream in the moonlit night, saying nothing for a very long time.

Chapter 6

They emerged on the other side of the river in a thick stand of trees, and walked on for some time before Shandiin called a halt. "Cold camp," she ordered. "No campfires yet, as we don't know if there is anyone close enough to see it. I need morning for us to go on, so I can check landmarks."

At least the ground was soft with years of fallen pine needles, and their packs made a decent pillow. But none of them were able to fall asleep.

"Khalen," Verity finally broke the silence, "would you have armed those women if you had known what they would do?"

Khalen laid with his arms behind his head, staring up in fascination at the stars netted in the tree branches above. The kitten slept in the curve of his neck.

"I was raised by a woman who is a soldier," he answered. "You met her; her name is Egypt. You also know Shandiin. I do know they are not typical of their gender, but my education has told me what the fairer sex is capable of. History has often warned soldiers not to be captured by the women."

"So you knew they would murder those men, and it didn't bother you? Have you no empathy?" Verity demanded.

"I knew there was a probability they would turn on the men who had treated them as less than human, who had raped even an innocent young girl, who very likely had killed the men those women had loved when they were taken hostage. Do I have empathy for the depraved monsters who did those things? No. And in the absence of law and order, I believe it was up to those who were wronged to determine what justice should be served." After a minute he added: "Shandiin, you knew what I would suggest before you asked me, didn't you?"

"Yes. I wanted to see if I was right. You were bred to be a leader, you and Khandor. I can see your rule wouldn't always be merciful. But I wonder about Khandor. He's an empath. How would he handle something like this, Khalen?"

"He would do what he knows is right. It's literally built into his genes. He couldn't do anything else, Shandiin, no matter how badly it would hurt him. And he would feel everything that resulted from his decision. He'd take responsibility for any decision he made." He sighed. "I don't know how he would bear it, Shandiin. I really don't know."

Morning found them away from the trees, climbing a graveled slope toward a wall of creviced rock with a lot of rough scrub at its base. Measuring landmarks, Shandiin walked up to a section that looked like everything else and started pulling out brush. The men quickly saw there were more loose branches than living plants, and moved in to help her.

After a lot of annoying, sweaty work, they realized that there was a cleft in the rock behind the scrub. Once at its mouth, Shandiin had them replace brush behind them to hide their passage, then she led them through.

The cleft opened onto a box canyon fed by a stream trickling from the rock wall to deep grass, a meadow with trees at the other end. Shandiin dropped her pack, then lifted her hands to her mouth and whistled, loud and long.

She waited then with hands on hips, looking concerned until they heard a shrill whinny in the distance. She grinned broadly when a huge black and white paint horse galloped out of the trees and toward them. The horse came to a plunging halt, then shoved his head against Shandiin, almost knocking her down.

She laughed, regaining her footing, and threw her arms around the thickly arched neck. The horse looked like someone had poured white paint over his black hide, even on his face. The eye surrounded by white was blue, half hidden by the long black forelock.

"Meet Nitch'i," she told them. "That's' Navajo for 'wind' though he's not as fast as some. I just like calling him Nitchi. Soon will come...ah, there he is. Chaha'oh...Navajo word, but you can just call him Shadow. He is a more refined heap of horseflesh than my Nitchi, though I love them both."

She spoke of the magnificent black stallion that trotted toward them, head up, mane tossing, tail bannered. He snorted suspiciously at strangers, reared and pawed. His coat was rough and dirty, but he was nevertheless beautiful.

Shandiin grinned at the men. "Can either of you ride?" she asked.

Khalen gazed avidly at the black stallion. "I have always wanted to see a horse. I would love to ride one."

"And I see you have already chosen Shadow. Good for you, Khalen."

"You aren't getting me on either of these beasts," Verity said. "I'm not all that fond of horses, especially playful ones."

"No worry," Shandiin laughed. "You aren't getting a horse. Meet Hannah."

Verity looked up to see a brown creature with very long ears walking toward them. It threw up its head and made a loud braying sound, then apparently lost interest and began grazing.

"What is that?" Verity asked.

"Haven't you ever seen a mule?"

"I don't believe I have, no. Isn't it half horse, half donkey?"

"You are a fountain of wisdom, Father Rowan."

Verity glanced at her sidelong, knowing her wicked grin. Then he noted Khalen standing with his arms crossed, feet apart, smirking derisively.

Verity studied the young man and, after a long moment of consideration, spoke with exaggerated soberness. "In the Bible, I believe a donkey is called an ass. Jesus rode into Jerusalem on an ass. I suppose that a priest can ride half an ass. Will that make me a half-assed priest?"

Shandiin snorted laughter. "That is an *awful* dad joke!" But she saw Khalen's surprised smile, and realized Verity had purposely used it to ease the tension between himself and the younger man. "But well done, Verity. Hannah's my pack mule, but she's trained to ride, and very sure-footed. Which you will appreciate, believe me."

Verity looked back at the mule. "You can't expect us to ride them bareback."

"I don't. C'mon; there's a shed with their equipment in those trees, and we can make a fire and have something hot to eat for a change." She started across the meadow. The big paint stallion walked with his muzzle at her shoulder. She was surprised to see Shadow walk with Khalen, who had a hand on his neck and the kitten peering from his pocket.

Later, Verity watched Khalen's first riding lesson with admiration. He had listened carefully to Shandiin, following instructions to saddle the big black stallion—which was in itself an event, as Shadow sidled and danced until Shandiin stepped up and snagged his bridle, thumping him between the eyes. The black's ears went back, then pricked, and he bunted her playfully but finally stood still as the saddle was cinched.

Khalen didn't wait, but was on the horse's back so quickly that Verity thought he'd missed something. The smile on Khalen's face as he looked down at Shandiin was brilliant, full of joy in the moment. He gathered the reins, listening still to Shandiin's directions, but that smile didn't change. Finally Shandiin carefully let go of the bridle.

Khalen lifted the reins and Shadow tossed his head and pranced away. Verity and Shandiin watched as he rode him in a circle, then a figure eight.

"He's a fast learner," Shandiin said. "I can't believe this is his first time. He—oh, shit!"

That exclamation came as Khalen leaned forward, lifted the reins, and put Shadow into a flying gallop across the meadow.

"I don't believe this!" She watched Shadow sweep over the tall grass, turning sharply with Khalen on him like a burr, riding like he was born to it.

Seeing Khalen's joy as he rode, Verity smiled. "That is the first time I have seen that young man happy."

But Shandiin just watched with her mouth open, and thought for some reason of a man on a city street corner who had smelled of soap and horses.

Shandiin warned the men that the canyon was not their final destination, but they took the day to rest, and made camp at the edge of the meadow with the promised campfire and hot supper from the rations Verity had supplied. Afterwards Khalen left the kitten with them and walked off to the horses.

The moon, just past full, peered over the canyon wall to paint the meadow with silver. Verity and Shandiin sat together by the campfire's embers, watching Khalen walk to the horses and sit down in the tall grass. It wasn't long before Shadow went to him and lowered his great head. Khalen stroked him and then laid back to stare at the sky.

"He's never seen a horse," Verity commented. "Yet he can ride like an expert, and the horse has obviously bonded to him. Who is he, really...and where does he come from, Shandiin?"

She sighed. "I can't answer your questions. Not even the ones I have an answer to. I can only tell you that he is seeing the world for the first time. He is enamored with the stars, because he has never before seen the sky except as an image, a hologram. He probably has an IQ off the charts, but he is like a child in many ways. I hope I can find a way to get him back to his people. He needs them...and I think they need him. Whatever you think of his origin, Verity, he is very human."

"I am sorry if I made either of you think I believed otherwise. I am just... uncertain of the morality of using science to change what God created."

"Do you truly think science is changing creation? I think it's just an avenue to discover what creation has made possible. The physicist James Jean said the universe begins to look more like a great thought than a great machine. I don't think we should restrict science to the outside of understanding while reserving the inside to religion. The two concepts may only be one, in the end."

Verity was silent for a long time. Finally he leaned back on his elbows, and studied her thoughtfully. "That should sound heretical, yet somehow it doesn't. Still...aren't you denying the reality of Christ?"

"No. I am not. If there's one thing I'm sure of, it's that I don't have all the answers, and neither does anyone else." She looked at him archly. "Including you."

He had to smile. Then something caught his eye, and he looked up. "Is that a meteor?"

She watched the tiny light traveling across the sky. "No. I don't think so."

After watching for a moment, he frowned. "It looks like the space station. But I thought that was destroyed about the same time as Washington."

Thinking it was probably the spaceship the Right Church was building, she looked back toward Khalen, who seemed to be asleep in the grass under the stars. She wasn't sure what she should say. "I think it's time we turned in, Verity. We have a long trip ahead of us."

"You've given us no explanation for where we are headed."

"We are going up. I have a place in the mountains that may be safe even if the end comes with a bomb or two."

"No underground bomb shelter for you?"

"No. I've made it safe as I can, but if it comes to that...I'd rather be able to walk out under the sky, in the end."

He watched her stand, but sat up and caught her hand before she could move away. "Is Leah safe with his people?" he asked.

"She is, yes. They are good people who are trying to save those the Right Church hasn't collected. Like Leah, like the children you were hiding in your church."

"Do you think they can? Save them?"

She thought of Zion and his family. "If anyone can, they will."

The next day Verity learned that the equines were what made the trip possible, at least for him.

The path was steep, and mostly invisible until they were almost upon it. Shandiin occasionally had them stop and wait while she scouted ahead, stating it had been a long time since she had come this way.

They purposely put Verity in the middle when the path narrowed to allow only one at a time. After that first day, he wasn't aware of much except the grueling climb—which the mule Hannah seemed to manage better than either horse—and the increasing chill in the air, and the fact that it was becoming harder to catch his breath. He didn't object when Shandiin took the mule's reins to lead her. Hannah followed her paint horse calmly.

He knew terror when the path seemed to give way under Shandiin's mount, and rocks rattled downhill while her big paint scrambled for purchase. Afterwards the stallion stood hard against the cliff face, snorting, while Shandiin twisted around in the saddle to regard the broken path and the men behind her.

"There's no way I can turn back," she told them. "So unless you want to go back without me, we have to go forward." She gave them a moment, then nodded when they said nothing. "Verity, there's a rope in Hannah's pack. Throw it to me."

He found it, a heavy length expertly wound, and tossed it to her wordlessly. He watched her tie it around her horse's saddle horn, then caught it when she threw it back. "Tie it around your waist," she told him. "Then give it to Khalen. Khalen, you do the same. If either of your mounts fall, you need to let them go, and trust me to pull you up."

"But...."

"Do it," Khalen said quietly from behind him. "Your Hannah is the most surefooted, and will probably cross without a problem."

The priest swallowed hard. He wound a length around his waist and tied it off, passing the rest back to Khalen, who paid out a longer length between them than Shandiin had allowed. When Khalen signaled he was ready, Shandiin met Verity's eyes, and read there a mix of fear...and surprising trust.

So she turned back and Nitchi started up the trail. Hannah stretched her neck, almost fighting the pull of the reins, but then stepped out to follow.

The mule stepped across easily. But Verity heard the scramble, the thud and rattle of rocks behind him, and would have stopped if Shandiin hadn't had Hannah's reins and kept going. Verity cried out when the rope tightened around his waist, but still Shandiin didn't stop. Verity clung hard to his mule, terrified that the horse behind him was falling.

He looked back to see Shadow gather and jump the broken path, landing barely clear of Hannah's rump. He met Khalen's emerald eyes and was shocked to see the man grinning as he patted his horse's neck in congratulation. Then he looked back as the path behind them began sliding away.

No return for them, then. Not the way they had come. Verity breathed hard, looked ahead, prayed for this ride to be over soon.

When they reached a wide ledge shelving deep into the cliff, Shandiin dismounted and came back to him. "Are you all right?" she asked. "You look a little pale, Verity."

"Scared half to death, that's all." He untied the rope from his waist, climbed down, felt his knees almost buckle when he tried to stand away from the mule.

Khalen was immediately there to put an arm around him, sharing his young strength until Verity caught his breath and stood steady. "Thanks," the priest acknowledged humbly.

Khalen just stepped back. "It's getting late. Can't we stop here, Shandiin?"

"I think we'd better. We can camp against the cliff wall, go the rest of the way in the morning."

"Are we close?" Verity asked.

"Yes." She looked at him pointedly. "I think it's best we stay here tonight anyway."

"Because of me?" Verity asked. "Look, I can..."

"I don't care," she interrupted him. "I don't care if you think you can go on. I don't like the way you look right now. The air is thin up here; there's less oxygen, and the altitude makes a difference. Do you have a heart problem, Verity?"

He scowled. "I may be pushing 80, but I'm strong enough. I don't appreciate being coddled."

To his shock she stepped up to him, put her hands on his shoulders, and kissed him softly on the lips.

Then she turned away, leading her horse toward the night's camp.

Verity just stood there, looking confused.

"I think she likes you," Khalen grinned, and followed her.

After a minute Verity followed suit.

Darkness fell swiftly as the sun set on the other side of their mountain. Verity ate because Shandiin gave him little choice, but balked stubbornly when she told him to lie down.

After a moment she spread a blanket, threw down two packs for pillows, laid down and held her arms out to him. "Come here."

When he just stared at her, she laughed. "I'm not trying to seduce a priest. It gets cold up here at night. Khalen's young; he'll be fine. I think we old people need to snuggle for warmth."

When Verity still hesitated, he heard Khalen snort. "Don't be a fool. If it's pride getting in your way, I'll point out that you're supposed to be the humble sort."

So Verity laid down beside the woman he had loved all his life, and...covertly exhausted...fell asleep with her warm against his side.

She followed into sleep soon after.

And she dreamed, believing she was awake.

At first she thought he must be Khalen, sitting beside her in the cold moonlight under a cathedral of stars, looking out over an unknown landscape of star-frosted peaks all around. But when he turned his head to look at her, she had no doubt who he was.

That enigmatic love was in his eyes again, but there was concern now, as well. She thought he was even more beautiful than Khalen or Khandor...or Zion, who had his likeness but not his aura, that nearly tangible presence of command...and something more personal. Her spirit responded to his with an emotion she couldn't name.

His velvet-black hair blew loose around his face, for there was wind on this unknown mountain. Moonlight swam around him; his emerald eyes fired with it.

"You might forget me in the long journey ahead of you," he said, "but I hope your spirit will remember even if your mind doesn't. Don't give up hope, Shandiin."

She woke weeping, knowing the greatest loneliness she had ever felt. She understood none of it.

"Shandiin," Verity whispered beside her. "What is wrong?"

When she didn't answer he touched her cheek gently and found her tears. "Tell me, Shandiin."

"I don't know how to. I don't understand myself, so how can I explain it to you? I used to believe in what is right and good. I've learned differently. I gave up all hope of anything to fill the emptiness. But then I met someone, just for a moment, and now I have feelings I don't understand. I think I am going crazy."

"Who is this person you met?"

"I don't know. I have no idea. But I feel his love like...like it's an object I can touch." She shook her head, covered her face with her hands. "He can't be real."

Verity's hand on hers was warm. "But what if he is? Shandiin, I told you...love is a miracle. Why must you turn away from even the possibility of love? Turning away from love is like turning away from life because you know death will come. Maybe you will find him in reality someday, Shandiin, and maybe you won't, but in the meantime you should let yourself love...and be loved."

She curled into his arms then, and he held her close while he stared into the darkness, saying a silent prayer for this woman of incredible courage who was nevertheless afraid of love.

She was her sovereign self again in the dawn, standing apart to take care of the horses while coffee boiled over the campfire. Khalen poured them each a tin mugful, grateful for Verity's supplies, and handed the priest a cup as he dropped to sit beside him.

They both watched the kitten exploring Khalen's boots.

"You'd never seen a horse," Verity noted. "Had you seen a cat before?"

Khalen smiled. "Yes, actually. Sarnath...one of my family has cats. He claims they are good pets for the children he looks after, but I think he loves them for themselves."

"So...this place where you come from...it already had children? Before taking in the ones from my church?"

"Oh yes."

"I assume they are the children the Right Church is trying to find. Are they all...like you?"

"Enhanced, you mean? No. About half are just kids. The rest have enhancements for health, and others have differences apparently more...acceptable...than what I have."

Verity thought that over for a long moment. "I guess it is all the same in the end, isn't it? Just a matter of degree." He looked back at Shandiin, her fiery hair gilded in the sun's early rays. "It's hard to believe she's as old as I am. She has to be enhanced like you."

"Maybe. I really don't know. But I gather you knew her all those years ago, before everything fell apart. You both watched it happen. I've been taught the history, but it had to be different, actually living it."

"It was an insidious change, Khalen. It started when we had a crooked president admired simply because he was born rich. He lacked empathy for anyone unlike himself, and anyone who disagreed with him in any way. He caused a great division among people already confused by a lack of trust in leadership. I thought that was the worst, but the division kept growing even when he was gone. Then along came a man who was brilliant, and handsome, and apparently honest because he was the head of a church with a huge following. He appealed to the many people who were sick of the division and the corruption in government. He seemed recalcitrant when called to run for office, but it was actually a well-executed coup."

Shandiin dropped down next to the men, reached for her own coffee. "Canard is a con, and the whole nation is his mark," she put in. "His platform was about starting over, starting clean, working for God. No more taxes! Only tithing for the good of those who trusted in God! Working alongside his cohorts who were elected with him after the fall of Washington, he did away with government assistance programs, saying it wasn't the job of the government to take care of people who should be taking care of themselves. Talked about loaves and fishes, helping each other, which the Church does well for its membership...while anyone who didn't join was left in the cold."

"And the poor couldn't join the Church," Khalen noted dryly.

Shandiin snorted. "How could they pay the tithe?" she wiped out her cup, rose. "Time to move. It really isn't much farther."

But Verity remained for a minute, deep in thought. When he stood to join the others there was deep sorrow in his golden eyes.

"While all that was happening," he said, "the Earth was dying, and it became too late to stop its death. There's a story in the Bible about a place called Eden, and how we fell from grace and were cast out. I wonder now if it is meant as a history or a warning. If in fact Earth is our Eden and we are cast out, where will our descent take us?"

Khalen looked very thoughtful as they saddled up. Shandiin glanced back at him as they rode out, remembering his purpose was to be an incorruptible leader. She thought it a worthwhile if impossible ideal, and felt sad that he would never have the chance to fulfill the duty he was created for.

She admired the people who had engineered him, but had no faith in their plans to find another world. Her faith stood upon the one thing she could rely on: herself.

The narrow path widened, and became a stone ledge that climbed until the nearest peaks were below them, and patches of snow shone from shadowed crannies. Then the ledge opened onto a plateau, and the men were stunned to see a concrete building and an antenna chained to the ground like a tripod.

Khalen was silent, surveying the wind-scrubbed mountaintop and blue sky and the distant miniaturized view of the city they had left so far behind...and below.

Verity was looking at the antenna. "Ham radio?"

"Yep." Shandiin began unsaddling Nitchi.

"Did you build all this?" When she nodded, he only stared. "How did you get all this up here? Not on that trail we just used!"

"There used to be a road, and I had a truck. When I was done building, I dynamited the road out about halfway down the mountain, to keep anyone from finding this place. But from up here the road's remainder drops to a valley where the horses can graze, and there's water."

"How is there water up here when it's so dry below?"

"Mountains hold water from centuries of rain and snow. Air is thinner up high, so clouds can't hold water vapor, so it rains more in the mountains." She hoisted her paint's saddle to her shoulder, looked up at him. "Need help getting down? You're looking pale again."

He didn't answer, just dismounted, glaring at Khalen who appeared ready to help him. Shandiin ignored them both, headed for the building.

She fired up the generator outside of it, walked through the unlocked door, dumped the saddle onto a waiting rack and gestured the others to follow suit. Walked through another door into a windowless room, turned on a lamp to reveal stacked bunk beds on one wall, a corner kitchen with small table and chairs, and radio setup.

"There's a bathroom, but I prefer you use the outhouse in the back unless we have to seal up," she told them, then grinned. "Hell, you guys can just pee over the edge of the mountain if you aren't afraid of heights. Unload the packs and stay awhile."

She dumped hers on the bottom bunk, gestured at the ladder for them, then went directly to the kitchen, where she demonstrated the sink's pump for water.

Khalen went to the radio, looked back over his shoulder. "High frequency?"

"Of course. It's to keep in touch with what's happening outside. I'm surprised you know what it is."

"I know that ham radios will work when everything else goes down due to loss of infrastructure. Everyone is reliant on internet, cellphones...electricity. How far does yours reach?"

"Worldwide. Repeater bounces it off the ionosphere."

He nodded. "What powers your generator?"

"Gasoline at the moment, until I get out the photovoltaic panels. I didn't want to leave them out in the elements until they're needed. Verity, take the bottom bunk if you don't want to climb."

The priest considered, threw his belongs on the bottom bunk. He then went to the kitchen table and sat on one of the wooden chairs. "So this is home," he sighed. "For how long, Shandiin? What do you think will happen next?"

"We have to wait and see. But there's food here, and hunting not that far away."

"You happen to have a telescope in all this equipment?" Khalen asked.

"Yep. You can set it up outside. Are you wanting to look up or down?"

"Both. I thought I saw the Church's spaceship going overhead last night, and was hoping to keep an eye on the rockets we passed."

"Church spaceship? So that wasn't the space station we saw?" Verity asked.

Shandiin pumped two mugs of water, joined Verity at the table, gave him one. "No. Verity, the Church is building a ship to save its constituency off-planet. That fact alone makes me pretty sure war is coming, because they would know. I only suspected, but I started building this place a long time ago as a just-in-case, hoping it wouldn't happen, but here we are."

She looked up as Khalen joined them at the table. "Any chance we can reach your people with the radio?"

"No. They're sealed far below ground."

Verity scowled. "So...we three are alone, facing the end of the world?"

Shandiin looked from one man to the other. "Just my luck. There was a song during World War II that seems applicable." When they both looked at her in question, she grinned. "It seems all the eligible men left for war. The women left behind sang, 'They're either too young or too old.'" She laughed and got up to empty her pack.

"I don't know about you," Verity said to Khalen, "but I find that a little insulting." When Khalen only shrugged, he added, "You'll get older, so she may reconsider in time."

"I'm already taken. Monogamy is as much a requirement for my bloodline as celibacy is for your priesthood."

"Even if you are the last people in the world?"

"Even then." Khalen got up. "I'm going to take the horses down to that meadow, look around a little."

He left, and Shandiin rejoined Verity at the table.

He studied her. "You're trying to be upbeat, but you truly believe this is the end."

"'Woe to the earth,'" she quoted very softly. "We watched it start all those years ago, didn't we?" She picked up Khalen's kitten, set it in her lap. "All the arguing about whether climate change was real or not, until it became obvious that it was very real...and too late to reverse it. They gave up tomorrow's hope for their immediate convenience."

"And now we have tomorrow."

"I guess." She stroked the kitten. "Since it's here...I'm glad to face it with you, Verity."

"Even though I'm too old?"

She smiled. "Would it make a difference if you weren't? With the celibacy thing?"

"Is that a hint?"

"Maybe. We can always lock the door."

He laughed, shook his head. "You and your weird sense of humor. I've missed you, Shandiin. You don't know how often I've thought of you, all these years."

"Same goes, Verity."

Her preparations for the end of the world included an arsenal that both men found surprising. She watched Khalen pick up a hand grenade, pretend to throw it, then grin at her. She just shook her head.

The three settled into a routine that included listening to conversations on the radio, learning of people stranded all over the world who could find no answer from the authorities they had once depended on.

And one by one, day by day, the voices dropped away.

Shandiin pulled out cards and chips and challenged them to play poker. Khalen won every hand. "Whoa," Shandiin laughed at last, "are you counting cards? That's cheating!"

"It is?" he asked innocently, with a telling grin.

"I should have known. You have an eidetic memory loaded into that high IQ. We'll have to find a more random game."

As Shandiin stood, they all heard a low rumble, and a stack of chips slid apart on the table. The floor vibrated slightly under their feet.

They rushed outside, into the night. Khalen went to the telescope, but they didn't need it to see a layer of fire appearing far below, burning white below needled forms lifting from the fire toward the stars.

"So many!" Verity exclaimed in shock. "So many ships!"

They watched them lift away from the earth on their fiery tails, taking the righteous with them, until that distant rumble was gone and only memory was left.

Shandiin went inside with Verity, where the radio quickly came alive with the news, voices full of anger as the rest of the world realized they had been deserted. But Khalen didn't come back into the cabin, so Shandiin finally went back out to check on him.

He remained standing by the telescope, looking down instead of at the sky as she had expected. He didn't change position when she stopped next to him.

"That should have been their signal," he said. "Zion's plan was to leave right after the Church did. If he can."

"How? And where's their ship?"

"He's been working on the 'how' for a long time, developing a superconductor that can use the earth's own magnetic field to repel a ship. It's called the Meissner effect. You could call it anti-gravity I guess; it's been known about for ages, but it took Zion to harness it. Egypt started to touch on it when she said they could come and get us when they have the ships. But they have to get away first, or it's all for nothing."

She frowned, understanding only part of his explanation. "I don't get it. Why would they wait until the others leave, if there was a way to go?"

He didn't look away from the city below. "Because Zion...none of us...wanted to destroy the people of the Right Church. They had to be gone first."

She heard tension in his voice, and worry. She stared at him, confused.

Then she felt the rumble. Felt the earth move under her feet.

It was much more than when the rockets had lifted off. This was much more. When she stumbled where she stood, Khalen reached to pull her against him, held her steady while his eyes never left the land below.

There was enough moonlight for her to see the impossible. The distant white city of the Right Church, empty now, seemed to lift; in fact it seemed the earth was growing under it, like a mountain was being born.

The mountain rose, and the white-walled city fell apart from its summit, and something else came through. Something that gleamed with moonlight as it climbed, shedding the city and the earth and rocks that had existed beneath it.

It kept rising. Big as the walled city had been, this impossible thing.

"It's a flying saucer!" Verity cried behind them, and Shandiin looked back to see terror on his face. "Where did it come from? What's happening?"

"It's Aztlan," Khalen answered quietly. "It's my people, and it came from where it was built, beneath the Church's own city. Shandiin has been there." He watched the ship continue up, as the rumble stopped and silence fell again over the world. "It's using the expulsion of its magnetic field against the earth's, to lift it out of the ground, out of the atmosphere. When it reaches space, it will wait for the others that have been built around the world, that should be rising even now to join it. Zion's plan is working."

He turned finally to smile at Shandiin and Verity. "It's working. He's saving thousands of people, as many as could be found and trusted, to be brought into the underground ships."

Shandiin watched as the disc rose, darker than the sky now, a mysterious shadow that blocked out the stars blooming in the night sky. When she could no longer see it, she turned and went to the trembling priest, took his hand in hers, and led him back to the warmth indoors.

The voices on the radio held more than anger, now. They held terror.

Those left behind in the world mankind had ruined now faced the final insanity of annihilation.

Nuclear bombs were falling everywhere.

Seeing the devastation in Verity's golden eyes, Shandiin silenced the radio. With a despairing glance at Khalen, she talked her childhood love into the bottom bunk and climbed in with him, drawing the blanket over them both, and listened to his whispered prayers for the lost people of Earth, until he finally fell asleep in her arms.

In the dark hour just before dawn Khalen heard her cry out, and went to her where she embraced Verity's lifeless body and wept.

He touched the priest gently, and knew he was gone. Leaving Shandiin to her sorrow, he lit the lamp and went to make coffee, waiting for her at the kitchen table until she dropped into a chair across from him, tears done, but her breath still catching and broken.

"I think," he said gently, "that one inch away from love wasn't far enough, was it?"

She shook her head, blew her nose. It took a while for her to find words. "Verity was a good man. Good right to the bone. Not because he was a priest. It was just his nature. I came closer to loving him than anyone else in my life. He was the only good thing that happened to me after I was taken away from my family on the reservation." She inhaled shakily, met Khalen's eyes. "They thought the Navajo were not good enough to have me, because I wasn't like them physically. Just because I have red hair and grey eyes. But I wasn't like any of the people who took me, either. The people who took me, and put me into a system where no one truly cared. I lost all of who I had been, Khalen. Verity tried to give it back to me. He worked very hard at teaching me to trust, to love." She sat back, shook her head. "And then they took him away, along with the babies that were ours."

Khalen hesitated, then reached across and took her hand. "I am sorry for your loss." He looked back at the bunks. "And for mine. I learned from him. I learned to respect a belief different from my own. I learned to admire a different kind of love, for an ideal transcending humanity's faults."

The next day they buried him in the meadow, under a sky already growing dark with nuclear death. Shandiin tried to read aloud a passage from his Bible, but when her voice broke Khalen took it from her and, to her surprise, held it closed against his chest while he recited passages ending with, "'All go to the same place; all come from dust, and to dust all return.' Rest in peace, Verity."

"So you know the Bible."

"And the Quran, and the Torah, among other religious and spiritual documentations. Sarnath required it. It was Solomon who talked about the dust, and he was the great King of the Bible they wanted me to emulate." He smiled a little. "Zion compared that passage to quantum physics."

"He would, and I guess he's right. We're all created from the same stuff, whether it's dust or—what do they call it?— quarks?"

She lifted her eyes from the new grave, regarded Khalen thoughtfully. His hair had grown to brush his shoulders, and he had put on enough muscle during their hard journey to strain the seams of his shirt. When he looked at her his emerald eyes were sad still, but she thought him as handsome as Zion.

She refused to compare him to a dark stranger she wanted to forget.

She sighed. "Egypt said they would come for you. I guess that's not happening. I'm sorry, Khalen."

"Don't count them out, Shandiin. They have small ships that use the Meissner effect just like the big ones do. And they can locate us through the biochips. They are busy right now, but they won't abandon us."

"I hope they don't abandon you. But I won't go with you if they come."

He turned to her, surprised. "Why not? You can't stay here alone!"

She shrugged. "I can't live on a ship in space. I was claustrophobic in your Aztlan when it was under the earth, and I think space is scarier."

"But it's only temporary until..."

"Until what? Your new world? A lifetime from now, if ever? No. I'll stay here, and die with the Earth." When he started to speak, she shook her head. "You can't change my mind. Now please...I think I will sit here awhile, with Verity and the horses, if you don't mind leaving me for a bit?"

"I understand. I'll go see what I can hear on the radio." He left to climb up the road to the cabin.

She sat down in the grass, and tried not to think.

Of course that never worked. She couldn't stop his voice in her head. *Don't give up hope, Shandiin.*

Hope for what? She wondered. *There's nothing left.*

She looked up at that sky already turning dusky from debris cast into the atmosphere by the bombs. She blinked.

A great creature of steel was rising over their mountaintop.

It bore an insignia, a white ankh.

She stood slowly, staring, then hearing the *whap-whap* of the helicopter's rotors she cursed and took off at a dead run uphill for the cabin and Khalen.

They didn't all leave. That's not Khalen's people. That's the Right Church, and they have homed in on my radio receiver. They will take Khalen. They will kill him, or worse.

While she ran she cursed herself for letting her guard down. She had a complete arsenal in her cabin, but had left with only her habitual pistol.

The helicopter had landed before she could reach the mountaintop and the cabin. She had her Glock, but the Warriors of God had better weapons, and they wore the white armor that the Glock's bullets couldn't penetrate.

They were still spilling out of the helicopter when she stopped yards away, boots planted apart, and began firing at the faceplates that were their only weak point.

But of course, she knew. She knew they would kill her. She could only try to kill enough of them to give Khalen a chance to handle the rest.

When their assault rifles turned on her, her last thought before the darkness was that she would never know the dark stranger who had smiled at her on a street corner once, a long time ago.

PART 2: HIRAETH

"One thing I have learned in a long life:
that all our science, measured against reality,
is primitive and childlike.
We still do not know one thousandth of one percent
of what nature has revealed to us. It is entirely possible
that behind the perception of our senses,
worlds are hidden of which we are unaware."
—Albert Einstein

CHAPTER 7

*N*ot dead.

Shandiin awoke devastated, because she didn't want to wake. She felt an ache in her heart and tears behind her eyelashes as awareness returned.

I'm still here. The thought flickered away as she felt a small weight on her chest and throat. It was warm, and alive, because she could feel it vibrating, a miniscule hum that shifted toward her face. It touched her cheek, and it tickled.

She opened her eyes to the golden gaze of a white cat huddled cozily at her throat. It was purring. It had a small black spot on its forehead in the shape of a heart.

They stared at each other for a long moment. "Hey," she greeted it finally, and her voice was barely a whisper. "You grew up."

"Chan!" She recognized her daughter Leah's voice. "Are you on Mother again? Get off!"

Shandiin lifted a shaky hand to stroke the cat's head. "Leah?" her voice was a little stronger. She swallowed and tried again. "Leah, is that you? Where am I?"

Her daughter's face appeared then, looming over the cat's. *Her face is almost as pale as the cat's*, she thought distractedly. *How odd.*

"You're awake!" Leah cried, and then Shandiin found herself embraced, her daughter's cheek warm against her own. The cat was trapped between them, but seemed fine with it. It didn't move as Leah drew back. "Oh, Mother, I'm so happy you're awake!"

A male voice announced, "I have advised Medical that the patient is awake." Shandiin frowned, vaguely recognizing that voice as a computer called Phil.

"Leah," she rasped, "Where am I? Am I in a hospital?"

"In a manner of speaking, yes. You've been asleep for a terribly long time. How do you feel?"

Shandiin thought about that. "I'm not sure. I need to get up."

"You should wait...oh, here's Zion! I'll get you some water. Zion, she wants to get up."

Leah moved away, and Zion's handsome face took her place. His emerald eyes were worried. "Give yourself a minute, Shandiin. You've been in a coma. Leah, can you take the cat?"

Shandiin put her hand protectively over the furry creature. It immediately purred louder. "I like the cat. Is it the kitten Khalen rescued? Where...where the hell am I, Zion?"

He managed a smile that didn't reach his eyes. "The cat obviously likes you, too. He keeps coming in here. Yes, it's the same cat. You've been asleep a very long time, Shandiin."

She looked from him to the cat, back again. "How long?"

"You've been in a stasis chamber. We took you out a few days ago when your EEG readings changed. You're bound to be weak..."

"What the hell is a stasis chamber? And how long, Zion? Just tell me where the hell I am and how long I've been out!"

Zion closed his eyes briefly, took a deep breath. "You're inside a ship in space. And you have been in stasis for close to ten years. You were removed from stasis and have been in a coma for the last week."

It took her several very long moments to process his words. Once she had, she returned her attention to the cat. "Okay. None of that seems real. I need time on that. Leah, will you take him now...is his name Chan? I thought I heard you say Chan."

"Yes," Leah gently lifted the cat away. "Are you all right, Mother?"

"I don't know. The last thing I remember...oh, God. Verity. Leah, your father is dead. I'm so sorry."

"I know, Mother. Khalen told me."

"Ten years. Is that even possible? To me he...he just died last night. Khalen..." Shandiin looked at Zion. "He's okay? But...damn it, I told him I didn't want to come on the ship!"

Zion grimaced and shook his head. "He saved your life, back on that mountaintop. He said it was the bravest thing he'd ever imagined, when he saw you standing there with nothing but a pistol. You distracted the Warriors of God long enough for him to take them out with grenades from your arsenal. You were badly wounded, but he kept you alive long enough for us to find you both and bring you to the ship. He saved your life, and yes, he told me you didn't want to come, but what was he to do? Leave you there to die?"

She put her hands over her face, took a deep breath. Then lowered them and was stunned to see Zion's eyes sheened with tears.

"Hey," she said. "I didn't mean to sound ungrateful."

"I don't care about gratitude. I'm just...overwhelmed. Glad you are awake, Shandiin."

She sighed. "I think I'm just rattled. This is so strange. Will you help me sit up, please?"

"Of course." She felt the bed lift her to a sitting position, and became dizzy for a moment.

Thirstily drinking the water Leah offered, she took a moment to look around the room, saw machines and monitors, none of them turned on. Looked down at herself, in a simple white gown. Lifted her arms, saw the bruising.

"Intravenous fluids and feeding," Zion explained. "We shut everything else down when we saw your vitals go to normal. How do you feel?"

"Shaky. And a little embarrassed. Um...were you my doctor?"

"Sarnath has been primary, and Leah's been your nurse. We've...tried to ensure you were treated with dignity, if that's your concern."

She bit her lip, nodded. *Always the gentleman,* she thought. *That's almost as weird as his genealogy.*

She looked up as the door opened and Sarnath entered. He said, "Leah, Zion...I need you to go now, so I can talk to Shandiin."

Zion seemed to hesitate, but after meeting Sarnath's eyes he nodded and left with Leah. Sarnath regarded her silently for a long moment, then sat in the chair next to her bed. "Phil," he commanded, "turn off communication for this room. Do not listen."

He looked toward the door, and she noted a small light above it. It winked off.

He returned his somber gaze to her. "What has Zion told you?"

"That I was in something called a stasis chamber for ten years, and in a coma after that. Why did you tell Phil to turn off?"

"Sometimes I prefer privacy."

"Do I still have the biochip? Doesn't it just listen in all the time?"

Sarnath shook his head and held up a device with a blinking light. "Not when I have a jammer."

She felt an immediate release of tension...and so let go. "Sarnath, you made a...a prophecy that I am critical to this project. You have to be wrong. I didn't even want to come on this ship. I don't understand anything that's happened, or why."

"That's why I am here, Shandiin. I can try to help you. But first you have to tell me why you don't want to be alive."

She immediately burst into tears.

In the days that followed, Zion was kind to the point of tenderness. She thought he and Sarnath had reversed roles, with Sarnath as doctor and therapist, while Zion was more concerned with her on a personal level.

She had been wary of Sarnath on their first meeting back on Earth. But that initial wariness now morphed into trust, and she never told Zion what she and Sarnath had discussed. Sarnath had given her a lot to think about, and she didn't believe Zion would understand.

Even if he did, it was none of his business.

Nor did she ask a lot of questions, though she had many. There was too much change, too sudden. She needed to come to terms with her own feelings about leaving Earth, about being a passenger on a ship in space. She had learned long ago that worry about things she could not control was mental pollution. So she lived one day at a time, instead of questioning how far they would travel, where they were going, what the plans were upon eventual arrival.

The others didn't crowd her, but reacquainted themselves carefully. Shandiin accepted it when Egypt showed delight at her awakening, yet seemed distant and uncharacteristically reticent in answering the few questions Shandiin ventured.

She had a long talk with Khalen at the first opportunity, and asked if he had told the others about Diane's abuse, as it was her intent to do so if he had not.

But he begged her for silence. He'd broken it off with Diane immediately upon his return to Aztlan, and the thought of anyone knowing what had happened to him was humiliating. She argued, but when valiant Khalen succumbed to tears she gave in, telling herself the victim had a right to privacy.

That was a decision that she would regret bitterly much, much later.

She and Diane ignored each other. It was easy to do, as the core group of engineered family had never truly included her, and her skills were no longer needed for the project.

Khalen was openly grateful to her for the time they had shared. He told her he was indebted for having been given his only experience outside of a confined world that was, in fact, the ship she now lived on.

His innate longing for freedom was something she understood. She missed that freedom even though a great deal of
the ship had been carefully designed to counterfeit nature, to
countermand any claustrophobic effect on the human psyche
on their long journey to another world she still couldn't quite
believe in.

Leah had become a favorite and, along with Sarnath, accepted as a kind of counselor to the people.

Khandor was the biggest surprise. He was no longer a boy,
but a young man, and spent most of his time among the
colony's membership rather than with the three she thought
of as Zion's core family.

Khandor's role as leader among the members was palpable.
After seeing his interaction with a dissenting few, she thought
he had a deeper understanding of people than most men twice
his age. She learned from observation and a few conversations
with others that his authenticity of character was absolute.
Everything he said, everything he did, matched who he was.
Trust followed naturally.

Even her own. She felt a deep admiration for him. She
knew Khalen's qualities, and had a great affection for him, but
Khandor was...more. He was not arrogant, but wore confidence
and even command like his own skin.

He in fact faintly echoed a dream she'd had once, of a dark
stranger on a street corner.

She wondered if Khandor's differences could all be from his
unusual DNA, and was curious enough to ask Sarnath about it.
"He seems so much older than his years. Do you think that's
from his engineering?"

Sarnath had...typically for him...responded with a question.
"Do you think our spirit is separate from our mortal body?"

"I'm not sure," she'd answered after a moment of thought.
"But I know some people seem to have a brightness about them
that has nothing to do with what they look like."

He had smiled. "Then I believe you have glimpsed their spirit. What some call a soul. And a soul is ageless, Shandiin, if it exists at all."

Roland had been left behind. "There was no way to get him off the Church's ship," Egypt told her sadly. "But if anyone will make the best of a bad situation, it's him."

"Is there any chance the people will be able to get off that ship?" Shandiin asked. "Won't Earth be habitable in places, at least?"

Egypt had looked at Zion, who said, "It's time to show you something."

So they had taken her to what they called the observation room.

One wall appeared to be a window into space. Zion clarified that it was monitor providing a view from the ship's cameras, but it seemed like a window. Shandiin settled into one of the big chairs and looked out upon a symphony of stars in black space. There were billions of them, hard points of light with no separating atmosphere to make them shimmer. Beyond the local Milky Way, billions more were patterned as galaxies.

That miracle of stars burned behind a series of metallic discs Zion explained were the rest of the ships traveling with them.

"Here's how it looked as we left our world behind." Zion switched to their last view of what had been a beautiful blue world, now dark, it's atmosphere polluted beyond redemption from planet-wide nuclear firestorms that had released debris, soot and smoke. Red glowed through in places, like embers in a dying fire.

It was, she thought, exactly like looking into Hell.

She didn't realize it, but tears were slipping down her cheeks. She started to ask him to turn it off, but then a silver sphere caught her eye, bright as the moon beyond its orbit.

"Is that the Church ship?" she asked. "Are all the Church members on that ship?"

Zion nodded, his expression sad. "They escaped. The Right Church got their people out. We got our people out. But we had no choice but to leave them behind, apparently forever in orbit around Earth."

"You did what you could," Egypt reminded him. "Without your work they wouldn't have had that ship at all. You know that."

"It still seems wrong, just leaving them there. But they would never see us as anything but enemies."

"Turn it off," Shandiin said, and refused to speak of it again.

The children she'd seen playing baseball that long-ago day were adults now. The place that had once been a baseball field was now a park with trees and flowers and grass, and it was well used by many.

Including Shandiin. She found a measure of solace there, because true nature had been combined with invention. She could feel the grass under her feet and hear the leaves rustling in the engineered breeze. The sky, with sun or stars as scheduled, seemed as real as another had, on a world lost forever.

She walked the park with Zion, several days after her awakening. She was regaining health and strength so rapidly she knew there was more to her recovery than she had been told, but she was still remaining careful to let explanations unfold along with her new life.

On this day she looked around at the people who shared the park. "I think I know which ones have been blessed with your genes, Zion."

He looked across at her in surprise. "Not just mine. We've combined genomic material from all of those engineered by Damon Alexander. Well, those that survived the cleansing, as they called it."

"Well, it's obvious which of them are related to the lot of you. Much of your colony appears to be of the fairer races. The people with your family's genes are darker, I'm guessing mostly influenced through Roland and Egypt...and they are better looking in general. Some even have Sarnath's slightly Asian features. Do any of them have the emerald eyes?"

"No. So far that mutation has only shown up in Khalen and Khandor. It may show up in the future, if their descendants intermarry with those who also have our genomic material in their ancestry. We aren't planning to require that," he smiled at her lifted eyebrow, "though we would hope the bloodline for leadership could continue through intermarriage with those of similar heritage. We keep computer records of the colony's genetics, but not for some required breeding program. And we're done with open genetic tampering. Roland told me once it's like we've created a new race. He called them the Royals, and everyone else the People. Needless to say, I didn't approve. Not even as a joke."

She laughed, then looked around. "Not a lot of redheads," she noted, "but there are some mixed in. Even with the Royals."

He shook his head. "Don't you start calling them that, Shandiin. Please. As for redheads...they are normally only about 2% of the population, and it requires a recessive factor from both parents to get one. Lilith was a redhead, so some is from her."

She heard the sadness when he spoke of his lost sister. "What was she like?" she asked gently. "Typical fiery nature, per all the cliches?"

He smiled. "Oh, yes. She could be fiery, and had pretty definite opinions of her own. She hated the biochip as much as you and didn't like Phil at all. She didn't trust artificial intelligence."

"Could that be why her chip quit working?"

"I'm sure that's just a coincidence," he shrugged.

Shandiin tucked this away thoughtfully. As a cop, she had never believed in coincidence...especially when things went wrong for no apparent reason.

And she remembered Sarnath's electronic jammer. She had a list of questions that she would ask as need unfolded, and decided to include asking Sarnath if he had suspicions about Lilith's biochip as well. Suspicions about Phil.

She asked, "How about me? Did you check my DNA, Zion? Egypt thinks I'm engineered, like you. I've often wondered if I have Navajo blood…what's wrong?"

He had flinched at her question. She stopped walking, so he had to stop.

When he turned to her, his expression was troubled. "No. Not Navajo. And not like us. Do you really want to know all of it?"

"Crap. So I'm really an alien?" At his expression, she sobered. "Yes," she said. "Whatever makes you look like that tells me I should probably know."

He led her to a bench under a tree, and sat down with her. He smiled at her expression, but it wasn't a happy smile. "Don't worry. You aren't an alien. You are human." He sat back, sighed. "We did do a complete analysis. We couldn't determine your heritage from your DNA, Shandiin. That puzzled me so much that I looked at other things. I studied your MtDNA, which is mitochondrial. You see, according to MtDNA, everyone who existed on earth during our time is descended from one woman. She lived a long time ago, some say between 50,000 and 500,000 years ago. But she wasn't the only woman who ever lived in that time. Something happened. Some cataclysmic event killed off almost everyone. Only her descendants survived." He met her eyes. "You are not one of her descendants, Shandiin. You are a bloodline unrelated to anyone existing on the earth during your lifetime."

She felt a hard slam of her heart, as though she'd been startled by a physical threat. Waited for it to steady.

"Why…" she began, then swallowed. "Why did you bring me back, then? I don't belong. I never have. I guess now I know why."

"Why wouldn't I have tried to save you, Shandiin? Don't you think I understand what it is, to be so different?"

But you are not one of a kind, she thought. *There are others like you.*

"What about Diane and Leah?" she asked.

"They both carry your mtDNA, which comes down only through the female bloodline. Their father's very normal DNA is also apparent. Diane has also inherited your unusual youthful longevity, while Leah has not. That's the luck of the draw, with natural genetics."

She sighed, secretly wishing it had been the other way around. "Leah was dismayed by your creation of Khandor. She said it would be hard, being one of a kind. I understood that, because I've always known I was different. So did my Shimá Sani, my grandmother. She told me the spirits had brought me to her for a purpose, and wanted me to be glad and to reach for some great destiny. But how can you be glad when..." her voice trailed off, and she looked up at the holographic sun sparkling through the leaves. Then she started over. "At least Khandor is the good kind. He doesn't lie, and he understands people. I think he even loves them. I'm not the good kind. Just...different. Maybe that is why I can't love anyone."

"That can't be true, Shandiin. From what Khalen told me, you loved the father of your children."

She shook her head. "I cared for Verity, quite a lot. But he loved me, and I could see the difference in what I could not give back to him. I don't think I'm a sociopath. I do have a conscience. But I know I'm not normal. I think maybe you've found out why."

He shook his head. "You are human. Maybe more than I am, if you look at the science."

"It isn't the science I worry about. It's the spirit. You're a good person who has helped to create an even better person. All I've ever done...." she shrugged, looked away.

"Look at me, Shandiin." When she complied, he took her hand in his, and asked, "Do you know what Egypt calls you?"

She laughed shortly. "Other than her bitch-sister?"

"She calls you a hero without a cause." He looked into her surprised face, and finally smiled fully. "Khalen agreed. You are a hero without a cause, because you defend everyone but yourself. You save people. Then you're gone like—what's that old story?—the Lone Ranger."

She thought about this, and smiled sadly. "She knows me pretty well. I don't love, and I don't stay." She met his eyes, those strange and beautiful emerald eyes that somehow stirred her heart. "I tried to warn you," she added softly.

"I have an advantage. I'm not so easy to leave behind. Where else can you go from here?"

As the days passed Shandiin recalled why she hadn't wanted to join the people on the ship called *Aztlan.*

Zion was right. There truly was nowhere else to go. The only possibility was in the stasis chambers that many of the colonists had chosen over wakefulness during their interstellar journey.

She'd already spent too many years in one of those. She'd come out of it filled with a profound sadness only Sarnath had recognized. They had discussed it the day she awakened, the day he had stopped Phil from listening in.

"You were made for a purpose greater than yourself," was his answer to her despondency. "I see only a reflection of your destiny, but it's beauty makes my spirit sing...while it makes you miserable, because you need it more than life, and it eludes you. You need to look outside of yourself, Shandiin."

"What? No. I don't believe in destiny, and you know how I feel about religion."

"We all have a destiny, but our life's choices can change it for good or ill. That is free will. You aren't religious, but I find you to be strongly spiritual. How do you perceive the difference?"

She considered. "I guess they're both about a higher purpose. But religion makes rules and prophecies, and searches for miracles in inexplicable events outside of natural law or science...while I think the true and only miracle is in all of existence, including natural law and science. Our very existence and what we make of it is the inexplicable miracle."

He smiled. "So," he had said, "Somewhere in your miraculous and inexplicable existence, you will find your purpose. You are the daughter of your own prophecy, Shandiin."

So she had stayed out of the stasis chamber, and tried connecting with the other passengers on this strange journey. In doing so she soon found a buzz of excitement that stirred her curiosity.

They were excited because their ships were nearing the heliosphere's boundary with interstellar space. She learned that the heliosphere was created by the solar wind, a thin gas of electrically charged particles blown into space by the sun. It protected the solar system, Zion explained, from most interstellar cosmic rays.

"So why are we leaving the heliosphere for the dangers of interstellar space?" she asked. "And how long will we be there until we get to a planet that is probably a few million light-years away?"

"I guess it's time for a return trip to the observation room. I have a surprise to show you."

"You are full of amazing surprises, Zion. Didn't someone say technology, when sufficiently advanced, is indistinguishable from magic?"

Khandor overheard her remark as he walked up to them, and laughed. "Perhaps we shouldn't call Zion 'Doctor.' Maybe his real title is Sorcerer."

"I'll go for that," Egypt put in from nearby. "I think a lot of people would like to join you, if you're taking her to the magic show in space?"

Zion just smiled, and soon they were settling into the comfortable chairs in front of the ship's 'window' into space. Shandiin looked out at the stars with wonder while more people filled in around them. Khandor, settling into a chair beside her, winked when she turned to him. "This is a big deal," he said. "We've seen it before, but not when we're this close."

"This close to what?"

He smiled. "Have patience. The Sorcerer is about to speak."

Zion stood to face the room. "Most of you know this, but I'm repeating it for those who don't. A very long time ago, Dr. Damon

Alexander discovered a wormhole just outside the heliosphere. Wormholes—tunnels connecting distant points in space—were considered theoretical, but this one was recognized by its magnification of light. What appeared to be a bright star was in fact light magnified more than a hundred thousand times. The light comes from an extremely distant star system that mirrors our own." He turned to the monitor. "Phil, please show this onscreen."

"What you are watching," he continued as the screen changed to show a very bright light in the darkness of space, "is the video from a small, unmanned ship sent into space more than fifty years ago. I am going to have Phil speed it up, as the old technology required all fifty of those years to get past the heliosphere." The light grew until it filled the screen. Shandiin heard Sarnath softly narrating the events on the screen to Leah as they unfolded.

Then a dark hole appeared within the light. It grew until there was only darkness, space and stars. It approached a single star, with planets around it.

It drew near to a planet that was blue streaked with white, and had a moon.

"The ship went through," Zion continued. "It found this planet, and entered its atmosphere, where it burned up. But these images and data were already on their way back to Earth."

They watched the planet grow bigger, a blue and white globe with a large land mass, until the picture fractured, winking out of existence.

"It looks like Earth!" Shandiin exclaimed. "Almost just like it!"

"We analyzed every bit of data the ship returned to us. It meets our specifications. There is a healthy ecosystem, but no evidence of civilization or the kind of sentient beings to build it. So...it's our new home." He had Phil reverse the video to stop at a still view of the beautiful planet.

"You have found Hiraeth," Shandiin said in wonder.

Zion looked at her in surprise. "What an appropriate name for our new world."

Leah asked, "What does that mean, Mother?"

"It's an ancient Welsh word. It stands for a spiritual longing for home, a home that perhaps is real only in a person's heart."

Her eyes met Zion's. "It's like a place in your soul that you grieve for and hope for at once. Well done, Zion. Well done, indeed."

Their ship would go into the wormhole first, and alone. Zion was confident they would emerge safely on the other side, since the ancient drone ship had done so, but he wanted to ensure the other ships could return to Earth's orbit if they did not.

Most of the people aboard the *Aztlan* knew this was the plan, but a few chose to be transported to one of the other ships to await the fate of the lead ship. Some elected to go into a stasis chamber and sleep through it. The more adventurous would ride it through wide awake.

Shandiin found herself among the adventurous, so when the time came, she sat in the observation room with the others. At first she was a little disappointed that there was nothing to see but light.

Until the light became a kaleidoscope.

She quickly turned her face away from the monitor with its broken patterns of color, and found that they were not just on the monitor, but in the room. The people around her flashed in and out of the pattern...and were colored with it, seemingly through it.

Then they disappeared, along with the room and the colors.

She looked around at a landscape under a night sky. She stood in a grassland, a sea of grass silvered by starlight from unfamiliar constellations.

Then it changed, and she was standing on a mountaintop, under a clear and moonless sky.

The stars are so brilliant their light ices everything, including him...shining light through his long black hair, firing the emerald of his eyes as he turns to me with love and sadness. My dark stranger.

Then he was gone. She felt a terrible emptiness as he faded away into nothing.

She had never known such loss.

The room was there again. There was nothing else.

It was silent except for the broken sounds of people weeping.

After a few moments, both Zion and Sarnath rose and looked around the room. The monitor now showed only stars, a central one larger than the rest.

"We've all experienced something unexpected," Sarnath said. "If anyone needs help or counseling, please come to me."

Zion nodded. "Thanks, Sarnath. Please, all of you...it's apparent we've all experienced hallucinations, probably caused by some unfamiliar element as we passed through the wormhole. I'd like volunteers for an examination, to determine if there is any sort of physical damage to the brain. Please be calm; I am only being cautious. Many things can cause such hallucinations. They are even common, for instance, in people on the edge of sleep. We'll meet back here tomorrow to determine the next steps."

This was met with silence, until people began to rise and walk out, and then there were only quiet murmurs. Shandiin left with the rest, and went to her room. Exhausted, not understanding why, she dropped onto her bed and into sleep.

When she woke the clock told her it was hours later, and the middle of the ship's scheduled night. She knew she wouldn't sleep more, so went out.

The park was empty under a brilliant moon. She followed her moon-shadow across the grass to the bench she had shared with Zion before.

He sat there, as though waiting for her. He glanced up as she sat down beside him. "Are you all right?" he asked.

She hesitated. "Yes. I just can't sleep anymore. How about you?"

He looked down. She frowned, as it seemed he was avoiding her gaze. "I'm not sure. I've examined several people, and found no physical problem. The hallucinations appear to be benign, though they've caused some mental distress."

"You're quite sure they are hallucinations?"

"Call them waking dreams, if you prefer. Sarnath called them visions, but he leans to the paranormal, as you know. I think they were dredged from our own subconscious, and may include memories some would rather forget. Several people told me flatly they didn't want to talk about it."

Nor do I, Shandiin thought. *And I'm not so sure I disagree with Sarnath.*

"Can you tell me what you saw, Zion?" she asked.

He'd been sitting with his wrists on his knees, toying with a small stick that he flicked away as he sat back. Moonlight struck emerald fire from his eyes as he studied her.

"I saw you," he said. "I saw myself falling in love with you out there on the streets of hell. Standing by a police car, and stupidly asking you to dinner."

Stunned, Shandiin struggled with a response. Came up with, "So that was a pick-up line after all?"

"I have never been so embarrassed as when that came out of my mouth. Have I shocked you, Shandiin?"

"Yes," she admitted. "And I have warned you, Zion. I do care for you, but I don't think I am capable of falling in love."

He studied her thoughtfully. "Then I must accept that I've taken the fall for both of us. Will you allow me to hope you will join me when you can?"

"Zion, you don't even know me."

"I feel like I have always known you. Like my strange twin, I guess, who somehow knew your name."

She shivered a little. "That feels like a dream. At the moment, so does this."

"Let me try to make it real, then." He put his hand on her cheek, leaned in...and when she just waited, kissed her lips very softly.

His lips were warm, and brought a different kind of shiver. After a moment she returned the kiss. She didn't open her eyes when he finally drew away. Then she blinked at him, wondering at the mix of emotions he brought.

Desire. Certainly, desire. Affection, surprisingly deep, but not quite love. What she felt was, she somehow knew, just short of that.

And a stranger's ghost stood between them.

But the stranger wasn't real. She may have seen someone who looked like Zion, but she told herself she had added otherworldly and impossible values to him, as one did in a dream.

The wrenching loss she had suffered from seeing that ghost again told her she needed to give up the dream.

So she looked instead to the man who was real and present, who deserved so much. Who waited for her to say something.

She gathered her thoughts carefully. "Zion...I never pretend. I don't change my colors for anyone or anything." She sighed. "But you honored me," she went on, "with what you just said. I am guessing they were words you've never said to anyone else. I just want you to understand that I will probably never say I love you. I don't know if I can love anyone the way you want. But I think I could come very close to it, with you. You honored me, and I want to honor you with what I can give...even knowing it isn't enough, that *I* am not enough for what you deserve. I tell you this with all honesty, because I will not mislead you, and I never want to hurt you."

His smile made him even more beautiful. She thought of Verity's words about the miracle that was love, of the amazing fact that she was here...that miracle of existence Sarnath had reminded her of.

She reached up to curve her hand through his hair, and brought her lips to his. Then she stood and took his hand to take him to her bed.

He knew how to make love. In fact, he was very skilled at it, as he seemed to be skilled at so many things. She responded, fully, surprised at the pleasure he brought to her, and tried to return it as best she could.

But what brought her the greatest wonder and the greatest sorrow was the love in his eyes and in his every touch.

When they were wrapped together in the warm aftermath of lovemaking, she held him close and promised herself she would not hurt him.

Her sorrow came from knowing she probably would anyway.

When those who had witnessed the transition through the wormhole met again the next day, Shandiin noticed Khalen sat with his head down, looking miserable.

Several people told Zion flatly they didn't want to talk about their memories, Shandiin thought. *I bet he remembered being sixteen. I'd like to punch Diane.*

She was surprised when Khandor dropped into the chair next to her. "I saw you," he whispered.

"What? Where?"

"It was on a prairieland of grass. You were standing there under the stars, with a big paint horse behind you. You wore leather armor, and carried a golden sword. Like a pagan goddess."

A prairieland of grass? "I did have a paint horse, named Nitchi. Was he left behind?"

"If Khalen knew about him, he's somewhere on the ships. Khalen made sure your animals were rescued. This was more than a hallucination, Shandiin. I swear it."

"Did you tell Zion?"

Zion interrupted by calling the meeting to order. Khandor looked at him, back at her, shook his head no. That puzzled her.

What he then told Zion puzzled her even more.

"I saw a city," Khandor reconstructed the rest of his vision for everyone in the room. "It was behind a wall, but it wasn't like the Right Church. This wall was the boundary of a medieval city. It spread beside a sea, and at the sea's edge was a tall black palace looming over everything else. There were sparkles like stars moving on its walls, on its towers. Did anyone else see anything like that?"

For some reason, Shandiin looked toward Diane. What she saw was quickly hidden surprise, and she was sure it had some meaning for her.

No one else spoke of anything like Khandor's vision. Their visions all seemed to have more personal roots. Sarnath reported that the recorded brainwaves of those in the stasis chambers showed they also had extreme sessions of dreaming at the same time they had gone through the wormhole.

"Everyone's exam came back fine. I tested all systems through our main computer," Zion announced. "Nothing was changed by our transition through the wormhole. So I am sending permission to the rest of our fleet to come through, and we will continue to the planet we've now named Hiraeth."

But the dreams didn't stop. Shandiin thought her nightly walks through the starlit grasslands were more like visions; she could clearly feel the tall grass whisking around her legs, the breeze on her face. But everyone else called them dreams. Strangely...to everyone, she thought at first, but her...they became accepted as normal, becoming little more than interesting topics of discussion.

The ships that followed them reported the same events, the same odd dreams. The night-visions became more vivid as they traveled, until some found them more real than waking moments.

Shandiin had moved into Zion's quarters, and so walked in unexpectedly while he was in a heated argument with Khandor.

"You are lying to people," Khandor was saying. "These are not just hallucinations or dreams."

"What else could they be?" Zion flung back. "Yours especially, Khandor, with palaces and medieval cities! Very vivid dreams, perhaps, but still not real."

"Then how do you explain the similarities?" Khandor demanded. "Several have seen the same prairie landscape."

Zion was dismissive. "They probably caught the idea from each other. Please, Khandor, people look up to you. Do you want to cause a panic with this nonsense?"

"Zion," Khandor replied so quietly it sounded dangerous, "that's an argument for secrecy used far too often by governments, and you know it."

"Things are strange enough without people thinking their brains have been invaded by some outside source."

Khandor stood his ground. "I believe they have been, and I think we should be addressing that instead of ignoring it."

"I'm surprised at you. You sound like Khalen, second guessing me." Zion stopped, as though noticing Shandiin for the first time. "Certainly you agree with me, Shandiin?"

He obviously expected her to support him. She lifted her eyebrows in surprise. She would not allow their relationship to color her opinion...and she had warned him she changed her colors for no one. "I've seen that grassland too, Zion. So have Leah, and Khalen and Khandor. Haven't you?"

He scowled. "No. I have not. Neither has Sarnath, who I questioned thoroughly, as he is the most likely to be on the other side of this."

"Did you ask Egypt?" Shandiin asked.

"She laughs about it. Says she saw some handsome redhaired man taller than her. I think everyone is stressed, which isn't surprising when losing a world and going to another. The dreams are probably some kind of release."

The problem wasn't resolved, as Zion was the undisputed leader on this journey.

Judging by the look on Khandor's face when he left, Shandiin thought that would change once the colony had landed.

Whatever was causing them, the dreams didn't go away.

Shandiin worried about Leah, who spent most of her time in her quarters with the cat in her lap. She sat quietly smiling for hours. Shandiin interrupted her occasionally, but she didn't answer questions. All she said was "I am fine, Mother. Probably better than I have ever been. I can see, over there. I can see everything, and it is beautiful."

So she spent extra time with Leah, making sure she awoke to eat, to exercise a little. Sarnath shared her concern, and after several days decided to put Leah into stasis until they arrived at Hiraeth. Leah woke barely long enough to agree and beg for the cat to go into the chamber with her. Softhearted Sarnath complied.

"Do you think the visions will stop when we get to Hiraeth?" Shandiin asked him.

"I can only hope so." For once he looked almost grim. "I don't know what to expect. Neither does Zion, for all his skepticism about the dreams coming from somewhere external."

Diane behaved much like Leah. It surprised Shandiin, for Diane had always seemed the realist, unencumbered by mysteries that couldn't be measured by science...or manipulated for her own benefit. Now her dark daughter rarely seemed awake, finally asking to go into a stasis chamber where she could dream uninterrupted. She never shared what she dreamed about.

Khalen and Khandor would provide leadership for the colony's transition down-planet, with Zion, Egypt and Sarnath staying aboard the flagship *Aztlan* to coordinate transport of people, livestock, and the many supporting supplies.

More and more people chose to go into stasis for the short remainder of their journey to Hiraeth.

Shandiin observed, and finally asked Zion the question that had been lurking since her awakening. "Why wasn't I in a terribly weakened condition? I was in one of those things for ten years. Will they all come out like me?"

"Yes. Stasis maintains their condition at entry. Your minor weakness was a result of your days in a motionless coma, not the stasis chamber. And you have excellent health, which returned far quicker than expected."

He wasn't looking at her as he answered. She considered, then flicked him on the ear. "Hey. I'm fine now. But you and Egypt keep treating me with kid gloves. There's something else you aren't telling me, isn't there? Something besides being an alien?"

"You are not an alien. Your genealogy is just different." He put a hand up to protect his ear from a second flick. "All right, Shandiin. Your genealogy is very different. It's why you haven't aged."

"Neither have you."

He ran a hand through his hair, drew her to sit beside him. "Those of us who are fully engineered have a very long life span. Damon...Dr. Alexander created a system of ongoing resets in our genetic makeup against the normal breakdowns of aging. We don't yet know how long our systems will continue to work. Khalen and Khandor have been engineered to live about 300 years, which is not unusual for the enhanced. They both agree with our reasoning; they live long enough to ensure stability for the colony they will lead, but not so long they are seen as inhuman by a colony that has accepted genetic enhancement. Most of the others related to their bloodline will also have extended lifespans to varying degrees. Do you want the whole scientific explanation?"

"I wouldn't understand it anyway. Why am I different from all of that?"

"All cells have various mechanisms for DNA repair...to maintain the integrity of its genetic code. Yours are far more powerful than any of ours. Shandiin...you were badly injured and nearly dead when I put you in that stasis chamber. My only hope was to keep you alive until I could figure out a way to put you back together. But amazingly, your body began its own repair while you were in stasis. We waited to see if you would come back all the way.

You did. We took you out of the chamber so you could wake up." He shook his head. "You may be immortal, Shandiin, and I didn't know if I should tell you. You see things differently than I. I didn't know if you would see that as good news or bad, especially after telling you your mysterious origin."

Shandiin was quiet for a long moment, then just said "Wow."

Zion lifted his eyebrows. "You reacted a lot more strongly to the news about your genealogy. I'm surprised."

"Zion...I think everyone lives like they're immortal, even with the facts in their face. You haven't changed that basic attitude for me. For now, I am trying to stay in the present moment."

But she decided it was time to quit being in denial about her own role...if she had one. The first step in that direction was to find out why Egypt had been so different around her since her awakening from stasis.

She found her friend working in a free-fall chamber that curved gently away, it seemed, into eternity.

Shandiin hadn't thought much about the fact that they lived in normal Earth gravity. Science was very similar to magic when it rose to Zion's level, as she had pointed out. But she was fascinated by this area that didn't contain 'artificial' gravity. She watched on a monitor as Egypt hung mid-air, working on some piece of machinery. Receiving permission to join her, Shandiin stepped through an interlock to come out beside her.

Egypt looked over in surprise, then smiled. She closed a metal door and shoved the object...was that a small ship?...back into a space obviously made for it. Then she signaled her to follow, and expertly began the journey down...or was it up?...to a different exit.

Free-fall, Shandiin quickly learned, was not like falling at all. Without momentum, her body just drifted. Without planned momentum, it drifted oddly.

Egypt gave Shandiin a hand to exit the chamber, where she almost collapsed upon having weight again. "It takes a minute to recover," Egypt laughed. "I can't believe people used to spend months in free-fall. What are you doing here, Shandiin?"

"Looking for you. What was that you were working on? And does that free-fall tube go all through the ship?"

"It doesn't go through, but around. It once included our parking garage, so you've seen part of it. Just now I was working on a small ship that can be used to transport people to other ships, or down to the planet when we get there. We have them in various shapes and sizes. I'm in charge of deployment and I just like to make sure things are in working order. Come on to my place, it's closest."

Once there they settled at a table with cold drinks. Shandiin was glad to see her friend's warm regard as they clicked mugs before sipping cold root beer.

"Did Zion finally tell you everything?" Egypt asked.

"I think so. Did you know all along I am a one-of-a-kind weirdo?"

Egypt shook her head. "You're no more weird than I am. He told us to remember the basic fact that you are human. The rest makes you different like us, just not in the same way." She lifted an eyebrow, studying her friend with those emerald eyes. "I would like to know where you come from, though, since Zion's so sure your origin isn't a laboratory."

"Is that why you have been so distant toward me, Egypt?"

Egypt frowned. "No. But I guess I have been distant, haven't I? I'm sorry if that made you unhappy. You were down for a long time, girl. I gave you up, and was surprised that losing you hurt me so badly. I didn't think you could come back from the kind of injuries you had. But Zion wouldn't let go. Bringing you back was like an obsession with him. I was worried about him, and then...well, frankly shocked when you came back. Then he told me to hold back on telling you what he'd learned about your origin, and I just couldn't make myself be so secretive around you. It felt wrong." She leaned back, sighed. "He fell for you so hard, Shandiin. I love him. I also love you. I didn't know what to do or who to kick or not to kick. But you seem to have worked it out."

She picked up her mug and grinned over the rim. "I understand you are now sharing his quarters."

"His bed is bigger. Are you having the weird dreams, Egypt, like everyone else?"

"I had a weird vision when we went through the wormhole, but nothing since."

"Let me guess. A plain of grass, stretching to the horizon?"

Egypt shook her head. "No. It was a man I'd like to dream about again. I mean, he was so damned pretty. Taller even that me, with the green eyes..." she pointed at her own, grinning wickedly. "But a redhead, like you. He wore his hair past his shoulders, all braided with leather and some kind of gold wire."

"Wow. Didn't you have a nostalgia thing like everyone else, though? What was yours?"

"Him." Egypt picked up her mug, sipped again. She looked away with an uncharacteristic air of melancholy. "When I saw that redhaired stranger, I felt like he was my home. It makes no sense at all."

Shandiin thought of her own dark stranger, and the awful feeling of loss that had come with his last disappearance. She asked, "Would you like to dream of him again?"

Egypt shook her head. "Like some people do, going into the stasis chambers? No. I think going away from yourself like that is like taking drugs. Besides, I need to be awake and sharp for planetfall. Zion, Sarnath and I will oversee while everyone else goes down to the surface."

"So you will come down last."

"We'll be taking turns. Someone has to stay on *Aztlan*. We'll do rotation duty. The other ships will land, but we want to keep Aztlan in orbit and operational for any future need. You don't just dump this kind of technology."

Those words would come back to haunt Shandiin.

They would haunt her for a thousand years.

CHAPTER 8

Shandiin dreamed that night, the most vivid dream yet. And the most unsettling.

She dreamed she was on the sea of grass again. She looked down to see she was wearing leather armor, as Khandor had once described seeing her.

She had asked him why he hadn't told Zion about that vision.

He'd frowned, and appeared to choose his words carefully. "Because you belong to Zion. Or he thinks you do. What I saw was a free and independent goddess who belongs to no one. And I think that's much closer to the truth."

"He was right," a woman's voice said in answer to her memory. *"You belong to no one. And you are different from all the others."*

There was warmth in that voice, and familiarity where there should have been none.

She turned around slowly, trying to find the woman who had spoken to her.

"I am here," the voice said. Shandiin realized it came from no direction, but was inside her head. It was like wearing head-phones. *"I am everywhere here. I am what you named Hiraeth."*

After a moment of shock, Shandiin spoke aloud. "You are the planet? How can that be? And...why do you sound like my Shimá Sáni...my grandmother?"

"I needed a voice to speak to you with. Your grandmother's was in your mind, and I recognized her. She served my sister, who some

called Gaia in the world you came from. But she had no way to protect my sister. I will protect myself, with your help."

Shaky with astonishment, Shandiin lowered herself to sit in the cool grass, and looked up at stars that were becoming familiar. "You are the planet," she repeated in awe. "Why do you need protection?"

In answer she saw, vividly, the shrouded hell that had been Earth. She shuddered, and it vanished.

"The people with you have brought that death to me. They carried it from the place where my sister died at their hands. I am taking measures to ensure it cannot harm me."

Shandiin felt a chill of fear. What measures? "These are not the same people who caused Earth to die! They come in peace, and are only searching for a home."

"I have been looking inside the people that came with you. I see that such journeys do not end in peace, even among themselves. They take whatever they want, without regard to harm. This appears to be the pattern of their history, and that includes the history of the nation you claimed as your own."

Shandiin knew it was true. Native Americans were not the first to have felt the tread of conquerors who took away their land, their people, their freedom.

But she feared Hiraeth's anger against Earth's survivors. "I don't think these people are the same. Please, they need a home."

"I am not without pity. I do not plan to harm them. They can stay. But I do not trust them. Even as I try to look inside, to know them, I find more reason to mistrust their chaos. Humans are a collection of strange beliefs they don't even share with each other. There are things they call superstitions they scoff at, but still believe. There will be some difficult results, as these things incorporate with my magic."

"Magic?" Shandiin wheezed. She felt like her head was going to spin off her neck.

"That is what most of your people call it, though some call it miracles, others metaphysics. Here, it is a law of nature. Where

you come from, it seems to be anything that cannot be explained by material observation."

Forcing herself to calm, Shandiin agreed. "Yes. Among my people, 'I have to see it to believe it' is a common phrase. But scientists know that reality goes a lot deeper than what is visible. Is that what you mean?"

There was a brief silence before the response. *"Not exactly. You are referring to what is called physics, the framework of your world. My magic is separate from that, and has separate laws."*

Shandiin wished Zion or Sarnath were here for this discussion. Her initial chill of fear had become biting cold with the certainty that this was neither dream nor hallucination.

She had to understand what was happening. "Hiraeth...can you give me an example of a magic law?"

"The manifestation of intent is the most basic, and is the greatest concern as it mixes with the various belief systems of humans. Even as I rid myself of the material threat to me, I see timelines where wrong intent creates new threats. This is something I need to address."

"Wait! Whoa! Back up! You just hit me with a double whammy. How can an intent be manifested? And can you see the future?"

"Intent is already being manifested, by one who shares part of your birthright. She is creating a place of great beauty, built of darkness stolen from the light. She calls it Penumbra."

Shandiin couldn't understand any of that. As was her way, she set it aside to ponder in depth while she addressed the more immediate. "Can you see the future? Can you tell me what will happen to this colony?"

"It depends. You all think time is a straight line, but it isn't. It rides the universe in waves, and changes with their speed. Events from before and behind ripple through to what is now. Choices change the future, and the bedlam of humanity makes it even harder to see. There is no single destiny, but many. I have to control that, for myself and for the people who came with you."

Shandiin felt distrust and shoved to her feet. "Control it? How would you control our destiny, Hiraeth?"

There was no answer. "Hiraeth?" Distrust became a stabbing fear. "Why are you telling me this? Are you telling anyone else?"

The voice answered, but it was fading. *"You are the only one,"* it said. *"Because you are the only one I can trust."*

She woke alone, in a cold sweat. She had to find Zion. She had to tell him what she had learned.

But even while dressing, she decided it was Khandor she should tell. Zion wasn't having the same experiences everyone else did, and he denied their reality.

So she went to Khandor's room. The door opened before she could knock, and he stood there sleepily, his dark fall of hair in disarray around that handsome face, barefoot in tee shirt and jeans. His smile was questioning. "Phil told me you were coming. Come in, Shandiin. I was just getting some coffee."

She stepped in as he turned away, and watched him pour two mugs.

She grabbed the offered coffee and gladly slurped. "Um...has Hiraeth spoken to you?" she asked.

He considered her carefully as he leaned back against the counter with his coffee. His emerald eyes were dazzling in the brilliant overhead light. "No. You mean the planet itself is sentient?"

And there, she thought, was the difference that was Khandor. Straight to the heart of it, no question of her veracity, recognizing the impart of her question.

She exhaled. "Yes. And she is magic."

He frowned. "I thought it must be something like that. It's in the paranormal for so many of us to be sharing the same visions. Just how magic is...she, you said?"

"She spoke to me in a woman's voice. My grandmother's. I think she took it from my memory. Khandor, she isn't just giving us visions. She's searching our minds. She told me she plans to control us, because she knows what happened to Earth, and is afraid of us."

His eyebrows lifted. "Did she say how she plans to do this?"

"She said we brought Earth's death with us, and she will take measures to protect herself from it. Then she said she could see danger ahead, so she had to control us. She didn't say how she would do that, Khandor." She straightened. "I think she told me about that magic palace you saw. She said someone is magically building a place of great beauty, built of darkness stolen from the light."

He set his cup aside thoughtfully. "Khalen shared the same image. He told me it is named Penumbra."

Phil announced, "Khalen is at the door."

"Tell him to come in," Khandor said, and to Shandiin, "He rooms next door."

Khalen stepped in, looked at the light over the door, said "Phil, do not listen."

The light went out. Shandiin recognized the jammer in his hand, the same as Sarnath's.

Khalen frowned at them both. "Phil told me what you're talking about...Hiraeth and magic. I wanted to warn you to be careful of the computer. He hears everything, and tells Zion everything."

"Why wouldn't we tell Zion?" Shandiin asked. "He can only deny the facts for so long, when we have evidence."

Khalen scowled. "What evidence is that? If I bring up anything related to a vision or a dream, Zion shuts me out before I finish. It's as though he doesn't *want* to believe."

"He does the same with me." Khandor crossed his arms. "He's always been a skeptic, even in the face of Sarnath's psychic abilities. He would listen to Sarnath, but neither Sarnath nor Egypt are having the same experiences we are. It's as though those three are immune or something."

Shandiin nodded. "Egypt's had an odd dream, but not like ours. Oh! She said they are not going down to the planet with the rest of us, that they are keeping this ship in orbit while everyone else is landing. Could that be why they aren't receiving the same visions? Khalen, Hiraeth told me she is going to take measures to protect herself. I think she's worried about the technology being brought to her. There could be danger to the ships that will be landing."

The two men looked at each other in understanding. "It's been too strange," Khandor agreed. "No one but the three of us seem to realize there is the potential for danger in these visions. But it's time we challenged that, I think...and Zion is most likely to listen to Shandiin."

Khalen lifted the jammer, watched the light over the door blink on. "Phil, tell Zion we need a meeting with him, Sarnath and Egypt. Now."

It was Shandiin's first visit to the ship's operation center they called the bridge. There were three work stations below several monitors providing data and images from space and all of the ships. One of the ship's leaders was always present here; all three were here now at Khalen's request.

Zion looked annoyed, glancing from her to Khalen and Khandor as they entered. "What's going on? Phil says you've been shutting him down to have secret meetings."

"Perhaps they just aren't comfortable with Phil's constant monitoring." Sarnath set a big hand on Zion's shoulder. "Don't look for deceit from our sons, Zion. It isn't in them."

"I agree." Egypt looked to the two she also called her sons. "So, guys...why are you cutting Phil out? Do we need to do it now, so you can tell us what's going on?"

Khandor shook his head. "No. I think Khalen just wants to talk in private sometimes. Phil's just a computer, but one that always has Zion's ear."

"So that's why you've been so secretive?" Zion snapped. "Khalen, why do you think you have to keep things from me? Phil said Shandiin went to Khandor with a tale of a talking planet, then you joined them and turned him off. Why?"

"That's why we're here." Khandor answered calmly, with a warning glance at Khalen. "You should listen, Zion. Shandiin, tell him what you told me."

She did so. No one interrupted, but she saw Zion's face grow hard when she finished with her concern about potential danger to the ships slated to land.

Zion shook his head. "What is your suggestion, Shandiin? We came to colonize this planet. We are within days of establishing orbit to begin that process. Are you saying we should give it up?"

"No. But perhaps everyone shouldn't go down at once. I don't know all the answers, Zion, but Hiraeth said she would take measures to protect herself. We need to know what measures those are."

"Can you ask her?" Sarnath asked, and Shandiin turned to him with relief. He showed none of Zion's disbelief or aggravation.

"I can try, assuming she comes to me again. She faded out, I think because my body was trying to wake up. It was like coming out of a nightmare, because she was starting to scare the hell out of me."

"How dangerous do you think she is?" Egypt asked.

"She said she is not without pity, and she didn't plan to harm us...but..."

Zion crossed his arms, scowling. "Why hasn't she spoken to anyone else?"

Shandiin turned back to him with a sigh. "She told me I am the only one she trusts. And no, I don't know why. Please, Zion, don't kill the messenger. I'm not trying to start a fight, and I don't understand why you are. I am not lying about any of this."

He looked dismayed at that. "I'm sorry. I didn't mean to insinuate you were. It's just...hard to take in."

"Because you refuse to believe," Khalen snapped. "You've been fighting the idea anything could hijack your great project!"

"Stop it." Khandor stepped calmly between Khalen and Zion. "Arguing resolves nothing. Sarnath, do you have any suggestions?"

Sarnath nodded. "We could try hypnotism. Shandiin, have you ever been hypnotized?"

"No. Are you thinking of putting me to sleep so we can ask questions?"

"Yes. Would you be willing to try?"

She looked around at the group. "Um."

Sarnath understood. "Just you and me. Too much energy flying around otherwise."

"Just you and me," Shandiin agreed. "Turn Phil off, too. I'll relax better. Still, I don't promise I can do this."

But she could, and she did.

Reclining comfortably in a dim room with Sarnath standing guard, Shandiin opened her eyes to a night sky. The constellations had become familiar to her, especially one with straight lines that looked like a horse's bridle. She realized she had actually become comfortable with that sky, that landscape...and it didn't feel like a dream. It felt real, and she was somehow discomfited by the fact it felt almost homelike.

She reminded herself she was not really here, but it didn't seem to matter. So she accepted, and looked around for answers.

A huge white moon hung at the horizon, and she saw a small cottage silhouetted against it, the only feature in that endless sea of grass.

She walked toward it, hesitating at the gate of a picket fence where the grass stopped. Roses grew on the other side, and a covered porch just beyond. A figure in white sat in a rocking chair, gently rocking. She was luminous even on the shadowed porch.

"Do come in," a woman's voice said. This one was different than Hiraeth's. It held a kind of music, hinting of a choir. *"Hiraeth said we need to speak. I've been waiting for you."*

So Shandiin walked through the gate, through the roses, up the stone steps to the porch. The figure, robed in shimmering white, gestured to the rocking chair next to hers, so Shandiin sat down and studied her.

The strange figure's long white hair fell like a cloak over her shoulders. She was blindfolded, and a white cat curled sleeping in her lap. She smiled. *"You are so lovely. I am glad to finally see you."*

Shandiin blinked. "Who are you, and how can you see, when you are wearing a blindfold?"

"I do not need eyes to see. I am the goddess Liethe, though you know me somewhere else by Leah's name. I was sightless in that other place, but here I can see you. The blindfold is a symbol of my true vision. I do not recognize evil, for I am its opposite, and see only the good, the light of life and love. I will be a healer, in our new world, and try to give hope to the lost."

"So you share memories with Leah?"

"Yes. She is yet to become me."

Shandiin felt cold at that. "What do you mean...become you?"

"She will finish my being, when she wakes."

"I don't understand what you mean! Did you say you are a goddess?"

"Yes. I am one of the deities of Hiraeth's new people. There will be four."

"Deities? You mean four gods? Has Hiraeth created these?"

"Three of us are being created for the purpose of protecting Hiraeth from intent that can harm her. We are constructs from the dreaming minds of those who travel with you."

Shandiin tried to bring her focus back to the questions she'd agreed to ask. "Do you know how Hiraeth plans her protection? Will she destroy the ships that come to land here? Should they not come?"

"They may come, and they may land, and there will be no harm to the people as they come forth from them. The deities will watch over them, and ensure they follow Phaelon's Law."

"What's that?" Shandiin demanded. "Who's Phaelon?"

"Phaelon is the God of Order. He hasn't fully arrived yet."

Liethe's statement was followed by a rumble of thunder. Shandiin looked around for clouds, but the sky was clear of anything but stars and moon.

She turned back. "So there is no danger to the colonists?"

"Not from Hiraeth," Liethe said. *"But you should beware Daimaine."*

"Daimaine. Okay, you are the Light, so what is she...the Darkness?"

"Yes. She is the Goddess of Justice, and will also be called the Deathqueen. Like me, she awaits completion. She walks out there now." Liethe lifted an arm, indicating the grass that surrounded them to the horizon. As she did so the cat rose and stretched, and Shandiin saw the tiny black heart on its forehead.

Then it spread wings, and became a bird that lifted to glide over the roses, over the picket fence, over the grass. It seemed to grow as it flew, until from the bird emerged a white horse that landed lightly on the grass, and galloped silently away toward the rising moon.

"That is ChanDethe," Liethe explained. *"He is my messenger, and that of the fourth deity. He will bring no harm to any."*

The thunder came again, a little closer. But there were still no clouds.

Shandiin turned back again. "Why do you say we should be wary of Daimaine?"

"She is the opposite of my Light, and cannot be trusted. She may do harm."

"But I thought Hiraeth wouldn't harm us!"

"She will not, but Daimaine might. Diane will finish her being, but she is built from the darkness of the people, as I am built from the light."

"Won't Hiraeth control her?"

"Daimaine is a construct with her own will. Her only constraint is against harming Hiraeth. There is no other constraint...unless she restricts herself for her own reasons."

"So we brought evil with us," Shandiin muttered. "Great. What about the fourth one? Is that another goddess based on Earth's mythologies? Is she evil too?"

Liethe smiled. *"No. She alone is not a construct of the people. Hiraeth says to tell you she is the only one she trusts. She is Chaos. She is you, Shandiin, and she needs you to come to her."*

Shandiin floundered out of hypnosis, out of the reclining chair into Sarnath's arms. The big man caught her close as she gasped, her heart pounding. When she began to calm he settled her back into the chair, gave her water, gave her time while he kept a hand over hers...and waited.

When her trembling eased, he asked, "Are we in such grave danger, then?"

"I don't know." She ran her hand through her hair, struggling to think. "There are gods down there, Sarnath. A god, and goddesses meant to control the people. They are constructs, she said, from dreaming minds. All but one of them. All but me! It makes no damned *sense*."

"All but you." He studied her speculatively. She thought she saw a flash of knowledge that he quickly hid, just as he had done when he had first met her, when he had announced her vision of a dark stranger.

But Shandiin had no time for mysteries. She shoved to her feet, determined to check on the stasis chambers that held Leah and Diane. The others were on her heels the minute she strode out of the room ahead of Sarnath. When they arrived at the stasis center Zion asked, "What is it? Are you all right, Shandiin?"

"They are both alive in there, right?"

"Of course they are."

She turned to him, ready to battle his ongoing skepticism. They faced a reality none of them could have expected, but it was reality nonetheless. "You have to keep them on the ship, Zion. And I'm not going down either. Hiraeth is trying to turn me and my daughters into some kind of gods to control the colony...and no, don't act like you don't believe this either. I am telling you, neither I nor they can go down there. There's another god too, but I don't know who that is. It's the one she called Phaelon, the God of Order. We have to find out who that is, and the four of us all have to stay on the ship, or the colony will be under their control."

She turned from his scowl to the others. "The deities are being created out of several different mythologies. I think the one she called Phaelon is being built as a monotheistic god of all, and will be setting down the laws everyone has to follow. Then there are three goddesses. Two represent good and evil...and somehow Leah is Liethe, and Diane is Daimaine."

"A triad of goddesses?" Sarnath asked.

Shandiin pushed her hands through her wild mass of hair. "She called the third one Chaos. She said it's me. She said I am Chaos. I refuse to be a goddess, for whatever reason!"

Zion put his arm around her, and she was shaky enough she let herself lean into him until he said, "Shandiin, you have to know this is not making any sense. You are overwrought."

She broke away angrily. "Don't try that crap on me, Dr. Alexander. I'm not some hysterical female."

He looked confused and hurt, but she couldn't care, and spun back to the others. "I'm staying on the ship. So are Diane and Leah. We have to figure out who Phaelon is, and keep him here too."

Egypt came to her. "I see no reason why you can't stay on the ship along with your daughters. You need to talk to Hiraeth again, find out who Phaelon is." She frowned at Zion, at the rest of the men. "It makes sense to take precautions. Go on back to the bridge, all of you. I'm staying with Shandiin for a minute."

Egypt waited as they left, her eyes on Shandiin's. "This doesn't seem real, but I can tell it scares the hell out of you. And you don't scare easy. So it's real."

"Hell yes, I'm scared. Think about it. All the myths, the awful beliefs people had, becoming personified! Liethe may represent good, but how will that be interpreted down the road? If gods become real, people become playthings."

"But you would be one yourself?"

"Egypt, I find that the most terrifying thing of all. That kind of power is corruptive. I already battle the faults I know I have. If those are magnified..." she shook her head. "No. I won't chance it."

"Who do you think the God of Order is?"

"The one called Phaelon? I don't know, but it's probably someone asleep. We have to find out who. I think Diane and Leah are projecting as visions, apparently without material impact. I can only hope that if we stay on the ship, there's no danger to the colony."

But the dreams stopped for her, and neither hypnosis nor her dreams brought more information on Phaelon.

Plans for landing and disembarking moved forward in the press of expectation of the colony that saw no reason to wait...especially since their leader saw none either.

Shandiin moved in with Egypt.

Chapter 9

Shortly before the day Egypt called planetfall, Shandiin walked into the stasis center to find Sarnath arguing with Zion.

"They are not dead," Sarnath was saying. "I saw the same anomaly with Shandiin when we first put her into stasis. When she came back, you decided it was a malfunction of the readout." He turned to Shandiin, who looked into the chamber and saw Leah, apparently still asleep.

"What anomaly?" she asked, shaken.

"They're in an irreversible coma, Shandiin." Zion spoke as gently as he could. "There is no cortical activity in their brains. I've checked everything. I'm sorry to tell you they are both gone."

But Sarnath shook his head, put a hand on her shoulder. "You came back, Shandiin. It is not irreversible. The part of the brain that controls lungs and heart and blood pressure is still working."

"But...are you saying their bodies are alive, but their minds are gone?"

"I believe consciousness has left their bodies." Sarnath looked meaningfully at Zion. "Gone from here, but still in existence somewhere else."

Zion shook his head angrily. "You are talking about an out of body experience. Sarnath, you shouldn't lead her on like that, giving her false hope. OBE's are nothing but hallucinations. There must have been a failure in the chamber that caused brain damage."

"I know astral projection is real," Sarnath argued. "How can you deny another person's reality—something you cannot personally share—as hallucination? That is sheer arrogance, Zion."

Shandiin clutched Sarnath's arm, drawing his attention back to her. "You think they've gone to the planet. To become the goddesses Liethe and Daimaine." Her voice was shaking.

"I do. I'm sorry, Shandiin. I think Hiraeth has taken them both."

Before she could respond the ship's speakers turned on, and everyone else in the room heard the voice of the planet for the first time.

"They are with me, Shandiin. They are safe here."

"No!" Shandiin looked into Leah's face, and ignored everything but the voice now so familiar to her. "Send them back, Hiraeth!"

"They are bound by my magic now, and cannot return unless their purpose no longer exists. I need you as well, Shandiin."

"Well, you aren't getting me. I am not going to let you take my mind. And without me your pantheon of deities is broken, so you might as well send my daughters back!"

"I need more than your mind, Shandiin. I need you, as you are. You must come down from your ship."

Shandiin shook her head in denial. "I will not leave this ship physically or mentally. I will not manifest as one of your damned gods, do you hear me?"

"You are already Chaos. You are the goddess who will be named Sunqueen, and your power comes from the sun."

Shandiin dragged her hands through her hair. "Agh! None of that makes sense. A goddess of the sun? Where'd you get that one?"

Sarnath turned to her. Even now he remained calm, unlike everyone else. "Most mythologies include a deity that embodies the sun, and it's usually the most powerful one of all. But I don't understand why the others are manifested through spirit, but you have to go as you are."

"She belongs here. She belongs with the son."

They heard a click as the speaker disconnected.

Egypt broke the ensuing silence. "Well, that's a relief to me. I was afraid she could take your mind or spirit or whatever it is when you are sleeping. But if she needs you both mind and body, you just need to stay on the ship."

Zion was staring at the stasis chambers, obviously in shock. But he looked up to ask, "What did she mean—that you belong with the sun?"

"I wonder if she meant son as in offspring, not the star." Sarnath was thoughtful.

Zion shook his head. "None of it makes sense to me. None of it."

Aztlan hung above the planet as the rest of the fleet landed on the eastern coast of the major continent. The ships settled along the sea's edge where the beaches were long, smooth, and very wide. Those beaches sloped finally into hills that rose into a range of mountains. The mountains were divided by a great rivered valley opening to the continent's nearly featureless central plain of grass.

The central grassland ended against a forested plateau in the west. That highland's forests meandered through open, rolling hills to the continent's other coast. The western coast was green and lush, with mountains rising in the north. Beyond those verdant mountains and valleys, the continent's farthermost north was a massive elevation forever snowbound. The southern part of the continent was tropical, and prone to storms.

The computer had designated landing on the gentler western coast as the best probable site. Zion had overridden it. The eastern land was far more rugged inland from the beach, but it also appeared to have more in the way of natural resources, being heavily forested; trace monitoring also showed it rich in metal ores, even near the surface.

The landings went smoothly, and the four watching through the ship's monitors knew relief as the last ship settled onto the beach without incident.

"It's beautiful," Khalen announced happily from below, activating his body camera as he walked away from his ship.

The camera panned around as he turned. Those watching through it from above saw people emerging from the ships, looking up at the sky, laughing in joy at a warm yellow sun on their faces. A sea-borne breeze stirred their hair and clothing.

Shandiin smiled through her own exhaustion. She'd slept only fitfully since Zion had given the go-ahead for landing three days before. It seemed to be going well despite her fears.

With all ships down safely, Egypt stepped back from her station and joined Shandiin where she sat observing from behind the work stations. The station in the center was the ship's own camera; *Aztlan* had changed from orbit to stationery, holding its position over the landing site while the process unfolded. Khalen's body-cam images were quickly joined by those of other project leaders.

Shandiin looked up and took the coffee Egypt offered as she sat beside her. "Thanks."

Egypt nodded toward the monitors. "It looks like bedlam down there, but I'm sure Khandor and Khalen will get everyone's mind back on the job after a few minutes of celebration."

"Which one is Khandor's camera?"

"He didn't want one; he only has audio communication. He said he would be surrounded by others with cameras so we could spy on him all we wanted." She laughed at Shandiin's raised eyebrow. "He told me he said that to get Khalen's ire up, since Khalen thinks Phil is Zion's spy."

"Have Zion and Khalen always been at odds with each other?" Shandiin asked, watching a colonist run sand through his fingers like a child.

"Not always. I figured it was just a teenage thing, when Khalen first started getting his back up."

Shandiin turned to look at her. "Sixteen?" she asked.

Egypt frowned. "Yes. It started when he was sixteen, come to think of it."

Shandiin hesitated. *Not my secret to tell*, she reminded herself. *But still...* "I think it may spring from jealousy over Diane. From something he said, I believe Khalen thinks Diane wants Zion."

Egypt was quiet for a long moment. "I should have seen that. I should have known that. I suspected he had a crush on her, but after your trip with him I've watched him turn to you instead." She smiled at Shandiin. "You care for him, as I do. I think that has been good for him, because you are nothing like her. He respects you."

"You don't mean he's crushing on me? I'm too freaking old for him!"

Egypt shook her head. "I think some of biology's choices arise from visible age differences, not chronology. Diane looks young though she isn't. She obviously got that trait from you." She glanced back at the monitors. "Look, there's Khandor. He's got the secondary project leaders surrounding him, so there's a lot of him to watch, as he predicted."

"I've been so involved with other things I haven't asked about this part of it. Will they move on, or live on the ships for a while?"

"They could have, but Khandor took a poll, finding most want to move on immediately. They will be offloading supplies and livestock into trucks to carry them to the valley just to their west. It's not that far, and they can camp there where they will begin building their new lives. Think about it, Shandiin. We are watching history unfold."

"Only because of you three and Roland," Shandiin reminded quietly. "Without you, all these people would probably be dead."

Unloading and transport took all of that day, but as twilight fell Khalen reported on the trek to the nearby valley. He stood atop a rocky knoll, where he could see the first stars blossoming over a cobalt sea. "It's so beautiful. Egypt, Sarnath...you should come down now. It's so beautiful here."

"Two of us will come down tomorrow," Sarnath radioed back. "Status?"

"Everyone's off the ships. The last holdouts are riding with the supply trucks, and a couple of the smaller Meissner ships."

"They are not allowed," came Phil's voice, strangely altered. *"Such machines are not the natural order of things, on Hiraeth."*

Stunned silence followed.

"What the hell?" Egypt broke the silence. "Phil, what are you talking about?"

There was no answer.

"Phaelon!" Shandiin exclaimed. "Phil, are you Phaelon?"

There was no answer.

"Phaelon?" Zion asked.

Shandiin came to her feet. "Hiraeth's God of Order! Liethe told me about him. Now I realize it must be Phil. He is an AI, right? An artificial intelligence. I think Hiraeth's magic has used him to construe the 'one god' of monotheistic beliefs."

"This is insane." Zion shook his head. "How can a computer become a god? I really don't follow all of this, Shandiin."

"Dammit, Zion, quit being so freaking blind! This planet is not Earth, no matter how much it looks like Earth. This planet is *alive*, and she said she would take measures to protect herself. Now she's hijacked the AI that controls all of the technology!"

"Including our auxiliary Meissner ships," Egypt put in. "They are all offline. Phil, what are you doing?"

There was still no answer from the computer. Zion was checking it manually, finally turned back, his face pale. "Life support systems are operational, but Egypt's right. We are all stuck up here."

Shandiin shook her head. "It makes no sense. She said she wants me there, but makes it so I can't go down there even if I wanted to."

Egypt was still watching the screen. "Phil is using remote control. He's removing them from the valley, back to the beach with the bigger ships."

Shandiin watched fearfully. "Hiraeth has a reason for this. She doesn't want technology on planet. I'm afraid she's going to do something to the ships."

Hiraeth's voice came over the speakers again. *"All technology will be taken where it cannot harm me. But you are needed here, Shandiin."*

"No!" Shandiin cried. "Hiraeth, you have to give the people their freedom back. I will not become one of your gods, so don't bother sending a ship for me!"

But Sarnath walked over, put his hands on her shoulders. "I think there's a way for her to take you down there without a ship...if she is not respectful of your own free will. You must be prepared, Shandiin."

"What the hell are you talking about?"

He shook his head. "I know it sounds impossible. More so than astral projection," he added, flicking a glance toward Zion. "But she has magic that obviously controls energy fields, and everything is energy. Including your body."

Shandiin poked herself, then him. "I feel solid to me, Sarnath. I don't think she can 'beam me up' like Scotty in the old Star Trek shows."

"While it seems alien to us, it's absolutely true that a thing can be two things at once. Light is both a wave and a particle. You are both matter and energy. And now...she is magic. Shandiin...I think you should consider listening to her. You know I've always believed you are critical to this mission. This may be the purpose you've been looking for."

She just stared at him. "You want me to be a goddess?"

"I think you already are."

Hiraeth's voice interrupted, coming again through the ship's speakers.

"The wise one is right. You are the goddess Chaos." There was a brief silence before she continued, and her voice changed in pitch. *"Something has happened I that do not understand. Phaelon believes you are Satan. Phaelon is initiating the Law of Order...but it is senseless. These people will be given a thousand years of peace under his Law, during which time your powers will be bound, and when you are released at the end of that time he will bring war that could destroy all the people. Why is he doing this?"*

"It sounds like Revelations." Shandiin was horrified. "He's tapped into the Bible. A thousand years of peace under the rule of God—his version!—and then Satan is released. Stop him, Hiraeth!"

"I cannot! Magic's intent cannot just be undone, even by me. The other gods are rational, though they reflect humanity's many faces...but he is a broken reflection from a shattered universe. He is terrible! You must join the people to save them, Shandiin."

"What the hell can I do about it? How do I stop a god?"

"You are the most powerful of the gods, the only one who can stop him. But he has bound your power against him for a thousand years. He has to release you at the end of that time, but he will bring a bloody war to destroy any who do not serve him. You can't stop the war, but now you are the only one who can give the people a chance. Please come!"

"A thousand years under his rule? And then war? Hiraeth, make him stop!"

"I tell you again I cannot...but this is NOT the destiny I would have chosen for your people. Why doesn't he have a soul, Shandiin? He has no soul!"

"Because he isn't alive!" Shandiin raged. "He is a product of technology, an artificial intelligence! He is not one of the people!"

She felt Hiraeth recoil from her truth. The speakers went dead.

Shandiin pushed Sarnath away, and ran from the room.

After a brief hesitation, Zion went after her. He found her leaning back against a wall, her face in her hands. He had never before seen her cry, and he reached for her automatically, pulling her into his arms.

"I'm sorry. Oh, Shandiin, I am so sorry for everything I have said and done. I've been a stubborn idiot about all of this. I just...found it so hard to accept. It goes against everything I've ever thought was true." He drew back to look into her eyes. "I love you, Shandiin, and I hate what's happening to you. I should never have doubted you and what you are dealing with. Please don't go down there, Shandiin."

She gave in to what he offered, leaning her head on his shoulder while she wished for the impossible. "I think I have to go. She said I'm the only one who can stop Phil—Phaelon."

"Shandiin...a thousand years? How could you even consider such a thing, even to save them all? God, Egypt is right. You are a hero. But please don't."

After a moment she whispered, "I don't think have a choice, Zion." She drew back to look into his handsome face. "When I woke up from that coma, I told Sarnath I believe the true and only miracle is in our existence and what we make of it. He said I would find my purpose in that belief...that I would be the daughter of my own prophecy. I have to accept this, Zion, as what I am meant to do."

She pulled away to walk back to the bridge, and after a moment he followed her. Hiraeth spoke again as they entered.

"I will soon remove all ships from the land, to be swallowed by the sea. Those of you watching from above must warn the people of this."

Egypt was studying the instruments at her station, and swore loudly. "I see what she's done! There's been an earthquake out to sea. It's caused a tsunami...the computer model says the water will take the beach, and the valley where the people are settling." She opened her own comm. "Khalen! Khandor! Get the people to higher ground! Tsunami!"

Shandiin's knees went weak. "No, no, no—Hiraeth, stop! Listen to me! They will all drown!"

"They will, if you don't come to me now. I didn't want it to be like this, Shandiin, but I need your help, and cannot bring you here against your will. So I have given you a choice."

Shandiin closed her eyes. "How can I come to you? All the ships are disabled, with Phil gone."

"You have no need of a ship. You can transition from where you are. And you must come, Shandiin. The water is coming to take the machines."

Shandiin shut her eyes, took a deep breath. "How do I transition?"

"You know. You are Chaos, and you know your own magic."

"Hiraeth—dammit, will I be able to come back?"

"To save them, you must join them. You will then be trapped here for a thousand years."

She opened her eyes to see Egypt and Sarnath staring at her. Zion watched her with such open pain it nearly broke her heart.

She huffed. "I have to do this. Goodbye, everyone. Dammit."

They watched her turn into sunlight, and shimmer out of existence.

CHAPTER 10

The tidal wave was heralded by the recession of the sea, but no one was around to observe it. The people were too busy trying to climb out of the valley in the tsunami's path. They were hampered by darkness and confusion, many trying to help the less able and the children among them. Others tried to carry along supplies, terrified of being with nothing in an unknown wilderness.

Their terror was briefly escalated by a white light so brilliant many fell to hide their eyes.

"Here is the way," came a voice from above, and it sounded like a choir of angels. *"Come here...to Liethe...to me!"*

They looked up to see a glowing figure in white, her arms open in welcome. A clear path was set alight below her, and the people in the lead took heart and climbed toward her. But it was apparent to everyone looking back that those in the valley would not escape in time. The tsunami had flooded the beaches and rose rolling through the foothills, drowning everything in its path.

Then came the goddess made of fire.

A vast figure of flame rose over the valley, wearing a living sun in her hair. She turned night into day.

The goddess Chaos called on her newfound magic to set a wall of flame at the valley's entrance.

The wall of water met the wall of magic fire at the valley's narrow entry, and turned to steam. A great fog drifted up to obscure the stars until the wind shredded it away.

When it was done, the valley lay untouched, unthreatened.

The brilliant light of Liethe remained until the people were again safely downhill, and then it dimmed and vanished. A few people thought they saw a great white bird fly away into the stars.

The sea slowly receded, having swallowed the technology that had brought the people from the sky. The path of the tsunami was scraped clean, all evidence of the people gone. The beach was empty save for one person who walked alone, wondering if the journey from Earth would become only a myth, a story few would believe in the distant future.

A future she would come to know.

"Is there no way out?" she asked Hiraeth, though she knew the answer in her heart. "Must I stay for a thousand years? You did this. You made us. Can't you just send all us gods back where we came from?"

"What has been created by magic cannot be undone, so all remain while Phaelon rules for a thousand years. I would not have allowed Phaelon to become a god, had I known he is part of the...what you call technology. The killing things."

"I understand your fear of technology. But it is only dangerous when used for dangerous purposes. You have reduced these people to a primitive level."

"It is done. It cannot be undone, even if I agreed with you."

Shandiin sighed. She stopped walking and turned to look out over the sea, its waves calmed now to soft exhalations against the land. A full moon hung just above the horizon, and she remembered the cottage in the grass. "Was my meeting with Liethe a vision, or is she real?" she asked. "Leah is still on the ship above us, as is Diane."

"They are not visions. The gods are constructs from many minds, but now hold the reality of a human life...all except Phaelon, who has no solid reality but only a jumbled set of agendas. Like you, each has their own magic."

"I never wanted magic, though that fire superpower came in handy."

"You have magic you have yet to explore. But you are con-strained while Phaelon rules. To keep you safe, I give you the ability to hide your magic. I foresee that you will find your own people, and I will ensure that you and they will be immune to the magic of the gods. So you can walk freely among mortals until Phaelon releases you in a thousand years."

"Thanks," Shandiin said dryly. "It will be nice, not being called Chaos to my face."

"Only Phaelon and those he rules will call you that."

Shandiin decided Hiraeth didn't understand sarcasm. "Can the gods make the people obey them?" she asked. "Is there no more free will?"

"There are limits. The gods will rule through promise and pun-ishment, and through fear. Phaelon can cast out those who are brought before him as corrupt. Daimaine can bring death as she may choose. But free will exists, for those brave enough and willing to suffer for their courage. Free will cannot be taken except by permission of the individual."

Shandiin filed that away for careful consideration. "What will happen at the end of the thousand years?" she asked. "How do I get rid of Phaelon?"

"I do not have clear vision yet, because he has not completed his Laws of Order. Nor have the other two goddesses finished their own magical intent."

"Can my magical intent be that they don't have any?"

"No."

"Can't blame me for trying. Hiraeth, I want these people to be free of gods. They should be able to live their lives subject only to their own accountability. Isn't there some way you could be safe without gods to control them?"

"They might again develop the evil technology."

"I tell you, the technology isn't what's evil!"

"Then I would have to trust the people themselves. Perhaps, in a thousand years, you will find a way for that to happen. Then you can leave, and take the other gods with you."

Shandiin felt a small rise of hope. "So we gods and all our magic could leave in a thousand years, if you found us unnecessary?"

"Yes."

After a moment she asked, "Where would we go?"

"You would all return from where you came, to the ship that remains in the sky."

"It would still be there in a thousand years?"

"Yes. To the people still on the ship, it would only be minutes from when you departed."

Shandiin fell silent then, deep in thought. Then she turned, and began walking to the valley she had saved. "You timed the tsunami so that I would have to come here, thinking I wouldn't come otherwise."

"Yes."

"Why? Why am I so important...and why am I different from the other gods?"

"You are necessary to the son, and you belong here."

"I don't understand," Shandiin said plaintively.

Hiraeth did not respond.

"You told me there will be a war at the end of the thousand years that could wipe out those who do not follow Phaelon. If I leave and take Phaelon with me, will the war still happen?"

"Yes. It is Prophecy, and so shall come to pass. Shandiin, while I understand your heart's wishes, I think you are reaching for things that are not possible."

"Can you see the future clearly enough to be sure of that?"

She felt a wind pass over her, and thought Hiraeth had sighed. *"Not yet."*

The colony's secondary leaders worked with Khalen and Khandor to return the people to their valley campgrounds. As dawn began to break the colony was finally calm, and many slept the sleep of exhaustion. The livestock that had been left behind grazed or slept on, apparently unaware of the peril that had nearly killed them all.

Khandor left a briefing with his fatigued leaders to see Shandiin walking toward him. She wasn't wearing leather as in his vision, but even in jeans and a faded denim jacket he recognized his pagan goddess.

He stopped and waited for her, smiling faintly. "Some of the people are calling you the Sunqueen," he said. "In case you were wondering."

She stopped and looked around. "I was hoping no one recognized me."

"Probably just Khalen and me. Your face was barely discernible in the flames enveloping you, but he and I had advance warning from what you told us on the ship. Thank you, Shandiin. That was nearly a disaster."

"Yes." She took a deep breath, exhaled. "It was. Do you have anything to drink?"

"Of course. Come with me. I guess even goddesses deserve a reward."

"Crap. Don't call me that, okay? Not even in private." As they entered his camp and he began digging through some belongings, she dropped to the ground to sit cross-legged next to Khalen, who was staring silently into the fire. He looked up as Khandor handed her a bottle of water, which she took gratefully.

"I thought you said there were four gods," Khalen said to her as Khandor settled on her other side.

"There are. The goddess Daimaine hasn't shown up yet."

"Let me get it straight. Phaelon is the God of Order. We haven't seen him yet."

"He's the AI you called Phil." Shandiin scowled. "Hiraeth didn't know that in time to stop it. He's a construct from the monotheistic beliefs."

Khandor nodded thoughtfully. "That explains Phaelon. Now, you...you are the Sunqueen...the goddess Chaos, you said. Then there's good and evil. The one with white light, who was up on the mountain. She must be the good one."

"Liethe. Goddess of Life and Love. Leah is part of her."

"And who is Daimaine? Is she Diane?" Khalen asked.

Shandiin turned to him. "I think she may have been, but now she's a construct of magic. Both Daimaine and Leah are physically aboard the ship, but their consciousness exists here, in Liethe and Daimaine. Khalen...Liethe doesn't trust Daimaine. She warned me about her."

"Did she say why?"

"She called her the Deathqueen, and that her only constraint is against harming Hiraeth." Shandiin frowned. "She said Daimaine can put other constraints upon herself for her own reasons...but I don't get why she would do that."

Khalen looked thoughtful. "It's my guess there was a reason for Liethe to say that. It seems like everything magic has some reason behind it, even if we can't see the logic. Will the people no longer have free will, Shandiin?"

"Hiraeth said free will cannot be taken without the individual's permission. The gods will rule through promises and punishment, and through fear." She scowled again. "Daimaine also has the power to kill."

Khalen flinched at that, and Shandiin briefly placed a hand on his arm in understanding.

"Tell us what else you know," Khandor said.

"I hope Khalen's right about there being some logic. I sure as hell don't see the logic behind Phaelon's thousand-year plan. He seems to have ripped it out of Revelations and made himself the hero...and he's cast me as Satan."

They were both quiet as she explained what she had learned, but she knew their genius minds were working. She also noticed Khandor in particular seemed to continually watch the people, which was possible since their tent was set above the valley floor. After she finished speaking and he still watched, she asked, "Do you feel responsible for them all, Khandor?"

He turned those emerald eyes back to her. "Yes." She thought she heard a note of despair in his voice. "And I haven't figured out how to help them get started on the new life we had all looked forward to. The gods are an element we never anticipated...along with losing every bit of technology."

"One day at a time," she said.

He almost managed a smile.

Khalen and Khandor both left during the next day to check on colonists and livestock. Khandor came back as night fell, still dealing with worried people with questions. "Just rest for now," Khandor told them. "We'll get together tomorrow, after everyone has a chance to rest and adjust."

The questions were often, "But how will we get food?"

To which Khandor's answer was always, "There's plenty for now. Don't start projecting for the future; we'll deal with it. I've told everyone to share what they have, and set everything they don't need aside in a common area."

"Share what they have? Loaves and fishes?" Shandiin laughed when he scowled at her. "Oops. I gather you don't want to be their messiah." He didn't look amused.

Khalen returned just then, settling down between them where they sat at the campfire.

Khandor reached over to pluck the tiny camera from Khalen's leather jacket. "Why do you still have this? It's useless now."

"I guess it's just hard to give up. I'm worried about the ship, with all communication gone."

"It's fine." Both men turned to Shandiin, waiting, so she continued. "I told you I'm stuck here for a thousand years, but she said that only minutes will have passed on the ship when I return to it. Magic time is different, or she can stop time...hell, I don't know. But I have to take her word for it. So don't worry about the ship. All the life support systems were working when I left. Including the stasis chambers."

Seeing Khalen's relief, she placed a gentle hand on his arm. "They are all fine."

Khalen met her eyes, and she saw in his a terrible sadness. "I did come to realize Diane is a sociopath without conscience. You told us she is an evil goddess on Hiraeth, and she can even kill people. That terrifies me. I didn't see her last night. I looked for her..."

It was like an invitation. The air turned cold around them, and his voice trailed away as a shadow spread over the night sky, it's darkness stealing the light even from the moon. They all looked up, to see the great shadow falling toward them; it became a woman of living darkness, her streaming black gown and hair laced with stars.

Then she stood over them. Her beautiful face was pale as starlight, outlined in sparkling runes of amethyst and sapphire. A crescent moon glowed from her forehead. Her eyes were frozen starfire, gazing avidly upon Khalen. *"I am Daimaine."* Her voice was like the night wind. *"I am the goddess of Justice and Death, and I have come to tell you I've made you a King."*

Khalen came slowly to his feet. "Diane? Is that you?"

"I am not." The goddess shook her head in denial, and stars rained from her hair. *"Diane is an unimportant memory. I am the Deathqueen, the power behind your rule of the people."* She turned her gaze on Khandor, who also stood. Khalen nudged him back protectively. Daimaine's smile was cold. *"This has been my magic's intent, and cannot be undone. You are also mine now, Khandor. You and all of your blood, the bloodline of the High Kings, are mine."* When Shandiin began to rise, Daimaine hissed at her. *"You have no purpose here!"*

"Don't interfere," Khalen told Shandiin. "Please, Shandiin! Just wait."

Shandiin settled back grimly, realizing her magic was hidden even from Daimaine, and that she was bound from using it against her or Phaelon...for a very long time. She also suspected Khalen was the one who could handle this.

"Please tell me," Khalen asked the Deathqueen, "what you mean about making me a King."

Daimaine's smile was stunning. Shandiin thought she looked like an impossibly beautiful witch from an animated film...and realized that might have been her construct.

"You and your bloodline will rule the realm Phaelon has creat-ed, the realm he has named Azlatan. There will be seventy-seven Dominions, each with their own King, but your bloodline will be High King over all. I give to you a magic sword..." and it appeared between them, a sword floating in a fog of starlight, stars glittering in a swirl along the bright blade. *"Only your bloodline may wield it. It's stroke will bring death, and it will protect your life in battle. With it you will rule the people of Azlatan, and you will live in Penumbra, the beautiful palace I have already created for you."*

With her words the transparent vision of a dark palace rose into the sky, living stars crawling upon its towers. It faded even as it appeared.

Khalen seemed unmoved by the vision or the magic sword. He stared through its starlit fog into Daimaine's cold eyes. "And what do you want in return, for these gifts?" he asked her.

She smiled at that. *"I already have what I want. I am the power behind your rule, and I own your soul and that of all the High Kings that come after you."*

"Do you own us while we live?"

"Your souls are mine, and will come to me after death." She lifted her hands as though in offering. They glittered with runes of moonlight. She spoke softly, seductively. *"But you could allow me to take you now. You would never have to die. You would belong to me for all time. I would own your heart and your will. You would serve me alone, as I choose."*

"No!"

Khalen ignored Khandor's cry. "I gather you need my permis-sion for that," he told the goddess.

Daimaine's eyes widened with keenness. *"If you give me per-mission to take you now, I will give the bloodline of High Kings the power to command with just their voice. People will recognize power in their very presence, and worship them as gods."*

Khalen shook his head in denial. "Our voices should be heard, but not necessarily obeyed. People must always have free will, and leadership does not always mean command. Nor will we accept worship. We are mortals, like our people."

She shrugged, and stars fled. *"As you wish. If the people do not obey the command of a High King, I will smite them."*

"No." His rejection rang strong. "I require your promise that you will not harm the people unless directed by the High King. And you cannot control a High King through any means, as long as he is living and aware."

She stiffened at this. *"You would restrict my power thus? To be at the command of mortal men?"*

"At the command of your High Kings, yes. That would be my requirement, before I would agree to come to you now, to belong to you, to give up my free will. To serve you alone, as you choose."

Her smile became feral. *"Then I give to the High Kings my gifts: this sword named Star Blade, the palace named Penumbra, the voice of command that is always heard but does not require obedience, the recognition of your powerful presence...and charisma and respect in place of worship. In return you have my promise that I will harm no people unless directed to do so by a High King. Nor will I control a King through any means, as long as he is living and aware."*

Khalen reached out then, and took the dazzling sword.

If his hand trembled on that blade, Shandiin couldn't tell. Understanding his sacrifice, her vision had become blurred with tears.

He offered the hilt to Khandor, who refused it until he recognized the desperate intent on his brother's face.

Khalen was enslaving himself for the protection of the people they had been created to lead.

There was terror in Khalen's emerald eyes, and courage beyond understanding.

Khandor took the sword, and dropped to his knees to honor him.

Daimaine took Khalen's hand, and they both became shadows that melted into the night.

Shandiin took Khandor into her arms, and he wept bitterly for a long time.

Chapter 11

S omehow they knew.

The people approached Khandor the next day with an attitude of reverence, and called him "Your Highness." He accepted it without comment, just as he had accepted waking in new garb...unadorned black leather. He wore a simple belted tunic with a tall collar over black breeches. It looked like a uniform, she thought, a symbol of soldierly allegiance to a higher authority. Even the plain black boots that rose midway to his knees were unremarkable. Nothing in his new clothing appeared regal, yet there he was, unmistakably the King of this new world.

He told Shandiin that black was the color sacred to Daimaine, and only he and those he chose for his service could wear it. As he strapped the Star Blade to his hip, Shandiin asked how he felt about it all.

"I'm still working on that." His emerald eyes turned once again to survey the valley below their camp. "It's not what I would have wanted. But it has to be accepted, and with Khalen's changes it may be workable." He sighed. "She had too much power. He took it from her, and gave it to me and my descendants. It has to be workable, or his terrible sacrifice was for nothing."

She studied him as he stood in his imposed black garb, his long black hair blowing around his face. He was still a young man, but he seemed to have aged overnight. He'd allowed a sleek beard to grow since their departure from the ships; it defined his strong jaw. The narrow mustache accentuated the sculptured lips, set grimly now. She thought him the most handsome man she had ever seen...outside of a dream she'd had.

"They're all waiting for you to say something," she pointed out quietly.

He shook his head. "It's not time yet." He turned to face her. "I can feel the magic coming. It's like a chill wind inside my skin. Be glad you are immune."

She frowned and looked from him to the people in the valley. They had all fallen silent, many standing to peer around them as though searching. But what they sought came from above.

A cloud descended over the valley's western exit. There was a rumble of thunder, but instead of lightning a single sparking ball of electricity grew on the side of the mountain, becoming so bright it outshone the sunlight.

The burning bush, she thought with resignation.

And Phaelon's voice, a thunderous roar, came from it.

"I am Phaelon, the God of Order. I have come to give you my Law!"

And as he spoke, his words appeared in great glowing letters carved into the air.

1. I HAVE PREPARED FOR YOU THE LAND OF AZLATAN IN THE FAR WEST, A REALM OF SEVENTY-SEVEN DOMINIONS, EACH RULED BY A KING.

2. THE ONE HIGH KING SHALL HAVE AUTONOMOUS RULE OVER ALL PEOPLE IN ALL DOMINIONS. HE MAY CREATE LAWS FOR GOVERNING THE PEOPLE THROUGHOUT HIS REALM, EXCEPT FOR THOSE I HERE PROVIDE. I SHALL CHOOSE THE WOMAN TO BECOME THE HIGH QUEEN FOR EACH HIGH KING, BETROTHED AT HER BIRTH.

3. THERE SHALL BE TWO RACES AMONG YOU. THE MASTERS ARE THE RIOCH, WHO SHALL BE SERVED WITH HONOR BY THE SERVANTS WHO ARE DUINE.

4. The Rioch and the Duine shall not lie together. If this Law is broken, the Forbidden Child and both parents shall die. This shall be enforced without exception by those Duine I name Anzihi, whose identity shall be known only to me.

5. I give to you a High Tahmond to serve as advisor on my Law, and to oversee the people's compliance with my Law. The High Tahmond may sanctify lesser Tahmonds as their service becomes necessary.

6. I am Phaelon, the God of Order. I am the only God. There exist also two goddesses, Liethe and Daimaine, who serve their own purposes in healing and judgement. Liethe shall also sanctify a High Tahmine. The only Tahmond to Daimaine is the High King, and she owns his soul.

7. Be it known that if my High Tahmond, the High Tahmine, and the High King, should in Council bring to me any person found to be in violation of my Law, I shall cast that person into the eternal void. If the High King is the person accused, Council shall include seven Dominion Kings and the High Tahmond and High Tahmine.

8. The goddess Chaos shall not be served in Azlatan, for she is the enemy of Order. She has been bound for a thousand years, and Azlatan shall know peace until she returns. It is my prophecy that upon her return, a forbidden child will come forth, my protection of Azlatan's borders will end, and there will come a great war.

9. If the Forbidden is allowed to live, Duine will rise up to kill all Rioch. No magic can save them. Thereafter, all will die who disobey me.

The ball of lightning exploded with a terrifying roar, and the storm cloud shredded to nothing.

Khandor turned back to the valley where people seemed to be struck dumb. One man broke away from the crowd below and began the climb toward them, a man with shining blonde hair.

"Zion didn't approve the computer's choice to land on the west coast." Khandor spoke bitterly as he watched the distant man's approach. "Now I have to lead all of these people and everything that goes with them through these mountains and across the central grasslands to the west. But why the hell did he divide the people into two races?"

"He's named them in Gaelic, or what he sees as Gaelic. Without his software, it's skewed." When Khandor looked at her in question, she explained. "Rioch is a version of the word Rioga, which is Gaelic for 'royal.' And Duine is 'people.' When I mentioned to Zion that the people with some of the engineered genes were different in appearance, Zion told me Roland jokingly called them the royals, and the rest the people. Apparently Phil was listening in. My guess is the engineering project that created you was a priority in his database. He's divided the races according to their genealogy, and assigning the wives for the High Kings to ensure the purity of your bloodline."

Khandor shook his head, fury in his emerald eyes. "And is that why he's said a child of the two races will be 'Forbidden,' and must die along with the parents?"

She frowned. "I think that's because there was a child born in history who changed the course of some religions. Phaelon may have a fear of that, because he thinks he is God. I believe his memory and even his logic, without the technology to support it, is fragmented."

"Yes, and it just makes him more dangerous."

Shandiin met his eyes in concern. "He also singled out the High Kings, setting up a council of Dominion Kings, Tahmond and Tahmine to judge a High King accused of breaking his Law."

"Believe me, I picked that up. It is obvious to me that Phaelon believes he should be the only one with autonomous authority.

He was denied that because Daimaine manifested her intent before he did."

She watched him frown, clearly in deep thought, before he continued. "Phaelon is a real threat, Shandiin. I have to find a way to keep his influence separate from leadership...for myself and my heirs. The people must retain their right to their own minds, to their own respect."

While Shandiin considered the burdens Khandor and his bloodline would carry, he turned away from her as the blonde man walked up to him and dropped to a knee.

"I am William," the man said. "I am your Duine servant. What service may I give you, Your Highness?"

"The first thing you can do is get up, William. If you kneel every time you approach, you'll drive us both nuts."

The man stood, and waited for the next command. Khandor sighed. "We'll be working together from now on. Please bring your tent closer, and include your family." He looked past William to the secondary project leaders who were also approaching. "We will be organizing for a very long journey."

As William left, Shandiin set a hand on Khandor's arm. "You must never tell anyone, not even your future heir, about my role as Chaos," she continued their discussion. "Phaelon also made it clear my magic cannot save anyone in that war he prophesied. Your bloodline cannot depend on me as a goddess. Don't allow them false hope."

Unable to respond, he could only nod as the project leaders approached, and she turned and walked away.

To leave him alone.

As he realized he and his bloodline would always be alone, in all the ways that mattered.

The exodus to Azlatan took five years.

Shandiin stayed with the colony, riding her big paint horse, and Khandor the black stallion named Shadow. She noted that Khandor, like Khalen, had an innate talent with the horse, and rode as though he ridden all his life. She wondered where that could have come from. No connection to DNA she could think of...but then, she didn't understand the science of his engineering, and realized in getting to know Khandor that she shared Sarnath's belief in a human spirit.

Because, beyond his physical beauty and strength, beyond his superior intelligence, his spirit impressed her. While accepting the homage people paid him as necessary to fulfill his role, he nevertheless treated everyone with respect and consideration, no matter how annoying she thought they were.

And there were a lot of annoying people, quarreling over the infinitesimal while facing the challenge of a new world, a strange and unexpected life.

"Sometimes," he smiled when she brought this up, "it's easier to be distracted with the small stuff. Most of them are just plain terrified, but you can only hold onto that for a minute or so before going out of your mind. Human nature, I guess."

Early in the journey she studied him as they rode knee to knee over the grasslands beyond the mountain valley where she had come to him after the tsunami. His emerald eyes continually scanned the people around him, and watched for those further away, who were hunting the wildlife of the steppes. His black hair blew free over his shoulders, and he had maintained the sleek beard she found attractive.

Not that anything about him was unattractive, she admitted to herself with a sigh.

He fascinated her. She knew he was a genius, but he had merely lifted an eyebrow when she asked if he thought other people were stupid. "That's a mean word," he frowned. "Have you ever noticed how some words judge things as good or bad even as they describe it? Words like honor and mercy are good. Stupid is bad, as surely as brutal is bad. No, Shandiin, I do not think that someone of lesser intelligence than mine is stupid. And even the word 'lesser' is judgmental. No one is 'lesser' because they don't have the same gifts as others. People are who they are, Shandiin, each with different gifts. They are all important and each one deserving of respect."

"I get that. But it must often be like being the only adult among a bunch of children."

He considered that, finally nodded slightly, but made no further comment, and she knew he wouldn't.

"You're an empath," she said to him now, and watched him turn that emerald gaze on her almost warily, waiting. "I know you are, and I heard your unhappy opinion of it when you were just a child. It must be hard, having all that emotion laid bare to you. Is that why you mostly stay apart from people?"

He thought a moment. "It helps, although I can block out their feelings most of the time. Sarnath taught me well. But it can get troublesome when—" he stopped mid-sentence, suddenly turning in his saddle toward William, who was talking to a woman some distance behind them.

"Stop, William. You're about to make her cry, and she doesn't deserve that."

The man looked around in shock. "I'm sorry, Your Highness!"

"It's not me you should be apologizing to." Khandor turned back. "You don't have to be mean to hurt someone," he added for Shandiin's ears only. "It only takes an absence of understanding. He has no idea she's in love with him, and every time he carps at her it breaks her heart."

"Why don't you tell him that?"

"Because it's really none of my business. They'll figure it out or they won't. But I had to say something or tell them to move further back. I can't be blocking all the time when I don't know if there is danger around."

"So you felt her heartbreak."

He sighed. "Yes." He met her eyes. "I can't feel anything from you, Shandiin. Sometimes I wish I could."

"I think that's a blessing. For me, anyway."

"I suppose so." He studied her for a long moment, her wild red mane fired by the setting sun. "Do you have any idea how beautiful you are?"

"Jesus H. Christ. Where the hell did that come from?"

"Um...from my heart? I'm sorry if I embarrassed you."

"Pissed me off, is what you did. It's terrible when a handsome High King says things like that. Makes me want to punch him."

He grinned. "Go for it."

"Sure. And have your subjects take me down like a pack of wild hyenas. Which reminds me...what are they hunting for, out there?"

"I don't think they know. I regret that the wildlife we tried to bring as embryos didn't make it; they were lost with the ships. But Hiraeth's wildlife is surprisingly similar to Earth's, and it's probably good for Hiraeth's ecology that we've added no new species."

Shandiin smiled. "Ying and yang, good and bad. The gifts in life are always two-edged."

He lifted an eyebrow. "How poetic. Did you see that lioness that's been trailing our livestock? She must be one of your two-edged gifts. She's dangerous, but beautiful." He hesitated. "Like you, I think. You remind me of a lioness."

He laughed when she rolled her eyes, and turned back to watch the hunters. "Hopefully we'll find big game out here as well, so we don't have to eat all the livestock. The hunters are learning archery."

"We have bows and arrows?"

"I and a few knowledgeable others have taught people to make them. The Duine in particular learn the craft quickly, but they won't hunt."

"Why not?"

"They tell me that is the role of the Rioch." He shook his head. "Many of Phaelon's laws aren't imposed from the outside, it seems, but sown from within. I can't overrule those, so I have to work around them." He scowled. "Civilization has to be rebuilt within them. I'm having all written material from Earth's history collected to that end, but there's not enough. Most of the writings that would help us are gone, or at least beyond our reach as it would take our vanished technology to read them."

Shandiin nodded. "I know you've been having people write their knowledge on whatever medium they can find. But a lot of knowledge is useless here as it's based on technology that no longer exists...and stuff Hiraeth wouldn't allow anyway. I personally think that's a good thing, when it comes to weapons."

"No weapons of mass destruction, certainly. But you were once a police officer. Are you against any kind of firearms?" He smiled when she refused to answer. "Since we are talking about weapons...Zion told me you're an expert in medieval history. Do you by chance know how to make a sword?"

She glanced at the scabbard strapped to his saddle, thought of the magic sword inside of it. Knew he was more concerned for his people than himself. "I actually made one once. Took lessons from a blacksmith, and there's surely a blacksmith in the colony. I can give you the basics. You already knew how to make a bow and arrow?"

"I read about it once out of curiosity, and I don't forget things. I don't like the idea of swords, but since Daimaine gave me one I'm guessing they will be needed. So I'd appreciate anything you can tell me."

He listened while she explained, and she knew he would remember every word even while he continued scanning his people near and far. When she finished he nodded thanks and silently continued to watch his people.

She thought he needed a break from that continual sense of duty, so she asked, "Are you looking forward to your beautiful palace in Azlatan?"

It was his turn to be surprised. "Where the hell did *that* come from?" he mimicked.

"Just wondering. There are some perks to being High King. Daimaine gave you that sword, and a palace in your promised land. Have you even thought about that?"

"Not really. I'm too busy trying to get everyone and every-thing *to* Azlatan." He halted Shadow, and everyone behind them immediately stopped on cue. "It will soon be dark. Time to make camp, and let the wagons and livestock catch up with us." He turned in his saddle, spoke to the man who immediately rode over to him. "Dante," he said, "get them started on camp, and get people to help with the wagons. William can set up my tent here."

The man saluted and turned to obey while Khandor looked over at Shandiin. "Want to go with me to get the hunters back?"

She immediately kicked her Nitchi into a run, and gave a rebel yell to urge him on when Khandor's stallion caught up with her. The two rode like maniacs over the tall grass, and she looked over to see Khandor laughing along with her as they raced.

She thought it was good to see him have a moment of joy. He didn't seem to have many.

The hunters heard them coming, and stopped, looking con-fused when the two raced past. They both galloped on a little further before starting a slow, curving turn back.

But then she heard a scream, and Khandor was gone imme-diately, breaking straight back to the hunters.

Her paint horse bucked when she tried to turn him, and she realized he was spooked. She finally fought him into submis-sion, and followed the High King.

She could see through the deepening twilight that one of the horses was down and shrieking. Men were also screaming as they tried to control their terrified mounts. A tawny lioness, as big as any horse, rose from the fallen steed and roared. Shandiin watched in amazement as Khandor's black stallion didn't shy off, but galloped right for it.

A galaxy of stars exploded around horse and rider. Khandor had drawn the Star Blade.

The lioness fell back from the flare of magic, from the black horse and rider silhouetted in the bright fog of light and stars coming straight at it. It ran, and she saw that there were others of its kind waiting in the tall grass. Their eyes reflected brilliant green in the magic light before they all sprang away.

She rode to the fallen horse and rider. They were both still, and she could smell death. Khandor was already there, on foot, the sword still in his hand. He glanced up at her almost distractedly, handed the Star Blade to her before he dropped to his knees beside the prostate man. She quickly rode to Shadow and slipped the Star Blade into its scabbard.

I think he's the only one who is supposed to hold that sword, she thought. She would have to warn him about that; a mortal who touched it without Daimaine's permission would surely die.

Khandor stood as the hunters surrounded him. "Daryl's gone." His voice held grief and restrained fury. "That creature killed both horse and rider. Didn't any of you see it before it attacked?"

They all denied having seen it, but didn't attempt to explain themselves. The King's courage had shamed them all.

He shook his head wearily. "Bring the body to camp. We'll leave his horse for the wild things to eat, because I just can't...not a horse. But strip the saddle and bridle. We need them."

Khandor mounted his stallion, and Shandiin fell in next to him as they turned back toward the main group. "Beautiful and dangerous," he muttered. "Damn it, Shandiin."

She could only be sorry for his grief, but hoped to soothe his anger. "Your people aren't at fault. Those beasts were hiding in the grass. I only saw them when you pulled the sword, because of their green eyeshine. It's not unlike your own, Khandor."

He looked across at her. "You're kidding."

"I am not. Kind of scary."

"Those creatures? Or me?"

"Both of you. That was a hell of a ride, right at an animal big as your horse and weaponized with tooth and claw."

"I had the magic sword." He shrugged. "We'll have to be more careful, since no one else has one. I'll call Council tonight, and get the word out about these creatures. I should have realized they were dangerous to more than livestock."

Of course he blamed himself. She sighed. "Did you know the man who fell?"

"Yes. And now I will have to tell his wife."

He left her then, riding ahead to do what he had to do, and she rode back alone, slowly and thoughtfully.

This land was beautiful, she thought. With hidden danger, yes, but still beautiful. She liked the open horizon, the sky with stars above now blazing almost as brightly as the Star Blade's.

It beats living on a ship, she told herself. *But I have a very long time to worry about going back to that.*

She found Khandor's tent where William had set it up and threw down her bedroll outside, as was her preference. She was cooking a slow and unlucky ground bird over the campfire when Khandor finally showed up to sit next to her with a weary sigh.

She tugged the cooked bird apart, handed half to him. He looked from it to her. "What were you, a Girl Scout?"

"My grandmother taught me how to live from the land. My people were Navajo. Native American."

"I know who the Navajo are. Were. Damn. They're gone too, with all the other people of our world. I'm sorry, Shandiin. I never got out of Aztlan to see that world and its people, and I'm sorry for that too."

She said nothing, but chewed the unlucky bird, and looked up at the stars.

He followed her gaze. "I've watched every night. The ship *Aztlan* is bigger than Earth's old space station, which I understand could sometimes be seen from the ground. But I've never seen our ship orbiting. Are you sure they are all right, Shandiin?"

"I believe they are there. But perhaps not in the same reality we are."

"What..."

"Don't worry about that. You've enough on your mind without worrying about realities or dimensions or whatever the hell they are." She finished her meal, wiped her hands on rags she figured William had left for them. She looked over at Khandor, was sorry to see him still grim, and decided to change that.

"This isn't a proposition, Khandor, but if I asked to share your tent tonight, would you?"

He almost choked, swallowed, looked at her in shock. "Do you mean for sex?"

"I guess I do. I'm not proposing. Just asking."

He threw bird bones into the fire, wiped his own hands. "I'm not sure what to say."

"I hear you always tell the truth." She grinned because he was rattled.

After a moment, he sighed. "Okay, then, I'll tell you. I might, if I weren't already engaged, so to speak. I would for certain, if it were you I'm engaged to. But things being as they are, I have to say no. And that's a damned shame, because I think I've fallen for you." The last was said with some irritation. "Don't you dare laugh."

"About what? About you falling for me, or turning down sex?"

"Either one."

"Hm. Well, I'm..." she remembered what she had said to Zion, and it hurt a little. "I'm actually honored, that you think you might love me. As for turning down sex, I am guessing you feel monogamy is important, unlike the thousand other men I've known."

"My God. Did you sleep with all of them?"

It was her turn to be shocked, until she saw his smirk. "Only half," she laughed. "So you are monogamous?"

"Until the world's morals changed, and even afterwards for many people, it was expected that women would save themselves for marriage. Why not men?"

And that reminded her of Verity. "Yes. Why not?" But she regarded Khandor thoughtfully. "So, no matter what, you...your bloodline, that is...can only have one woman in your life?"

He looked away, took a long minute before he answered. "You have to understand something about my bloodline. I know we are not normal. We are frankly abnormal. I would never expect or want my people to be like me. We were created for their benefit, not our own. I respect and revere my people as they are...so wonderfully human, with choices and experiences we cannot share. We have standards that may make no sense except as idealistically moral role models for our people...but that's not the reason those standards exist. Those standards ensure that our purpose cannot be corrupted. And our purpose owns us."

He looked back, his beautiful emerald eyes meeting her own, and she saw in them the truth he carried with a heart far bigger than his subjects would ever know. "It is necessary for us to be one of a kind, Shandiin."

It hit her then. Azlatan's High King lived in a cage. He and his bloodline would always live in a cage engineered by science and fused by magic, different from anyone else...and thus forever alone. His lack of moral choice, of the human gift of free will, was what made him incorruptible...and that difference, which he understood too well, would keep him forever apart. Alone.

She wondered if that were Zion's true reason for limiting their lifespan, if he gave them that gift out of kindness.

She remembered Leah's anger about tampering with the human spirit.

The enormity of it depressed her on Khandor's behalf, and she was quiet for a long time.

Forever alone, she thought.

"At least you will have a wife," she murmured finally. "Though it's a shame that you can't choose your own bride."

"She doesn't have any choice either, but I'll try to make sure she's not sorry she got stuck with me."

Definitely not normal. Better, she thought with a sigh. *Infinitely better than normal.*

But still caged.

The lions didn't return to threaten the hunters, but they heard wolves howling, and saw their green eyeshine when they lurked near enough to the campfires. Torches were set around the perimeter each night, more guards established, and children and livestock were kept in the camp's center.

Shandiin watched with interest the relationship between Rioch and Duine. Phaelon's Law required that the Duine "serve with honor," but it was friendship that most often bonded servant and master. Convention was served in certain formal behaviors, but there was a partnership of understanding, and not the slavery she had feared.

Khandor's separate law established the requirement for respect between all people, and it was understood that this applied to both of the 'races.' His correction of failures was swift and just, and taken to heart. His people looked to him, and trusted him, because his boundaries were few and always fair. He did not try to control anything that existed within those perimeters. Free will, he explained to Shandiin, is no less than chaos, and humanity's history was overwritten with the failed intent to control it.

The journey to Azlatan was leisurely, as Khandor would not travel faster than the slowest of his people. There were many people, and most were on foot. They had built wagons when wood had been plentiful in the valley they had left behind, but the wagons were too few for all to ride. Most were used to carry supplies and carry small animals like chickens.

The people learned to make do, even weaving cloth from the tough grass fibers as well as sheep's wool, and finding wild plants as well as animals for food. Livestock was herded in their wake, and guarded closely.

Shandiin always slept on the ground, outside Khandor's tent. She wouldn't tempt him or herself with anything closer, and she enjoyed being under the stars. Nitchi grazed nearby; she didn't have to tether him or Shadow, for both horses seemed to know where they belonged.

A long time into their journey, the voice of the world woke her up. She sat up abruptly, looked around at the peaceful night, then heard it again.

"Shandiin. Listen to me now."

She didn't bother to speak, but only thought her response. "Hiraeth. I am listening, though I'm surprised...I haven't heard from you since the tsunami."

"Shandiin, I have foreseen the intent behind Phaelon's Prophecy War. He plans the destruction of the people he calls Rioch, and all others after who do not obey him. He could end all of human existence. This is never what I intended."

Shandiin leaned back on her elbows. "What do you want me to do about it? Will you let me leave with Phaelon now?"

"I tell you again I cannot change what has been done. Phaelon will rule for a thousand years. When your time approaches, a Forbidden Child will be born, there will be war, and the Duine will rise up to destroy the Rioch."

"And he said no magic can save them. So even if I turn into the Sunqueen and I were willing to kill the Duine, I couldn't? I wouldn't do that anyway, Hiraeth. This war isn't their fault, it's Phaelon's. It's why there should be no gods!"

"I see now that the High Kings would not permit the destruction that took your world. So the gods are not necessary... and I would not purposely have allowed what Phaelon has done, what he means to do."

"But there's nothing you can do to stop his damned Prophecy War?"

"No. But you are the hidden goddess, who will rise at the prophecy's fulfillment. You will be foretold in myth as Prophecy's Daughter, who will come to give them freedom from the gods. Such magic requires some foreknowledge, but it must be hidden from Phaelon, so it will be seen as a myth."

"I can finally take the gods, but there will still be a war that could end them all." Shandiin was bitter with anger. "It's wrong, Hiraeth, to have allowed this to happen, and then leave them with so little hope."

"There is hope. The seventh High King may win the war... if he lives past his youth. If he is a warrior King with hardened heart, unlike his ancestors. You must help him with both, before you leave with the gods. Before you leave him here to fight the Prophecy War."

Shandiin thought about Hiraeth's dialog throughout the next day, and that night she asked Khandor to join her at the campfire. He laughed when she offered wine and conversation, but she read caution in his eyes; he'd come to know her well.

As they both settled in, she took a long breath, swallowed some of their carefully rationed wine, and began explaining Hiraeth's concerns...and the prophecy about the seventh High King. She explained her role: to defend and teach the King, and to take the gods away from Hiraeth, freeing the people.

He listened without interruption, then sat for a long time in thought.

"The seventh High King," he said. "That will be my grandson four times removed. Her foresight does, at least, give me hope for my bloodline."

"Wouldn't that be five times removed?" she asked.

He shook his head. "Khalen was the first High King. I will ensure Azlatan's history begins with him, even though he gave up his rule before our arrival." He sighed. "A thousand years. You will wait a thousand years, and then you must defend and teach the High King who will face the Prophecy War. That's more than a long time, Shandiin. It sounds impossible...unless you are immortal, which is necessary for your mission...my God, you really are a goddess."

"I will need your help to do it. Yours, and your descendants. The seeds of rebellion against Phaelon must be sown secretly and carefully within your bloodline. You cannot openly speak against him, or tell his truth...that he is a mad thing, a distorted intelligence without a soul."

Khandor surprised her. "Liethe knows. She came to me in a dream last night, and pledged her support to the High Kings, and said she will protect the Forbidden Child. She does not believe any child should be forbidden."

He set down his cup. "Of course I will help you with your thousand-year vision, Shandiin. But we can't do anything now but live within the construct of the gods. This world, with Phaelon's Laws of Order, will sadly be the only world my people know. In a thousand years, Earth will be no more than a myth."

He looked around at the sea of grass, at the people camped within it. Then he turned his emerald gaze back to her. "But remembering Earth isn't what matters. What matters is what we should have learned before we left it. The intrinsic curse of Earth's civilizations was the acceptance of evil as commonplace, and good as the exception. My bloodline is charged with changing that."

CHAPTER 12

During the next year their route grew rocky and sloped slowly higher, until a near-vertical cliff barred their passage. It stretched from north to south as far as they could see. They realized that Azlatan awaited them on the plateau atop this cliff.

Khandor and Shandiin rode ahead of the colony, finding a break in the cliff with a switch-backed upward path that was not too steep, but narrow. It reminded Shandiin of a road that had once existed on the mountain she had shared with Khalen and Verity, a road she had taken out with dynamite to keep her hideout safe. She wondered if it had been taken from her own mind, a gift from Hiraeth.

They rode up together to find the plateau edged with grass and trees. They rode through the trees to a grassy meadow, stopping at its far perimeter to scan the land dropping gently away in rolling hills and lush forests. Sunlight sparkled from a waterfall not too distant.

"It's beautiful. Your Azlatan is beautiful, Khandor. I'm guessing it's like this from here to the western sea where your palace awaits you."

"You sense it too. That cliff is the boundary."

"Yes."

She turned to see he was smiling at her instead of the view.

"We're here and you're still with me," he answered her questioning look, then gave her no chance to respond. "We don't have to bring them up single file, but we will have to divide into confined groups, and the heavier wagons may have difficulty." He scowled. "It will separate the colony, possibly for weeks, as we get everyone across. We'll need a semi-permanent camp up here."

"You need a second in command."

This time it was him looking at her in question.

"You've been treating me like a general," she told him. "But I am not one of your people, and I'm not sure I am destined to finish this journey with you. I know you have been carefully choosing your Dominion Kings, but you need more than that. You need someone you can rely on completely, to understand your purpose and carry out your orders. Not just for now, but in the future. I'll point out that's kind of how you have been using Dante."

He nodded thoughtfully. "Yes. You are right. Dante is ...like a compatriot. He and I grew up together. I trust him, and people listen to him."

When they rode back to the colony Khandor called Dante over, and Shandiin watched the young man with dark brown hair and blue eyes as he was given the new title of Compatri. Dante drew himself up in amazed pride, but began immediately helping with strategy. He would help people on the trail up the ridge, where Khandor would manage. He and Shandiin would organize from the bottom of the cliff.

She had noticed long before that some of the people had dropped away from the traveling colony, and found as they organized the climb that many of the horses had been taken with them. She brought this to Khandor's attention, but he was undisturbed.

"Many didn't see the need to keep traveling west." He shrugged. "They saw fertile land, especially back there in that mountain valley, and felt they could settle there without the hardship of a long journey. Phaelon's attention must have been elsewhere, as he didn't object, and I saw no reason to fight them about it."

"You wouldn't. But the horses will be missed. I think they took the best, the ones of Arabian blood."

"They were the best?" Khandor leaned over Shadow's curved neck, gave him a pat. "I rather prefer the heavier animals."

"He's Friesian. Heavier, but not like the draft horses we have pulling the wagons. The Arabians are the fastest, and have more endurance. There are a few left with your stock, however, and I think you should combine their bloodlines. Most of the hotblooded breeds trace back to the Arabians, and a new infusion will make them stronger."

He lifted a perfect black eyebrow.

"What?" she asked.

"You know more about horse genetics than human."

She laughed. "In nature, animals are easier to breed. They don't let emotions get in the way, and they only fuck in season."

He wrinkled his nose. "That's such an ugly word. I know animals aren't exactly making love, but still."

She smiled at him, thoughtful. "One of the first things I noticed about the men in your family is how unusual you all are...not just from being engineered, but because you are so decent in a world that has set aside old-fashioned things like gentility in behavior and speech. I hope that is something you never lose. In fact, Khandor, I hope it is something you will keep in mind as you establish the land of Azlatan. Lead them to be like you, not riff-raff like me."

She was surprised at his somber response. "You are neither riff nor raff, Shandiin. Because I do not like a word that you used has nothing to do with my respect for your true heart and brave spirit. For you I will gladly set the standard for Azlatan to be civilized in speech and manner...but I want you to never change, Shandiin. In a thousand years you will be the only one to remember who we were, and I never want you to change who you are."

When he held out his hand, she offered her own, and he took it gently...and lifted it to his lips, a brief kiss.

She watched curiously as he rode off. She hadn't been able to read the expression in his eyes just as he turned away.

Then she felt a warming, a resonance that she recognized was connected to Hiraeth itself. She would recognize it over her long years as a kind of loving magic. Their simple pact was made part of the relationship between her and the High Kings from that day forward.

Shandiin didn't realize that it had also shaped the structure of a new world.

Some of the horses had to make the climb twice, being brought back down to pull the heaviest wagons. Shandiin handled most of that, glad after several days of struggle up and down the ridge that it was nearly done, and Khandor finally could stay above to oversee the main colony.

She was helping with the last horse teams when a rider came down at a dangerously fast gallop, heading right for her. He was yelling before his horse came to a halt. "The King needs you!"

She rode Nitchi hard uphill, to find Khandor standing alone in his simple black leather, facing a strange man wearing robes black on one side, white on the other. His hairless head was also painted in the same manner. The man's eyes were like white marbles, and he held a staff that sparked with electricity.

Before she could make a move toward Khandor, Dante stopped her. His eyes were terrified, but he stood strong as he said very quietly, "The painted man is Phaelon's Tahmond...that's what he calls his priest. The High King doesn't want you in that fight. He wants you to help the people the Tahmond's enforcers want to kill."

She slid down from her horse and surveyed the scene. Most of the colony peered from the trees where the camp had been set. Those present stood well back; only a few braver ones ranged behind Khandor.

Behind the Tahmond were angry members of the colony, armed with axes and spears, with bows and arrows, with any weapon they could find. These surrounded another group bound in chains, most on their knees. There were hundreds of prisoners, she realized in shock, and many were dead on the ground, obviously killed while chained and defenseless.

Every one of them had red hair. Like her.

She moved immediately toward the prisoners, and when one of the men guarding them saw her coming, he threw his spear at her.

She'd long past learned that Hiraeth had gifted her physically. Swift as a cat she caught the spear mid-air, and broke it over her knee. She threw the pieces to the ground, striding to stand between the guards and the prisoners.

She stopped in front of a prisoner much taller than her six feet, powerfully built, bound with heavy chains. Even chained, it was obvious he was a warrior. Arrows were lodged in his arms and shoulders; he was both bloody and bruised. He stood defiantly with an arrow aimed at his heart, between the archer and several children huddled on the ground behind him.

The archer's eyes narrowed in fury when Shandiin stepped in front of him and snarled, "Lower that arrow, or I will shove it up your ass."

He fired the arrow.

She caught it, and when she stepped forward with it in her hand he ran like a rabbit.

During all of this she was also listening, watching the standoff of the High King, furious she could not openly reveal her Sunqueen power to help him—and wondering where the hell that weird Tahmond had come from.

"Phaelon has demanded them gone!" The painted Tahmond slammed his magic staff against the ground to emphasize his words, and lightning flashed.

White brighter than lightning exploded next to Khandor. Liethe's figure glimmered within the haloed light, and her voice rang like a church bell. "You are not Phaelon. The High King rules here. All mortals within Azlatan must obey him."

The Tahmond startled visibly, stepped back, caught himself. "Phaelon said these people are marked by Chaos, and shall not be allowed in Azlatan!"

Khandor stood beside Liethe with boots braced apart, his eyes pinned on the Tahmond in fury. "Phaelon did not say to kill them, but you have ordered otherwise, and you have further ignored my command to stand down. This will not endure."

"The prisoners belong to Chaos," the Tahmond bellowed, "and are immune to magic! *I* say they die!"

Khandor unsheathed the Star Blade, and this time the Tahmond did step back, several feet back. The King's voice was cold. "I am Tahmond to Daimaine, goddess of Death and Justice, and I call on her now to stand with me and with Liethe. The prisoners *will* live. You *will* stand down!"

Shandiin wanted to stop him, was terrified for him, as Daimaine's darkness infiltrated the air next to him and the beautiful Deathqueen grew into being.

The High King now stood between two goddesses, enveloped by both light and darkness, holding a sword that bathed him in stars. The Tahmond backed away further.

"The prisoners will leave Azlatan as Phaelon requires," Khandor said. "But you shall not harm any more of them. You are the one who has brought chaos to Azlatan. Daimaine could wreak her justice upon all of you for your disobedience."

After a long moment the Tahmond turned slowly back toward the captors and their prisoners. "Stand down," he told them. "They are exiled from Azlatan. That shall suffice."

"It shall *not* suffice," Khandor snapped. "You, and these men who are your enforcers, have defied my order and spilled blood in my realm. I command exile for all of you!"

"You cannot!" the Tahmond cried.

"He can." Daimaine's laugh was a chorus of wind. "The High King has only to ask, and my magic will send you into exile...or destroy you."

Don't, Shandiin thought frantically. *Don't ask her, Khandor! Don't give her that foothold to your realm...to you!*

But Daimaine's threat was sufficient. The captors threw down their weapons and bolted, heading for the road down from the ridge.

After a moment, the Tahmond ran after them.

Shandiin turned to the big man behind her, reached for his chains, and to his shock broke them in two with her bare hands. She smiled grimly as she dropped his bonds. "What is your name?" she asked him.

"I am Rowan." He rubbed his wrists as he tossed back his thick mane of red hair.

"I name you now as Roinn, and your name will be remembered from this day forward, because of your great courage." As she spoke, she broke the chains of the children he had fought to defend.

"Who are you?" he asked in wonder.

"I am Shandiin. And all of you..." she looked around at the prisoners, "...*all* of you will come with me, to our own place in this new world, to our own freedom from the tyranny of the gods."

She remembered Hiraeth's words, which she hadn't understood until this moment. *"I foresee that you will find your own people. I will ensure that you and they will be immune to the magic of the gods."*

Now she understood.

She turned as Khandor stopped beside her, handing her a bolt cutter, which she immediately gave to Roinn so he could start freeing others. She saw Dante, and Khandor's other chosen people, handing out more tools and helping free the captives.

Satisfied, she turned back to Khandor. "I'm not sure if that was courage or stupidity, calling on Daimaine. You know damned well you can't trust her."

"It was necessary. I am sending horses and supplies with you. Use the wagons and whatever else is still down below."

"Where the hell did that Tahmond come from?"

"He was an odd man, always kept to himself, watching everyone with judgement in his eyes. I saw a bright flash of light and he became as you saw him. Phaelon's doing." He looked toward Roinn. "You have named that man, who is truly a hero, and I believe made these people your own. I think you are a queen now."

"I am not!" she exclaimed. "I don't believe in royalty, Khandor...well, except for your star-crossed bloodline. I'll have no heir to take any title they didn't earn, and no subjects. If they follow me, it will be their own choice."

"Then what will you be?" he asked.

She studied the redheads, old and young, tall and short. "They were chained. I'll make sure they remember that they were chained and helpless, and that you stood for them. I will teach them to fight, so they will never be chained or helpless again. I'll ensure they will remember it all." With a little smile, she added, "To help that along, I'm naming them the Chaine. And as their leader, they may call me simply *The* Chaine. Did you know they were collecting those with red hair?"

"I knew people were gathering in one place. When I realized they were being taken prisoner, the Tahmond argued they were neither Rioch nor Duine, and their hair marked them as belonging to Chaos. When he tried to use Phaelon's magic to control them he realized they were immune, and that made him turn vicious. I didn't stop him before some were killed. I failed them, Shandiin, and I am sorry."

"You didn't fail them, Khandor. You stood for them, when you knew, and you saved them. You have my word we will be Azlatan's allies, when the Prophecy War comes to Azlatan. In the meantime...watch out for Phaelon's Tahmonds. Unlike Daimaine, Phaelon chooses really crappy priests." She frowned. "Khandor, the fear of Daimaine is a valuable tool for the High Kings. I don't think you want Phaelon's Tahmonds to realize Khalen purposely restrained her. The next step would be their realization that you won't use her savage powers at all."

"Yes. I had already decided that. But it means Khalen's sacrifice has to be secret as well." He shook his head sadly. "Secrets...and prophecy. A thousand years from now, you will be allies not to me, but to my distant descendent. Damn it, Shandiin...I know there's no choice now, but I don't want you to leave." She saw his emerald eyes had dulled to jade. "You understand me. You have made me...not alone." She was shocked when his voice broke.

She felt a lump in her throat, the pressure of ready tears. After a brief inward battle, she reached up to frame his handsome face with her hands, and kissed his lips very softly.

Then she stepped back, forcing a smile. "That probably wasn't the proper thing to do. But I want you to know part of my heart will always be with you, Khandor. I'll somehow find my way back to Azlatan, though I will have to be in disguise. When Liethe names her High Tahmine, work with her to take any more children who may be born with red hair. I will get them away to safety."

Unable to speak, he could only nod assent.

She left him there to his lonely rule, and thought it was one of the hardest things she had ever done.

Chapter 13

S handiin, and the people she had named the Chaine, returned to the eastern mountains where they settled in a lush and rivered northern mountain valley. Roinn became her second in command, and served in that position for a couple of centuries. She was surprised to find that her people had the same normal lifespan as the High Kings, and wondered if her unknown benefactor, that voice of the planet, had made that happen.

They were also uncommonly strong, her Chaine, though none as strong as she in her hidden goddess guise. Shandiin taught them the martial arts she had learned on earth, but made it clear that they were only the basis for what they would need in a real battle where there were no rules to follow. So they learned how to fight dirty, and over the epochs combined it all to create their own fighting style. She would, in later centuries, bring their technique to Azlatan.

There was always a Roinn.

The Chaine were long lived, but not very fertile; children were a rarity and so cherished...but there was always a Roinn. The story of the first Roinn's courage was one of the things that kept the Chaine people proud, as Shandiin intended. They established a competition testing wit, integrity, and fighting skill, to determine who would be awarded the name that became a title.

Shandiin was pleased, over the long centuries, that three of those recipients were women.

Her people built their own culture over the eras, but she set the foundation...with the spirit of Azlatan's High Kings as an ideal, but with her own free-ranging anarchy at its heart. Their story was recorded by certain citizens through the centuries, with herself as the legendary heroine. She occasionally complied with their pleas to add some of her adventures from her point of view. With secret amusement she thought of it as her people's heretic bible.

She was the only person in her nation who never read it.

In the high valley that was their first home, the Chaine mined an ore different from anything that had existed on their planet Earth. It would centuries later become known as Chaine gold because of its color, but in their early days her people used it only to forge unbreakable swords. It was tradition to include bits of the iron from their broken chains into those blades.

The smelted metal was stronger than steel. In time Chaine gold was also used to make a tightly-woven mail armor that no arrow could penetrate, and a kind of lovely jewelry that overlaid their leather armor to strengthen it.

Shandiin left her people at times, trekking in disguise to Azlatan to retrieve the red-haired children kept for her by Liethe's High Tahmine. She also for long periods wandered to meet other people on the steppes and the mountains that they had crossed. She found a nomad nation similar to the natives of the American southwest, and stayed with them for a time. The oldest among them recognized her as the goddess who had stopped a tsunami. True to Hiraeth's word, they called her the Sunqueen, and honored her even though she asked for nothing. She came to love the Sundancers, as they called themselves, and gave them a special gift with the help of Liethe; the horses they bred were a special kind, descendants of the magic steed called ChanDethe.

Hiraeth gave the Sundancers their own prophecy through Shandiin. It told of a future hero who would deliver them from their enemies, riding a horse with ChanDethe's name.

Shandiin passed on this foretelling from Hiraeth while hoping greatly that they would not be drawn into the war with Phaelon when it finally came. These were a peaceful people, who respected nature and lived in harmony with it.

But they did have enemies, who occasionally raided their camps to steal women and horses. She tracked the raiders to a city named Xanthe in the far south, but she didn't enter it. She felt Phaelon's presence there, and saw evidence of his Law in the hard-eyed men and the cowed women who served them. She realized these were the descendants of the murderers Khandor had exiled, and gave them a wide berth. She feared her interference would alert Phaelon to her existence, and thus draw the god's dangerous attention to her beloved Sundancers.

She traveled alongside the cliff that was Azlatan's eastern border, finding it ended at the snowclad mountain range of the north which would become known as the Everwhite. A verdant valley at the southern boundary of that range became Azlatan's northernmost Dominion, which she would later learn was named Ordhold. Over time, in her ongoing guise as Shan the Wanderer, she became friendly with the rough-hewn people who settled there.

She didn't guess how important that place would become to Azlatan's future.

The woman titled simply 'The Chaine' eventually led her people through the Everwhite and the Everwinter Pass north of Ordhold, immigrating to the western sea to settle on a peninsula that jutted far to the northwest of Azlatan's own sea-border. There they settled again, a few centuries after their exile from Azlatan, in a strange and verdant forest of golden-trunked trees. They used the strong golden wood to build the ships that would, in Azlatan's ninth century, sail to meet Azlatan's sixth High King.

Shandiin did not take her people into Azlatan before that sailing, but did herself slip in and out of Azlatan disguised as Shan, a man of the Rioch race. She traveled through the countryside as it was settled by the colonists' descendants, watching the settlements grow as the centuries passed. Khandor had not, as Zion had planned, founded the first home of his people as a centralized colony. Instead, he had scattered his chosen Dominion Kings throughout his realm, and the first of them were farmers and herdsmen sent to Dominions appropriate for the seeds of agriculture they had brought with them from faraway Earth. Working from memory of the areas they had surveyed from orbit, Khandor ensured from the beginning that his people would be fed and clothed even into the distant future.

She found, when she approached the central edge of Azlatan's far western sea, that a great forest had been razed, and from its wood and stone a city had been built. The city was called Cabre, known throughout the realm as the King's City. The leveling of that forest had created a vast plain circling the city's towering outer walls. Through that barren flat converged the many roads connecting what became the seventy-seven Dominions of Azlatan.

More interesting, to Shandiin's thinking, was the fact that the empty plain made it impossible for an enemy to approach the city unseen. Knowing the intelligence of the High Kings, she was sure this was not by accident.

The High King's palace, Penumbra, dominated Cabre, being visible from every vantage of the city. It's obsidian towers rose from the black sea-cliffs at Cabre's southwestern edge. Its lowest level held Daimaine's sunless Temple, and at night Penumbra's dark towers held their own stars.

At the city's northern edge, Liethe's ice-white sanctuary of healing ascended from a spreading fan of steps, it's back half built into the cliffside of a mountain.

The plain stone temple that was Phaelon's squatted in the center of the city itself, equidistant from the other two.

The city bustled around these dominating monuments to the deities, which were made commonplace by their familiarity.

The goddess called Chaos was not recognized in Azlatan except as myth and as a curse word.

Shandiin had met Khandor's son, but the third High King Khastiel had known only an androgynous man with short, shaggy black hair and strange silver-grey eyes. His gaze upon her had been full of speculation, which she supposed was because he could not read her with his gift of empathy. They had even struck up a brief but enjoyable friendship, which she abandoned before he could deduce too much. It was too soon, she knew, to make contact as herself.

Khandor's death had driven home the curse of her own immortality: the loneliness of outliving every person she cared for. She regretted that she had never seen Khandor again, even though he lived to 275. His wife had not been brought to him until he was nearly 200, and had died in childbirth not long after. He had raised Khastiel alone.

She had looked into the son's emerald eyes, and thought sadly how much he resembled his father.

She made a point to travel back to Azlatan in disguise during the rule of each of the High Kings, living among the people for a time, learning that it's culture reflected Khandor's intent...as much as it could, considering humanity's chaotic nature.

More importantly to her, she saw that the incorruptible character of each High King remained true even as their personalities differed. Azlatan flourished under the bloodline's benevolent rule: from friendly Khastiel came gentle Ashtari, came grave Mordane.

It was almost a thousand years before she brought her people to Azlatan, in the reign of the sixth High King, Mordane's son Allasar.

PART 3: THE KING'S DEFENDER

"There is one who is secret.
You will know her when you see her.
She will be the King's Defender.
She will bring the people who will be your allies
in the war Azlatan faces when the prophecy is fulfilled.
Trust her.
She will make you not alone.
Nonetheless, guard your heart."
—High King Khandor

Chapter 14

Shandiin looked across the bow of her small craft and turned back to the people rowing it toward the shore. "There's a reef here," she warned. "Don't ground the boat, but wait for me; I can wade in the rest of the way."

Roinn the Seventh frowned at her. "I would prefer you didn't do this alone."

She just grinned at him. "Don't be a worry-wort. There isn't an army waiting on that beach."

She looked behind him to the great golden ships dancing lightly on the blue sea under the blue sky. Her people had built those ships, and she thought—not for the first time—that they looked like Viking ships. Glancing back at Roinn, she thought the similarity didn't end with the ships. He wore his long chestnut hair partly braided, with wire of Chaine gold woven through. She thought that the Vikings, like her own Chaine, had probably dressed in leather and fur.

She pulled her fur cloak from her shoulders and unstrapped her sword and knife, dropping it all at Roinn's feet. The look of alarm he gave her in return made Shandiin shake her head. "Think about it. Would you want an armed person walking into your home?"

"No. But nevertheless." He eyed the beach warily.

She climbed easily from the boat, dropping her booted feet into water that came almost to her knees, and started wading across the reef toward the beach. The sea was cold on her legs even through heavy leather, while the sun was warm on her strong, bare shoulders and arms. A stiff sea-breeze unfurled her shaggy sun-fired hair.

As she walked she studied the lone figure that waited for her on the sand, a tall man in simple black, and the palace towering from the rocks at the beach's end further down. Far behind him a low wall separated the town proper from the beach, and a crowd had gathered behind it. She was sure the arrival of her ships had to be a shock, and probably a terrifying one. She smiled at that distant multitude, watching the High King stand bravely alone at the water's edge, and thought things hadn't changed that much in nine hundred years.

As she came nearer, she saw the jet-black hair blowing free about his shoulders, and the familiar glint of emerald eyes, and for just a moment hope pierced her heart...but as she drew nearer she saw that he was not, as she should have expected by now, the dark stranger who had haunted her through too many years to count.

Neither was he the High King she had expected to find. She had known Mordane briefly, though it had been at least a century before. This must be his son, and she wondered about that, because Mordane had been fairly young at her visit. A High Prince didn't ascend to rule until his sire was dead...gone to Daimaine, as his subjects said in sorrow, for the High Kings were all revered by their people.

This man was familiar nevertheless, for she had known his emerald-eyed family from its earthly beginning, and found them dearer than she could have imagined in all her lonely years that had begun on a lost world called Earth.

So she was smiling when she walked up to him from the water, and his—of course—impossibly handsome face held an expression she couldn't read until the emerald fired with warmth and he smiled back, very slowly.

"Hello, Your Highness." She did not kneel, for she wanted Azlatan to know from the beginning that she was not his sub-ject, nor were her people. "I am Shandiin."

"I didn't know your name," he responded, "but I know who you are. I am Allasar." His gaze lifted from her to the ships. "You have traveled far, I think, to amaze my people. They have believed until this moment that they were the only people in the world."

"But not you?"

"I had reason to believe otherwise. Will your people wait, for a time, while we walk and talk?"

She nodded, turned back toward the sea, and gave the broad arm signal that told her people all was well and they should wait.

Then she and Allasar turned together and walked toward Penumbra like old friends.

She knew, however, that he was studying her as she studied him. He was taller, she thought, than those who had come before him, and wondered if the four generations of female blood added to his bloodline had made that difference. Glancing at his profile with its sleek, narrow mustache and beard, she saw there had been no diminishment of beauty.

What a funny way to think of a man, she thought. *But it fits, and makes him no less masculine.*

"We will go to the Temple sacristy," he said, "where we can speak in private."

"I'm guessing not many people use it."

He glanced over, lifting an eyebrow. "What makes you think that?"

"Because I'm pretty sure they're all terrified of Daimaine. As they should be. I hope that you are also wary of her, because..."

"Because she isn't to be trusted," he finished her sentence.

"I see Khandor sent the warning down through his son."

"He did. Along with other things we don't discuss with anyone not of our bloodline."

She walked along with him for a long moment before commenting, "That must be a lonely wait for conversation, since there's mostly only one of you at a time."

He gave her a sidelong glance, but did not respond.

They came to stairsteps that led up, across a bridge toward the sea-cliffs, and then down again to a walkway at sea level. The palace's black stone wall ran along one side. The other side was a march of arched windows, with the sea at high tide washing and whispering just below each open stone sill. The walkway led to a pair of giant black doors, but the High King turned off before they got there, and they entered a room that was dim and quiet when he closed the door behind them.

He lit a lantern, and she saw the room was comfortably furnished with a thick rug over the cold stone floor, and a fireplace laid in wait for a fire. He glanced at her boots. "Would you like me to light the fire? You must be wet, if not cold."

"Not really. We use the same resin on our clothing that we use to waterproof the ships."

"Ships. Yes, I know that word, from some of the histories in Penumbra's library. Please, have a seat, Shandiin."

She dropped into a comfortable chair, and watched with some interest when he reached for the Star Blade strapped to his hip. "I hope that's not for me," she said mildly.

He laughed. "That would be an ignominious end to your journey, wouldn't it? It's not the Blade I need, but something that is kept in the scabbard with it." He drew out a small scroll, and handed it to her. "It's a fine hiding place, since no one but a High King can touch this particular sword."

She took the thinly rolled leather, unwound it, and read:

There is one who is secret.
You will know her when you see her.
She will be the King's Defender.
She will bring the people who will be your allies
in the war Azlatan faces when the prophecy is fulfilled.
Trust her.
She will make you not alone.
Nonetheless, guard your heart.

Khandor's signature was clearly scripted at the end, and her vision was a little misty when she looked up at the High King named Allasar.

"Is this why you said you know who I am?" she asked.

He lowered into the chair facing her, took the tiny scroll back as though to read it anew. "Yes," he said. "Though I thought from its content that you would show up in my son's time, not mine." He looked up. "The Tahmond say Phaelon promised a thousand years of peace when the goddess Chaos killed the first High King. I hope that time isn't yet over."

"Your hope is truth, but your history is wrong. Chaos didn't kill Khalen. Khalen sacrificed himself to Daimaine, in return for giving up her ability to control and kill without direction from your bloodline." At his sad nod of agreement, she sat back. "So you knew that truth, at least. I imagine a lot of history has been revised in nine centuries. I'm not here to correct it unless it matters."

"There were other secret letters." Allasar leaned forward to meet her eyes. "Some have decomposed during the centuries, but the Kings have tried to keep the truths of our world by recopying what is left. This one alone remains as it was, I believe through the magic of the Star Blade. I would wish there was more explained about you. But I'm more interested in the present than in the history. Why do you come to Azlatan now, if we have time yet before the Prophecy War comes to pass?"

"I thought it best to get ahead of it. We need to prepare."

Before he could respond, there was a knock at the door. He leaned back, palming the scroll. "Enter," he called.

A man stepped in, his pale aging skin wrinkled, his eyes a piercing blue. His cap of hair was white, yellowed by the lantern-light. "My apologies, Your Highness. The High Tahmond has sent an urgent message."

Allasar met Shandiin's eyes, and she saw a glint of humor. "Not unexpected. Shandiin, this is Canon, my bonded Duine. Canon, this is Shandiin, who is..." he halted, lifted an eyebrow.

"My people are Chaine," she supplied. "Among them I am known as The Chaine."

Allasar nodded politely, eyes on hers. "This is The Chaine," he finished. "What is the message, Canon?"

"He...requests the stranger be brought to Phaelon's Temple."

"Of course. Although I expect it was a demand, not a request." He smiled at Shandiin. "Do you think I should respond by inviting him here instead?"

"That's your choice of course, Your Highness. I and my people come as your friends and allies, but we have no interest in religion."

Allasar sat back, regarding her steadily. "No interest? Are there no gods or goddesses wherever you come from?"

"It doesn't matter, as we are immune to magic."

And that, she saw, sparked his interest immediately. "Immune?" he tapped the Star Blade, still at his hip. "This is the Star Blade, given to the first High King by the goddess Daimaine. Are you immune to its magic?"

"I believe so, yes. Would you care to test it?"

Canon began to back out the door.

"I think not," Allasar laughed. "Canon, stop that. She wasn't issuing a challenge...I don't think. Please advise the High Tahmond I request he meet us in Daimaine's Temple."

"As you wish, Your Highness."

Shandiin noted Canon didn't look happy as he closed the door.

"Will the Tahmond give him trouble?" she asked.

"No. He is 'only'..." and he held up both hands to emphasize the word, "a servant Duine, and therefore beneath that Tahmond's notice. As you may have guessed, the High Tahmond is rather arrogant, and tests me at every opportunity." When he smiled she thought the emerald sparkled a little. "But I can be far more arrogant than he, as he should well know by now. He's very uncomfortable in Daimaine's Temple, so that gives us an advantage as well."

"I see. It will also give you a fair idea about my immunity to magic, I think. Or at least to my lack of fear about it."

He just smiled.

"You don't lie," she chuckled, "but you are cagey. Does Daimaine peek into your mind, Allasar?"

"Not without me being aware of it, and I am always aware when awake. Could you explain something about Khandor's message?" he asked as he stood, tucking the scroll back into the scabbard.

"If I can."

"I understand most of it, except for the last part. *She will make you not alone,*" he quoted. *"Nonetheless, guard your heart."*

"I can't explain that. I have no idea what he meant."

Allasar's eyes were narrowed when she looked back at him, and she noted they were slightly tilted, as though his bloodline had been infused with Asian blood.

"You just lied to me," he said flatly.

When she didn't respond he seemed to let it go. "Come, Shandi-in, let's go to Daimaine's Temple. We could enter from this room, but I think for your introduction we should use the formal entrance."

He spoke as they strolled again down the sea-walk to the giant black doors at the end. "Azlatan's histories say there is somewhere in the world a likeness of each of the goddesses, so that they might be known to anyone wise enough to behold them. The location of such likenesses is known for only two, and since all mortals must recognize Daimaine through Death, or perhaps even through Justice, her image is here for all to see."

He pushed through the plain black double doors into a foyer, lit by a magic chandelier that looked like the moon. It threw an eerie silver light. When he closed the doors behind them, they faced a second pair of doors.

She followed him through the second doors into a cavernous chamber, and realized it was both the Command Hall of the High King and Daimaine's Temple, and that the sun never came here. This was the heart and core of Penumbra, and here the obsidian called Nightstone lived, lit by the galaxies wheeling across its high walls and ceiling. From the far side of the expansive black floor towered the statue of Daimaine, seven times higher than a man, with the stars brightening as they climbed her height, until at last they blossomed to silver flame within the black crystal of her hair. Her face was living moonlight, so terribly beautiful that her audience looked away after one frantic glance, and for long moments after bore the afterimage of her sign: the blazing sickle she wore upon her forehead, both moon and scythe of souls.

She looked from that face to High King Allasar's, and found him watching her. "Am I supposed to kneel or something?" she asked.

He grinned. She saw in that moment his resemblance to Khandor, to Khalen, and it warmed her heart. "No, though most people do." He offered his arm, then, as though they were going to dance, and they walked together across the black glass floor while she gazed around at the whirling stars and privately thought the whole thing was really great theater.

She didn't mention another statue in her own likeness, in a cave across the continent. It was made of Chaine gold. It was from that cave her people had mined the ore for their swords and armor, though Hiraeth had closed off the cavity where her statue stood, so that even her own people couldn't guess her secret. Only she could access it; it was her private space, and she had occasionally communed with Hiraeth there.

She was surprised to see five simple black chairs at the foot of Daimaine's statue. The row of chairs sat atop the statue's raised base, which she assumed was meant as an altar.

"Where is your throne?" she asked as they walked toward it.

He looked at her in question. "What is a throne?"

She laughed a little. "An assumption, apparently. I should have known the High King of Azlatan, who wears no crown, would need no throne. It's unimportant. But I am guessing you usually sit in the center chair."

"Usually. The High Tahmond and the High Tahmine sit at each side of me, for formal gatherings, and the High Queen and High

Prince at each end." At her questioning look, he added, "I have neither Queen nor Prince yet. My promised bride will soon be traveling to Cabre, and I am to marry her here at Starfall."

She calculated; Starfall, she knew, was the beginning of winter in Azlatan. Not far off, then. "Your Highness..."

"Allasar, please."

"Allasar, then, and thank you. If what I ask disturbs you, I will drop the question...but I would like to know what happened to your father. I had expected to meet Mordane."

They took the two steps up to the altar, and he gestured her to sit before himself taking the chair next to her. He crossed his boots at the ankle, leaning back. "My father walked into the sea in about the same place you walked out. We recovered his body three days later."

She was stunned. "Mordane...he killed himself?"

He looked across at her, and she noticed the emerald was subtly dulled. That made her recall Khandor's eyes darkening to jade when he had told her goodbye all those centuries before.

"He wasn't the first. Khandor did the same thing, but his son elected to keep that secret, since he was alone when he discovered his body, and brought it back to Penumbra himself with no explanation. People assumed it was a natural death. Khandor was High King for 250 years, longer than any King since, and I'm sure Khastiel was concerned about instability in the realm at his passing...particularly if people learned he had suicided. It was also kept quiet when Ashtari walked into the sea in the year 670. His crypt is empty."

Shandiin couldn't speak for a long time. His words were a horror to her. Half of these caring, gifted Kings dead by suicide. In particular she thought of the loneliness of a friend, her very dear friend Khandor, as he spent 250 years serving his people and his purpose, and almost all of it without his promised bride. She finally managed to speak, but her voice broke. "I am so sorry, Allasar. More than you know. And for you...I am sorry for your loss of your own father."

"He had his own pain when my mother died, and it's rather a curse that we also share the emotions of our people. I've been luckier, as I am more able than he was to block that out. Now...will you tell me why you lied, Shandiin, when I asked about Khandor's message?"

"I would truly be guessing."

"You knew him, so I think it would be more than a guess."

"What makes you so sure I knew him? That was almost a thousand years ago."

"Why else would he be so sure that his descendant would know you on sight? You are unique, Shandiin. We Kings know uniqueness."

"Huh. I guess you would." She frowned. "May I ask that you give up that scroll that tells about me? I can't explain, Allasar, but it's better that your future son doesn't know too much about me."

He contemplated her for a long moment. "This has to do with his role in the Prophecy War?"

"Yes."

He looked away. "Then it's really going to happen. I knew it, but you've just made it very real. Yes, Shandiin. I will destroy Khandor's scroll, and my heir will only know you as The Chaine."

She took his word. She knew the veracity of The Kings. And she carefully changed the subject. "You've indicated your father was an empath, as I know you are. I also know that you can't read my emotions like you can others. So why are you so sure I was lying?"

"Empath. Is that what you call it? My father said it was one of our bloodline's curses, even though occasionally useful. Being flooded with all that confusion, anger, hatred, sadness, even joy...it is frankly overwhelming, particularly when there are a great number of people. I am able to set up a mental block against it. So I just observe. People often tell more by their small behaviors than they do by speaking. You looked away when you said you didn't know what it meant."

She had to laugh, even while wondering what other 'curses' the High Kings experienced. "I should know better than trying to fool a genius. I read a liar by that same method. I call it body language."

He seemed intrigued by her laughter or her words, but a bar of magic moonlight appeared as the double doors were opened and a figure stepped through, followed by three men.

The Tahmond's staff sparked, but the sparks were not very impressive here in Daimaine's star-filled temple of power. The man himself, painted and robed vertically half-black, half-white, strode across the floor toward them with anger obvious in every step. He stopped at the base of the altar steps and struck his staff against the floor, causing a flare of lightning and a rumble of thunder, while the men behind him knelt.

Allasar, who had straightened respectfully upon their arrival, raised his eyebrows at the show of temper. Shandiin kept her face impassive.

"Welcome, Your Honor," Allasar said mildly. "And to you, Majesties. I didn't expect to see Dominion Kings so soon after our meeting yesterday."

The three stood up, looking more than a little nervous.

"Never mind that," the Tahmond snapped. "I brought them because it appears your realm has been invaded, and they should know..."

Allasar sat forward, his face intent. "Have Phaelon's wards fallen from the border? Please excuse my interruption, Your Honor, but I find that rather alarming, since I wasn't aware of it." He looked to the three, who Shandiin assumed were Dominion Kings. "Have any of you received some word of an invasion?"

They looked at each other, and one said "No, Your Highness. Only the summons by the High Tahmond, which he said is related to the strange objects in the sea, which he was unable by his magic to send away."

Allasar returned his intimidating emerald gaze back to the High Tahmond. "Do the wards stand, then?"

"Of course," the Tahmond said irritably. "Phaelon's powerful magic guards Azlatan's borders, as always."

"Did you try by magic to remove the ships that brought new friends to Azlatan, and why?"

"Ships, you call them? Of course I did! I have never heard of such a thing! They are outside of the natural order!"

"I see. But your magic failed?"

"That failure is also outside the natural order!"

"Is it? Have you never attempted magic against an animal, and had it fail?"

He snorted at that. "Animals are inhuman by their very definition, and so immune to magic."

"Are they outside of Phaelon's natural order?"

"Of course not!"

"I agree, they are not. And neither are those ships, nor this friend beside me, who commands those ships. So I fail to understand your concern. Let me introduce The Chaine, as known by her people who are called Chaine. She has claimed no connection to royalty, and comes in peace."

Shandiin spoke for the first time. "I also come bearing gifts, as we would like to make trade with the Dominions of Azlatan. I believe it will be a mutually beneficial relationship."

"You can't accept gifts from this creature!" the Tahmond snapped at the High King.

"I don't see why not." Allasar sounded surprised. "We take gifts from the animals, do we not? For food, for clothing, for labor, even for companionship. Frankly, Your Honor, I think your concerns are invalid, and I do not accept them." Shandiin jolted a little as his voice changed to what she would later learn was the bloodline's 'command' voice: *I respectfully demand that you stand down on this matter.*

It wasn't a tonal change, but magic that penetrated the brain as the words were spoken. She thought of headphones, earbuds. She was surprised she heard it, as she was otherwise immune to magic...but then realized that it wasn't just magic, but part of his genetic heritage, and magic had only amplified it.

It's impact was clear when the Tahmond stepped back, blinking. "Fine. Do your business and your bartering, then. I have nothing to do with animals, and do not care to be introduced to them." With that he turned and left, showing arrogance but none of his previous umbrage.

Shandiin considered what she had just witnessed. She recalled Daimaine's attempt to give the High Kings the ability to command obedience, which Khalen had rejected. Daimaine had changed that to simply ensure they would be heard.

She had just seen evidence that the Kings would, in fact, be heard.

Allasar had turned to address the Dominion Kings. "Majesties, I am setting a meeting for tomorrow, when The Chaine and her people will bring to us their gifts and proposals for business. Please return to Penumbra tomorrow at noon, all of you...in the Council Hall, not here. Bring your Duine and your officials; I'll be sending messengers to others in Cabre who might be interested in some new business ventures."

"May I ask what you bring to us, Your Majesty?" Dominion King Parmenas asked Shandiin.

Her response was clearly addressed to a person she considered of equal standing, but it was given with a respectful nod. "My people are Chaine, and we do not have royalty. As their leader I am simply referred to as The Chaine. We do not use honorifics. I am called by my name, Shandiin. We bring armor and weapons, tools, jewels and furs, and horses."

Allasar turned to her at that. "Horses?"

She smiled. It seemed that all of his bloodline liked horses. "Yes."

"Then I will make sure my stables are ready, and those interested can meet us at the stable yard before we go to the Council Hall. Thank you for coming, Majesties."

Recognizing dismissal, the three men bowed and left.

Allasar turned to Shandiin. "My apologies if it appeared I was calling you an animal. It was meant as a metaphor, to get past the High Tahmond, who could make your visit very uncomfortable to Azlatan."

She just smiled. "I've been called worse."

"You didn't mention gifts."

"You didn't ask." She shrugged, then tilted her head. "I am wondering if you used your empathy...what you call your curse...to read the High Tahmond just now."

"He always reads the same. Nothing but anger, cold or hot. I don't know why Phaelon always chooses such as him as his Tahmonds. Most are also lacking in intelligence, and I'm never sure if that makes them more or less dangerous."

"How many Tahmond are there?"

"More than I care to count. I wish there were as many of the Tahmine, who are far more useful to Azlatan."

"How is that?"

"The Tahmine serve the goddess Liethe, and they are healers. The High Tahmine is...I guess I could say she is a good friend. I trust her, as Khandor told me to trust you."

"I hope you will find in me a good friend as well, Your Highness."

He studied her. "I told you before to use my name. You are not one of my subjects."

"I am absolutely not one of your subjects, but I think the honorific appropriate, as your very bearing is inherent to who you are. I do hope to be your friend. I will leave you now, Allasar, and return in the morning with some of my people and a lot of gifts."

She knew it would be the horses that won the High King's heart, so decided to send them off the ships first. She rode her own big paint descended from her earthborn Nitchi.

From his back she led the best of all the thirty horses she had brought, a black stallion bred from centuries of melding Friesian and a breed kept by the faraway Sundancers, the nomad people known only to her. Shashata was her special gift to the High King, as unruly a spirit as her own, as he proved by fighting the lead-rope as they swam from ship to reef, plunging and playing in the water from reef to shore. Her huge paint was the only other horse who could handle him on lead, being even larger and much heavier.

Allasar's handsome face was full of delight as he watched Shashata being led from the water to dance across the sand with his high, free-springing step. Shandiin stopped in front of the King, and wordlessly offered the lead-rope.

Allasar stared up at her. "For me?" he asked, almost like a child, and she felt a rush of warmth for the High King that made her think she should guard her own heart.

She just smiled, and Allasar took the lead rope. She watched the big stallion immediately lower his head to bunt the King's chest, and Allasar had to step back while he laughed in obvious joy.

She directed her people to take the rest of the horses to the High King's stables, where she dismounted to stand with him, watching as each beauty was led past them to the readied stalls. Allasar still held Shashata's lead rope and stood stroking the black's great curved neck.

His eyes shone as they moved from the horses to Shandiin. "They are all amazing. I have never seen their like, and I thought I had the finest of horses already in my stable. I thank you from my heart for this horse."

"He answers to Shashata," she smiled.

"Shashata," he repeated, and shook his head as though in wonder at it all. "What would you have me do with them all, Shandiin?"

"Shashata is my gift to you. I had hoped that you would in turn gift some of the others to the most important of your Dominion Kings, to help ease them into accepting our invasion..." she grinned at his laugh, "...and use Shashata and the rest to improve the stock for your army."

He looked surprised at that. "I do not have an army. I've never needed..." his voice trailed off, and he looked away, suddenly sober. "I'll need one, won't I? Or my son will."

"You're quick. We'll talk about that later." She looked around at the crowd gathering in the royal stable-yard along with her own people, who were already busy displaying their wares. "It seems you've already spread word about us. May I stable my horse here?" she asked.

"Of course. We'll have him put next to Shashata, for company. I'll call my Compatri to take them in."

"He can take Shashata, but mine is an evil creature, and I think it best that my own second in command handle that."

So she introduced Roinn, who nodded with cool respect to a High King he considered no better than his own leader—no matter what she said—and they watched the horses be led away.

"Your man doesn't care for me," Allasar noted without rancor.

"Roinn is very conservative. He doesn't like many people. But he is also concerned about our acceptance in Azlatan, starting with you."

"I'll have to win him over, then, because it's my intent that the Chaine be fully accepted. We'll wait for him to join us, and go to Council Hall. I see that many of my people are already getting to know yours."

They watched as her leather-clad, red-haired people displayed their wares to his citizens, who were obviously as fascinated with them as the materials they brought. When Roinn returned, they went on to Penumbra.

A great market square fronted the palace, and Shandiin guessed it was usually very busy, but that the events in the stable-yard had drawn many of the shoppers away. Shopkeepers and their customers watched avidly as she and the High King walked through with Roinn and the King's Compatri behind them. She noted that the people bowed or knelt when Allasar went by, realizing once again that the High King needed no ornate trappings. As magically powerful as his command voice, his presence conveyed his ultimate authority.

She also noted that no one approached him without invitation, guessing that was tradition, and that the High Kings had probably established that for their own protection in view of Allasar's noted curse of empathy.

There were few Duine visible. Most of the people here had the dark hair, some had darker skin. Glancing at Allasar, she thought that the colony's Rioch race...and wasn't that a joke?...had melded smoothly from its diverse beginnings, as shown by the High King's own tip-tilted eyes. The paler Duine, she guessed, had a heritage less rich, or perhaps just less obvious.

A broad fan of wide, shallow steps led up to the imposing entrance to Penumbra. The relief sculpture above the great doors looked Egyptian to Shandiin's earthly eyes, but the sickle moon on which it stood marked it as Daimaine. There were guards stationed at the doors and within the entrance hall. They were dressed exactly like the High King in unrelieved black, except unlike him they wore metal trim at shoulder and wrist, and braid edging the cloaks some wore. She guessed that the various symbols in silver, gold, and emerald signified rank.

They walked straight through the atrium to more double doors, which the guardsmen swept open before they had to slow a single step. She realized the High King had purposely kept their initial meeting private, free of this smooth procession that was otherwise a normal part of his life.

The Council Hall was already populated with people who stopped all conversation at their entrance, bowing to the High King and moving to their seats in rows facing an elevated table. Allasar indicated to her that she should sit at the table on his left, settling himself into the central chair.

"Welcome." He addressed the room, and a quick shiver went down her spine. He spoke quietly, in his normal low tone, but his commanding voice carried powerfully. This time it brought back that strange sense of authority in the voice of a dark stranger she had met, once, on a street corner before the Earth died.

She swallowed, trying to return her focus, as he introduced the Dominion Kings and Guildmasters who joined them at the head table. She sensed rather than saw the change in his demeanor when a woman entered the room, seeming to glide toward them in opalescent robes and veils.

To her surprise, all of the men stood at her arrival, including the High King. He took both of the woman's hands as she stopped in front of him, and kissed them before settling her into the chair on the other side of his.

"The High Tahmine," he introduced her in a voice that held something like reverence. "The Chaine," he announced, with exactly the same tone.

He remained standing as the two women faced each other across his chair, and the Tahmine slipped the veil from her face and hair, revealing a face aged, yet beautiful as a sunrise. Her white hair was caught back in a smooth curve at her nape. Her eyes were sea-green and filled with magic, and smiled even as she did.

"Welcome." Her voice was soft and somehow musical. "I am Tariah, and I invite you to visit me at the Temple of Liethe."

"Thank you. I am Shandiin, and I will gladly accept your invitation." She looked up as Allasar took his seat between them. "If it please the King."

Allasar glanced at her sidelong. "I have no intention of ever coming between the two of you," he said for their ears only, "except at this table."

Tariah laughed, and Shandiin immediately liked her.

The meeting went smoothly, as such meetings never did in Shandiin's earthly memory. The High King made it clear that The Chaine and her people were friends, that they had brought gifts to Azlatan, and that its citizens would profit from it.

Shandiin was quite sure no one was going to argue with him, whatever they thought.

When he stood, the meeting evolved from formality into a kind of cocktail party, as Duine came in serving drinks and food that could be eaten out of hand. Shandiin, who had always hated such gatherings, gritted her teeth until her augmented hearing picked up one of the Dominion Kings complaining that "She looks like she knows more than she should, and is always on the verge of amusement. She makes me nervous."

Well, she thought, *I should. I certainly should make them nervous.* It made her relax.

Allasar stayed at her elbow, so she was never overwhelmed with too many people, but the High Tahmine was the one who rescued her. "Would you consider coming with me now?" Tariah asked, and the sparkle in those sea-green eyes told her she understood that Shandiin was not a social person.

"Gladly," she agreed, and with a parting word to the High King she walked out of Penumbra to see the High Tahmine's carriage arriving at the foot of the steps. It seemed created of pearl and opal, and was drawn by horses of the same color, with eyes the color of the sky. By magic bred, they were silent upon the road; only the delicate chimes on their harness could be heard. The tiny bells flashed like diamonds through the drifting veils of their manes.

The horses floated past them, needing no driver to guide their silent pace, and halted so the carriage door was exactly in front of them.

"Holy crap!" Shandiin exclaimed, stunned out of using Azlatan's proper speech. "Those horses!"

The Tahmine gave her a puzzled smile, gestured for Shandiin to enter the magic carriage. "They are only half-mortal," she explained. "They were sired by ChanDethe, and have served every High Tahmine since Liethe gifted them to us upon arrival at her Temple in Cabre."

The carriage moved—Shandiin could see the people watching them go by, the buildings on each side of the narrow streets of Cabre—but there was no sensation of movement, not even a vibration. She sat on a soft bench directly facing the Tahmine, who was smiling at her reaction. "You seem more interested in the horses than the magic," she said. "Allasar is much the same."

"I think all of the High Kings have liked horses."

"Have you known them all, then?"

Shandiin realized she had spoken too freely, leaned back to consider the woman who watched her so closely. "No. Only a couple or so."

"And which couple would that be? Shandiin, you can be open with me. I am not an enemy. In fact, I am very much your ally. Liethe has foretold your coming. She said this: *In the days of prophecy, there will be one with hair like fire and eyes like silver, who will come to Azlatan to become the King's Defender.* Which King you are meant to defend she didn't specify, but we who serve her have also served and revered every High King for all of Azlatan's centuries."

Shandiin was surprised, then thoughtful, remembering Liethe's defense of Khandor when he confronted the first High Tahmond. "No one else knows that, do they?"

"Allasar advised me that he had a similar message about you from the second High King. We have spoken of this to no one else."

"Allasar told me the Tahmonds teach that Chaos killed the first High King."

"Which you and I both know to be untrue. Daimaine took the first High King before the people crossed the Plain of Admech."

Shandiin exhaled. "So you have the history right. I think the High Tahmonds have been rewriting it. Is that what they call the steppes outside Azlatan's eastern border? The Plain of Admech?"

"Yes. The Tahmond also teach that the goddess Chaos is an evil entity kept away by Phaelon's magic borders. We have little information about that goddess, except for Liethe's own prophecy that Chaos will return when the Forbidden Child comes, and that he will ride a mortal horse named ChanDethe."

"The immortal ChanDethe being the magic horse who sired yours." Shandiin smiled inwardly, for she knew of this magical creature. He was ancestor of the horses of the nomads of the eastern plain Azlatan called Admech. She said nothing, for it was her fervent hope those people would be spared from that damned Prophecy War.

"Yes." High Tahmine nodded. "ChanDethe is not just a magic horse. He appears in other forms as well, and generally awaits his call while asleep in Liethe's arms."

"The cat!" Shandiin exclaimed at her memory of Liethe on a cottage porch very long ago. "She was holding the cat!"

Tariah's eyes widened. "You have seen Liethe!" she exclaimed.

"Yes," Shandiin admitted.

"Then you are doubly welcome," Tariah breathed, "for you have been given the highest of honors."

They arrived at the lovely white temple that was Liethe's, alighting on its steps and entering into a place illuminated by the purest light Shandiin had ever seen. Liethe's statue was not hidden below-ground, like Daimaine's, but stood at the entrance, just as tall, seemingly created from a single opal. She stood draped and veiled from head to toe, smiling down at the cat in her arms. She wore a blindfold. Shandiin looked up at that lovely smile and thought of Leah, and felt comforted.

Tariah's chambers were surprisingly small, and not all in white as Shandiin half expected. The High Tahmine shed her veil upon their entrance, and offered tea, and they settled into comfortable chairs together.

Then she immediately shocked Shandiin with her words. "I know the High King's power. But no matter how you feel, he must not turn away from the wedding at Starfall."

Shandiin stared, confused.

Tariah tilted her head. "Haven't you seen how he looks at you? Can you truly tell me you haven't fallen in love with him?"

Shandiin very carefully replaced her teacup in its saucer, set it on the table between them. "Your Highness..."

"That title is reserved for the High King. I am generally called Mother, but I prefer Tariah. You seem at a loss for words, Shandiin."

"I guess I am. What the hell are you talking about? I can definitely tell you I am not in love with anyone, and that includes Allasar!"

"I see. Forgive me, then, for my assumption. Your immunity to magic must include his."

"He has magic?"

Now Tariah set her cup aside. "He does. It particularly affects women."

Shandiin frowned, recalling Daimaine's words, all those centuries ago. "Daimaine wanted the Kings to be worshipped, but Khalen rejected that. So she gifted them instead with charisma and respect in place of worship. I believe that's where their authoritative presence comes from. But are you telling me that gift causes some people to fall in love with them?"

When Tariah didn't meet her eyes, Shandiin sighed in understanding. "I am immune, but it seems you are not."

"I am not, no. I fell in love with him fifty years ago, the first time I saw him. Of course he doesn't know, for it is unseemly of me."

Shandiin looked at Tariah's lowered head, and thought: *Oh, he knows all right, but he will let you keep your dignity while he unwillingly holds your heart.*

Yet another curse for the High Kings.

Shandiin moved away from that the subject. "So...he is to marry at Starfall."

Tariah looked up, then, composure regained. "Yes. Phaelon chose his bride upon her birth, the Princess of the Dominion of Alaura. The High Tahmond and I will conduct their wedding at Starfall, in Daimaine's Temple. She will be High Queen, and mother of the seventh High King. I believe that is the King that you will be called to defend, Shandiin, for he is the one to save us from the horror of the Prophecy War."

"And why would he need a defender?"

"That I cannot say. And my concern is more immediate." The Tahmine met her eyes meaningfully. "Allasar looks at you, Shandiin, and I see his love already, though you are just arrived. I fear you are a danger to his marriage."

Shandiin sat back. "I'm sure you must be wrong, Tariah."

"Are you?" There was challenge in those lovely eyes. "Ignorance is not wise, Shandiin, unless it is purposeful."

Shandiin blinked. "Okay. I gotcha." At the Tahmine's puzzled expression, she shook her head. "Sorry, thinking out loud. Well, I plan to do some traveling, so I won't be seeing much of Allasar before the wedding." *Why are those handsome green-eyed men always crushing on me?* She wondered. *Even Khalen, according to Egypt way back when. But he never let on.*

Tariah smiled. "I wish you safety in your journeys."

CHAPTER 15

Azlatan was a large realm, many of its Dominions heavily populated, but less so as The Chaine and her people traveled farther from Cabre. Word of their coming preceded her in every town they visited. Interest was mostly in the weapons of Chaine gold, and those were snapped up in the barter system quickly established, trading for goods the Chaine could use but not make themselves, such as the silk that came from the warmer southern Dominions.

The horses she had brought went to some chosen Dominion Kings as a gift from the High King, who sent with them some of Penumbra's black-clad Guard to recruit soldiers for the expanding forces that had traditionally served only Cabre. Shandiin saw some curiosity about this, as there had never been a central army in Azlatan, or a need for one; the High King's rule was, after all, undisputed. She learned, however, that the second High King had set down a law that each Dominion was required to have a standing military, whose warriors were trained in horsemanship, swordsmanship, archery, and hand-to-hand combat. These skills were generally used in competitions between Dominions rather than actual warfare.

She blessed Khandor's foresight, knowing he had realized military skills would be needed when the Prophecy War came to pass. However, Shandiin found that while the prophecy was known about, fear of it had faded with the centuries. Few paid any attention to it. Those that did were sure nothing could happen until the year 1000, and that was a long way...they thought...from the current year 965.

She knew better on all counts. Years always passed more quickly than people thought they would, and the count had begun when Phaelon announced his Law of Order, five years before Khandor arrived in Azlatan...their calendar's year 1. She thought the prophesied rising of the Duine against the Rioch would come to be in the year 995, only thirty years away.

The people were generally peaceful and complacent, although she saw fire in a younger generation that wanted to learn the more expert skills of the Chaine, skills that quickly became renowned as her people conquered every scheduled competition...and every challenge for a rematch that immediately followed. Word that Chaine skills would be taught to Cabre's Guards brought Allasar many new recruits, as she had planned.

The fact that the Chaine warriors included women as well as men was also intriguing to the populace, as Azlatan was...in Shandiin's opinion, at least...a misogynistic society. She even saw the separation of roles between Rioch and Duine as reflecting some of Earth's histories. The Duine served as good 'wives,' she thought privately, to the proverbial 'husband' Rioch.

Without the sex, of course. Phaelon had seen to that.

When Shandiin deigned to compete herself, she was never defeated in archery, in swordsmanship, in horsemanship...or in hand-to-hand combat. She smirkingly recognized that caused women of the Rioch to look at things a little differently.

But underlying all of Azlatan's fascination with these strange immigrants was the perception of their cultural difference. Chaine culture was anarchistic, based on cooperation instead of authority, and on personal honor rather than fear of or orders by any ruling deity. The Chaine people did not marry; they found personal relationships to be just that, not a bond ratified by an outside agency. Their creed was reason and accountability. They were seen as stoic and apparently unemotional.

These things, and fascinated speculation, led to rumor that they had no word for love, and so were soulless.

Shandiin and her people did nothing to change this widespread opinion. They had come to Azlatan at the behest of their leader, who had warned them of the differences they would find, and the fact that they would be changing Azlatan not for philosophical purposes, but in anticipation of a war that could destroy at least half of these blameless people.

When she was summoned back to Cabre, however, it was not due to war, but economics. Many of Azlatan's Guilds felt they were being undermined by the Chaine's new enterprises. Some had gone to their Dominion Kings, who...out of uncertainty...referred their concerns to the ultimate judge: the High King.

So Shandiin returned to Cabre after three years away, to find changes there since her absence. There was a new High Tahmond, and a new High Queen.

And a High King she thought sadly changed. He had lost his easy demeanor, and carried an unease she couldn't quite identify.

The Guilds were disappointed with his dismissal of their concerns, though he had listened carefully before his ruling. "Competition," he told them, "should be a healthy thing, making you improve your products or sell your labors in ways that benefit the people as well as yourselves. Perhaps you should take note of how and what the Chaine are doing that you could emulate or make better, instead of wasting your time and mine with complaints."

She was a little surprised at his bluntness, seeing that it openly angered those who were not simply chagrined at being reprimanded by the High King. After the ruling, he asked her to join him for a talk in his private library. There she spoke frankly as he handed her a cup of wine and they settled into chairs in front of the fireplace.

"Don't you think you were a little harsh?" she asked him.

"Do you think so?"

"The part about wasting your time was a surprise. I've heard nothing but good about the High Kings, your fairness, your patience."

"None of that means I shouldn't be decisive."

"I also hear there's a new High Tahmond. Did he weigh in on any of the issues today?"

"He did. He's not as unconcerned about your people as the last one, and told me flatly he thinks you are a destabilizing influence, and I shouldn't have supported your immigration."

"Hm. Immigration instead of invasion sounds like an improvement."

"No. It's just a more political way of saying the same thing. He's very intelligent, and that concerns me, as it makes him more believable in his pronouncements."

"Is he the real reason you called me back to Cabre, Allasar? Because it's obvious to me you didn't need me here while you made your decision about the Guilds. Now you've dismissed your Duine, and I see you have that very heavy door guarded from interruption. What is truly bothering you?"

He was quiet for a minute, looking into his wine as though there were a message there. "I figured out part of what Khandor meant," he said.

"Don't you dare say anything about your heart."

"But that's what it's about. I didn't guard it well enough, Shandiin." He was silent for a long moment, then looked up at her. "It's not about you. I have loved you since the day you walked out of the sea, but I am wise enough to know that had to be set aside like hidden treasure. I have always believed I was wise about matters of the heart." He sighed, and ran a hand through his long black hair. "I don't know how this happened. I couldn't tell anyone this, but you...you understand our bloodline is different. I don't know exactly how or why, but you see us, and you understand us. No one else does that. No one, Shandiin. I don't think even my beloved understands, or else..." his voice broke, and he looked away. "Or else none of this could be happening."

She waited for him to go on, but when he didn't, she asked gently, "What is happening, Allasar?"

"I don't even know how to explain it. I shouldn't try. I shouldn't tell you this, not even you, but then I shouldn't feel this, either. I've never..." his voice broke.

He carefully set his cup aside, got up, and went to the fireplace. He braced his hands on the mantel, looking up at the painting of his father that hung above. "He walked into the sea," he said. "I can't do that, because I don't yet have a son to take responsibility for my people. I have to go on, but I don't know how to face what I have done. I don't know what to do."

There were warning bells in her brain, and she felt a chill. "What, exactly, have you done, Allasar?"

"I've fallen in love." He turned, and looked at her, and she saw such pain her own heart squeezed in sympathy. "I've fallen in love with my wife, and her bonded Duine. And they are both with child."

His words seemed to echo in her head, and her chill turned to ice.

Phaelon's Law, she thought.

And she repeated it aloud, for both of them to remember.

"The Rioch and the Duine shall not lie together. If this Law is broken, the Forbidden Child and both parents must die. This shall be enforced without exception by the Duine Anzihi, whose identity will be known only to me."

She was silent for a moment, watching Allasar lower his head before the portrait of his father.

He knew as well as she did that a Forbidden Child heralded the Prophecy War.

She thought, *I never for a moment thought that a High King could be the father of the Forbidden Child. But here we are, and my heart breaks for him, because his very nature is in ruins, and the women he loves do not, cannot understand just how impossible this is for him, how devastated he must be. What was it Khandor said? "We have standards that may make no sense except as idealistically moral role models for our people...but that's not the reason those standards exist. Those standards ensure that our purpose cannot be corrupted. And our purpose owns us."*

He is trapped in an engineered cage alloyed by magic, and now it is crushing him.

She yanked back her emotions, a little surprised at herself, and set out to approach the problem with the logic she had trained into her own people. She asked, "Has it ever happened before, that Rioch and Duine have had a child?"

"It's happened."

"And then what?"

"In every known case, the Duine Anzihi...Phaelon's enforcers...they have killed them all. Father, mother, and child."

She closed her eyes briefly. "Phaelon's enforcers? Where do they come from...who are they?"

"No one knows who the Anzihi are. They must have magic, because the deaths occur, but no one is witness, and no one has ever seen them. Historically there is no escape, and they can find their quarry anywhere."

"How do they find out if a woman is pregnant in violation of Phaelon's law?"

"No one knows that either."

She looked up at him. "You said the enforcers have killed everyone in all known cases. Is it possible that some have happened, but never discovered?"

He frowned. "I suppose that's possible, but...well, of course I've not heard of it. If no one ever found out, I wouldn't know either, would I?"

"Does your wife...do both women know about the other?"

She was shaken when he laughed, because it sounded a little insane. His emerald eyes gleamed with unshed tears. "Oh, they know. They came to me together. My wife...my beloved, beautiful Queen Rhiathe...she knew I was attracted to Mia. Her Duine, Mia. She had guessed it, though I had hidden my shame, and certainly never meant to act on it. But Rhiathe learned Mia had fallen in love with me. She was determined that I should love both of them. They came to me together, and I..." he trailed off, shook his head.

"They seduced you? They purposely seduced you!"

"How can I blame them for my own weakness? I love them. I love them both, as wrong as it is. I want to protect Mia. I wouldn't care for myself, but Azlatan...my people need their King. I have assured my own destruction, Shandiin, and I am...I am lost."

She rose and went to him, looked up into those beautiful, tormented eyes. "You are *not* alone," she told him fiercely. "We'll face this together, Allasar. It's why I'm here, remember? I am the King's Defender."

The High Queen of Azlatan waited in the front room of the chambers she shared with her husband, located atop the westernmost tower of Penumbra. Deep rugs covered the floor, and art and weapons were displayed on the stone walls. There was a mammoth fireplace burning at one end of the room, and great fur-covered chairs grouped to face it.

Rhiathe rose from one of the chairs as her husband entered, holding the door for the tall woman in armored leather who followed him. The Queen saw a powerful female warrior with a sword at her hip, shaggy hair spilling like wildfire over her bare and sculpted shoulders, and eyes like bright, hard steel.

Rhiathe was nearly as tall as Shandiin, and every curvaceous inch was regal. Her eyes were deep moss-green, so dark they were almost as black as the gown she wore. Her hair was the color of good rich earth, and fell in heavy waves to her waist. She was beautiful, as beautiful as the High King was handsome, and that simple fact gave Shandiin a shock.

Allasar went to his wife immediately, leaning down to kiss her in greeting. Rhiathe looked up at him with such love it was almost a physical presence in the room. She then turned to Shandiin with a smile undisturbed by that warrior's piercing gaze. "Welcome to you. I have heard so much about The Chaine, yet you are even more than I had imagined. Please, come and sit by the fire."

Shandiin busily adjusted her expectations to the reality. Magically beautiful, obviously in love, and unintimidated...which was the most surprising thing of all, for Shandiin was and had intended to be intimidating. She glanced at Allasar, who held his wife's hand protectively, and sighed. "Sure. I'll sit. I am Shandiin. Do I call you Your Highness?"

"Only if you want to," Rhiathe smiled. "Please..." she gestured, and Shandiin walked to the fireplace and dropped into one of the big chairs.

Rhiathe turned back to Allasar with a look of concern. "Do you want to stay?" she asked him. "You must know I will say nothing to her that I would not say to you."

He took a deep breath, looking from her to Shandiin, who sat back and tapped the arms of her chair while she scowled. "I think Shandiin wants to talk to you alone. Since we need her help, I'd like to accede to her wishes."

Shandiin frowned at the term 'we,' watched as Allasar left them and Rhiathe settled into the chair across from her.

The beautiful High Queen studied her for a moment, and then addressed her with surprising insight. "You are angry. I can understand why. This is very hard on Allasar, and he says you are his friend." She angled her head. "More than friend, I think, but not as a woman to a man."

"You would be right about that. All of that. Where is your Duine?"

"Mia is in the next room, behind a closed door. I wanted to see you first."

"*You* wanted to see *me*?"

"I guess he didn't tell you that part." Rhiathe sighed. "He's been forgetful, very unlike himself."

"I think you know why."

"Yes. He is a good man, torn with guilt over a simple thing like love."

"Bullshit."

Rhiathe's perfect eyebrows climbed in question, and Shandiin leaned forward in her chair. "None of this is simple," she snapped. "He's far more than just a good man, and he is more than torn with guilt. His very foundation is gone. He does not *do* this. *How the hell did you make him?*"

"I made him do nothing," Rhiathe responded calmly. "I only told him truth, and he recognized it. I love him. I love him beyond words, my lady Chaine, and he loves me. But so does my Mia, and she is like a sister to me. She has been my sister since I was born. She admitted her love for the High King, and told me she had to leave me, to return to what had been our home, for she believed her love to be an evil thing. I disagree that love is ever evil. I did not want her to leave me, and I could not bear her misery or his, so I simply put two people together who needed each other."

Shandiin stared for a long moment, then sat back.

She recognized truth. She had expected a villain, but found instead an unselfish spirit. It was also apparent that the Queen didn't really know her husband as well as she thought, if she just saw him as being torn by guilt. Shandiin knew the destruction to Allasar's spirit went deeper than that.

Well, Shandiin thought, *I think I am the only one in this world who understands his bloodline. I guess that's why I'm his Defender now.*

"You don't believe in Phaelon's Law of Order?" she asked.

"Mia is my sister," Rhiathe said again. "She is not a servant, though she must pretend to be when we are among those who believe otherwise. I not only do not believe in Phaelon's Law, I despise it."

Shandiin's eyes narrowed. "Do you despise it enough to rebel against it—perhaps to destroy it?"

"You are speaking of the Prophecy War. A Forbidden Child may bring death to all called Rioch."

"Yes. Was it your intent that this Forbidden Child be fathered by the High King?"

Rhiathe's eyes brightened with sudden tears. "I would cut out my own heart, if it could only be otherwise. I fear it will be the death of him, my lady, which is why I asked him to speak to you openly. We need your help." When Shandiin only scowled at her, she lifted both hands as though in pleading, and continued. "I went to the High Tahmine and told her of our plight, and she told me to call on you, because Liethe has said you are the King's Defender."

"Good God almighty," Shandiin muttered, still scowling. "What about your Mia, Highness? I hear the Duine Anzihi kill both parents. And if they determine you are involved, you're in danger as well."

Rhiathe's hands swept that away. "I am not a part of this. I will die with the birth of my son, and my story ends at that moment. My concern is for Allasar and Mia."

"What makes you think you will die?"

"She knows things," came a soft voice from behind her, and she and Rhiathe both looked up to see the slim blonde woman walking in, wearing a simple blue gown that matched her eyes, and a flush of pink in her cheeks when Shandiin's gaze fastened on her. "I couldn't wait and wonder any longer. I'm sorry, Rhiathe." She went to sit on the arm of Rhiathe's chair, and the Queen took her hand reassuringly. "I am Mia," the blonde introduced herself to Shandiin.

"I managed to sniff that out. What do you mean she knows things?"

"Rhiathe has always known things. When we went to Ord-hold with the High King, she told the Dominion King that his new wife was already pregnant, and he would have a son. She was right. Rhiathe is always right." She looked at the woman who called her sister with great sadness. "She says she will die in childbirth, and I believe her."

"What we both hope," Rhiathe put in, "is that Mia will be able to help Allasar through the loss. She has to be able to stay here, in

Penumbra, after I am gone. Allasar is already grieving. I...there's nothing I can do to help him."

At that Shandiin had to get up, and began to pace. "Does Mia have a steady boyfriend?" she asked. "When she starts to show, tongues will wag. Hell, they'll flap at both ends."

"There's no one." Mia spoke just as Rhiathe looked toward the chamber door. A second later it opened, and Allasar came in.

He went directly to Mia, and Shandiin watched the High King kiss his wife's servant while his wife watched, smiling. He turned to Shandiin. "I had to come back. I need to know if you have any idea what to do."

Shandiin stood with crossed arms. "I do, but you won't like it. Mia can't stay in Penumbra. I'm sure someone else has the same gift as Rhiathe, and can tell when a woman is pregnant before she shows. That must be how they find out. Every second Mia stays here is inviting the Duine Anzihi."

Allasar put a protective hand on Mia's shoulder. "I won't just send her away. They could find her anyway, and she would be without my protection."

"Dammit, Allasar. If she's here, they'll connect it to you. Would she be in danger if the father were Duine?"

"No. Generally, only matters that involve racial boundaries are subject to Phaelon's Law instead of mine. But maybe their magic lets them know." He looked at Mia, stroked her hair. "I have to keep her safe. But...I don't know how."

Shandiin shook her head. He wasn't even thinking straight at this point, he with the greatest mind on the planet. "There's only one answer, Allasar. Mia has to go to the High Tahmine, who already knows about this, since she sent Rhiathe to me. And she has to go now." She held up a hand before he could object. "That's not sending her away. It's putting her in protective custody."

At his confused expression, she dropped both hands to her hips, sighed, rephrased. "Allasar, the High Tahmine will take care of her, especially if you ask her to. I have no doubt of that. I think Mia will be safe from suspicion when she is in the Temple, under the High Tahmine's protection. You and Rhiathe can even visit her there."

"What about the child?" Mia asked.

"We'll have to ask the Tahmine's help on that, too." She crossed her arms again. "But you must know you can't keep the child. Apparently Phaelon's enforcers nose out things of this nature."

Mia looked up at the High King, and he simply pulled her from the chair into his arms. "I am so sorry," he murmured, gathering her against his chest.

She curved her hand against his cheek. "It's what must be."

Rhiathe was already thinking along practical lines. "Should we say Mia is sick or something? How will we explain her absence from Penumbra?"

Shandiin huffed. "We have to be more devious than that." She met Allasar's gaze. "It has to be something they won't question, and it has to be something the High King won't have to lie about, since he won't. Or can't. Whatever the hell. You're all going to have to let me handle this, and that's going to require your trust."

Allasar still had his arms around Mia. He looked at Shandiin, nodded. "As Khandor advised, then. I will trust you."

Shandiin looked from one woman to the other, saw their acquiescence. "Say your goodbyes, Mia, and come out to meet me when you are ready."

Without a backward glance, Shandiin walked out and closed the door behind her. Then she just waited on the landing at the top of the very steep tower stairs. Her mind was spinning.

What am I doing? By helping them, am I initiating the prophecy of the Forbidden Child? Is this right or wrong? Does it even make any difference, since the Prophecy War will happen no matter what I do? And...what I am going to propose is dangerous, if Mia will even agree to it. She could die. Crap. It all comes back to the damned prophecy, doesn't it? If she dies, that's the end of it, except Allasar will stop trusting me or worse. If she doesn't...well, then, it's destiny, is it? So much for free will. Except...it will be her choice to make.

Two things she was sure of. First, Phaelon's Duine Anzihi would destroy Allasar and Mia and the unborn child if she didn't help. Second...she couldn't allow that to happen.

She believed Allasar's love for Mia was real, no matter how wrong he thought it made him. What she was going to ask of Mia would test her love as well. It would also test her courage.

Mia came out, closing the door quietly behind her, and listened while Shandiin told her what she thought had to be done.

Both love and courage were proven when she understood and agreed to Shandiin's plan that would take her without question to Liethe's Temple and its healers.

Shandiin pushed her down the very high tower stairs.

CHAPTER 16

S handiin had a dream the night Rhiathe gave birth to the seventh High King of Azlatan.

She dreamed she was standing atop a mountain. She recognized it as the northernmost tip of the continent, because the Chaine had passed here long ago, on their overland journey to the western sea. There was always snow in this high place, so the world spread white until it met the edge of the night sky, where the arc of Hiraeth's home galaxy sparkled from horizon to horizon. The nearest stars blazed like beacons.

She turned in a circle, gazing up at that cathedral sky, until it suddenly flashed white.

Her dark stranger appeared beside her as the white light faded. The stars were so brilliant their light iced everything, including him, shining light through his black hair, firing the emerald of his eyes. Once again she stood looking into those dazzling eyes, and once again she saw that unaccountable warmth.

But also sadness. "I cannot come to you again," he said. "The path before you is your own. I can only tell you that I am sorry, for it will be hard and lonely."

"My path has been hard and lonely for a thousand years. I hoped you might finally come to me in this reality, so I wouldn't be walking it alone."

He smiled, and she felt his warmth through his sadness. "I know, and I am sorry, but even though you couldn't know it I've been behind you, Shandiin, every step of the way..." the smile faded, "until now. Now I must step aside for the seventh High King of Azlatan. He is here, and he needs you. You must be his defender and his mentor. You must teach him to be what none of his ancestors have been: a hard-hearted and skeptical King, a warrior, even a killer. The fate of many things depends on it."

"Must I?" she asked, and at her dark stranger's nod, she thought of the true and benevolent spirits of the green-eyed Kings, and felt a great sorrow. "Then I will do what I must."

"I know you will. I know your strength, Shandiin. But listen well. You cannot let him love you. You cannot bind him to you in any way. You are not his mission here. You must guide him to his destiny, and leave him there. He has to meet his fate without you." He hesitated. "And...Shandiin...guard well your own heart, to keep it whole."

She felt like stomping her foot. "Why? Why is that heart guarding thing so important to all the High Kings, and now to you?"

He studied her. "You truly don't know, do you? But some part of you is aware, for you've kept yours guarded all your life. Love can be deadly dangerous, Shandiin, for it is the most powerful thing in the universe. You have to stay strong. He needs your strength and your courage, but you cannot give him your love. Do not let your love bond him to you, for the sake of his world."

He began to fade, but lifted a hand as though he wanted to touch her face. "I am so sorry," he said again, and dropped the hand after all, turning as though to leave.

"Who are you?" she cried. "Will I ever know?"

He looked back over his shoulder, and she tried to memorize his face against that sky, his midnight hair blowing around his face, the stars like his crown. She thought she would never forget his beauty, or the love he...inexplicably...still held in his eyes.

He didn't answer, and then he was gone.

She woke thinking: *Love can be deadly dangerous.*

Well, it almost had been, hadn't it? But High King Allasar lived yet.

Mia's injuries had been severe, but not mortal. The High Tahmine had told them gravely that the child she'd started had died in the fall, and Mia grieved for it, so remained in the Temple to heal both body and spirit.

The Duine Anzihi had not made an appearance.

Allasar was distant, devastated by Mia's injuries, suspicious of Shandiin's part in her accident...but it was himself he would not forgive. Shandiin was sure he would never forgive himself for any of it, and the changes in him as time passed often brought her near to tears, for he did not deserve the pain she frequently glimpsed.

Rhiathe suspected the truth, she knew, but she had shown no rancor toward Shandiin.

In fact, she and Rhiathe had become friends. It began because they were both concerned for Allasar, who became withdrawn even while his Queen grew great with child and Azlatan celebrated the coming of another High King. Rhiathe's prediction of her own death haunted him, and Rhiathe had asked Shandiin to remain in Penumbra.

"He'll need you," she told Shandiin. "Mia won't come back. She told me she regrets...not her love, but her pregnancy, because it could have caused Allasar's death. I begged her to help him through this as we originally planned. I even asked her to be the one to take care of my son, but she refuses that too."

"She lost her own child, Rhiathe. I can understand why she won't take yours."

"Yes." Rhiathe rubbed her very pregnant stomach absently. "I know. But my son will need a mother."

"Don't look at me." Shandiin held up her hands, palms out. "I am definitely not the mother type. I'll talk to the High Tahmine, see if she has someone else who can foster your child."

But no one had come forward, until the night Shandiin woke up with the knowledge the child was born because a vision had told her so.

She had been staying in Mia's old room at Rhiathe's request. She stepped from there to the door of the royal chambers, and knocked softly.

"Come in," said a woman's voice, and she found the High Tahmine herself in her opalescent robes, a baby carefully wrapped in her arms.

"Rhiathe?" Shandiin asked her, knowing the worst.

"She has passed on." Tariah's voice was sad. "And Allasar has already asked for you. But first..." Tariah turned with the infant, showing him to Shandiin, who was startled to see those precocious emerald eyes in a tiny face under a shock of black hair. "Meet High Prince Khedran, who will be the seventh High King of Azlatan."

The emerald eyes looked directly into her own, completely aware.

She was flooded with the uncanny and terrifying sensation that there was something she should know, something she should remember, something from the past and the future at once. She felt a chill like she had never known, even in her first contact with an unbelievable sentient planet.

Stunned to her core, Shandiin stepped back.

She fought for equilibrium, finally won. "I thought newborn babies didn't see well," she managed.

Tariah was watching her curiously. "I believe this one sees everything."

"Have you found a foster mother for him?"

"I have decided that role will be mine, as I just promised his dying mother. Come, Shandiin."

She followed the High Tahmine into the bedroom, grimacing when she saw Allasar sitting in a chair beside his Queen's deathbed, his head in his hands. She stepped to the bed and looked sadly at Rhiathe, then gently dropped a hand onto the King's shoulder.

He looked up at her, and she saw his eyes had dulled to jade. Then he stood and held out his arms to take his son from Tariah.

To Shandiin's shock, he immediately offered him to her.

"Um," she said, backing up.

"Take him. I want to tell you something." Allasar's voice was thick with tears.

She swallowed, then took the baby carefully.

As soon as she did, she saw the light. It shimmered through the tiny form she held, a spirit brighter than sun or moon or truth.

She almost cried out in denial of the promise she had made. She would tarnish, darken, even ruin this bright spirit...because she had to teach him to be what none of his ancestors had been: a hard-hearted and skeptical King, a warrior, even a killer.

It was apparent she was the only one experiencing the strange vision. As it faded, she lifted her eyes to Allasar, fighting tears, knowing her lips were trembling.

"You have been my defender," Allasar told her. "Even when I didn't properly appreciate you for it. For that I thank you. But now I ask you to be his. I ask you to be his defender, his mentor." His eyes pleaded. "And I don't want him to be alone."

Shandiin swallowed. "He won't be. He will have a Queen, chosen by Phaelon, as Rhiathe was chosen for you. As we already agreed, I will send one of my people to be defender to his betrothed until they are married."

He sighed. "All that is very well. But I said what I meant. I don't want him to be alone. I know what Khandor meant when he said 'She will make you not alone.' You have an understanding, a kinship with my bloodline, something we have with no one else...not even our Queen. I want that for him. And I want you to teach him your wisdom and your ways, because he will face a world Azlatan has never seen before. The High Tahmine will be his mother, at least until he reaches a certain age..."

"And forever after, when and if he ever needs me," Tariah put in.

He nodded thanks. "But he needs you, Shandiin."

She looked down and saw the child was sleeping, his black lashes soft against his cheeks. "He needs all three of us. You will teach him, Allasar, how to be a High King, a skilled leader as true and noble as you. Both you and Tariah will give him the unconditional love he deserves. I will protect him until he no longer needs my protection. And I...I will teach him the hard things of the world."

Allasar placed his hand over hers as she cradled his sleeping son. "I must have your oath...realizing, Shandiin, that I put his safety above my own, and mean for him to be your priority above all others...including myself."

She looked up into his grieving eyes, still fighting the battle with unfamiliar tears. "You have my promise, Allasar."

She gave the sleeping infant to the High Tahmine and left abruptly for her room.

There she closed the door, put her back against it, and slid to the floor. She put her face in her hands, and for the first time since her Verity had died more than a thousand years before, she grieved from the deepest part of her being.

And wept, for a very long time.

When finally there were no more tears, when she could breathe again, she closed her swollen eyes and sought a way to make peace with herself. When she opened them, she saw the sky through the window in the opposite wall, and watched the constellation called The Bridle turn red, bleeding its light onto the world.

She knew then the time of prophecy had begun, and would end with the Prophecy War. She knew with certainty that even as the brightest spirit had come into the world, so had the one who would be called the Forbidden Child.

She lied to me, she thought. *The High Tahmine lied. Mia did not lose her child. He is here, and he is Khedran's brother.*

Her intent since coming to Hiraeth was to free humanity from its gods. But this was more. Now she had pledged to be more than a defender to a King. She had to deform a pure spirit, an empath, into a hard-hearted and skeptical King, a warrior, even a killer. To do that, it seemed, she had to be cruel and heartless to a child. Worse, she had to teach him to be cruel and heartless.

To be able to kill his own brother, to save his people.

That was worse than killing him. That was distorting him into something he was never meant to be.

She couldn't do it. There had to be a way to accomplish her objective, to help him save his people, without destroying that bright spirit. She had to walk a tightrope from this day forward, but she would find a way.

Guard your heart, the dark stranger had told her.

But it was already in shreds.

CHAPTER 17

"I think he deserves a day off," Allasar said without looking up from the work on his desk. "The boy is exhausted by the end of the day as it is."

Shandiin was leaning in the doorway with her arms crossed. "Right. Like you didn't drag him on a learning mission through your seventy-seven Dominions before he was twelve, and have him sitting Council at thirteen. You've never been protective of him before, Allasar. What's the big deal with him turning sixteen?"

The High King finally leaned back, looking up at her with some irritation. "You know a lot about my bloodline, but not everything, and I do not believe it necessary to share everything. Just give him a day to rest, Shandiin."

"If I tell him I'm not going to train and he has a free day? The first thing he'll do is head for the stables. He won't rest, and he needs to work on combat."

"He is not a Chaine, nor a Guardsman. He doesn't need..." Allasar stopped midsentence when his son stepped into the doorway next to Shandiin.

"May I speak, Father?" Khedran asked.

Allasar all but rolled his eyes. Shandiin just waited, eying the lanky boy in black, his thick black hair disheveled, his boots covered in mud. There was lately something familiar about him, and she realized the older he got the more he looked like his beautiful lost mother.

Khedran was already as tall as Shandiin, and his voice had changed. But while he was still a boy, he had never seemed young to her. Sarnath would have said he had an old soul.

Another beautiful green-eyed boy, she thought, *with the mind of a sage.*

"Judging by your disagreeable appearance, you've been working with the horses," Allasar accused. "I thought you were going to stay in this morning."

"My apologies if I misunderstood a command, Father."

Allasar looked at him wryly. "You know very well it wasn't a command. It was a suggestion, and I should have known better. What did you want to speak about, Khedran?"

"I overheard you saying I might have a free day. I wanted to request that I have my regular combat training."

"Why?" Allasar demanded.

"Because," Khedran threw Shandiin an oblique glance, "one of these days I am going to take her down and sit on her."

Shandiin grinned. "You still haven't forgiven me for that, have you? Well, you have to beat Roinn first. You won't have a chance against me if you can't take him."

"And I'll do neither if I don't practice." He looked back at his father, and for a moment they locked eyes, King and Prince. "It's all right," Khedran added very quietly. "You need have no concern for me, Father."

Allasar studied his son, nodded. "Then do as you will."

Curious, Shandiin looked from one to the other, but neither said more. She raised her eyebrows, then straightened preparatory to leaving. Stopped. "Did I see the High Tahmond in here earlier?"

Allasar sighed. "You did. He is concerned because I am allowing you to teach the High Prince your Chaine ways. He thinks that it is inappropriate."

"And your response?"

"That your training has my full approval."

"Which 'Chaine way' was he concerned about, exactly?"

"I'm pretty sure he's just against critical thinking in general. But he made specific reference to the term 'amhara' which I have never completely understood."

Shandiin looked at Khedran. "Can you explain it to him?"

Khedran nodded thoughtfully. "It's the Chaine word combining 'love' and 'respect.' It has two meanings. In the first, it describes a relationship between people. Respect is possible without love, but love without respect is not. Love with respect is *amhara.* In the second meaning, it is a word of requirement relating to everything, and includes a note of gratitude."

"Everything?" Allasar asked.

Khedran smiled. "Yes. I feel *amhara* for our people, and also for the world that supports our people."

"And mainly," Shandiin added dryly, "you feel *amhara* for the horses you can't stay away from."

His smile turned into an open grin, and his long emerald eyes sparkled. "Not mainly, but it's pretty strong. Shall we go to the courtyard? I saw Roinn waiting."

"Yes. Go ahead, I'll be along."

When he was out of earshot she asked, "Did I also see Mia here earlier?"

"Yes."

When he said nothing more, she frowned. "Are you playing with fire again, Allasar?"

"Not at the moment," he said mildly. "Among other things, Mia came to tell me the High Tahmine has concerns about Khedran. Much the same as I have. He is at a very difficult age."

"I have the feeling there's more to it than that, but yeah. He's a teenage boy. What's he doing, chasing girls?"

She was surprised when Allasar looked up sharply. "He is of the bloodline. He would not."

"I see a touch of anger, there, Your Highness. What does your bloodline do, then, when your sexuality comes to call? Sixteen is a difficult age, all right."

"It's really none of your business, Shandiin."

"I see." She frowned. When he remained silent, she huffed. "Be careful with Mia. That's none of my business either, but you've made it clear Khedran is, and anything you do will impact him."

With that she followed Khedran to the courtyard, speaking briefly to Allasar's Duine, Canon, as she left.

Penumbra's courtyard was central to its four corner towers, and open to the sky. It had once been a garden area, but was now a place for training with sword, with bow, and—as Chaine ways combined martial arts with street brawling—any combat requiring skill, strength and wit. Shandiin walked in to see Roinn and Khedran circling each other with an audience of other trainees, new recruits for the Cabre Guard.

Plus one Duine, the son of Allasar's Canon. Camion was Khedran's bonded Duine, and being much older, he took his role very seriously. Shandiin went to the bench where he sat and joined him. "Hello, Camion."

He glanced briefly at The Chaine. "Hello." He was polite but cool.

"Are you here in case he gets injured?"

"Of course." Camion's eyes were glued to the High Prince.

"You know he hates that, Camion. He's no longer a child to be coddled."

"He is the High Prince. He shouldn't even be touched without permission, much less pounded on by people."

"Is that what Canon has taught you?"

Camion turned his head, looked directly into her eyes. "Yes. It is what has been true for all of Azlatan's history. There are rules surrounding the High King, and these should apply as well to his son."

"I would think that you'd have accepted by now that Khedran's intent is to be different. He wants to be able to defend himself and his people."

"Why would defense be necessary? Who would dare to attack him, now or when he is King? And as for his people...Phaelon's magic wards guard our borders. No enemies can enter."

She didn't tell him the border wards had disappeared the night Khedran and his forbidden brother were born. It was the High King's choice whether to make that public, not hers.

She sighed. "Camion, I think your concern is about more than Khedran having combat training. We should get that settled, you and I."

He visibly steeled himself for confrontation. "It is I who should guard his door at night. Just as my father guards his Rioch's."

"That's what I thought this was about. Camion, what would either of you do if someone entered to do harm to the High King or the Prince?"

"We would defend them with our lives."

"A noble cause," she said drily, "to die on their behalf. But that wouldn't help your Highnesses, would it? Because you would be dead, and the intruder still alive. Because you have no training in fighting or killing, and would surely be unable to stop someone who does."

"Tradition." But his frown became thoughtful.

"Tradition wouldn't save them. This would." She pointed to where Khedran had just taken down Roinn.

Unfortunately, Roinn was up immediately, and Khedran went down with a thud that made the audience flinch in sympathy.

Camion was on his feet, but she gave him a gentle push back and strode onto the courtyard to stand over the High Prince with her hands on her hips.

He rolled onto his back, swiped blood from his face with his sleeve. "Almost had him," he said.

"Almost won't keep you alive." She tapped the toe of her boot against his ribs.

Quick as a cat, he swept her other boot from beneath her, toppling her on top of him.

And held her there, her face inches from his. His grin was bloody. "Got you."

"Do you?" She rammed her knee into his crotch.

She stood while he curled up, and saw that Camion had gone pale. She looked back down at her charge, who was biting back a groan.

"Remember that move, Khedran. I won't hold back next time."

When she looked up again, she saw Canon signaling her.

"Take care of the Prince," she told Roinn, and went to Allasar's Duine, who stepped behind a pillar, saying simply "The High Tahmond. He is back, and with the King."

She strode back to Allasar's office, Canon trailing.

"Where is she?" the High Tahmond was demanding.

"In Liethe's Temple, I presume." Allasar was leaning back in his chair, still at his desk while the High Tahmond stood. "She wasn't here long."

"She was Duine to your High Queen," the Tahmond rumbled. "What was she doing here now, after leaving Penumbra more than sixteen years past?"

"She was here to bring a message from the High Tahmine." Shandiin heard the uncharacteristic anger under Allasar's words.

Shandiin stepped in, stopped by the High Tahmond, looking down at him while he glared back from his lesser height.

"You do not belong here," he sniffed.

"Why not? I was invited. Were you invited?" she asked.

"Insolent vixen."

"Isn't that a female fox? I think they're cute."

"If you weren't immune to magic like the animal you are, I would bury you."

"You could try." She moved closer, invading his space, and watched the white marbles of his eyes bulge a little. "Without magic."

He stepped carefully away, turned back to the High King. "You continue to ignore my warnings," he told him. "You allow insolence against me in your presence. This behavior could be brought to High Council."

Allasar look bored. "I find that doubtful. I hardly think that impolite disagreements are worthy of Phaelon's attention. I believe we are quite done, Your Honor."

"For now." The Tahmond turned, black and white robes swinging, and marched out.

Canon peeked in. "Close the door," Allasar told him, and he did, staying outside.

"Did you talk to Canon about the High Tahmond?" he demanded of Shandiin.

"I did. I asked him to let me know if he was lurking about. He's watching you, Allasar, and I heard him asking about Mia. I want the truth without evasions now. Have you been seeing her?"

After a moment he stood up, walked around his desk, propped a hip on the edge and faced her where she stood with her arms crossed.

"I have. For sixteen years, Shandiin. The High Tahmine knows, for I go to her in Liethe's Temple."

Shandiin gritted her teeth. "You don't lie, but you sure know how to keep a secret. What was Mia doing here today?"

"Bringing word from the High Tahmine, as I said." He placed a hand over hers where she gripped her own arm so tightly. "And to tell me goodbye. The High Tahmine is sending her away. I am sorry, Shandiin, for not telling you before. You understand so much, but I don't think you know how much she means to me." He closed his eyes fleetingly. "Has meant to me."

"Why is the High Tahmine sending her away? To protect you from yourself?"

He dropped his hand, met her eyes. "Do you remember our plans, should anything happen to me before Khedran comes of age?"

Her stomach clenched. "Dammit, Allasar."

"Do you remember?" he repeated.

She shut her eyes briefly, yanked herself back to neutral. "You want me to take him to Ordhold."

"To King Randmar. Yes. Randmar is my closest ally, and answered my request long ago by offering his home and his protection. Further, you can depend on him to come to Cabre, with his forces, when Khedran reaches eighteen and comes back to take his rule as High King. For Khedran will need his forces, Shandiin, until he can cement his place, and build the army we have only begun. You know the High Tahmond has been steadily chipping away at me, at you. I don't believe he will stop at Khedran. I think it is his well-hidden intent to replace the High King with himself. If I could ask Daimaine, she might stop him, but..."

"You don't dare. I agree, you can't ask her. If the High Tahmond has Phaelon's ear, I don't think Daimaine could stand against him anyway. But Allasar...if you were gone...who would rule until Khedran's return?"

"By Khandor's Law, in the absence of the High King there would be joint rule between the High Tahmond and the High Tahmine."

She studied him for a long moment. "You seem very calm, especially for someone who just said goodbye to his lover."

He nodded. Stood up to face her. "I've lived for too long waiting for the other shoe to drop. I lost my wife, my Queen, and I'll love her forever. I am losing now the only other woman I have loved. Save one." He put a gentle hand on her cheek, and to her surprise he kissed her lips lightly. "I've loved you as well. For your strength, your loyalty to both me and my son. You promised, at his birth, to make him your priority. I remind you of that. I also ask that you not mourn me, should the worst come to pass. When the other shoe drops, perhaps Daimaine will allow me peace at last. My spirit has known no peace for twenty years, Shandiin. I am a weak man, and do not deserve to be King or father."

When she began to speak, he shook his head, touched her lips gently. "You can't make me feel differently, though I know you want to. I need to talk to Khedran now. Will you send him to me?"

Chapter 18

Ordhold was the northernmost and largest Dominion of Azlatan. It's southern boundary included the range of mountains separating it from the mainland of Azlatan, and it was not an easy journey from one to the other.

Shandiin led her companions between walls of stone from the last mountain pass, into the great valley at the Dominion's heart. They rode through the encircling forest to the valley's open floor. It was deep and wide, a fertile place where man and horse could thrive. Small cottages lined the pasture fences, and a narrow river wound through the verdant center.

The road was well-kept, easy on a horse's feet. They rode past gardens and lawns, an occasional chicken squawking out of their path. And always, behind the houses, sometimes alongside the road, there were pasture fences, for the horses of Ordhold were many and famous. Once a band of playful yearlings raced with them as they went by, until they were thwarted by the fence's end.

Shandiin turned in her saddle to watch Khedran, who had been silent for most of their journey. She saw he was watching the yearlings and was glad for him, that there was something joyful to see, if even only for a moment. The boy was entirely too smart, and Allasar's excuse that he wished to visit a Dominion King before he could join them rang false. Allasar did not lie, so his visit to a neighboring Dominion was a fact...but his goodbye had said more than his words.

She didn't think Allasar would be coming to Ordhold to join his son. She knew Khedran had sensed it, but she had refused to answer his questions. He'd grown very quiet then, and she saw a puzzled anger when he looked at her.

She was a hard teacher, and he had often been angry with her. But this was different.

Stables and small cabins sprawled around King Randmar's home, a castle walled and turreted, yet more homely than any other Dominion King's palace, for Randmar was a man of the land and the walls were green with living things. She knew Randmar fairly well, as she had traveled with Allasar and Khedran to this land before. He and his realm seemed untouched by the boundaries of Azlatan's rituals, pristine and uncomplicated. The folk of Ordhold were a different breed, who dealt with the harshest realities of nature as equals, and rarely turned to magic instead of their own minds and hands. Perhaps that was why they offered welcome to the people called Chaine, who dealt with magic not at all.

Randmar's support was the surest stone in Azlatan's foundation, cemented by a respect for Allasar that Randmar would never give to a lesser man. Shandiin secretly thought Randmar would have defied a High King unworthy of his rule. Such a thought approached heresy, for no Dominion King could claim separation from Penumbra. Allasar's son would have to pass a very high standard as well.

Knowing the son, Shandiin thought that standard would be well met.

They passed through the outer ramparts of the castle. Here were the stables for the King's favorites. Great trees embraced the roofs, and pale flowers grew in the glossy wall-ivy. A young man, scarcely older than the High Prince, stepped out to greet them.

"Welcome," said Prince Jon, Randmar's oldest son. "We only received word you were coming yesterday, but Father is very pleased that you've come to visit."

He spoke only to Khedran, so Shandiin sat quietly on her big paint horse and waited.

Khedran dismounted, trailing a hand over Shashata's great neck as he went to offer his hand to Jon in greeting. "Thank you." As was his habit, he spoke quietly. "Can we stable our horses here?"

"Of course." Jon looked at the big black stallion, and Shandiin saw puzzled recognition in his frown. "Isn't that Shashata...the High King's own horse?"

"Yes." Khedran offered no explanation. "The Chaine and I should see to our own mounts, as they are both capricious. I think the rest can be handled by your stablemaster."

Jon just nodded and led the way. Shandiin listened to the boys' voices fade as Khedran took Shashata to a box stall. She unsaddled her horse, taking a leather-wrapped object from her saddle and carefully placing it under the straw in the corner. No one would enter her horse's stall unless they wanted to be kicked or worse, but she stopped by Roinn and told him to keep an eye on him anyway, and to settle the rest of the Chaine...about ten of her people on this trip...in the cabins normally used for housing Randmar's soldiers during training exercises. She motioned Camion to join her and Khedran as they followed Prince Jon.

They emerged from the stables to cross a courtyard ringed by flowered walls and trees. A symphony of birdsong greeted them as Jon lead them toward a wide veranda where Randmar waited, standing to greet them as soon as they were in sight.

Shandiin thought Ordhold's King a handsome man, big and rugged as he was, with dark hair shot with grey, and fierce blue eyes under bushy brows. He went to Khedran first, started to offer his hand, then saw something in the boy's face that changed his mind. To her surprise he stepped in and wrapped his arms around the High Prince. "It's good to see you, Your Highness," he said as he stepped back from the hug. "I hope your father will soon be here as well."

"As do I." Khedran turned to smile at the younger, second Prince who waited beside his father. "Hello, Brend." They shook hands, and Jon led a girl...probably about Khedran and Jon's age, Shandiin thought... to meet him.

"This is Rani." Jon put his arm possessively around the pretty brown-haired girl. "She is my father's ward, as she lost her parents some time ago."

"Hello, Rani." Khedran gave her a soft smile. "I'm sorry for your loss."

"Thank you." She glanced into Khedran's handsome face only briefly, then at Jon. "We should tell them they can serve breakfast." She ducked under Jon's arm toward the castle entrance. Jon began introducing Khedran to several other teenagers who stood about looking awestruck.

Randmar turned to Shandiin with a friendly grin. "And here is The Chaine herself. You are still defender to the High Prince? I thought Allasar only hired you until he grew up."

"He's still growing," Shandiin said drily. She noted Camion's smirk, as she'd just been nonchalantly designated by Randmar as hired help, but she knew Randmar meant no disrespect. It was just his way.

"Go." Randmar turned to the group of youngsters, waving them away, and including Camion in the gesture. "Go sit over there. They'll bring out the food and we will eat. I first want to talk to this beautiful woman before my wife catches me."

As soon as the others had walked away chatting, he turned back to Shandiin. "What has happened?" he demanded in a harsh whisper. "That boy looks like he has lost everything. Has he, Shandiin? Where is Allasar?"

"It's a long story, and not all of it is mine to tell. But you may have the High Prince as a guest for some time, if things happen as I think they might. He may be in exile, Randmar, because Cabre is no longer safe for his father or him. The High Tahmond has designs on becoming ruler."

Randmar scowled. "I've heard you called the King's Defender. Why aren't you with him?"

"Because he's made Khedran my priority." She met Randmar's eyes. "That's the only way I would have left Allasar, Randmar. Now it's my hope you will remain loyal to the High King no matter what may come. He needs you to support his son...now, and when he returns to Cabre to take his rightful position as High King."

Randmar stared for a long moment, took another moment for sadness. Then he lifted his chin defiantly. "Of course. If Khedran is half the man his father is, I'll follow him to face Chaos herself."

Shandiin had watched Khedran grow from beautiful child to stunning teenager. She had often thought she saw in him a similarity to Sarnath, the guru of his ancestors. He wasn't psychic, but had a depth of understanding far beyond his years, and sometimes, she thought, that very wisdom brought his greatest sorrow, for he saw need in every person, and knew that it was beyond anyone's ability to fill the hollow places in the human spirit. It was more than empathy. It was his nature.

It also set him apart from everyone, another gift, another curse for his bloodline.

She had hoped he would make friends here in Ordhold, as Jon and Brend had a myriad of cousins their own age. But her hopes diminished as he remained quiet, and after a long first day asked to be excused to rest.

She walked him to his cabin. "Are you all right?" she asked as he turned back at the door.

"I'd be better if I knew why I've been sent here." He studied her face. "When did my father hire you?"

She blinked at the question. "The night you were born, he made me promise I would be your defender and your mentor."

"Does he pay you for that? I've always just accepted your presence. I never thought about why you are here."

"Khedran..."

"Please. I think I deserve to know this much, at least."

She sighed. "I swore I would be Azlatan's ally. That oath has now been extended to becoming...whatever I am to you. There has been no monetary payment. My people and I are guests of the High King, and my oath is part of that."

"And whatever are you...to me? I had thought, all my life, that you were my friend as well as my teacher and defender. I guess I thought I was more than a duty."

"I see." She took a deep breath. "I'm guessing you are annoyed because you can't read me like you do other people."

His eyebrows went up, and she smiled.

"You didn't think I knew about your gift? You can read emotions like others read words. Your father calls it a family curse, for all of the High Kings have been empaths...that's what it was called, a long time ago. I would think it's a handy thing. For example, people can't get away with lying to you."

"You could."

Her smile vanished. "Do you think I've lied to you?"

He considered, watching her closely. "I've never thought so, until now, when you won't answer my questions, or even look me in the eye when you refuse."

Ouch. "Khedran, refusing to talk isn't lying."

"It's not being truthful, either." He started to turn away, then asked, "Are you going to sleep out here tonight?"

"That was my plan."

"You have a cabin."

"I've given that to Camion, unappreciative as he is."

"He thinks he should be guarding me, not you. But things have changed, haven't they?"

She sighed. "Yes, I guess they have."

"Well. You've admitted something, at last."

He stepped into his cabin, closed the door behind him.

She stood a moment in the darkness, staring at the door, then turned back as she heard Roinn approaching.

He dropped her bedroll by her feet, looked from her to the door and back. "Does he know yet?"

"No."

"You should tell him. He has a right to know, Shandiin."

"Allasar told me not to. He doesn't know for sure that Phaelon's Duine Anzihi would actually target a High King. It's...almost inconceivable."

Roinn shook his head, his bright braids swinging over his shoulder. "The boy is going to be devastated, if his father dies."

"He will be a High King at eighteen, if his father dies. He would be the youngest ever, but he has responsibilities. He can't afford to be devastated."

He met her eyes. "You are a hard woman, Shandiin. He's still only a boy."

There was no way to make him understand the awful duty she had so unwillingly accepted. So she turned away from the disapproval of a man who had been her friend for nearly two centuries, and said nothing.

Khedran remained serious over the next few days, interacting politely with the others while he ignored Shandiin, who nevertheless remained near as his defender. King Randmar took him under his wing, and one morning announced he had a gift for him. Shandiin followed them on the walk to the royal stables.

It was morning, and the stone stable was cool, with sunlight angling through the high windows under the eaves. Randmar led them to a box stall where stood a beautiful black mare in a deep bed of straw. Khedran looked at Randmar, puzzled, but the King just grinned and opened the stall door, gesturing him in.

As soon as Khedran stepped on the straw, a tiny black foal peered at him from behind its mother. It's newborn legs were far too long for the rest of him, but it walked nevertheless...straight to the High Prince.

Khedran dropped to the straw and the foal collapsed into his lap, legs akimbo. When the boy looked up at Randmar, his emerald eyes were wide and brilliant. "For me?" he asked, and Shandiin's heart squeezed at the memory of his father asking her the same question when she had given him Shashata, more than twenty years before.

"His sire is Shashata," Randmar said. "Your father planned this foal for you, Khedran, and he was born just this morning. His name is Chandar."

Wordlessly, Khedran put his arms around the tiny colt, curving over him with his head down. His black hair slid forward from his shoulders, hiding his face.

When the boy didn't move from that prayerlike position, Randmar turned back to Shandiin. "Let's give him some time alone." He smiled, but his voice was thick with emotion.

Khedran didn't come out for the rest of that day.

The next morning she was waiting at his cabin door as usual, but she broke the pattern they had set and wouldn't step aside when he opened the door. He stopped in the doorway, meeting her eyes levelly.

"It's time you resumed your training," she told him.

"Fine. But I would prefer Roinn as trainer."

"So be it. But you can't avoid me forever, Khedran. I'm not leaving you."

There was a flicker of shock. "I never thought you would. You gave an oath."

"Well, there's something else you can hate me for then." She turned to walk away.

She hadn't gone two steps when he said, "I don't hate you, Shandiin. Daimaine knows I've been angry enough to try, but I can't. I don't think you can hate someone you love."

She heard again the warning on the night of his birth: *You cannot bind him to you.*

She didn't turn back to face him, but lifted her chin and closed her eyes while she spoke as coldly as she could. "You don't love me, Khedran. You are sixteen, and you don't know what you love other than that beautiful colt Randmar gave you. Whatever you feel for me, it's a tangled mess, but it isn't love. I'm the hired help, remember?" She didn't, couldn't turn back to see his face. "I'll tell Roinn to set up your training."

She walked away thinking the lump in her throat might choke her to death.

The pack of teenagers...for a pack is what she considered them...crowded against the fence to watch Roinn's lessons, and it didn't take long for them to start begging the big man's attention.

"Will you train me as well?" young Prince Brend was the boldest, and the first to ask, but the others followed suit quickly. All but the older Prince Jon, who was reticent in his dignity.

Roinn threw Shandiin a desperate look, so she decided rescue was needed. She stepped into the training arena, picked up a bow. "We'll start with archery, then. The High Prince already has a planned schedule, as he is continuing advanced lessons."

"But I want to fight!" Brend exclaimed.

"Yes," another boy put in. "We've heard about the Chaine way of fighting. That's what we want."

When the others agreed, she shook her head and looked at Roinn meaningfully. "Go ahead as planned. The others can watch, and if they still want to learn, I'll get the rest of our people involved. They can all train."

So they watched, and as she had expected a couple of boys discretely left after seeing the reality. Shortly after, Khedran executed a spin-kick that missed Roinn by inches—followed by a right cross that didn't. Khedran went down a moment later, was agilely back on his feet before Roinn could follow up with more damage, but it was obvious he was dazed.

When Roinn started to back off, Khedran swung again.

Lost his balance, went down, did not get up.

Shandiin sighed, climbed through the fence.

Camion was beside Khedran's prostate form before she was, terror in his eyes when he looked up at Shandiin. "He's been killed!" the Duine exclaimed.

"He just got his bell rung. He'll be fine." She nudged Khedran with the toe of her boot. "Get up," she said.

Khedran stirred, rolled onto his back. She noted the bruise on his temple, looked at Roinn.

Roinn immediately turned to the pack of boys. "Looks like his lesson is done for today. Who wants to go next?" he asked, and this time it was Jon who stepped forward, fists clenched in fury.

"Is this how you treat a High Prince?" Jon demanded. "Putting him in the dirt like some animal?"

"That animal," Roinn said stiffly, "is twice the fighter you could ever be, young man."

Shandiin saw Jon stiffen in outrage, but returned her attention to Khedran, who was trying to get up. She grasped one arm, Camion the other, and together they pulled him upright and standing.

Khedran was blinking in confusion, but shrugged off the arms that held him and stood alone, though swaying a little. Shandiin shook her head. "You may have a concussion. That's the end of training for today. Camion, take him to his cabin. I'll send a doctor."

"What is a doctor?" Camion asked. "He needs a healer, a Tahmine!"

"I don't think there are any of those available. Khedran, can you walk?"

"Of course I can." Clarity was returning to his eyes, along with embarrassment. "I'll be fine."

"Yes, you will. And you won't fall for Roinn's side-kick again. Now go."

He didn't look at her, but walked toward his cabin with Camion jittering at his side. She watched, frowning, then went in search of the Chaine who knew what to do about concussions.

And shortly thereafter faced Randmar's concern, as Jon had reported the incident from his point of view.

"I understand Prince Jon's anger," she told the Dominion King. "Khedran's Duine feels the same way. But the training is done at Khedran's request and with his father's approval."

"It's too uneven. Your Chaine man is twice his size," Randmar scowled.

Shandiin grinned. "Yes. And Khedran has put him in the dirt more than once."

The scowl turned to interest. "Truly? And this is a skill you have taught him?"

"Roinn and I together, yes. We've also been training the High King's Guards, but Khedran is the best student we've ever had. Your son Brend has shown an interest."

"Has he, now? And what's your opinion of that?"

"I think we would start him slowly, without kicking him in the head," she smiled.

Randmar nodded thoughtfully. "It would be good for all of them, to learn how to defend themselves as well as your Chaine."

So Ordhold's youngsters began a new education, and when Khedran returned to resume his own, it was obvious he was their hero. He handled their adulation with composure. He wasn't humble...Khedran was never humble, in Shandiin's opinion...but his pride was never maintained at anyone else's expense.

He seemed to be losing some of that constant dour stress, but his expression when he deigned to look at Shandiin told her he was still waiting for the other shoe to drop.

The same thing, she mused sadly, that Allasar had expected for so long.

Jon took the training, as Randmar expected him to. He worked harder at it than anyone else, but when he noticed the girl Rani watching Khedran instead of him, he took exception.

And challenged Khedran to fight him.

Khedran frowned, said "No," and began to turn away.

He'd been taught well to watch his back. He pivoted, caught Jon's fist in his hand, pushed it away. "Stop."

Shandiin straightened, surprised to hear his bloodline's command voice. Jon obeyed immediately, stepping back, then saw that Rani was still watching.

He lunged.

Khedran stepped aside, and Jon's face plowed dirt.

Khedran waited, looking down at Jon as he turned onto his side. "I won't fight you, Jon. It would therefore be dishonorable of you to continue trying, and I know you are honorable." He reached a hand to help him up, and Shandiin watched closely, because she knew Jon could use it to yank Khedran to the ground.

She was sure Khedran knew the same thing.

After a moment Jon grasped the offered hand and got up. "I guess I need more lessons," he managed.

Khedran smiled at him. "It's taken me all my years. You could be proficient in far less time, the way you focus."

Rani came to Jon, took his hand, and led him away. Khedran turned to see Shandiin watching.

She noted the deep weariness in his eyes before he turned away, and decided it was time to talk to him.

Khedran rarely slept more than a few hours, and she had often followed him when he left his cabin to go to the stables, where he sat in the straw with the colt Chandar. That night, for the first time, she entered the stall behind him, and sat cross-legged to face him as he leaned back against the wall.

He waited, saying nothing.

So she did. "You don't rest. There's more bothering you than being dragged here without explanation. It's time you told me what your father was so concerned about, the day you turned sixteen."

He frowned. "I would rather not discuss it."

"I'm asking you to tell me anyway. I'm your defender, Khedran. I need to know everything about you, or I won't know everything to defend against."

He seemed to consider. Then looked down, toying with a piece of straw. "I'll tell you part of it." He waited a beat, sighed. "There's a curse on us. It starts at sixteen. People...most usually girls. They think they are in love."

She grimaced. "I knew about the thrall. I had no idea it started so early. Has it happened to you?"

He nodded. "That's why Jon was so angry. He said Rani was mooning after me, and I was leading her on, which I shouldn't do because I have a betrothed and I can't consider anyone else." He looked up, met her eyes. "I'm not interested in her. I haven't led anyone on. But sometimes I don't know what to do. I can't exactly get angry with them."

She exhaled. "That's got to be tough. Did your father have any advice for you?"

"Not really. He said he just ignores it, but that hardly feels right."

"What would *amhara* tell you to do?"

He lifted his head at that, his expression thoughtful. After some consideration, he said, "To respect them. To love them, as part of all that is, but to respect them first." His thick black lashes fell over the emerald briefly, lifted again as he nodded to himself. "To give them time to come to their own balance, to find their own self-respect." He met her eyes. "To let them see themselves with their pride intact. Just as you do for me."

That surprised her. "I do?"

"Oh, yes." He got up, brushed straw from his clothing. "You could destroy me when I am foolish. But you don't, and you wouldn't."

He got up and left her there, bewildered. She couldn't recall him ever being foolish, and realized how odd that was in itself.

Shandiin froze when she saw the black-clad man at the castle gate.

Black was sacred to Daimaine. Only the High King and those sworn to him could wear it.

She knew that, as did the High King's son.

She looked around, saw Khedran turn toward her from the far side of the courtyard, and went to the gate to greet Allasar's messenger.

"Farbet, isn't it?" she asked him.

"Yes, ma'am." His faded blue eyes were somber. "I've come with a message for the High Prince."

She looked at the emerald star on the tall collar of his black uniform. "You are very young to be Compatri to the High King."

He swallowed. "He gave me that honor the day before the Duine Anzihi came for him."

The expectation his words confirmed made it no easier to accept. Her knees threatened weakness, and her vision blurred. She was unable to speak even when Khedran stopped at her side. She could only watch as Farbet dropped to one knee, offering him a scroll banded with the seal of the High King.

Khedran took it, motioning Farbet to rise. He broke the seal, unrolled it carefully.

He read the long message without expression.

He looked up at Farbet. "They came for him."

"Yes, Your Highness. He was killed in his bed, in the castle of Dominion King Eleban. He was found with the Anzihi's knife in his heart. His Duine...Canon...was found dead in the room by the same kind of knife." He held out a thin-bladed knife to show the symbol of the Duine Anzihi carved into its handle, the lines of stars depicting the Bridle constellation.

Khedran made no move to touch the knife. "I must tell Randmar," he said after a long silence. "And I have to find Camion, to let him know about his father."

Shandiin watched him walk away, realizing after a moment that he had handed her the scroll. She lifted it with a shaking hand, and read it.

My beloved son, I am sorry. If you are reading this, it means I have been killed by Phaelon's Duine Anzihi. Shandiin knows why;

do not blame her for her silence about this, as I have asked her not to explain anything until and unless this happens.

I ask of you...no, I beg of you...not to take vengeance. No one knows who the Anzihi are. It could be any Duine, anywhere, and the Duine make up fully half of your realm; they are woven throughout the fabric of Azlatan, and they are your people, they are yours just as certainly as the Rioch. Any attempt by you to find the few who are the Anzihi would destabilize your realm. Azlatan is already endangered and will be more so, for the time of prophecy is coming.

Azlatan is weakened by my own actions, will be even more weakened in the years it will take for you to step into your rightful place, for the High Tahmond...even with the High Tahmine to keep him in check...will replace our rule without compassion. Your people will be afraid and confused, for they have always and rightfully expected a King's mercy while accepting the need for Daimaine's justice.

That Azlatan is gone. Your rule must be different than any other. You cannot be a velvet hammer, but a sword forged by the Chaine.

You must have faith in yourself even when your own people turn against you, because your duty is to save them all. You must accept the homage of those who are loyal, because their faith in you is necessary to the same duty. You must accept it all, my son, knowing they may well die for you when you call them to defend Azlatan.

I understand what that burden means to you. Only Shandiin will truly understand in the same way. You can trust her.

I hereby release Shandiin from her promise, so that she can tell you why this has come to pass. I have known for some time that they would find me; it is my own fault, my own sin against everything the High Kings have stood for.

It is now your duty to repair my sin and save our people.

I am sorry. I love you.

The news flooded Ordhold even as, Shandiin was sure, it sent shock waves throughout Azlatan. Shandiin stayed as near Khedran as she could while he was offered condolences he didn't want, comfort that didn't comfort.

True to his word, he had found Camion immediately, and held his sobbing lifelong companion in his arms before easing the older man's return to dignity.

She waited for him to break, to show something other than the distance she saw in his eyes and his manner. When he remained unchanged at nightfall, she watched him go into his cabin, then went quickly to the stable and removed her hidden parcel from her horse's stall. When she returned with it, she shunned her bedroll and just sat against the wall by his cabin door, looking up at the bright moon as it journeyed across the stars.

Much later she heard his door open, and he came to her silent as a shadow. He sat down beside her, resting a hand across an upraised knee. He spoke very quietly. "I'm sorry I was angry with you, Shandiin. I don't agree that I should have been left in the dark, but that was my father's choice, not yours."

She saw with an oblique glance that he was looking up at the moon, and waited without answering.

It was a long moment before he went on. "She must have done something to him. Whoever she was, she must have had some magic trick to corrupt him."

He doesn't need to know the details. She had already decided that. How could she help him understand what she couldn't? For Allasar's failure was a mystery to her even yet.

"Do you believe love can be corrupt?" she asked.

He turned his head toward her, moonlight firing the emerald gaze. "Do you?"

She shook her head. She couldn't bring herself to answer, but she thought: *It can be deadly dangerous.*

He returned his gaze to the moon. "I was taught to set a wall around myself. But...it's failing. The people hurt, for themselves and for me, because the High King is dead, and my wall is breaking. I can't even protect myself, so...how can I protect them from me? Shandiin, this grief has sent my thrall out of control, and it's flooding them all now, not just the girls. They feel my magic as surely as they could feel my fist around their heart. And it all comes back to me. This is a sea of pain, and the tide keeps coming in, and I...I am already drowning."

She was the only one who could understand, now that Allasar was gone. Allasar, who had called upon her to mentor his son, knowing why his own father had walked into the sea to die.

She knew the only things that would drag Khedran from his sea of pain.

His purpose.

And her resolve.

She'd worked relentlessly all his life to make his trust and faith in her absolute. Now she must exploit that trust, that faith, to overcome the empathy and compassion that were his nature.

Because he had to be more than all who had come before him.

His purpose came first. She reached for the bundle she had hidden so carefully, unwrapped it, and offered him the Star Blade, in its scabbard.

Khedran looked at it. Shook his head in denial.

So she gave him his father's words. "You must have faith in yourself even when your own people turn against you, because your duty is to save them all. You must accept the homage of those who are loyal, because their faith in you is necessary to the same duty. You must accept it all, knowing they may well die for you when you call them to defend Azlatan."

He met her eyes then, and his were filled with painful under-standing. Finally, hesitantly, he reached for the sword. She held the scabbard as he pulled the blade free, releasing Daimaine's cold and terrible light, the wheeling stars that marked his birthright.

The reality of his father's death, his father's *words*, lived in that light. He slammed the blade back into the scabbard and threw back his head, and he screamed his unbearable pain to the sky.

And she thought:

Fuck it.

She rose to her knees, buried her hands in his hair and dragged his face against her shoulder, where his tears made sodden her shirt while his arms wrapped around her so tightly she couldn't breathe. She swore a mantra to herself, over and over, holding him as he wept.

No. This one is never going to walk into the sea. Not him.

When he finally shuddered toward calm she still didn't let him go.

"I can't be King." His voice held so much misery it made her heart ache. "I'm not ready, Shandiin. I don't know how I can do this."

She forced his head up, bringing his face inches from hers.

His purpose. And my resolve.

She stared fiercely into those drowned jade eyes. "You will be ready. The day you return to Cabre no one will doubt you are the High King. You'll be the best there ever was. I've known it since the night you were born. Listen to me!" She hissed it, and her fists in his hair were a steel vise. "*You can do this.* You find a place inside yourself and build a shell of iron around it. Then fill it with cold. Freezing, numbing, stunning cold. Seal it and keep it. And when you feel the horrors life gives you and your people...the pain, the anger, the sorrow, any of the *things* that scorch your soul—you take that *thing* in your fist and you crack the seal just enough to shove it into that infernal undying cold and it will be gone. It will be *gone*, Khedran, *and your mind will be your own again.*"

She didn't let go until his eyes fired emerald, and she knew he believed.

Through the next two years in Ordhold, and still after his return to Penumbra, she watched him refine that belief.

He taught himself to contain his own empathy, his own emotion, his own pain and anger. He did this over and over, so that he could move forward with clear mind and purpose, and do what needed to be done.

There was an instant's inferno within that emerald gaze, and then the conversion. His people, enemies or loyalists, would come to know it well, and word of it would spread until the High King was given another name, a name that instilled both fear and confidence in his rule.

Wearing Daimaine's black, with dangerous, feral emerald eyes, Khedran became the Black Wolf, and his only purpose was to save his people.

CHAPTER 19

Khedran turned seventeen at the winter solstice, when an annual rain of shooting stars heralded the season the people of Azlatan called Starfall.

But the attempted assassinations of the High Prince began long before. It seemed Phaelon or his Tahmond could not believe the son innocent of the father's sins. And those they called the Anzihi were relentless.

Shandiin never left his back unguarded.

His training had always included swordsmanship, but now she demanded he perfect his use of the Star Blade without relying on it's magic. She would never trust Daimaine's magic... and her greatest hope was that he would be free of all magic when she left him.

They set up training in the huge barn-like structure that King Randmar used for training his war-horses. Here, the young High Prince again proved himself a far better student than any Shandiin had ever known, even among her own warrior Chaine.

His training was put to the test, and hard-won. Even when the killers began to arrive in greater numbers, he defended himself skillfully. Each assassin met death by her sword or his. She had trained him well, and he was a strong and powerful killer.

But she saw the toll it took on him. He stepped into battle with the feral fury of the Black Wolf, but turned away from the aftermath with the emerald fire of his eyes darkening to jade.

Because even though they had attacked him, they were still and always his people.

When she made him discuss the logistics of their defense, he told her he was always alerted to the danger before they struck, using the gift of empathy the High Kings had called a curse. He had read them, he said, but could not make sense of what they felt. He had not sensed evil, but only a kind of desperation, an insane need to kill.

The attacks grew less as the winter wore on and the days became longer and warmer. Then they finally stopped. When the snow had melted off, Shandiin and Khedran and Randmar, with a mix of soldiers and Chaine, walked together to the nearest pasture so that Khedran's young colt could finally enjoy freedom, sun and grass. Khedran walked out into the field to watch his colt more closely, and of course Shandiin followed, walking slightly behind and to his left as always. Randmar watched smiling from the fence.

The attack was swift and unexpected. Ten men erupted from the nearby woods, nearer to the High Prince and his Defender than Randmar and his people were. Eerily aware and synchronized, the pair spun to fight back-to-back.

It was a deadly devised dance, and their attackers were given no quarter. By the time Randmar and his soldiers reached them, the fight was finished.

Randmar went immediately to the High Prince. He glanced into those savage and firelit emerald eyes, wondering how one so young and kind could become such an innate killer. He said nothing for a long moment, but stood beside Khedran as Shandiin strode away briefly to talk to one of her own people.

Watching The Chaine walk away in her tawny leather, he commented, "You are both amazing, but watching her fight is like watching a lioness take down a lamb."

To Randmar's surprise, Khedran's emerald fire damped to embers, his expression gentled, and he looked back at Randmar with a half-smile.

"Yes. I know they call me the Black Wolf, but I have always thought of her as a lioness when she fights."

Randmar noted that the High Prince didn't look down at the carnage before them...something he had noticed before, but only Shandiin understood.

He was eighteen when the High Tahmine came to tell them he was needed in Cabre.

Khedran met her magic carriage, and when the door opened he simply lifted her out and held her, for a long moment, in his arms. Shandiin stood back, knowing the bond he had with his foster mother was stronger than anyone else knew. She was both warmed and concerned, because she knew there was a reason the Tahmine had come.

He's too young, she thought. And then: *No. He's who he is. He'll do what he determines needs to be done, and there's no one on this planet who can do it but him.*

For she had discovered much about Azlatan's High Prince as he had come to maturity, and knew that he would be the greatest of all the High Kings.

Although very possibly the last of them.

He walked with the Tahmine to Randmar's place of meeting, a cozy room with a fireplace and paintings of Ordhold's beloved horses. Shandiin walked just behind them, as she always did since Allasar's passing.

Never before had a High King been less than beloved by his people. If this had changed, the High Tahmine said, there was no way to know, for fear had infected the realm.

"The people are living in terror of the Anzihi," the High Tahmine said as she sat facing Khedran and King Randmar. Prince Jon was also in attendance, while Shandiin stood guard at the door. "There's no way to know who they *are.* Is it your neighbor, your friend...possibly even your brother? The Anzihi are fanatics, and so secretive no one dares to protest as they manically search and destroy those they *suspect* violate Phaelon's Law. There is no peace, Your Highness. With Penumbra vacant, Cabre is a morass of terror. Few will come into the city, and an awful dread is growing like a sickness across the land."

"What of the Dominion Kings?" Khedran asked. "Do any stand against the Duine Anzihi?"

"I think some would, if they dared. But three of your bravest have been assassinated themselves."

He nodded grimly. "I am aware of those murders. What is the High Tahmond doing?"

"He calls for peace. I do not know if he means it. He claims he doesn't know who the Anzihi are...and again, I do not know the truth." The Tahmine put a hand over Khedran's. "I fear for your safety there, Your Highness, but I think you must return. Without a High King, Azlatan is spiraling into madness." She looked toward The Chaine, who had not spoken. "Shandiin...you should bring your people with him. I saw you have many more here than I expected."

"Not just her people," King Randmar interjected. "Ordhold holds true! My legions will follow you to Cabre, to stand against the Anzihi, to witness your ascension."

Khedran nodded thanks to Randmar's loyalty, but disagreed with his strategy. "I don't believe all your legions will be required to witness my ascension. We will cross two Dominions as we travel, and I will speak to each Dominion King as we go, and see if they will join us."

"You should give them no choice!" Randmar's anger spurred him to the edge of impudence. "My legions are greater than theirs, and can hold them accountable!"

Unruffled, Khedran shook his head. "I will not go to war with them. They are my people too, Randmar, as much as you are. Either they will listen to reason, or they won't."

Randmar threw a sidelong glance toward Shandiin. "Reason? They are not Chaine, to be trusted with reason. If they disagree and you just pass through, you could be leaving enemies at your back."

"Why should Ordhold stand with you if you will not fight?" Prince Jon interjected.

Randmar visibly jolted with the realization that he had overstepped, and turned on his son. "I was wrong to speak to the High Prince so brashly, and you need to show respect. He is our liege, even if he has not yet ascended to High King."

But Khedran sat back calmly, regarding Jon. "Did I say I wouldn't fight?"

Jon glared at him sullenly. "It's known all over Azlatan. The High Kings have never had to fight, and they have never called on the goddess Daimaine to keep order, even though she is the power behind their rule."

Randmar was immediately out of his chair. He grabbed Jon by his shirtfront and jerked him to his feet. "You will apologize immediately!"

When Jon stubbornly remained mute, Randmar shoved him back a step. "Then get out. This is a meeting of adults, not spoiled children. You and I will have our own meeting later, but leave this room now."

Prince Jon straightened his shirt, while Khedran watched him without expression. He finally turned and walked to the door. Shandiin blocked his path.

Her furious eyes shifted from Jon to Khedran, who gave a nearly imperceptible shake of his head. She stepped aside, closed the door behind the departing Dominion Prince, and returned to her position at guard.

Randmar dropped back into his chair, looking miserable. "My apologies, Highness, for his disrespect. He will be punished."

"That is your choice, Randmar. But he only told the truth."

Randmar stiffened in shock, but Khedran lifted a hand to stop him when he began to speak. "No High King has ever fought against his own people," he pointed out. "Nor has one ever unleashed Daimaine upon them. Those are facts. Apparently Prince

Jon believes those facts are a result of cowardice rather than circumstance." He turned to the High Tahmine. "Do you believe that opinion is common?"

"I have heard it voiced," she sighed, and Khedran nodded.

"We live in a different world than the six High Kings who came before me," he told Randmar. "It became different when my father was murdered. I will of necessity be a different King, and I believe there will be a lack of cowardice." He smiled then. "Nor, Randmar, will I be stupid enough to leave enemies behind us as we travel."

"Then I will call together my legions," Randmar said.

"One only. Would you have Ordhold accused of invading another Dominion? One of your legions is sufficient to accompany us to the ascension, unless you have a problem with your neighbors."

"I will have," Randmar said, "if they do not join with you."

"Leave that to me. It's my duty to keep peace within the Dominions."

Randmar wouldn't argue, but he looked toward Shandiin. "You will at least take the Chaine warriors."

Khedran shook his head. "We have become accustomed to Shandiin's role as the King's Defender, but she is first and foremost the leader of her own people. Whether her Chaine warriors travel with us is her choice, not mine. If you would please give us the room, Mother and Majesty, I need to learn what her plans may be."

He stood as he spoke, and kissed the Tahmine's hand. She in turn placed it on his cheek and smiled, drawing Randmar with her as she left.

Shandiin closed the door behind them, and faced Khedran across the room.

She slapped her hands on her hips. "What the frigging hell?"

He lifted his eyebrows, amused as he frequently was by her strange speech. "After all this time, I still have no idea what that means."

"Jon is a piece of crap despite everything Randmar has done to make him a Prince. Why did you allow him to speak to you that way?"

"Apparently I haven't earned the piece of crap's respect...whatever a 'crap' is. He's of small importance against what I'm facing, Shandiin. I believe the High Tahmond is working very hard to undermine me. I have to go to Cabre, you know I do."

"Of course I know. And unless you want to throw us out of Azlatan, I'll bring my people along whether you want them or not."

"Of course I want them. You and your people would terrify any enemy more than all Randmar's Legions combined, and terror is a great deterrent to battle. I don't want to battle my people, no matter how badly misled by the High Tahmond."

She sighed. "And you won't set Daimaine loose either."

"Of course not."

"So what is your plan?"

He turned to the map of Azlatan gracing the wall between two horse paintings. "The Dominion of Rafel lies directly over the mountains. King Arafon will listen to reason, I believe. The next Dominion we will travel through...Sunhi...is uncertain. King Chindra was assassinated, and his son...now King Chonor...I only met once, as a child. I have some concerns about him." He paused and turned back to Shandiin. "I'm asking that you send some of your Chaine ahead of our group, with the High Tahmine. She'll go ahead of us, taking the route I plan."

"Do you think she is in danger?"

"If I am, so is she, even in her magic carriage. But I ask this for more than her protection. I wish to show Azlatan that the Chaine's allegiance extends to more than myself. You are friends of Azlatan, and the goddess Liethe is the most sacred to Azlatan's people, with good reason."

"I'll send Roinn and a some others with her," Shandiin agreed.

"Compatri Farbet will ride with us, along with a unit of Cabre's Guard. I have already sent a messenger to alert Cabre of our coming arrival."

"So you are letting the Tahmond know you are returning to claim your rule. Why do you want to give advance warning?"

His smile didn't reach his narrowed eyes. "Because it appears necessary to prove a lack of cowardice."

King Arafon was waiting for them, having been alerted by the High Tahmine who had already passed through his Dominion. He came out personally to meet them on the road, giving King Randmar a respectful salute.

He then dismounted and kneeled briefly in front of Khedran's black stallion. "Your Highness," he said. "I am glad to welcome you to the Dominion of Rafel. I understand you are riding to Cabre to take your rightful place in Penumbra."

Khedran swung his horse sideways, reaching down to take Arafon's hand. "My thanks, Majesty. Yes, that is my plan. Will you ride with us?"

"It will be my honor." The Dominion King stood back, a tall man with anger in every line. "I admired your father. I, for one, do not believe the lies about him siring a forbidden child. The continued assassinations by the Duine Anzihi only prove my belief. They are not soldiers of Phaelon's Law, but outlaws, and beyond contempt."

Khedran folded his gloved hands over the saddle-horn, and did not address the verity of Arafon's belief. "Are there others who agree with you?" he asked instead.

"Yes. The Anzihi... as they call themselves...must be stopped. I believe you are the only one who can see to that."

Khedran didn't make a speech; he simply nodded agreement. Thus assured, Arafon returned to his horse and led them to where his soldiers were already waiting.

Shandiin brought her mount beside Khedran's as they rode. "Perhaps the High Tahmond has overstepped. The attacks on you and those who support you may anger others on your behalf."

Khedran was thoughtful. "My father asked me not to take vengeance on the Anzihi. His reasons were valid, whether or not I agreed. It's the Tahmond I have to repudiate. My concern, if these assassinations are truly ordered by Phaelon, is whether this could result in the Prophecy War."

She scowled, wondering if the Duine would rise up against the Rioch before Khedran became King. "I don't think so," she decided. "The war is coming, Khedran, but Phaelon's thousand years of peace are not over until the year 995. That's seven years from now." *And there it is again,* she thought. *The number seven.*

"I think you must know more about history than our greatest historians," Khedran remarked. He regarded her with a question in his emerald eyes. Her only response was her familiar enigmatic smile.

The Dominion of Sunhi was known for its great fields of wheat, and always made Shandiin think of Kansas. She also thought the Dominion King's castle of blue-grey stone rising from the golden hills was like something out of a fairy tale.

It was not the King who greeted their arrival at his castle entrance, however, but a very nervous Duine. Khedran waited with his retinue as his own Duine, Camion, immediately asked to speak to the man first.

Camion came back to look up at Khedran, who had remained mounted while he waited. "I asked him why Chonor would so dishonor the High Prince by not greeting you personally. He stated Chonor does not wish to meet the same fate as his father who supported you, and demands we ride on without stopping."

Khedran looked toward the Duine at the castle entrance. "He was King Chindra's bonded Duine, was he not?"

"Yes. For nearly all his life, until the King was killed." Camion's anger was obvious. "He is humiliated by being sent to greet you.

He is also frightened; I think he expects to be struck down where he stands."

"Does he, now?" Khedran studied the tall white-haired man standing bravely just outside the palace entrance. Then, to the surprise of everyone in the entourage, he dismounted and walked to the Duine, who immediately dropped to his knees.

"Please rise," Khedran said, and the man obeyed. Khedran waited until the Duine's gaze met the famed emerald eyes. "Your name is Denin, is it not?"

"It is," the man said in surprise, quickly adding "Your Highness!"

Khedran nodded. "I am sorry for the loss of your King. I remember you laughing with him when my father and I visited here all those years ago. It was clear to me that your bond was strong, and one of friendship."

"I...I am honored that you remember me," Denin stammered.

"Why shouldn't I remember you? The Duine are my people, as are the Rioch, and your King was my father's good friend. Now I need your help. Will you advise me who should be the next Dominion King, with Chindra gone?"

Denin could only stare, and then an outraged voice bellowed "How dare you!" and a dark man, dressed in expensive clothing, strode from the castle.

"Hello, Chonor." Khedran spoke mildly. "Eavesdropping, were you?"

"Why would you ask a Duine such a thing?" Chonor demanded. His glare moved from Khedran to the mounted entourage, and he suddenly recognized two Dominion Kings and The Chaine. His face went pale, and he looked back at Khedran. Subdued, he said, "Apparently you do not realize I am King Chonor. I met you when I was Prince."

Khedran's eyebrows lifted. "Oh, I remember you. But you are not the King of this Dominion, Chonor. A Dominion King would not dishonor the bonded Duine of his own father, who was a good and just man." He turned back to Denin. "I ask again: who do you believe should be Dominion King of Sunhi?"

Denin's face went through several expressions: shock, question, tenuous hope. When Chonor stepped forward to argue, the High Prince simply lifted a gloved hand, and used the command voice of his bloodline. "You are not King of the Dominion of Sunhi. I have spoken, and in the absence of a High King, my word is law. If you wish to remain alive, you will step back, and vacate this castle. Now."

Khedran's other hand was on the hilt of the Star Blade, but Chonor never looked at it. He stared into the feral emerald eyes of the Black Wolf, and he stepped back, turned, and fled.

Khedran returned his attention to Denin, who was now smiling openly.

"The man who should rule is Handel," the Duine told him. "He is not related to King Chindra, but he is a distant relative of your bloodline, and a true and wise man all will trust."

"Where will I find Handel?"

"He is the stablemaster here."

Khedran nodded. "Take me to him, please. I would like to speak to him, to see if he meets my requirements as well as yours."

The man named Handel was young, muscular from hard labor, and had his black hair tied back for work. He wore the rough clothing of a workman, and was mucking out a stall when the great doors of the stable opened. He was surprised, as King Chonor preferred the doors closed against what he considered a bad smell too near the castle.

Handel stepped from the stall, turning toward the doorway. At first he could only see three figures silhouetted against the brilliant sunlight spilling in behind them. He quickly recognized Denin, but blinked in shock at the tall man in black walking in, and the woman just behind him with hair like fire.

Handel dropped immediately to his knees. "Your Highness," he managed to say, staring in disbelief at the black boots that stopped in front of him.

There was a moment of silence. Handel could not know that an empath was reading him as he brought his gaze up slowly over the plain black leather garb of a man built as powerfully as he was, to a face of unworldly beauty and eyes that gleamed like emerald jewels. When he met that gaze, Khedran smiled, and Handel's heart swelled with love for the man who would be his liege, the High King of Azlatan.

That day a legend was born, of a stablemaster who became a King. The most important part of the story was Handel's strong and benevolent rule over a Dominion that became one of the most important in Khedran's realm, and whose people prospered...all because the seventh High King had considered the heart of a servant.

It took time for the change in the Sunhi Dominion's regime, but not as long as it might have, for it's standing legion welcomed the change, and was glad to join the retinue accompanying the High Prince to Cabre. Still, it was time that the populace gladly accepted as it gave them the opportunity to gather along the route. The crowds quickly spread the story of the Dominion's new King, and a holiday spirit seemed to affect them.

Khedran rode vanguard of three Dominion legions, along with the Chaine warriors most people in these realms had never seen before. Riding through a crowd gathered in a small village, the procession was stopped by several men boldly holding villagers hostage. Khedran reined in sharply at the sight of a woman being held with a knife to her throat directly in the roadway. Other villagers were held behind her, one barely more than a child, and Khedran's eyes blazed as archers stepped through, bows drawn, with the clear intent to kill him.

His command voice rang hard. "If any one of you harms one of these innocent people, you will die."

Most of the hostages were immediately released, but the archers fired at him—and watched in disbelief as their arrows glanced off his black clothing, for he wore Chaine armor beneath.

Khedran's own archers quickly dispatched those who had fired on him.

There was immediate bedlam, as soldiers he'd seeded through the crowd went after assassins and hostage-takers who attempted to fight their way free.

Controlling her nervously sidling horse, Shandiin looked around to see the chaos settling, save for one group of villagers gathered around someone on the ground. When Khedran turned toward them, she extended a hand to stop him.

"I'll find out what that's about," she said. "Please stay with your defenders. There could still be more danger."

He looked both angry and worried, but met her eyes and nodded. She gestured for Farbet and two of her Chaine to stay with him when he turned his mount toward those captured in the attack.

She dismounted, handing off her reins to a soldier, and stepped through the small mob surrounding the fallen man. The people parted quickly, except for some who appeared stupefied upon seeing a Chaine for the first time. Shoving past them, she saw a young man who kneeled over a prone man.

Shandiin leaned over the kneeling man's shoulder to see he was using a leather lace in an attempt to tie a tourniquet above the deep wound on his patient's thigh. She frowned to see he knelt on the wound itself, and then realized he was purposely applying pressure to stanch the bleeding while he worked.

Seeing his struggle to tighten the ligature, she pulled a short knife from her belt and held it within his eyeline. "Use this," she suggested.

Wordlessly he snatched the sheathed knife from her hand, and wound the leather lace over it, then twisted the knife until the binding was sufficiently tight. He looked up as another young man shoved through the crowd and dropped an open bag within his reach. Shandiin could see the bag held bandages and other medical supplies unusual in this land of magic healers.

The newcomer had frozen in place, and she straightened to see a tall Duine man staring at her with eyes of dark gold. His fair skin was tanned from the sun, and he had cheekbones of steel. His hair was the color of pale sand, tumbling long around a face nearly as handsome as a High King's.

There was something familiar about him, and she felt a pang when she realized he resembled a love she had lost a thousand years ago. *Verity?*

The name was no sooner thought than she heard it spoken. But of course it was different. Her Verity was long gone.

"Varady," the kneeling man spoke as he hastily applied a bandage, "I can only do so much here. We have to move him indoors, where I can stitch this closed." He pushed to his feet, and Shandiin stepped back to give him room.

"Where did you learn to do this?" she demanded, for she hadn't seen such expertise in anyone but her own people, not in magic Azlatan.

"I taught myself." He answered brusquely, his mind obviously on his patient. "We don't have Liethe's magic healers in my small town." He glanced toward her as he spoke, then froze in the apparent shock that had become familiar to her in their travels. He turned slowly around to stare at her—eye-level to him, her wild mass of red hair fired by the sun, statuesque in her leather and gold.

What she saw was a lean young man with unkempt black hair and his shirt open because he had unlaced it to make a tourniquet. The tawny skin of the Rioch included a spectrum from medium to deep hues; his was a shade darker than Khedran's medium, and the artic blue eyes in that face were almost startling.

"What's your name?" she asked him, teetering between interest and concern about getting back to the High Prince.

"Um," he managed.

"Well, that's unusual." She glanced toward the Duine he'd called Varady. "Is he yours?" she asked.

Varady nodded, apparently quicker to get past amazement, and now merely fascinated. "He is Danon. He taught himself to heal in that manner, at first on animals, and now on people. You are Chaine."

"I get it. You've never seen one of us before. Can you help him get this injured man to where he needs to be?" She scowled at the onlookers. "Can any of you help?"

But Varady was still intent on her. "You are more than a Chaine. I know the legends. You are *The* Chaine. The stories say you have silver eyes."

She exhaled, having concerns other than stories. "Somebody has to help Danon." She looked back toward the young medic. He still hadn't blinked.

It made her impatient. "C'mon, Danon. Anyone who can do what you just did is smarter than that."

He flushed, and finally blinked. "Um."

She rolled her eyes. "Wow. I've heard of being starstruck, but you take the cake."

It wasn't the first time she'd used words unknown to Azlatan, and it added confusion to his daze. "What?"

"Well, that's an improvement. You said a whole word."

He flushed, embarrassed, and turned away from her to the onlookers. "We'll need a litter."

A couple of people scrambled to assist. Danon turned back to Shandiin, gathering his dignity. "I appreciate your help."

"I only handed you a tool. Do you know how to sew him up?"

"Yes." He glanced down at his patient. "He's regaining consciousness. I need to—"

"Then do what you need to do," she interrupted. "Look, I'm sorry I embarrassed you. I really think you are amazing. The High Prince could use someone like you in his Guard."

Danon shook his head. "I plan to go to Liethe's Temple, and become a real healer. My town needs one."

She scowled. "You are already a real healer. You have a talent, and you've advanced it into a skill. Why throw that away to rely on something outside of yourself?"

He looked amazed. "Magic is always better."

"No, it isn't." She looked down at his patient, who remained unconscious. "What would your people do if there was no longer any magic, Danon?"

"That can't happen."

When she looked back into those arctic blue eyes, she was hit with realization. If she succeeded in her mission, if she took away the gods of Azlatan, people like this young man would be key to survival in a world that had relied on magic for a thousand years.

"Think about it anyway. Magic isn't the answer to everything."

He frowned, returning his attention to his patient. "I am not a Chaine. From everything I have heard, you are not of my world." He glanced back briefly, her spell over him apparently gone and his dignity returned. "You are so very different, I don't think we could ever understand each other."

She watched him kneel again to his patient, and began to turn away...but was caught by Varady's watchful golden eyes.

"Your Danon is a different kind of man," she told him.

"He is," Varady agreed. "But I think he's wrong about being unable to understand each other. You seem human to me, despite the stories."

She was surprised, more by his warmth than his words. "You are big on stories, aren't you?"

"I am. And some of them contradict each other. They say you came from the west, so there must be a world outside of Azlatan. Danon and I live near the eastern border, and I've often wished I could cross over...but it's said the borders are closed by magic, and Azlatan is the only world anyway. How do I know what to believe?"

She hesitated, intrigued now by the Duine as well as his Rioch. Instead of responding, she asked, "You long for freedom, don't you? Is it hard...being Duine?"

That seemed to surprise him. He turned his gaze to Danon, who was helping move his patient to a litter. "Danon and I were raised together. He is like a brother to me. I can't imagine being without him." He looked back, and gave her a smile so beautiful she blinked. "Freedom isn't always necessary when there is love."

"I don't believe that. Someone told me once love is deadly dangerous. I think that's especially true when it keeps you in bondage."

She turned away, feeling unsettled, and was thoughtful as she rode back to find Khedran.

The High Prince turned away from a group of soldiers as she approached. "No one knows the attackers," he told her. "The others were villagers they paid to take hostages, tricking them with various lies. I could wish my archers hadn't killed the organizers so quickly, so we could question them." He frowned when she didn't respond. "You seem distracted, Shandiin. What is it? Was everything all right back there?"

She shrugged. "I met someone named Danon, and tried to recruit him for you. He's an amazing healer, but thinks he needs magic. Somehow, I found that sad. He's worth so much more."

Khedran studied her curiously, and she shrugged again. "I guess it doesn't matter. I just got a strange feeling about him and his Duine. I think perhaps we'll meet them again."

"You aren't usually one to make prophecies."

Her eyebrows went up. "No. I don't, do I? Forget it, Khedran."

But she looked back at the crowd before they rode on, and still felt sure she would see them again one day.

As they crossed the barren land that lay outside of Cabre's high walls, Khedran looked up to see in satisfaction that his soldiers, the Guard of Penumbra and Cabre, stood in wait on the ramparts. Beyond the gates the citizens of Cabre thronged the streets and climbed on rooftops to watch his return.

Shandiin, riding to his left, watched with a frown as he drew the Star Blade briefly and lowered his head before sliding it back into its sheath. "What are you doing?" she asked him.

He looked across at her, lifted an eyebrow. "Talking to Daimaine." He shook his head as she started to argue against what was already done.

She huffed, scowling, and looked toward the gates. "You know there will be an ambush. This is the High Tahmond's last chance to be rid of you, so he can become the new ruler of Azlatan. I know you are wearing Chaine armor under your leather, but..."

"We've already discussed this, Shandiin. I must enter Cabre alone."

When her gaze flicked back to his, he reached over and placed his hand on her sword arm. "You have been and always will be the King's Defender. I will always..." he closed his eyes briefly, shook his head as though in denial of what he had begun to say, and started over. "I will always be grateful to you. But my people's perception is critical to their sense of peace. They must trust me and respect me beyond any doubt. Even from here I read their terrible fear and dawning hope. It's my duty to give them what they need." His eyes of jeweled emerald were unreadable, so he shocked her when he added, "Do I have your trust and respect, Shandiin?"

She shoved away her fear and gave him her fierce smile. "Always." She meant it from the depth of her heart.

Reining in her horse, she fell back to ride with the three Dominion Kings, several lengths behind Khedran. Her Chaine, a unit of Cabre's Guard, and legions representing three Dominions rode five abreast behind them.

But she drew her sword and held it ready across her thigh as she rode through the city gates, scanning the crowds on both sides of the city's main street.

That long avenue emptied into the market square in front of Penumbra's wide fan of steps. Waiting on the top step was the black and white figure of the High Tahmond, with his hand on the staff that sparked lightning even in the sunlight.

Khedran rode alone toward him, through the long avenue, between the crowds who fell silent as he came. He continued sedately into the market square, halting his black stallion at the foot of Penumbra's stair.

As he began to dismount, a hail of deadly arrows filled the air.

Every arrow that neared him vanished in a burst of starfire. Daimaine's magic was dazzling even in sunlight.

The crowd was surging, screaming in terror, as badly aimed arrows fell among them.

Khedran's boot had no sooner touched the ground when Shandiin's Chaine and Cabre's Guards let fly their own arrows, and the assassins were taken out from their high vantages above the main crowd. Ignoring that phase of his strategy, Khedran went immediately to a child who cried over his fallen mother, then helped the woman up as others rushed to take her for healing.

He scanned the crowd to assure himself that soldiers were moving in to care for his people, as planned. Those he scanned fell silent as his gaze passed over them. Assured, he turned on his heel and strode up Penumbra's steps to confront the High Tahmond.

"Were these killers Anzihi?" he demanded, and with the use of his command voice every person in the marketplace heard him. Screaming fell away like water down a drain.

The High Tahmond wavered, looking into those furious eyes of emerald fire. Khedran read his hesitation, and those eyes narrowed.

"I demand to know if these assassins were sent by Phaelon." Khedran continued in command voice. There was a collective gasp from all who witnessed the confrontation, for no one had ever dared to challenge the High Tahmond.

The High Tahmond drew back in shock, but before he could answer, the very steps beneath his feet came alive with moving stars that crawled up the black palace behind him, alive and swarming. With Penumbra's new life came a wave of cold, an icy cold that heralded the presence of the Deathqueen, Daimaine.

Khedran stood unafraid, unlike every bystander, while Shandiin cursed under her breath.

Khedran spoke again in the voice always heard. "You may find yourself in audience with the Deathqueen," he warned the Tahmond, "if you refuse to answer my question. Are these killers, these assassins, Phaelon's Anzihi? Or are they simply outlaws who should be subject to *my* law, *her* justice?"

The High Tahmond stared into the eyes of the Black Wolf as a would-be King had recently done, and swallowed. "They cannot be Phaelon's, or he would have told me."

Khedran waited a beat, his gaze still pinning the Tahmond's, before turning back to the crowd. "They are not Anzihi," he proclaimed. "And they will no longer be a threat to anyone in Azlatan, for the Deathqueen will find them out."

A roar of joy rent the very air of Cabre as Khedran turned back to the Tahmond. "Your true Anzihi," he said for his ears only, "have not found my father's Duine woman, or her child?"

"Not yet." This time, gazing into those feral emerald eyes, the Tahmond added, "Your Highness."

"Then I give you warning...Your Honor. The Anzihi must cease their search. *I* will look for the woman and child, and you and your Tahmond may look for them, and if they are found they are to be brought, alive and unharmed, to me. *To me*. Do you understand? I swear on the scythe of Daimaine, no more innocent people will die because of the Duine Anzihi!"

"Brought to you? But...how can you know if the child is the Forbidden Child?"

Khedran's smile was as dangerous as the Star Blade he drew, bringing its dazzle level with the Tahmond's eyes. "By this Blade the child will be known. For only the child of a High King may touch it and live." As the magic fog grew around him, as the stars swirled, he snarled, "Do you agree?"

"Yes, Your Highness."

Khedran turned then, and watched the High Tahmine walk up the steps to join him within Daimaine's ghostly, starlit mist. She smiled at her foster son before turning back to the crowd, standing in Liethe's lambent veils beside Khedran, with the High Tahmond on his other side.

There would be a ceremony, but it would only be a formality. The ascension was done. It was apparent to every witness that the Tahmond and Tahmine stood with the seventh High King of Azlatan.

As the crowd's cheer and the celebrating began, Khedran's gaze found Shandiin where she stood at the foot of the stairs. She gave him a smile and salute, sheathed her golden sword, and turned away to join her own people waiting at the crowd's edge.

She did not see Khedran watch her walk away, or she might have found familiar the expression in his emerald eyes.

It would be years before she recognized the warmth of a man she had met once, on a street corner on a long-ago day before the Earth died.

The End of Book 1 of the Series:
PROPHECY'S DAUGHTER.
Turn the page for a sneak peek of Book 2:
PENUMBRA

The Journey Continues

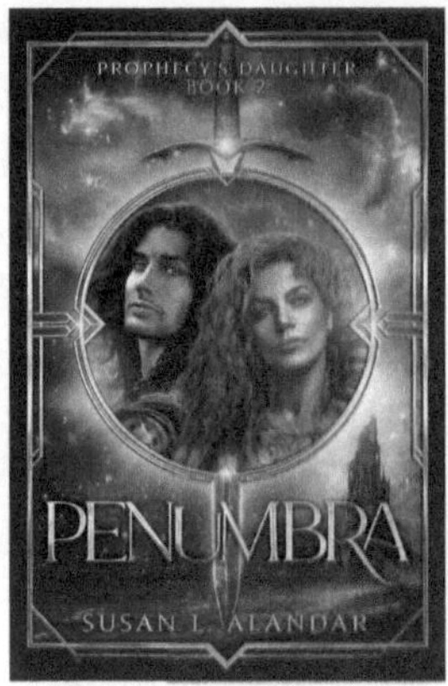

When gods are real, people become playthings.

For a thousand years Shandiin has lived among the people of Azlatan, biding her time until she can free them from the control of their divine rulers and return to what is left of her world. But even if she succeeds, she cannot stop the Prophecy War that will follow.

Hoping to save the people she must leave behind, she has turned a bright spirit born to mercy and compassion into a warrior. A killer. A King who could win a war.

Her defiance comes with a cost. The strange High King is feared as much as he is respected. Even as his strength grows, so does an invasion of insidious magic undermining the people's trust. Together he and Shandiin face the most powerful god of them all, a twisted being with no soul, whose magic threatens to destroy their entire planet.

 When the time comes and Chaos is unleashed, Shandiin must make a terrible choice – to risk everything for the people she has grown to love or walk away from everything and leave them to their fate.

GLOSSARY

Admech, (ad-MEK), the grasslands on the eastern border of Azlatan.

Allasar, sixth High King of Azlatan, father of Khedran.

Amhara, (am-HAR-a), is Chaine word combining 'love' and 'respect.' It has two meanings. In the first, it describes a relationship between people. Respect is possible without love, but love without respect is not. Love with respect is *amhara.* In the second meaning, it is a word of requirement relating to everything, and includes a note of gratitude.

Anzihi, (ANZ-zi-high), also Duine Anzihi, secret enforcers of Phaelon's law.

Ashtari, (ash-TAR-ee), the fourth High King, ruled 475-670.

Azlatan, (AHZ-la-tawn), the nation of seventy-seven collected Dominions ruled by a single High King, created by the god Phaelon for his chosen people. The western border is the sea. Northern border is arctic, southern tropical. The eastern border is a cliff dropping to a prairie, guarded by magic.

Aztlan, the mythical paradise from which the Aztecs came, is also the name of a secret project on Earth that created engineered people. It later became the name those people used for their project to save humanity, and the ship that took them from Earth to Hiraeth.

Bond or Bonded. When capitalized, this denotes a formalized union of individuals, Rioch (lord) and Duine (servant).The Duine are not slaves, but "honored servants" under Phaelon's Law, and friends in actual practice.

Brend, King Randmar's younger son, Prince of the Dominion of Ordhold.

Cabre, (Kah-bray), the King's City on the western sea, home to the Temples of the three gods deified in Azlatan (Phaelon, Liethe, and Daimaine.)

Camion, (CAM-me-on), the Duine servant Bonded to the High Prince.

Canon, (KAYnon), Duine servant Bonded to High King Allasar, father of Camion.

Chaine, (Chain), a powerful redhaired race of warriors who sailed to Azlatan from the west in the reign of the sixth High King. They are considered disruptive mercenaries by traditionalists and are immune to magic, but their metal called "Chaine gold" is sought for its strength. The Chaine's golden swords are in high demand, as well as armor of interlocking links. The Chaine people's clothing is often threaded with Chaine gold.

Chandar, (CHAWN-dar), Khedran's horse, sired by Shashata, his father's stallion.

ChanDethe, (Chan-DEATH-ee), the mystic messenger of the goddess Liethe; legend says the Forbidden Child will ride a horse by this name.

Chaos, the fourth deity, who is not honored in Azlatan.

Compatri, (Com-PAW-tree), Compatri are chosen by the King for personal reasons of trust and respect and are rare. They wear an emerald star on the collar of their uniform.

Council, a gathering for trial purposes in Azlatan, made up of the High King, High Tahmond and High Tahmine, and selected Dominion Kings. Meetings are held in the Council Hall of Penumbra. The High King's rule is autonomous, but he generally abides by the findings of Council.

Damon Alexander, the creator of Project Aztlan, which created genetically engineered superior people for the purpose of saving the human race. He was assassinated along with the majority of his creations.

Daimaine, (Die-MANE), also called the Deathqueen, goddess of Death and Justice. She 'created' the High Kings, giving them magic gifts; the souls of the High Kings belong to her. Her Temple lies below the palace Penumbra, and is the Command Hall of the High King.

Dante, (Dawn-tay), first Compatri, serving High King Khandor.

Deities of Azlatan: Phaelon, the god of Order; Daimaine, goddess of Justice and Death; Liethe, goddess of Life and Mercy; and Chaos, who is not deified in Azlatan because she is the enemy of Phaelon.

Diane Fairchild, Shandiin's Daughter, scientist, twin of Leah, becomes the goddess Daimaine on Hiraeth.

Dominions: there are seventy-seven of them in Azlatan, each with its own King, all ruled by the High King. Cabre is not a Dominion but is the city that is home to the High King. The other Dominions mentioned in this book are King Randmar's Ordhold, Alaura (ruled by Jairus), King Handel's Sunhi, and Rafel (ruled by Arafon.)

Duine, (Dinna), the name rooted from the Gaelic word for "people;" are the race of people named by Phaelon to be servants to the Rioch, usually fair-haired. The "races" are forbidden to mix, because prophecy says that their offspring (the Forbidden Child) would bring the uprising of Duine against the Rioch.

Duine Anzihi, (Dinna an-zi-high), the secret enforcers of Phaelon's Law.

Eleban, (Ella-bon), Dominion King. Allasar was murdered in his castle.

Everwinter Range, the mountains north of Ordhold, the northern border of Azlatan.

Egypt, one of the family of genetically engineered heroes, best friend of Shandiin.

Farbet, (FAR-bet), Compatri to High King Allasar.

Forbidden Child: Phaelon's Law is that Rioch and Duine shall not mix, and if a Forbidden Child of Duine and Rioch is allowed to live, the Duine will rise to destroy all Rioch, and no magic will save them.

Handel, a stablemaster who became Dominion King of Sunhi by Khedran's command.

High King(s), the handsome and intelligent autonomous rulers of Azlatan, were created through a combination of science and magic; they all have emerald eyes that mark their special bloodline. They are bred to be incorruptible, and they are empaths who can read the emotions of their people. Their gifts include a 'command voice' which is not a tonal change, but magic that penetrates the listener's brain as the words are spoken; a presence that causes them to be recognized as the realm's ultimate authority without need of insignia; and charisma that also causes a thrall to fall over most anyone who meets them, a thrall of wonder and sometimes love.

Hiraeth, (Hi-RITH), an ancient Welsh word expressing a spiritual longing for home, a home that perhaps is real only in the heart, a home that is everywhere and nowhere. It becomes the name of the planet colonized by some of Earth's survivors.

Jairus (Jay-rus), Dominion King of Alaura, father of Rhiathe, High Queen to Allasar and mother of Khedran.

Jon, (John), oldest Prince of the Dominion of Ordhold.

Khalen, (KAY-len), the first High King. He never arrived in Azlatan. During the exodus, he sacrificed himself to Daimaine in exchange for her promise to do no harm to the people without permission from a High King.

Khandor, (KON-dor), second High King, ruled years 1-250.

Khastiel, (Cass-tee-ell), third High King, ruled 250-475.

Law of Order, generally refers to Phaelon's law that Rioch and Duine cannot mix.

Leah Rowan, Shandiin's daughter. Becomes Liethe when the magic overtakes Hiraeth.

Liethe, (Lie-ETH-ee), goddess of Life and Mercy, healing; she appears with a blindfold because her origin is Shandiin's blind daughter, Leah, and because the blindfold is symbolic of her caring for others despite any faults they may have.

Lilith, one of the family of genetically engineered heroes captured by the Right Church, mercy-killed by Roland.

Marshall Canard, His Eminence, head of the Right Church.

Mia, Duine to High Queen Rhiathe, secret love of High King Allasar.

Mordane, (Mor-DANE), the fifth High King, father of Allasar, ruled 670-810.

Nightstone. Penumbra is built of this magic obsidian which at night is covered with moving stars.

Nitch'i, or Nitchi, is Navajo for Wind. This is the name of Shandiin's first paint horse.

Ordhold, (ORD-hold), the northernmost and largest Dominion of Azlatan.

Penumbra, (Pen-oom-bra), magic palace of the High Kings, given to them by Daimaine. Daimaine's Temple and the crypts of all of the High Kings are contained within Penumbra.

Phaelon, (Fail-on), the God of Order.

Prophecy War. The God Phaelon prophesied that at the end of a thousand years the goddess Chaos will be released, Azlatan's borders will fall, and there will come a great war. A Forbidden Child of Rioch and Duine will come forward; if the Forbidden is allowed to live, Duine will rise up to kill all Rioch, and no magic can save them.

Randmar, King of the Dominion Ordhold, ally to the High King.

Rani, (RAW-nee), young girl in Ordhold, fostered by King Randmar.

Rhiathe, (Ree-AH-thay), formerly Princess of the Dominion of Alaura, High Queen to Allasar, mother of Khedran; she died in childbirth.

Rioch, (Ree-awk), the name rooted from the Gaelic word for "royal," is the name for the ruling race of Azlatan, usually dark-haired; they are descended from the genetically engineered people of Earth. The god Phaelon ordered that the Riochs rule and the Duine serve. The races are forbidden to mix, because of prophecy that their living offspring (the Forbidden Child) would cause all Duine to kill all Rioch.

Roland, one of the family of genetically engineered heroes, who gave Lilith a merciful death by poison.

Roinn, (Rowan), hero of the Chaine people, is commemorated by his name being passed from one generation to the next. The name is given to the winner of a competition testing wit, integrity, and fighting skill. Three of the historical Roinns were women. The winner becomes second in command to The Chaine, their leader.

Sarnath, (SAR-nath), one of the family of genetically engineered heroes, who is psychic.

Shan the Wanderer, Shandiin's disguise during clandestine visits to Azlatan.

Shandiin, (Shan-DEEN), found as an infant and raised by the Navajo, she does not age and is of unknown origin. On Hiraeth she becomes The Chaine (title), leader of the Chaine people. See "The Chaine."

Shashata, the black stallion gifted to High King Allasar by The Chaine, Shandiin.

Star Blade, the magic sword gifted to the High Kings by Daimaine; it protects its wielder from harm and never fails an intent to kill. It is fired by stars and starlight when unsheathed.

Stareven, the warm season.

Starfall, the cold season, presaged annually by a fall of stars (meteor shower.)

Tahmine, (Tah-MEEN), priestesses of Liethe, healers. The High Tahmine is revered.

Tahmond, (TAH-mund), priests of Phaelon; the High Tahmond is feared.

Tariah, the High Tahmine of Allasar's reign, foster mother of Khedran.

The Chaine, mysterious leader of the Chaine people (Shandiin), also known as the King's Defender. She was charged with guarding and mentoring High Prince Khedran.

Verity Rowan, priest, once Shandiin's love and father of her twin girls, Diane and Leah.

William, Khandor's bonded Duine.

Zion Alexander, the genius scientist and leader of a family of genetically engineered heroes. He took his engineer's last name to honor him. Alexander's meaning is "defender of mankind."

MEET THE AUTHOR

Writing and art are my lifelong partners. I've written fantasy since I was a child, usually hidden from those who didn't understand why I was wasting my time on "nonsense." My best childhood friend was a pen pal (does that phrase still exist?) who did the same thing, and we shared our worlds through the mail until I lost her to cancer decades later. I still glimpse her turning a distant corner on my world of Hiraeth.

I grew up on Robert Heinlein and Ray Bradbury and Madeline L'Engle. I discovered epic fantasy (Tolkien, of course) about the time Heinlein broke into adult work with Glory Road. But what I wrote, the world that unwound in my own mind, was always apart from theirs. It's apart from today's wonderful writers, too, though I smile to recognize in all our work a certain genealogy from the classics.

I gave up the fragile hope of a writing career when I became an abandoned mother of two and needed a stable income. In retrospect I needed the raw experience of the real world. Back then misogyny and bigotry were openly accepted, and I (daughter of a rabid freedom marcher) was angry...a lot. But I was able to gain my foothold in the working realm because there were also people of honor and compassion. Humanity's nature is chaotic and fascinating, and the world has improved, but there are still shadows behind the light.

All of it has influenced my writing.

I still wrote fantasy in spare moments, because my best friend and I still exchanged our chronicles through the mail while I wrote nonfiction for a paycheck, and became good at it. I supplemented my income with my art, usually portraits of the horses I have always loved, and people's dogs and cats. Animals have always been a gift in my life (I currently live with three rescue dogs), and horses were like characters in my youth's secret stories...something reflected in the tales I write now.

So, as to what I write now. My fantasy world of Hiraeth is hard but beautiful. Hiraeth is an old word from the Welsh about a home we all long for. Perhaps it's only a dream, or perhaps that longing is seeded in a distant memory from childhood when we felt secure and loved, where there was always a sense of wonder...and yes, still a thrilling need to check under the bed.

My characters live in me, and evolved from experience and curiosity about what could be. How could a man be morally incorruptible and still be compassionate? In this case he believes he is less than human because he lacks free will. He has been created one of a kind, and so therefore completely alone. There is only one person who understands him, only one person he loves with all his heart, but she is like a dream that disappears on waking...always just out of his reach. I think his need for a love who understands is common to all of us, and gives him the humanity he doesn't realize he has after all.

My heroine Shandiin is his antitheses. Where he is magic, she is immune. Where he rules as a king, she is an anarchist. She questions everything there is to question. She distrusts everyone...until him. And she is the only one who understands him well enough to feel sad for him.

It all comes down to the chaos of humanity...free will. That is what has always fascinated me. Like Shandiin, we all write our own destiny in the choices we make.

Make wise choices.

Sue

Acknowledgements

When I was left alone at the death of my husband Jim (a bright spirit with honor and compassion), my two daughters encouraged me to return to the stories they had loved in their childhood but that I had finally put aside. So I dug out an old manuscript and started typing the words from paper into a computer. As I did, I found joy return to my spirit. I found enthusiasm, and purpose. Hiraeth and her occupants welcomed me home, and...because I understood more... they became more.

So I thank my beloved redhaired girls, Rose and Kimberley, for their faith in me. And I thank the wonderful person I found, Keri-Rae Barnum of New Shelves, who has guided me through the practical part of writing fiction. And, most importantly, I thank all three for supporting my newfound courage to quit writing in secret.